THE IDENTITY MINE

Dean Crawford

ISBN: 1517025184
ISBN-13: 978-1517025182

Also by Dean Crawford:

The Warner & Lopez Series
The Nemesis Origin
The Fusion Cage
The Identity Mine

The Ethan Warner Series
Covenant
Immortal
Apocalypse
The Chimera Secret
The Eternity Project

Atlantia Series
Survivor
Retaliator
Aggressor
Endeavour
Defiance

Independent novels
Eden
Holo Sapiens
Soul Seekers
Stone Cold

Want to receive notification of new releases? Just sign up to Dean Crawford's newsletter via: www.deancrawfordbooks.com

I

Fort Benning, Columbus,

Georgia

Major General Frederick J Thompson drove south along US Highway 27, the dawn sunshine flickering through the trees in a hypnotic dance that usually caused him to squint but now merely mesmerized him. The whisper of the tires along the asphalt hummed in his ears, a gentle lullaby that numbed his thoughts and caused his limbs to relax until he was barely holding on to the steering wheel as he eased down the off ramp toward the massive US Army training base nestled in Georgia's rolling hills.

A veteran of two Gulf Wars, Thompson was an iconic figure in the US Army, his square jaw and bright blue eyes framing a wide, silvery moustache that adorned his upper lip like a pair of twisted bayonets. Without conscious thought he followed the Old Cusseta Highway to the security checkpoints at the entrance to the base, saw two armed soldiers awaiting him, their rifles gripped at port–arms. One of the soldiers raised a gloved hand and stepped out into the road before a set of barriers, and Thompson slowed his vehicle and eased his window down.

Thompson glanced briefly at a photograph pinned to the dashboard of his wife, three children and extended family, all of them smiling back at him as though they understood. He was *sure* that they understood. Such a shame, that he'd had to kill them all.

The soldier stepped forward, his eyes concealed behind designer wrap around shades as was the fashion these days among the younger troopers, many of them battle hardened in Iraq's brutal deserts. Despite the shades Thompson was vaguely aware of the soldier's surprised expression as he leaned down and peered into the vehicle.

The trooper jerked upright and flipped a rigid salute at Thompson.

'Good morning, sir! Proceed to the main gate please, sir!'

Thompson slipped his vehicle into drive and crept forward as the barriers raised and he passed through without further interruption. He crossed 8th Division Road and cruised toward 7th Cavalry Road, then turned right toward the Brave Rifles Parade Field. There were no other vehicles on the camp's roads at this early hour, but he knew that new infantry recruits would be out in force on the parade ground, unarmed.

Thompson glanced again at the picture of his family. It had been pinned there since the birth of his first daughter Ellie, twenty eight years before, and he had simply updated it every once in a while as new children, and then grandchildren, were added to the family. Smiling faces, blue skies, their Colonial style house on the Alabama border, rolling fields and sunshine. The image blurred as he stared at it and he realized that he had stopped breathing. He knew that the image was important but suddenly he could not quite recall why.

Thompson blinked as he came upon a gentle curve in the road and followed it round, and his mind went silent again as he drove toward a parking lot on the parade field's south side and pulled in, then killed the engine.

Two squads of troops were marching up and down to the bellowed screams of two drill sergeants that marred the perfect dawn. Clouds of dust kicked up by their boots glowed in golden whorls as they paraded, half a dozen of them doing press ups in the dust nearby for misdemeanours or poorly timed manoeuvres, a third drill sergeant shouting at them. The roaring bluster of the sergeants' was at odds with the gentle lullaby of birdsong echoing through ranks of trees surrounding the field. Thompson reached for his car door and methodically stepped out, closed it carefully behind him and locked it. As he did so he caught his reflection in the window glass, resplendent in his dress uniform, ribbons and medals emblazoned across the dark fabric, his beret adorned with four stars denoting his rank, his parachute wings vivid on his right chest.

Pride surged through him but it faded rapidly until it felt distant, vague, like a dream.

Thompson blinked again, then turned and marched toward the parade ground, heard the cries of the drill sergeants take shape in his ears.

'Your *left*, your *left*, your *left right left…*'

The drill sergeants saw him coming long before the exhausted recruits, and their bellowed commands changed tone as they ordered their charges into parade formation. The drumming of boots on the hard earth slammed to a halt and the billowing clouds of glowing dust drifted away in the sudden silence as the drill sergeants stomped into position before the three squads of recruits and snapped to attention.

Thompson liked the silence that greeted him. As a recruit so many years before at this very camp he had learned to hate the sound of a drill sergeant's screaming; so unnecessary, so forced and uncompromising. He had often wished that he could pull a gun and blast their twisted, gruesome faces away, until over the months of gruelling training he realized how important they had become to him, how essential their hard work was in shaping he and his fellow recruits into the hardened soldiers they had become.

'Attennnn – *shun*!'

The squads slammed their boots to the earth and stood as rigid as telegraph poles, staring through the general as though he were no longer there. Thompson, his hands behind his back as he approached, nodded once. His lungs felt numb, his chest constricted it seemed by steel bands, his throat dry. He called out a single command.

'Comp'ny, about *turn*!'

Infantry training at all US Army camps was about breaking the recruit down and rebuilding them as the army required them to be. Utterly in the thrall of their commanding officers, they were conditioned to accept and obey orders without the slightest hesitation.

In an instant the three drill sergeants repeated the command and then the entire recruit company made a hundred eighty degree turn on their heels so that their backs were turned to Thompson. Their boots slammed down onto the earth once more in perfect time like a mortar round going off, the report echoing off the nearby barracks behind the general.

Thompson reached into his pockets and without conscious thought he retrieved a pair of M67 fragmentation grenades, pulled the pin on the first and lobbed it overarm into the nearest of the three squads. The second followed silently a moment later, and Thompson watched as the two weapons arced through the clear blue sky and plunged into the soldiers' midst.

Even as they landed he lobbed two more, and then as the first cry went up he pulled a ceremonial pistol from its holster at his side.

The drill sergeants turned first as they spotted the grenades plunge into the recruit formations and they opened their mouths to shout a warning, their faces stricken with the same kind of panic and horror that they inflicted daily upon the recruits under their instruction. But this time their voices were drowned out by the sudden blasts as the four grenades detonated with ear–splitting blasts.

Thompson did not flinch as he saw the grenades explode, though he felt the shockwaves from the blasts as they scythed through the platoons of recruits and cut them down in a hail of metal fragments like a thousand bullets. Screams of terror and pain screeched into the morning air as Thompson became aware of the three drill sergeants sprinting toward him, converging on his position with fury and hatred in their eyes.

Thompson did not flinch or panic as he lifted the pistol and fired at the first of them, the bullet smashing into the NCO's chest and hurling him to one side. The remaining two did not deviate from their charge and Thompson fired a second round directly into the screaming face of the second drill sergeant. The bullet smashed into his upper jaw and exited his right temple in a spray of bright crimson blood as the soldier tumbled to the ground in a cloud of flailing limbs.

Thompson turned to the third drill sergeant and fired again, this round hitting the man low in the belly at close range. The drill sergeant howled in agony and crouched over the wound but he kept coming, and Thompson fired again. The soldier's skull split as the bullet smashed through bone and sent the soldier sprawling across the ground to land at Thompson's boots, his shattered skull glistening with bright blood in the sunlight, pink bone protruding from his wound.

Thompson felt something wet on his lip and he tasted blood on his tongue as he licked at it. He briefly wondered whether it was his or that of his victims.

Thompson looked up to see the recruits in disarray, heard screams of agony and cries of alarm as a distant siren began wailing across the camp. Major General Thompson stepped over the bodies of the dead drill sergeant toward the platoons and began firing his pistol into their dense ranks even as many of them fled in terror. In his mind he instinctively counted down his rounds even as he saw dozens of recruits sprinting toward him with utter, desolate rage ingrained into their faces.

Thompson fired into them, saw men and women tumble to the ground as bullets impacted their bodies with dull thumps as though they had been punched. *Five, four, three, two…*

Thompson turned the pistol and pressed the searing hot barrel to his temple. He realized vacantly that he was smiling as he pulled the trigger once more.

***

II

Defense Intelligence Agency, Joint Base Anacostia–Bolling,

Washington DC

'He did *what*?'

Douglas Jarvis sat in a comfortable leather chair in one of the United States' most secretive locations just inside the District of Columbia: Anacostia–Bolling Air Force Base and the home of the Defense Intelligence Agency's DIAC Building.

Lieutenant General J. F. Nellis, the Director of the DIA, sat opposite him, both men scrutinizing files in their laps.

'He drove into Fort Benning two hours ago, discharged four hand grenades into recruit formations beating the parade ground and then shot dead three senior NCOs and nine recruits before turning the gun on himself. That occurred approximately two hours after he rose early and executed his wife, three children and his own father. His mother was injured but survived the incident. She's being cared for by the army and will be interviewed soon.'

Jarvis closed his eyes for a moment as he struggled to match the new information with what he knew about Major General Thompson.

'I met him in Kuwait in 1991,' Jarvis replied. 'He was a lieutenant back then and a damned fine soldier, a patriot through and through. He's climbed the star ladder like it's been going out of fashion. This just doesn't jive with the man I knew.'

'Agreed,' Nellis replied. 'To point out that this is out of character would be an understatement to say the least.'

Nellis was a former United States Air Force officer who had recently been appointed DNI by the current president. Jarvis, who was a former Marine Corps officer and later an intelligence analyst with the DIA, had been selected by Nellis to run a small investigative unit designed to root out corruption within the intelligence community while remaining beyond the prying eyes of senior figures on Capitol Hill. Jarvis had been chosen due to his prior success in operating a similar unit within the DIA that had conducted five investigations into what were rather discreetly termed as "anomalous phenomena," which had attracted the attention of both the FBI and the CIA and eventually been shut down. Jarvis had spent some twenty years working for the DIA and been involved in some of the highest–level classified operations ever conducted by elements of the US Covert Operations Service. Most of them he would never be able to talk about with another human being, even those with whom he had served. Jarvis knew the rules and had obeyed them with patriotic fervour his entire career.

'How many did we lose?' Jarvis asked finally.

Nellis sighed.

'As well as the three drill sergeants, nine recruits have died in total and a further nineteen are in hospital, several of them with life–changing injuries that mean their army careers are over before they've even really begun.'

Jarvis rubbed his temples wearily. 'Media?'

'They're all over it,' Nellis replied. 'We've initiated a ten mile no–fly zone over Fort Benning's existing borders to limit the amount of footage the news crew helicopters can obtain, but right now we're not even going to begin to conceal the core event. The US Army on site are handling the reporters, and for now are simply informing them that there has been a major incident and that details will be forthcoming.'

Jarvis knew what that meant: the public crucifixion of Major General Thompson's reputation, attacks on what was left of his family, his friends, those who might speak out in his defense, the law suits from the bereaved families of the dead recruits, the law suits from the victims maimed or otherwise injured for life.

'How long do we have?' Jarvis asked.

'The president has given us seventy two hours to figure out what the hell happened down there,' Nellis replied. 'After the investigations that you and your people have conducted in Peru and Nevada we have his ear and his support over and above any intervention by the FBI, CIA or NSA. He's keen to find answers to what happened so that he has something to say to the press and the people when the inevitable announcements are made. Right now, all he knows is that one of our most decorated soldiers committed cold–blooded murder and then killed himself. What he needs to know is that this isn't a case of domestic terrorism or the complete mental breakdown of one of our toughest and most senior military officers.'

'Why do you want us in on the case?' Jarvis asked. 'Surely this is straight forward enough, no matter how appalling? Thompson went off the rails even though none of us saw it coming? It happens sometimes – even the media know that.'

Nellis said nothing as he opened a drawer on his desk and lifted out a small, sealed plastic bag that he kept in his grip as he replied.

'Part of the rationale for involving the DIA, and yourself in particular, is the unusual nature of the case.'

'Unusual, how?'

'Firstly, the general had presented no outward signs of discontent with his role, his life and his future. In fact, he was extremely upbeat and looking forward to a position on the Joint Chiefs of Staff, which given his career success seemed highly likely to be approved by the Senate. We've spoken to members of his family who weren't present at the home, and believe me they're not only beside themselves with grief but are utterly unable to understand why he would have done something like this.'

'Mental breakdown?' Jarvis suggested. 'Post–Traumatic Stress Disorder or some other form of mental distress that he kept from them?'

'No evidence of that,' Nellis replied, 'and in fact he routinely sought advice after serving in combat theatres. He wasn't afraid of talking about his experiences and frequently encouraged other officers to do the same. He just doesn't fit the profile of somebody bottling up rage.'

'There must be something,' Jarvis insisted, 'a trigger action of some kind?'

'US Army Doctor Gordon Shrivener conducted an emergency autopsy of Major General Thompson within an hour of the shooting,' Nellis explained. 'During the attack, several witnesses reported noticing that the general was suffering a nosebleed.'

Jarvis thought for a moment. 'Maybe some kind of brain event, a stroke or something?'

'That's what the doctor thought, until he found this.'

Nellis slid the plastic bag across the table to Jarvis, who leaned forward for a better look at it.

The interior of the plastic bag was smeared with blood, some of which was darkening now as it congealed. In the center of the blood smears was a thin, ragged looking sliver of metal an inch long, from the top of which were two wiry coils that appeared to have decayed.

'What the hell is *that*?' Jarvis asked.

'That's exactly what Doctor Shrivener said out loud on the autopsy recording,' Nellis said, 'when he pulled this out of the general's skull after detecting it in an X–Ray. Our labs are running tests on it now and trying to determine what it's made of and what the hell it was doing inside his body. I can tell you what they've figured out so far.'

Jarvis looked up at Nellis expectantly, and the general continued with an almost reluctant tone.

'Given the object's length and the position the doctor found it in the general's nasal cavity, it would appear that the coils you can see on one end would have penetrated the frontal lobes of General Thompson's brain, reaching some way into his cerebrum. The material used is some kind of advanced semi–conducting alloy.'

Jarvis stared down at the tiny device and then up at Nellis.

'You're thinking that he was somehow driven to do what he did by this, *thing*?'

'Like I said, I don't know for sure,' Nellis replied, 'but Doctor Shrivener's opinion is that given Major General Thompson's otherwise immaculate physical health and the lack of any mental issues that could have driven him to snap and open fire on his own people, this device may be the key to explaining why he did what he did. Thompson joined the army on his eighteenth birthday and served his entire career, so any medical procedures would have been conducted by the army's Medical Corps or privately at the army's expense. Needless to say, there's nothing on the record about him having this contraption shoved into his head.'

Jarvis picked up the plastic bag and was surprised when he saw the needle–shaped metal object bend and break in even a gentle grasp.

'It's okay,' Nellis said as he saw Jarvis's concern at the break. 'The object is heavily decayed. Doctor Shrivener managed to X–Ray it and obtained a three dimensional scan.'

'This isn't the work of some lunatic on the street; this is high technology, something that only a country like ours could create.'

'Which is why you're here,' Nellis said. 'I want Warner and Lopez in on this.'

Jarvis looked up at Nellis again as he set the bag back down on the desk. 'Majestic Twelve?'

'It's possible they're involved,' Nellis said. 'As you said, this kind of technology doesn't just turn up out of nowhere. Wherever it came from and whoever inserted it into the general's brain, we've got about seventy two hours to figure it out and bring it to an end because as I'm sure you've already guessed, if a four–star general can end up killing innocent recruits in the middle of one of the largest infantry bases in the continental United States…'

'There could be more of them,' Jarvis acknowledged. 'And they could be anywhere.'

'We've already enacted a protocol, quietly,' Nellis said, 'and X–Ray scans of all military personnel are underway, but even so it will take weeks to clear our entire staff, and as for civilians there's no way we can scan three hundred fifty million Americans without causing a major panic. This has to be done under the radar Doug, and it has to be done fast. Your people excel at this kind of thing.'

Jarvis nodded. 'I'll get right on it. Will we have support?'

'From the top, just like I said,' Nellis confirmed. 'The FBI's Director may well attempt to oppose you, but with presidential backing he's going to have to figure out another way to carry out MJ–12's bidding, and if he does, this time we'll be there to catch him.'

***

III

Al Utaykah, Basra,

Iraq

Fear.

Kiera Lomas sucked in a mouthful of dusty air and coughed, her head bowed down so tight that her chin jabbed her chest as she choked. Her wrists were bound with coarse hemp rope that sheared the skin from her wrists, her hair hanging in limp fronds and her ankles shackled to a chain in the concrete floor of the cell.

She had been taken four days before, or that was as close as she could guess her abduction had taken place. The market district, strolling among the stalls, the smell of fresh goods on the air, warm sunlight, smiles of greeting, a rare break from the monotony of the next breaking report from the remains of a country that the rest of the world was trying to forget.

Then the looks of concern on the market traders' faces, the sudden scurrying away of other shoppers, shouts of alarm, and then they were upon her. A dusty looking truck or 4x4, she couldn't really be certain, had careered into the market and smashed its way past several stalls, braking to a halt within ten yards of where she stood. She had known then of course that she should run immediately, but her legs had betrayed her and the doors of the vehicle had burst open to reveal masked men armed with Kalashnikovs who swarmed upon her like demons upon a fallen angel, dragging her into the labyrinths of Hell.

Keira knew that she was underground, concealed in a pit beneath the floorboards of some old building likely bombed–out years before by her own countrymen. Basra had been the site of some of the war's most vicious battles between the forces of *Al–Qaeda* and both American and British infantry, alongside their fledgling Iraqi comrades. The masked abductors had bundled her into the vehicle despite her protestations that she was a reporter and not a spy or soldier, and within half an hour they had shoved her into a building that she presumed acted as some kind of safe house.

She had not immediately been placed into her underground prison, although now she wished that she had been. Instead, she had been dragged into a small room wherein a thin, stained mattress adorned an iron–framed bed. There, she had been bound to the headboard and her clothes sliced from her body using long–bladed knives that were frequently waved in front of her face to dissuade her from any opposition. Lying naked before the masked men, she had been forced to watch as they bartered cigarettes for the rights to her body, sniggering and jostling and arguing until a hierarchy had been accepted. One of her captors had placed a blindfold over her eyes before the men removed their masks.

She did not care to recall what had happened next, the memory buried somewhere deep inside a neural tract that she hoped she would never, ever revisit. Cut free from her bonds afterward, she was hastily dressed in a *burka* and then dragged into incarceration in the pit in which she now huddled in her own filth, her mouth dry from dehydration and her mind filled with terrifying hallucinations of what terrible fate awaited her at the hands of the captors whose identity she now knew.

Islamic State. They had been known to burn people alive at the stake, a fate so unbelievably barbaric it had not been witnessed since it had been routinely practiced by Christians in medieval Europe hundreds of years before. Islamic State, along with the Taliban and *Al–Qaeda* had beheaded Western journalists live in front of television cameras and broadcast the grisly videos to the world, shot schoolgirls, seemingly competing with each other in order to increase the barbarism they enjoyed inflicting on the innocent around them.

And now Kiera was in their hands.

A noise from somewhere outside sent shockwaves of fear pulsing like writhing snakes through her shivering body and she tried to stifle her sobs as she heard heavy footsteps stomping toward her amid angry bursts of Arabic and Urdu. A heavy latch was slid through its mounts and the trapdoor above her hauled open.

Rough, dirty hands hauled her up and out of the pit, the pitiful shawl around her falling away to reveal her nakedness once more, smeared now with bodily fluids. Gasps of disgust were followed with more angry shouts as Kiera felt something draped across her shoulders, felt a more gentle touch guide her away from her captors through the building.

Crippled by fear, Kiera allowed herself to be led, her bare feet slapping on cool stone. She could feel the man alongside her, could smell the scent of tobacco on his breath, could hear the sound of his breathing as he led her into another room and closed the door behind them.

'This way.'

She startled, the voice almost American, Middle East accented but recognizably touched with a New York twang. For a moment she wondered whether she was about to be rescued, but she quickly realized that such good fortune was not possible. This man was as much an abductor as the men who had raped her, was her enemy as they were.

Her thighs bumped against the edge of a bed and the man's hands guided her to sit down. Keira perched on the edge of the bed and suddenly she felt her ankles swung up onto the mattress and a strap pulled tightly over her legs to secure them in place. Her heart sank as she realized that she was once again to be raped and she was unable to stifle a sob.

'Quiet now,' the man said. 'You will not be harmed.'

She felt his hands unwrap the blindfold and suddenly light filled her vision. She squinted, trying to focus on the room around her. Slowly she noticed a series of lights set into the ceiling, the walls around her painted a clinically bright white that reflected the glare. She turned her head and saw that a man was standing over her. Dark skin, dark eyes, heavy beard, a white lab coat that contrasted with his tanned skin and the cruel gleam in his eyes.

Keira glanced to one side and a wretched fear twisted her guts as she saw a trolley bearing medical equipment; scalpels, needles and tweezers all gleaming in the light.

'Do not fear them,' the man said. 'Soon, you will fear nothing.'

Keira's limbs began to twitch erratically and her breath came in short, sharp gasps as she replied.

'Who are you? What are you doing?'

The man smiled without warmth or compassion as he turned away from Kiera and walked across to the trolley. He picked up a hypodermic needle that was filled with a clear fluid and flicked the needle to ensure no air was trapped before he moved beyond a muslin veil that shielded her view from the rest of the room.

She could hear movement outside the veil and she fell silent and still. Another noise, like two pieces of metal being tapped together, then that voice whispering in the darkness.

'Has he survived?'

Her breathing rasped and she could feel her heart trying to thump its way out of her chest.

'We have signals verified from the pre–frontal cortex.'

A figure moved past nearby and the muslin sheet rippled and parted enough for her to see into the room beyond. Some ten feet away was a metal gurney upon which lay the naked form of a man. Tubes protruded from his body and she could see his chest rising and falling. An intravenous line rose up to a saline bag suspended above his head and she could see that his nose was swathed in blood–stained bandages.

Kiera started to twist her hands back and forth, seeking a weakness in her bonds. Her wrists were narrow and her hands small, perhaps small enough to squeeze free. She forced the thumb of her left hand inward and then pulled against the strap. The strap scraped against her skin but she felt the edge move. She pulled harder and the strap slipped further over her hand. She gritted her teeth against the pain and pulled hard.

The strap slipped across her hand and then it jerked free. She clenched her hand a few times before reaching across and loosening the strap on her right wrist.

'He's coming round.'

She sat up in the bed as she heard a faint whimper from across the room as though someone were crying out for help. She turned and saw the naked man's body quiver.

'He's almost awake,' the voice said again.

The body shuddered again as though live current were zipping through dormant muscles. Another murmur came from deep within the man that rose suddenly to an ear piercing scream of anguish that soared through the building. The body flailed, the naked man sobbing and screaming as he thrashed about on the table as the doctors sought to restrain him.

The man began frothing at the mouth, choking on his own saliva and his head began crashing violently against the gurney. Kiera's guts convulsed as she saw him suddenly snap his mouth open and shut with sharp cracks and a thick torrent of blood spill down his chin as he crunched through his own tongue.

The man's body convulsed violently once again and then suddenly it stiffened and then sagged, the limbs falling to its sides as the sound of a fixed–tone pulse monitor droned in the sudden silence. Kiera stared in horror at the corpse, its ruined tongue dangling by threads from his mouth and strings of blood drooling away toward the floor.

She heard a sigh, and then another voice.

'At least we still have the woman.'

Kiera yanked the restraints free and leaned forward in a desperate attempt to free her legs as a whimper of terror blurted from between her lips. The muslin sheet was whipped aside before she could free herself, and she cried out as two men wrestled her back down onto the bed and fastened her wrists back into place.

'Let me go!' she screamed. 'What are you doing?!'

The doctor smiled down at her without compassion.

'It would not matter if I told you who I was, why you were here or even what is going to happen to you, for you would not recall it anyway.'

Kiera whimpered as the syringe in the doctor's hand drew closer to her. 'Please, let me go.'

Again that cruel smile, fixed it seemed upon his face as he leaned in.

'That, my dear, is precisely what I intend to do.'

Kiera squeezed her eyes shut as she felt the needle slip with a sharp pain into her arm, and then a cold sensation flowed through her veins that chilled her to her core. Slowly, her rapidly beating heart and labored breathing faded away into blackness, and her last thought was her horror at feeling the man gently caressing her brow with one hand as she passed out.

***

IV

DIAC Building,

Washington DC

'This feels weird.'

Nicola Lopez stood at the security check point inside the entrance to the Defense Intelligence Agency as a pass was clipped to her shirt by a security guard, showing an image of her exotically tanned skin, dark eyes and long black hair. Even such a small photograph seemed to project the supressed anger she carried around with her like a talisman.

'Don't knock it,' Ethan Warner replied. 'It's better than all the sneaking around we've been doing these years past.'

The DIA's south wing entrance, in front of which was a fountain before broad lawns, made up only a tiny part of the agency's sprawling complex. Huge, silvery buildings with mirrored black windows contained some of the most sensitive intelligence gathering equipment in the world, including vast 24/7 *Watch Centers* manned by specialists monitoring events across the entire globe.

It had been a long time since Ethan Warner had set foot in the building, a long series of controversies separating Lopez and he from their official work for the DIA. Years in fact, ever since the events in Idaho. Only now, with presidential support for the DIA's operations under the control of Doug Jarvis, had they finally been able to come back in from the cold.

In all they had conducted seven investigations for the Defense Intelligence Agency since Ethan, a former Marine Corps Lieutenant and later vagrant, had been plucked from Cook County Jail by his former platoon commander, Doug Jarvis, and given a new life working for one of the most clandestine units ever created by the intelligence community. Despite the trials they had faced over the years, he had to admit to himself that it felt good to be officially working for the good guys once again, if that they could be called.

Lopez led the way through the intense security measures, including full–body X–Rays and pat down searches. Ethan glimpsed their own images on monitors in the security stations: Lopez's diminutive frame, radiating an attitude as usual that he was surprised didn't show up on the X–Ray screens as a glowing red halo. His own rangy form followed, unkempt light brown hair, wide jaw and a loose–limbed stride.

They finally passed through the last of the checks in time for Jarvis to meet them in the main foyer of the building, the polished tile floor emblazoned with a large DIA emblem in the manner of all the senior intelligence agencies. Ethan wondered whether it helped them to remember which agency they actually worked for.

'You made it through without being shot at,' Jarvis observed laconically. 'That's a first.'

'Why are we here?' Lopez demanded, her arms folded. She had never been a fan of either Jarvis or the DIA, but the call to the headquarters had been sufficiently unusual for her to make the trip. As the new boss of the renamed *Lopez & Warner Inc*, their bail–bondsman outfit, she had become somewhat inclined to getting her way.

'Come with me,' Jarvis replied. 'I'll show you.'

Ethan followed them, aware of the large number of civilian staff walking through the building. Uniquely to a highly secretive intelligence agency, two thirds of the DIA's seventeen thousand employees were civilian, which allowed select freelance operatives like Warner and Lopez to act in concert with official employees like Jarvis. Represented in some one hundred forty countries and with its own Clandestine Service, to which Ethan and Nicola were now attached, the agency's only flaw was a lack of influence in law enforcement, forcing Ethan and Nicola in past cases to work alongside police and federal law agencies around the country.

Jarvis led them to an office on the third floor, which to Ethan's surprise was emblazoned with the old man's name once again.

'Don't tell me they've let you back in the door for good?' Lopez asked with a resigned tone.

'Such warmth, such happiness,' Jarvis replied as he led them into the office. 'It's a wonder you don't burst with joy every morning, Nicola.'

Ethan stepped into the office and Lopez kicked the door shut with a back–flick of her heel.

'You've taken the fun out of my life one too many times,' she shot back. 'Spill the beans or we're out of here.'

Jarvis sat down behind his desk and glanced at Ethan. 'I might put you up for some kind of medal for coping with this every day.'

'Just send me into a war zone for a break every now and again,' Ethan suggested. 'What's the story?'

'Assassinations,' Jarvis replied. 'I take it you've seen the news reports coming out of Georgia?'

'The army general, ran riot and murdered a bunch of recruits,' Lopez replied. 'Tragic to say the least. What happened to him, PTSD?'

Jarvis shook his head and slid a series of photographs across the desk to them.

'No. *This* happened to him.'

Ethan looked down at the images, all close up shots of a sliver of metal an inch or so long according to the dime placed alongside the exhibit, which was sealed in a plastic evidence bag.

'Wow, he must have been good. The general killed all those people with this little thing?' Lopez suggested.

'In a sense, yes,' Jarvis explained. 'This was extracted from his frontal lobes during autopsy and sent here for analysis. Director Nellis briefed me on the case an hour ago, which was when I called you.'

Ethan felt something cold ripple like insects crawling under his skin as he digested what Jarvis had said.

'It was in his brain?'

'The frontal lobes,' Jarvis repeated. 'It's made from a metallic alloy and is designed to be ejected from the body after death, upon receiving no further signals from the brain. It would have been lost had the general not been autopsied so quickly after his death.'

'What did the lab say about it?' Lopez asked.

'That's where it gets creepy,' Jarvis said. 'The device is a highly complex transmitter and receiver and was essentially plugged into the general's brain. The guys in the laboratory are convinced, and have actually signed their report together, that this device in effect is a form of remote control.'

Ethan looked up sharply at Jarvis. 'You're kidding?'

'Two dozen Fort Benning recruits are dead,' Jarvis replied. 'I wouldn't be kidding about something like this. I know how insane it sounds, but that's what the guys are telling me and I've got no reason to doubt them.'

Lopez picked up one of the images as she spoke.

'So, you're saying that this general was not in control of himself when he opened fire on his own people.'

Jarvis nodded slowly.

'He killed his own family too, people he was well known to dote upon. We've never seen anything like this. The technology is of the highest order and is something that our own agencies like DARPA have been working on but have yet to make any serious headway. Right now they've been limited to hacking the brains of bees and rats, not taking over the minds of senior military leaders.'

Lopez startled. 'You're saying that it's possible to hack a brain?!'

'The technology is in its infancy but yes, it's possible. I'll let the geeks downstairs explain all that to you, but right now our main focus is on figuring out where this thing came from and who the hell put it in the general's head.'

Ethan put aside his amazement at what he had just heard and began thinking quickly.

'We'll need to retrace his every step to figure out when this thing was put inside his head.'

'And the general must have endured a medical procedure that he was expecting,' Lopez pointed out. 'He can't have failed to notice somebody shoving this up his nose.'

'Army personnel are already in contact with the general's personal and army physicians, but so far they've drawn a blank,' Jarvis replied. 'The general hadn't seen any physician for at least three months, so I can't see how it could have been implanted through normal procedures.'

'He must have known,' Ethan surmised. 'Do you think that he might have consented to such a procedure, perhaps under duress or the belief that it was for another purpose?'

'I doubt it,' Jarvis replied. 'I knew the general from back in the first Gulf War, and he was bright as a button and not a man easily fooled. I have no reason to doubt that he'd changed much in the intervening years.'

Lopez frowned, still looking down at the images.

'What about the control method? If this stuff is even possible, that means that it must have been remotely activated. Can we track down what frequency it might have used?'

'Outstanding,' Jarvis replied to her. 'The techs are already looking into it, and we have teams studying X–Rays of the device. You'd better check in down there and get up to speed before you deploy.'

'What's the rush?' Ethan asked, and then he realized immediately. 'Damn, if this thing got into a senior army officer then they could be anywhere.'

'That's right,' Jarvis replied, 'and right now the president can only keep a lid on this for a couple of days before the storm breaks under its own momentum and the media pounces on anything it can find. Can you imagine the panic it will cause if it's revealed that these things even exist and that they could be in the heads of any one of our senior military figures, even the administration itself?'

Ethan turned for the door.

'What's waiting for us downstairs?' Lopez asked.

'You're going to have to see and hear that for yourselves to believe it,' Jarvis said.

***

V

'Hellerman!'

Jarvis led the way into the Defense Intelligence Agency's *Advanced Research and Intelligence Engineering Section*, known as ARIES, allowing Ethan his first glimpse in a long time at one of the most secretive departments in the US defense arsenal.

Created to support to the work of other agencies such as the NSA, CIA and DARPA, ARIES was specifically tasked with emulating the technology of other nations that had been uncovered by overt overseas operations, for the purpose of finding effective defenses against those technologies. In a world where cyber–warfare was becoming more widespread with each passing year, with foreign hackers accessing everything from the computers of major film studios to even the Pentagon and other defense installations, the risk of exposure and manipulation of sensitive material and equipment had never been higher.

Hellerman was a short, bearded and bespectacled operative who had long been Jarvis's right hand man at the agency. He hurried over, his cheerful demeanor infectious.

'Hi guys,' he beamed, and then at Lopez. 'Ma'am.'

Unusually Lopez, more than used to fending off the attentions of men, fawned over Hellerman and hugged him tightly.

'What's up, brainbox?' she asked.

Hellerman, his cheeks flushed with color as Lopez pulled away and a slightly vacant glaze over his eyes, blinked and beamed again.

'Quite a lot, actually. Has Doug brought you up to speed?'

'We know about the implant and what it does,' Ethan said as he shook the scientist's hand. 'But we don't know the *how*.'

'Then step this way,' Hellerman said as he guided them through the laboratory.

Although not quite the marvel of technological fecundity seen in a *Bond* movie, it was hard not to draw comparisons to *Q's* infamous contraptions. Ethan could see scientists experimenting on numerous highly classified objects, including body armor woven from spider web silk and what looked like a self–reassembling, shatter–proof window.

'It's a window made from a temperature sensitive fluid contained within a silicon film,' Hellerman explained as they passed by the sealed lab. 'When a bullet strikes the window, the heat released by the impact causes the fluid within the film, which is solid at room temperature, to melt and stretch.

The heat from the impact is dissipated through the fluid, the fluid begins to solidify, and the bullet is captured in mid–flight and contained by the surrounding film. It all happens in milliseconds, of course. It's a nifty way of protecting the interiors of vehicles and identifying the offending bullet's origin and direction of travel all at once.'

Hellerman led them to a busy little office in one corner of the lab and gestured to something on his desk.

'Check this out,' he said as he reached for a small black box with a dial and a couple of switches mounted upon it.

Ethan saw Hellerman activate a switch and then he flinched as from Hellerman's desk a large bee suddenly lifted off, its wings buzzing loudly in the small office.

'Jesus,' Lopez uttered as she stepped clear of the bee, 'how did that get in here?'

'Don't worry,' Hellerman said cheerfully. 'It's entirely under my control.'

Ethan watched in amazement as Hellerman guided the bee around the periphery of the office using the control box, speaking as he did so.

'The guys at DARPA have been working on creating miniature synthetic drones for decades, mostly copying from nature itself and funding civilian programs to assist them. Some bright spark at the University of California, I'd like to think a guy a bit like me, had the idea of simply attaching their control system to a live bee instead of trying to build replica creatures.'

'Genius,' Lopez mumbled as she ducked to avoid the buzzing insect. 'They're going to sting our enemies to death? How does it work?'

'The bee has a small rig glued to its belly that contains a microchip, which itself connects to the insect's brain and flight muscles. Then, we control it via a laptop computer and this remote unit. Engineers at a place called the Center for Robot Assisted Search And Rescue, at Texas A&M Engineering Experiment Station Center, are developing these little guys to help complex search and rescue missions and disaster relief, flying them into danger zones or small cavities in collapsed buildings to look for survivors.'

'What happens if the bee gets too tired?' Lopez asked.

'Ah,' Hellerman said, 'they stop flying, but we can monitor their wing beats and if performance starts to degrade then we simply fly them out of the danger zone and across to one of these advanced devices.'

Ethan watched as the bee hovered over Hellerman's desk and landed gently alongside a large spoon filled with a clear fluid.

'Sugar water,' Hellerman announced, 'the world's cheapest fuel. The bee takes a drink and is soon ready to get back into action.'

Lopez watched the bee suspiciously as she spoke. 'It's not exactly a stealth bomber though is it, and the technology is not complex enough to control a fully grown man?'

'No,' Hellerman admitted, 'but this is a simpler program that's not a part of DARPA's Black Budget research. That stuff really is top of the line.'

Ethan knew that the US Government's Black Budget was a vast sum of money annually presented to the defense community for development programs so secret that even Congress was not informed of their purpose or content.

'You think that somewhere in the Black Budget there might be an answer to what happened to General Thompson?' Ethan asked.

'For obvious reasons we don't know much about what happens deep within DARPA's most classified projects,' Jarvis replied for Hellerman as he joined them in the office, 'but I do know that DARPA runs a program called Robotic Challenge, and that recently a robot named ATLAS that was part of the program "went dark". It was also being developed as part of programs inspired by the Fukushima nuclear disaster, creating an ability to send machines into areas that would be hazardous to human beings, but I've heard rumors that ATLAS is now being militarized into the world's first fully combat–capable robot. A *Terminator*, effectively.'

'General Thompson wasn't a robot,' Lopez pointed out. 'Could somebody have figured out a way of doing to him what you're doing to that bee?'

'It's a question of complexity,' Hellerman said. 'There's a company in the US that's selling something called *RoboRoach*, which is the first commercially available kit that allows people to remotely control a cockroach. There's an uproar at the moment about the ethics of all this, but official programs have developed various insect drones. A species of beetle named *Mecynorrhina torquata* has been controlled using pulses directed to the insect's optic lobes, with batteries harvesting energy from the insect's own movements to power the pulses. Something closer to a human application involves Dogfish sharks that have had electrodes implanted into their brains which were then used to control their movements, with an aim to using them as underwater research vessels or for seeking out mines in hazardous waters. Even birds have been controlled, with researchers at Shandong University of Science and Technology in China implanting micro–electrodes into a pigeon's brain and flying it at will. Again, much furor among animals rights' groups over such research.'

'But wouldn't anybody controlled in such a way just shout out that they were being manipulated?' Ethan asked. 'A pigeon or shark can't protest what's being done to them, but General Thompson certainly would have done had he been able to do so.'

Hellerman gestured to an image pinned to the wall of his office that depicted a human brain via a CAT scan of some kind, the various regions of the brain highlighted.

'According to the autopsy report, the artifact was removed from General Thompson's brain and had originally penetrated the frontal lobes, one of four main lobes in human brains and those of all mammals. The precentral gyrus, which is located near the rearmost border of the frontal lobe, contains the primary motor cortex which controls the voluntary movements of our various body parts. However, it also contains the dopamine sensitive neurons of the cerebral cortex which are associated with reward, short term memory, planning, motivation and attention.' Hellerman tapped the image of the frontal lobes with one finger. 'If you can control this region of the brain sufficiently, stimulating the dopamine sensitive regions while at the same time controlling the victim's motor cortex, then you won't have to worry about them crying foul when they open fire on their own family because they'll be smiling and dreaming while they're doing it.' Hellerman shrugged. 'They may even be asleep.'

'Asleep?' Lopez asked.

'It's quite common for people to conduct quite complex tasks while effectively being alseep,' Hellerman explained. 'Have you ever driven along a stretch of road for a prolonged period of time and then suddenly wondered what happened over the last ten minutes?'

'Occasionally,' Ethan admitted.

'Then you were in some respects asleep,' Hellerman replied, 'driving on autopilot. The processes involved were so natural and instinctive to you that your brain did not need to be fully involved and so it began to quieten down. I know that now and again I've been dreaming while behind the wheel and still watching the road in front of me at the same time. I'm not going to admit that to a police officer, but we all know that it's happened once or twice. If the people that developed the device that was found in General Thompson's brain had perfected a means of keeping their victims in a pliant state while controlling their actions, then they could have created the perfect assassin: an individual with access to anywhere, who could be controlled from afar and would raise no suspicions. Can you imagine what could be done with such individuals? *Area 51* workers could be sent into Groom Lake to find the aliens, or Wall Street financiers used to get the lowdown on the latest stock market developments, or senior government figures used to get into the Pentagon to gather state secrets.' Hellerman became somewhat sobered. 'Or scientists to sabotage nuclear facilities and create Hell on earth.'

Ethan peered at the image of the human brain and then looked down at the bee on the desk, still sipping from the sugar water.

'That's our clue,' he said finally.

Jarvis looked at Ethan. 'What do you mean?'

'They wouldn't be able to infiltrate Area 51, or a nuclear facility,' Ethan explained.

'Why not?' Lopez argued. 'If they can control an individual long enough to get them into Fort Benning, they could do the same at the Pentagon or even the White House.'

'It's not about the control,' Ethan said. 'We need to look at all photo and video footage of the Fort Benning attack, because our real killers will be on it.'

'General Thompson did the shooting,' Jarvis pointed out. 'His killers could be anywhere within signal range, many miles away.'

'No,' Ethan countered. 'All of these mind control programs have one thing in common. They control the body, even the brain to a point, but they do not control the *eyes*.'

Lopez raised an eyebrow. 'The hackers would need line of sight to control their victims.'

'To see what they see,' Ethan confirmed. 'It's possible they could attach micro–cameras to their victims.' Ethan turned to Jarvis. 'Have the lab people check out General Thompson's uniform, see if there's a concealed camera anywhere on it.'

Jarvis turned away as he reached for his cell phone and began dialing.

'You think they'd have to be close to the victims to make this all work?' Lopez asked.

'Think about it,' Ethan said. 'You've got a senior official under your control and you walk them straight into the Pentagon. If you're not inside the building with them then you're effectively blind and cannot control your victim, you can't see where they're going.'

'And they can't be allowed any degree of autonomy,' Hellerman agreed, 'or they'd break free and cry for help.'

'So they would need visual aids of some kind,' Ethan went on, 'either that, or they'd need further implants to see what the victim was seeing and further signals to relay that information to whoever was controlling the victim.'

Jarvis turned to Ethan.

'They found nothing,' he reported. 'General Thompson was in the open when he killed the recruits at Fort Benning, but he killed his family as they slept in their beds.'

Ethan frowned. 'Then how could his controllers see what he was doing?'

'Whoever did this, they're already in the country and they'll have more victims lined up because the technology must already be in place,' Jarvis said. 'I don't think that General Thompson's rampage was the main act. I think it was a test run.'

'Test run for what?' Hellerman asked.

'Something bigger,' Lopez realized. 'Much bigger.'

***

VI

J. Edgar Hoover Building, Pennsylvania Avenue,

Washington DC

No big deal.

That's what FBI Special Agent Hannah Ford kept telling herself as she stepped into the headquarters of the Federal Bureau of Investigation, the brutalist architecture of the high rise building basking in the bright sunlight outside, just a few blocks down from the White House.

Despite her clearly displayed identity badge and having the appointment booked for her, Hannah was still subject to the routine scanners, bomb dog and pat down before her arrival was recorded in the daily log and she was allowed inside the building. All around, in almost every hallway, were displayed images of the FBI's *Ten Most Wanted*, permanent reminders of the Bureau's endless mission to seek out those who had taken flight from US justice and bring them back to face the courts.

Hannah Ford felt the weight of that mission upon her shoulders in the presence of so many indicators of just how many enemies of the state were out there to make her task seem impossible. Since the events of September 2001, the FBI had tripled the number of intelligence analysts and altered its internal structure to streamline its intelligence gathering capabilities, all to counter the increasing threat from within America's shores, where Islamic militants and their sympathizers plotted and conspired to bring mayhem and grief wherever they travelled.

But today her meeting was not about Islamic State, nor anarchist groups scratching a meagre existence in the Nevada badlands, or biker gangs or drug lords. Today her meeting was about a former United States Marine, an ex–DC cop and a shadowy covert agent who was apparently both dead and very much alive. Hannah had found herself embroiled in a case so labyrinthine that she barely knew where to begin.

Hannah walked past an indoor gun range, the bullet proof window of the viewing platform frosted over to conceal the testing session ongoing within. Hannah could just make out the muffled *pop pop* of small arms fire as she passed by and then caught an elevator up to the fourth floor.

Despite having completed her training at Quantico almost ten years previously and having served loyally for a decade, Hannah had never met the Director of the FBI. In all fairness most agents didn't get to meet the DFBI, scattered as they were in field offices and consulate buildings across the globe. Hannah slowed and checked her appearance in the reflection of a door window. Her gray suit contrasted with her long auburn hair and green eyes, but her jaw looked a little too tense, her mouth a thin hard line.

Lighten up, she told herself. *They* asked for the meeting, remember?

Hannah took a breath and walked the last few paces to the Director's office before she knocked and entered. A receptionist looked up at her and without prompting keyed a microphone on her desk and spoke quickly and efficiently.

'Special Agent Ford is here to see you sir.'

'Send her in, Clara.'

Clara nodded at Hannah, who aimed for the next door, this one highly polished and bearing the name of Gordon LeMay. She opened the door and walked in to see LeMay sitting behind a large, polished desk. Two computer monitors adorned the desk along with pictures of LeMay's family, and the desk itself was flanked by the Stars and Stripes and a second flag bearing the FBI's seal.

LeMay got to his feet, surprisingly tall with heavy jowls and a belly that stretched his white shirt. His gray hair, eyes and suit gave Hannah the impression that LeMay was appearing before her in black and white. She shook his hand, firm and dry, saw him smile and was reminded of a great white shark.

'Please, sit down Agent Ford.'

Not so much a request as a command, LeMay's voice gravelly with age. Hannah sat down opposite the Director and waited patiently.

'I appreciate you coming here at such short notice,' LeMay began. 'Agent Jenkins said that she could not spare you for this meeting on company time.'

Special Agent in Charge Jenkins, the head of Hannah's Field Office in Virginia and a thorn in Hannah's side for the past three years, had done everything that she could to prevent Hannah from making the meeting. Jealous, angry and petulant, Jenkins had developed a deep hatred for her ever since Hannah had successfully apprehended a number of high–profile fugitives and foiled a major attack on a solar plant outside of Las Vegas just months before.

'Jenkins has her hands full,' Hannah replied diplomatically, not wanting to vent on the Director until she understood what the meeting was about.

'So I hear,' LeMay murmured in reply. 'The events at Crescent Dunes have propelled you into the Bureau's star agent list, and I suspect that Jenkins dislikes being outshone.'

Hannah chose her words with care. 'She has ambitions of her own.'

'But she doesn't have the results to back those ambitions,' LeMay countered, and then pointed a hooked finger at her. 'You do Hannah, which is why you're here.'

Hannah waited dutifully for the Director to continue.

'It's come to my attention that in the aftermath of the Crescent Dunes arrests you've been conducting an investigation of your own, off–books.'

Hannah could not prevent herself from startling somewhat and she raised her eyebrows in surprise.

'I didn't know that anybody was watching me off hours, sir,' she said with some resentment.

LeMay raised a hand to forestall her protest.

'This is not a rebuke, Agent Ford. Your persistence in this matter is appreciated, not condemned. You have been pulling files on a number of former fugitives from this agency by the names of Warner, Lopez and Meyer?'

Hannah nodded, figuring that there was no point in hiding anything. LeMay probably knew it all anyway and was testing her honesty.

'The Meyer family is clean and of no further interest to the Bureau but Ethan Warner and Nicola Lopez are something of an enigma. They were wanted by the Bureau and yet upon their capture, by me, they were promptly freed. I've dug as deep as I can in the official records and they're featured all over the place, but every document is so heavily redacted that I can't make head nor tail of who they're working for. All I have is Warner's assertion, in interview, that he works for the Defense Intelligence Agency. I checked him out and nobody at the DIA knew a damned thing about either Warner or Lopez, yet they're facing twenty to life in a federal prison and they're released? Last I looked, they were still working as bail bondsmen out of Chicago like nothing's happened?'

Director LeMay leaned back in his seat and cradled his chin on the back of his interlocked fingers as he regarded her for a long moment.

'Is that all?'

Hannah bit her lip for a moment before replying.

'Warner made mention of a homicide scene we were investigating that was connected to the Meyers. He seemed to know that there was a third person present at the scene who may have been the killer, despite not having been present at the murder. I couldn't figure out how he could have known that information, especially since he revealed the name of the individual: Aaron James Mitchell.'

Hannah was not attempting to analyze her own boss, but she saw the briefest of tremors in the old man's eyes, a sign of recognition.

'Did you pursue this matter further?' LeMay asked, his tone guarded.

'The FBI field team analyzed blood found at the murder scene that did not belong to the victim, and claimed that no matches were found in the system. Given all that was happening at the time, I decided to take a second sample off the books and had it DNA tested.' Hannah thought that she heard LeMay sigh softly as she continued. 'It matched Mitchell, whose official records at the Department of Defense state that he died some two decades ago.'

LeMay seemed to think for a moment before replying.

'And you've been attempting to hunt this Mitchell down?'

'No,' Hannah replied. 'I've simply been trying to figure out why he would have been at that homicide scene and why he would be listed as dead by the DoD and yet clearly still be very much alive and working for somebody. I'm assuming he faked his own passing and is now able to operate criminally with some level of impunity – it's tough to get caught when nobody's looking for you.'

LeMay nodded. 'And what of Warner and Lopez?'

Hannah shrugged. 'They're pretty much untouchable. I spoke to the Chicago field office and they did some digging. Warner was in trouble with the law for a short while some years back but has been clean as a whistle since. Lopez used to wear the blues of the Metropolitan Police Department here in DC, no criminal record, no nothing. Seems like they teamed up a few years ago and there's some anecdotal evidence that they've turned up at the scene of DIA investigations around the world, but again, everything's redacted. About all I can say for sure is that they travel across the country pursuing bail jumpers but they only have jurisdiction in Illinois. It's a thin cover, but for what I don't know.'

'Both Warner and Lopez were exonerated,' LeMay pointed out. 'Neither committed any crime and both were cleared of involvement.'

'Yes, but by *whom* were they cleared?' Hannah pressed. 'Who the hell has the power to quash a homicide investigation and at the same time order the release of two known fugitives involved in that same crime and a lot more besides? This should have been a slam–dunk case, even if Warner and Lopez were innocent and it turned out Mitchell was the perp'. Stanley Meyer was murdered, sir, and every suspect we have is suddenly untouchable? How does that figure?'

LeMay uncradled his chin and leaned forward on the desk, his big hands folded together and his eyes fixed upon Hannah's as he replied.

'There are forces at work here, Agent Ford, that extend far beyond the boundaries of the homicide in Virginia. I have been researching the same material as you, for some time in fact, and it has become clear to me that elements of the intelligence community have begun an initiative to subvert the authority of the FBI.'

Hannah stared blankly at LeMay. 'How, and why?'

LeMay took a deep breath and replied in what sounded to Hannah like a resigned tone.

'The FBI has long since ceased to be the most powerful of our country's agencies. In the wake of nine–eleven precedence has been given to overseas intelligence gathering, the work of the CIA, the National Security Agency and the Defense Intelligence Agency.'

'But the greatest problem for us is the homegrown terrorist,' Hannah said, 'the lone wolf nobody can see coming but us. Look at the attacks at the Boston marathon. The FBI's role can't be downgraded in favor of hunting down enemies of the state in countries thousands of miles away. If we're not patrolling our own back yard then who's going to stop the next bombing or another nine–eleven?'

'My sentiments exactly,' LeMay replied and slapped one open–palmed hand down on the desk between them in a display of satisfaction. 'But Congress is still trying to bust us down along with the other agencies, especially after the Edward Snowden affair. We've all been up in front of the Special Committee and explained that we cannot protect this country with one hand tied behind our backs. Increasingly, terrorist activities are being conducted by people who otherwise look, sound and act like Americans. We *have* to listen in on them, we *have* to pry into their lives, but if they turn out to be innocent…'

'Then they have nothing to fear,' Hannah completed the sentence.

She knew well the furor created by human rights activists appalled at how agencies such as the super–secretive National Security Agency could listen in to any phone call or monitor any digital communication they chose, breaching any number of privacy laws under the protective veil of the Patriot Act. But she also knew that the agencies in question did so in order to seek out terrorists, not to find out if somebody's aunty's grandmother had steak for dinner. The NSA's servers could monitor millions of communications every second, but it was a task far too gargantuan for human beings to pore over the immense reams of data the agency produced every day. Instead the data was scanned, analyzed and filtered by computers specifically programmed to hunt out only the kind of communications transmitted by those who might intend to cause harm to others. The human rights activists too often forgot that while fighting to protect the human rights of citizens, they could also inadvertently place them in harm's way.

Gordon LeMay folded his hands once more as he spoke.

'The Defense Intelligence Agency has seen fit to reactivate a covert intelligence operation that was shut down by the CIA and FBI some years ago. Warner and Lopez are a central part of that operation and have already escaped arrest on numerous occasions by operating beneath the protective umbrella of DIA undercover investigations. I want you to start monitoring what they're up to and report to me directly.'

Hannah almost fell out of her chair.

'What about the Virginia office?' she asked without thinking. 'Jenkins will do everything that she can to sabotage anything I do and…'

'I wouldn't worry about Jenkins,' LeMay said. 'I will ensure that she gives you all the support you require.'

Hannah composed herself, re–engaged her brain. 'Sir, you're effectively asking me to spy on a sister agency.'

'I'm asking you to spy on its agents,' LeMay corrected her. 'I can reveal to you that Warner and Lopez received a full presidential pardon after what happened at Crescent Dunes and appear to have a close link to the incumbent president that I was not aware of. I'd like to know more about that, with the aim of bringing the pair of them to justice for their crimes. If they do anything illegal, anything at all, I want them brought in.'

Hannah thought hard for a moment.

'What about Mitchell? He's in the frame for the murder of Stanley Meyer.'

'Use this operation to find out more about Mitchell,' LeMay said. 'I believe that the DIA are looking for him too. Two birds…'

Hannah nodded, not entirely sure of what she was getting in to.

'Report to me alone,' LeMay repeated as they stood. 'Let's bring this injustice to an end, and honor the values we swore to uphold when we joined the FBI.'

'Yes sir,' Hannah replied.

***

VII

DIAC Building,

Washington DC

'We've got something.'

Ethan looked up from where he and Lopez were searching through traffic camera footage from around Fort Benning, hoping to detect vehicle movements that would coincide with General Thompson's suicidal rampage.

'What is it?' Ethan asked Hellerman as he hurried over.

Hellerman was holding a flash–RAM drive that he plugged straight into a nearby laptop, accessing a series of files as he spoke.

'Traffic camera footage from Columbus, Georgia. We managed to pick up General Thompson's drive to Fort Benning on the morning of his death. He left real early out of Parkwood, his family home, so we spotted him easily.'

Ethan watched with Lopez as a series of stills appeared on the screen, each depicting the general's champagne–colored sedan making its way south out of Parkwood toward Fort Benning. It didn't take long for them to figure out what Hellerman had seen.

'There's a goods vehicle in all of the shots,' Lopez identified it.

A white van, non–descript, travelling in the same direction as the general's vehicle all the way to Fort Benning. Ethan leaned close to the screen, but the poor resolution prevented an identification of the license plates or the occupants.

'We already found the vehicle though,' Hellerman informed them. 'Local law enforcement found it burned out near a town called Preston, fifty miles south of Fort Benning. The vehicle had been stolen forty eight hours before in Alabama.'

Ethan frowned thoughtfully.

'That was a dumb move. The smart play is to simply abandon a vehicle, not burn it and advertise its presence to law enforcement. They could have driven it into deep woodland and it wouldn't have been found for months.'

'What're you thinking?' Lopez asked him.

'Professional, high–tech equipment used to reprogram a senior soldier's brain to commit an act of mass homicide, and yet the perps' are too dumb to conceal their vehicle? That smacks to me of hired help of some kind. Either our perps are not real smart and got somebody else to do their technical work for them, or they're very clever but are entrusting the actual trigger–pulling to local thugs.'

'It figures,' Hellerman said. 'The labs still haven't finished working on the implant device yet but they all agree that it's state of the art, literally. They haven't seen anything so advanced in their careers to date, and believe me they've seen some stuff you just wouldn't believe.'

'So have we,' Lopez pointed out. '*Project Watchman*, for instance. Maybe we could use that to check these guys out and find out where they went after they dumped the van?'

Ethan looked at Hellerman expectantly. He and Lopez had learned of *Project Watchman* during a previous investigation into a man who had apparently been able to see into the future. Desperate to get ahead of their quarry, Jarvis had enlisted the help of NASA and revealed *Watchman*, a program that enlisted spy satellites to record events on the continental United States in unprecedented detail from multiple angles, and compile the resulting data into a virtual world through which investigators could walk. Despite its flaws, *Watchman* could have revolutionized criminal investigations, but it was Jarvis who shattered the hope of using *Watchman* on the case.

'Watchman was deactivated last year,' he told them as he entered the room. 'Too high a risk of congressional investigations of human rights breaches by the National Reconnaissance Office. The Director of the NRO didn't want Congress knowing anything about our current spying capacity and seeing it spread across every news outlet in the western world.'

Ethan rubbed his temples.

'So we've got the tech' but we can't use it?'

'Afraid so,' Jarvis confirmed, 'welcome to a world where terrorist mass–murderers have human rights but their victims don't.'

Ethan shook his head and stared at the laptop screen for a moment as he tried to think of some other way to pinpoint the perpetrator's movements and pin them down.

'What do we have in the arsenal already that uses a similar technology to what we're seeing here? Is there anything that might point us toward a likely origin of this sort of technology?'

Hellerman gestured to the screen.

'A white van doesn't tell us anything about who's behind this, but it's fair to say that the technology has existed within the military for some time. Even today, you can go on–line and buy a brain–controlled toy helicopter that you fly with the power of your mind.'

'Seriously?' Lopez asked.

'Sure, they're not even that expensive,' Hellerman explained. 'The medical industry has spent decades developing prosthetics for amputees, but while legs have come on in leaps and bounds, pardon the pun, arms and grasping hands have been a major stumbling point.'

'You're a comic genius,' Lopez smiled at Hellerman, 'and you don't even know it.'

'It's a gift,' he replied, embarrassed. 'The point is that having a chunk of plastic powered by servos stuck to your shoulder wasn't working for the recipients, and so research in brain function resulted in the creation of prosthetics that actually connect to the brain itself via existing muscles, tendons and by extension neural networks, allowing the brain to control the prosthetic limb directly. If I recall correctly, a man named Igor Spetic was the first recipient to receive one of these radical new prosthetic arms and the effects were spectacular. The phantom limb pain he had experienced for years from his missing arm vanished, and when a researcher brushed the back of his prosthetic arm with one hand, Spetic *felt* his arm hairs rising in response to the touch.'

'How is that even possible?' Ethan asked.

'The doctors attached electrode cuffs to the arm and then attached those to the nerves that remained in the recipient's upper arm. Not only could he feel the touch, he could tell what it was that was touching him. Having the prosthetic directly attached to the skeleton and neuromuscular system, by means of what has been termed osseointegration, completely alters the wearer's perception of their prosthetic and in some cases they forget it's a replacement limb at all.'

'It's amazing, sure, but what's this got to do with General Thompson?'

Hellerman gestured to the screen and the image of the white van.

'I've been thinking about what happened to the general and of how anybody could control a human being so precisely. I mean, they couldn't just type in a command to a keyboard like: "kill yourself", and expect the recipient of the command to then turn a pistol to their own head. It involves too many competing neural pathways, too much to get in the way, too many things that could go wrong.'

'So, what then?' Ethan asked. 'You think that somebody in that van was sitting their talking Thompson through killing dozens of people?'

'No,' Hellerman said. 'I think that they were using the power of their own mind to send signals to the implant in Thompson's brain. I don't think that they were directing him at all – I think that they'd taken over his thoughts, that they'd literally hacked his brain.'

A moment of silence enveloped the room in the wake of Hellerman's statement.

'Hacked his brain,' Lopez echoed. 'How could anybody make an otherwise sane person commit such awful acts without stopping themselves?'

Hellerman got up from his seat and hurried across to a pile of journals stacked in an unsteady pile in the corner of his office. He fumbled through them for a moment, muttering as he went.

'There is a process known as transcranial direct current stimulation, or tDCS for short, that's become something of a phenomenon in recent years. There are freely available plans on–line directing people how to build these things, which mimic actual medical equipment, and attach them to their heads.'

'What the hell for?' Ethan asked.

'Ah, here we go,' Hellerman announced triumphantly as he produced a journal and flicked it open to a relevant page. 'TDCS is the direct application of electrical current to the brain in order to induce an altered state that enhances cognition, motor control and memory in order to manage chronic pain and motor, sensory and neurological disorders.'

Lopez frowned as she glanced at the page Hellerman was showing him. 'People are zapping their own brains for fun these days?'

'The currents are tiny compared to those used in electroconvulsive therapy,' Hellerman explained. 'The devices apply current for ten to twenty minutes and the results have been extremely encouraging. The theory behind it all is that a weak direct current alters the electric potential of nerve membranes within the brain, which is said to make it easier for neurons to fire. There have been reports that tDCS can reduce pain and depression, repair stroke damage and improve recovery rates from brain injuries, as well as improving memory, reasoning and fluency. And it's not a temporary thing – those improvements persist for days and even months.'

'And you think that this technology also applies to what happened to General Thompson?' Ethan pressed.

'Scientists at Duke University in North Carolina managed to link the brains of two rats together and showed that signals from one rat's brain could help the second rat solve a problem it would otherwise have no clue how to solve. The rats were in different cages with no way to communicate other than through electrodes implanted in their brains. The transfer of information even worked when one rat was in a lab in North Carolina and another was in a lab in Brazil.'

'So as long as a signal was available and able to get through,' Jarvis said, 'one person could technically control another person's brain from afar with nothing more than the power of thought?'

'Precisely,' Hellerman agreed. 'Brain hacking, or using electrical stimulation to control a person's movements or medical conditions, has been used for a long time and so signal control is only a modern version of the same principal. Scribonius Largus, a Roman physician who lived in the first century, prescribed the electric ray shock as a cure for headaches, and nineteenth century pioneers like Alessandro Volta and Luigi Galvani created bioelectric experiments with similar aims in mind. With today's technology it's potentially possible that a person could be completely remotely controlled from a distance, given the right conditions.'

Ethan leaned back against one wall of the office as he rolled what Hellerman had said through his mind. Thompson had committed a terrible atrocity, completely at odds with his character, before taking his own life. But Thompson had also been known as an extremely strong character, not somebody who would easily bend to wayward electrical impulses firing through his brain.

'Could they really have controlled somebody like Thompson in such a way? Wouldn't a four–star general have been able to mentally fight back?'

'That depends on what his mental state was like at the time,' Hellerman countered. 'Remember, the implant we found could have been capable of altering his mental state too. If he felt as though he were in a dream of some kind, barely conscious, then he may not have had any awareness at all of his situation. That's what this tDCS represents, the ability to directly affect not just mental state but actual cognition through electrical stimulation of certain brain regions. If this technology is good enough then one human being could come under the control of another human being and be completely powerless to oppose their commands not through a lack of will, but through a lack of *awareness* that they've been hacked at all. Like I said earlier, they may have felt as though they were asleep and may not have had any recollection of their actions at all.'

Ethan looked at the image on the screen for a moment longer and then at Jarvis, who was leaning against another wall and listening to the conversation.

'We can't track these people down,' he said, somewhat alarmed. 'We don't have a damned thing to go on and they could be out of the country by now.'

'We need more signals data,' Jarvis agreed. 'And for that, we'll need…'

'Another attack,' Lopez finished the sentence. 'Damn, we really don't know who or where they're going to strike next?'

'We're blind,' Hellerman confirmed. 'Just like their victims we don't know anything about the next target. Our country is facing lone wolf terrorist attacks where even the wolves don't know they're the enemy.'

'All we have is General Thompson's medical history,' Ethan said. 'He was targeted somewhere by somebody. We need to know how that implant got into his head.'

***

VIII

USS Carl Vinson (CVN–70),

Persian Gulf

'Razor Flight, approach vector, ETA overhead sixty seconds.'

Commander Sandy Vieron kept his gaze fixed on the F–18C Hornet fighter upon which he was formating as the two aircraft descended through broken cumulus cloud that raced past them, the wingtip of his formation leader barely eight feet away. The surface of the vivid blue ocean sparkled beneath them, cloud shadows drifting across it as Sandy changed hands on the control column and without looking pulled a lever that extended the arrestor hook from the stern of his fighter.

Beside him, he saw the lead F–18's black and white striped hook lower at the same time, a visual signal to the Landing Signal Officer that both aircraft intended to land after their overhead pass.

Bright sunlight flared between the clouds as Sandy switched his hands back to the throttle and stick, shadows flickering across the cockpit in quick succession as Sandy input tiny variations on all of the controls to maintain position in close formation with his leader as they levelled out below the broken cloud base, descending to eight hundred feet above sea level at three hundred fifty knots.

The mission had been an uneventful Combat Air Patrol some two hundred fifty nautical miles to the west of the carrier's position, close to the border of Iranian airspace. Now, close to *bingo* fuel status and tired after four hours in the saddle, Sandy was looking forward to some rest and a meal. The sunlight flickering through the canopy lulled his eyes and he felt the warmth from it, so hot and irritating up until now, suddenly cosset him in a blanket of warmth and safety. Sandy smiled beneath the plastic oxygen mask he wore as he held station alongside Razor One and saw their runway appear from the surface of the ocean before them.

The huge nuclear aircraft carrier USS Carl Vinson was a thin strip of dull metallic gray, her hundred thousand ton steel hull dwarfed by the vast and pristine ocean. The two Hornets were approaching the immense vessel from astern in close formation, and as they passed overhead Razor One called their position.

'Razor flight overhead for recovery.'

As Sandy held position and the carrier rushed by eight hundred feet below the flight leader's Hornet suddenly rolled onto its side, displaying to Sandy an oil–streaked belly and combat load of sleek air–to–air missiles and a pair of five hundred pound laser–guided bombs. The fighter pulled away hard, vapor trails spiraling off the wing tips as it broke into the pattern.

Sandy watched the Hornet pull away and then without thinking he rolled and pulled too, G–forces crushing him into his ejection seat as the fighter loaded up into the turn. Sandy blinked, coming awake as though from a dream as he pulled the fighter through the turn and heard his leader report his position, downwind to land.

'Razor One you're number one to land, report ball.'

Sandy levelled his Hornet out, now a nautical mile abeam the carrier as he rapidly selected his undercarriage, lowered the flaps and went through the pre–landing checks that he had carried out hundreds of times before, finishing with locking his ejector seat harness. As the G–forces eased he felt the warmth returning, began to smile to himself once more. He looked up through the Hornet's *Heads Up Display*, and through the flight information displayed on the glass he saw his flight leader turning onto his final approach.

'Razor one, you're at three quarters of a mile, call the ball.'

'Razor one, ball, clara one decimal eight.'

'Roger, Razor.'

Sandy listened as he heard the Landing Signal Officer, himself a fighter pilot, take control of the landing phase from the carrier's tower as the Hornet descended toward the rolling, pitching deck. He smiled as he watched his leader making a perfect approach, reveled in the warmth of his cockpit and fought the urge to sing a song as he flew by unthinking reflex toward the final turning point and eased his Hornet into the base–leg turn, the fighter's wings rocking on the wind currents and the G–force increasing gently again as he turned.

Hypoxia.

The word leaped into Sandy's mind and his brain sharpened once more as he glanced at his oxygen indicators. Hypoxia, the result of oxygen starvation to the brain, started with feelings of inexplicable comfort and then euphoria, swiftly followed by unconsciousness, coma and death. Sandy and all military pilots were trained to identify the onset of hypoxia before it became lethal but as he looked at his oxygen indicators he realized that both were in the green, normal flow, plenty of oxygen available. Sandy blinked, confused as he continued his turn and levelled out, his Hornet fighter now just four hundred feet above the ocean and a nautical mile astern the carrier.

'Razor Two you're at three quarters of a mile, call the ball.'

Sandy glanced at the *ball*, a series of lights on the port side of the massive carrier's deck called a Fresnel lens that indicated how far, if at all, he was high, low or adrift of the optimum glideslope to bring the Hornet slamming down onto the crowded deck and decelerate from one hundred forty knots to a standstill in the space of a hundred feet.

'Razor Two, roger ball, clara one decimal six.'

Sandy completed his final checks, the ocean sparkling before him and the sunlight flickering through the clouds drifting high above. *Fuel checked, harness locked, weapons cold…* Sandy's eyelids drooped even as he heard the LSO's gentle commands.

'You're looking good, a little high, ease off the power…'

Sandy's head drifted up to look once again through the Heads Up Display, and then his arm moved of its own accord from the throttle to the armament switches on the control panel before him. Sandy flipped the switch's security cover off and activated the Hornet's ordnance array as with another switch atop his control column he switched the HUD from landing settings to ground–attack display.

'Keep it comin', you're looking good.'

Sandy moved the control column and rocked the throttles without conscious thought, keeping the Hornet on a near–perfect glideslope designed to ensure that the fighter's arrestor hook snared the number three wire. Too low, and the aircraft risked smashing into the "fan tail" at the ship's stern. Too high, and it risked missing all the wires and shooting a "bolter" right off the deck and into the air again.

'A little high,' the LSO warned, *'come off the power.'*

Sandy could see his leader's F–18C taxiing across the deck, its wings folded up to conserve space on a deck crowded with crew and parked aircraft and helicopters, the ship an immense floating city and airport all in one. The movement and the aircraft's colorful tail markings, denoting the Commander of the Air Group's personal jet, caught his eye and his gloved hands twitched on the controls.

'You're high and wide,' the LSO called.

Sandy barely heard the LSO as he turned the F–18C Hornet and lined up the aiming reticule in his HUD onto the taxiing aircraft's gray fuselage. The voice in his ears grew loud and panicked.

'Razor Two, wave off, wave off, power!!'

Sandy smiled as he moved his thumb across the fire switch and slammed the Hornet's engines into full afterburner. The fighter lurched forward as flames blazed from its twin exhausts and the aircraft roared overhead the deck, and Sandy chuckled to himself as he squeezed the launch button twice in quick succession.

The Hornet's fuselage shuddered twice as powerful charges propelled the two five hundred pound incendiary bombs off the inner wing pylons. Sandy pulled back on his control column and reached out to retract the undercarriage and flaps as suddenly the Hornet rocked violently from side to side.

Sandy looked over his shoulder as he rolled to one side in a steep climbing turn and saw his bombs impact the carrier's deck with twin blossoming fireballs that raked across the parked aircraft. Two parked Hornets, their wings laden with live ordnance, exploded amid the massive fireballs and Sandy saw bodies hurled off the deck to spiral into the ocean below as his earphones screeched with horrified commands.

'Razor Two, desist immediately! Razor Two, do you copy?!!'

Sandy heard only a distant cacophony of cries as he held the throttles wide open in full afterburner despite his perilously low fuel supply. The Hornet climbed vertically away from the ugly clouds of black smoke billowing from flames sweeping across the carrier's deck, fuel lines and bomb trolleys ablaze as Sandy watched through the top of the canopy as his Hornet came off the top of a loop two thousand feet above the carnage.

Sandy kept pulling, kept the throttles wide open as he began to dive, keen to see the results of his efforts. The Hornet soared downward and accelerated wildly, and then suddenly the G–forces increased and slammed Sandy down into his seat, pulling the blood from his head and brain as his G–suit inflated to prevent his blood from pooling in his legs.

Sandy blinked as though coming awake from a dream, and before him a kaleidoscopic milieu of color sharpened into focus and he saw the deck rushing up at him and a scene of utter carnage, of running crewmen trailing flames, of bodies scattered in pieces across the scorched deck, of burning aircraft and helicopters and corpses.

Sandy's scream joined the terrible cacophony even as his Hornet slammed vertically into the carrier's bow with the force of a fallen angel at four hundred knots and vanished in a superheated fireball that spread across the deck.

***

IX

Zubayr, Iraq

'Fire team, cover Echo point.'

Lieutenant Larry Bryant of the 48th Infantry Brigade's Combat Team eased alongside the crumbling wall of an abandoned compound, the sun blazing off the baked walls and scorched earth, sweat beading on his forehead and itchy beneath his combat fatigues as he cradled his M–16 rifle and peered around a corner.

The desolate Iraqi desert stretched away to his right, while to his left meagre towns built it seemed from the very earth itself, the walls as crumbling and abandoned as the deserts, stood forlornly to reach up into the hard and unforgiving blue skies.

'Bryant, Echo, standing by.'

Larry waited for the command to enter the compound, glimpsing through his sunglasses the shapes of his fellow troops forming up into covering positions, their weapons held at the ready. There was minimal chatter on the RT, and when any voice was heard it was clipped and short, tight with tension that made Larry's jaw and temples ache.

The briefing had been just that – brief. A tip off. A location, abandoned, far out to the south of Basra. Unreliable source, a hostage sighting. *Proceed with extreme caution.* Everybody knew what that meant. As a former regular US Army soldier and now Georgian reservist supporting the fledgling Iraqi army as it fought to control the country against the ferocious rise of Islamic State, Larry was well used to combat situations, but this one was a tight–wire even for him. Just get us in there for Christ's sake and get it over with.

'Eagle eye, in position.'

The snipers were ready, covering from higher vantage points further back in the district. There was little wind and they were "sun down", the sun behind them and thus not restricting their vision, perfectly placed to pick off any ambush attackers.

There was a moment's pause and then the commanding officer's voice crackled down the radio.

'Entry team, fire team, go now now now!'

Larry burst into motion and dashed into the compound as behind him twenty more soldiers, all heavily festooned with webbing, weapons, water and other battle kit thundered across a deserted courtyard. Larry's eyes swept the scene as he moved, hyper–alert for any sign of a threat.

Debris was strewn across the courtyard, desiccated weeds poked from cracked cement, broken down walls surrounded open doorways that were as black as night inside. The walls were pockmarked with impact craters from mortars and small arms, the ageing signs of conflict from two major wars fought by US forces over the decades. No vehicles, few footprints, no enemy fire.

Larry made straight for the main entrance, the doors hanging from their hinges having been blasted in long ago by some other fire team, probably clearing the building of insurgents a decade before. He slammed against the wall alongside the entrance as two of his men hurled flash–bangs inside and took up positions alongside their lieutenant, eyes down, gloved fingers in ears. Larry pulled off his sunglasses, his eyes closed and one finger curled over his rifle's trigger.

A double boom thundered through the building and Larry whirled and rushed inside, his M–16 held before him as he hunted through the gloom. A cloud of gray smoke swirled from the flash–bangs as he plunged through it, all around him soldiers shouting as they advanced through the long abandoned home.

'Clear left!'

'Clear right!'

'Eagle eye, no movement.'

'Fire team, advance! Bravo, hold position!'

Larry's command echoed around the hollow walls as they moved, half of the fire team holding a defensive position as the rest of the men followed Larry through the building. He could already see the rear courtyard down a long hall, a bright rectangle of flaring sunlight, rooms splitting off either side of him filled with debris and the rusting springs of old beds. A hotel or guesthouse maybe, sometime long in the past.

'Enemy!'

Larry flinched and dropped down into a firing position as he saw a figure lunge into sight further down the corridor and the flash of an assault rifle muzzle. Bullets zipped past him as he fired, both of the men behind him likewise opening up on the silhouette confronting them with a withering hail of automatic fire.

The figure shuddered as multiple rounds tore into his body and slammed him onto his back on the ground, the rifle in his hands clattering down alongside him.

'Advance!'

Larry, his eyes and ears supernaturally attuned now as adrenaline soared through his bloodstream, advanced in his crouched posture to the edge of the doorway, which opened out onto a small courtyard and an outbuilding perched in one corner.

The body of the man before him was riddled with bullets, blood seeping from each wound and the man's chest rising and falling rapidly as he struggled to take his last breaths. Pink bubbles frothed around the corners of his mouth as blood leaked into his punctured lungs, and his dark eyes stared up into the hard blue sky above.

Larry watched him for a moment and then waved his men past. They bolted out into the courtyard, weapons aiming this way and that as a second fire team entered their field of view ahead, cutting off any potential enemy's escape route.

'North entrance clear!' Larry called into his microphone.

'South entrance clear!'

Larry advanced toward the outbuilding, its crumbling walls and shattered windows long abandoned. As he breached the entrance with his rifle held before him he was beginning to wonder if this whole thing had been a bust when he saw the bright white walls of the rearmost room to his right. He slowed, glanced over his shoulder and indicated to his men that he had seen something ahead. Then, he positioned them on the left side of the dark hall so that their weapons would more easily come to bear on anybody hiding in the room.

Larry crept to the edge of the door's jam and crouched down, then nodded his head once, twice and a final third time. On the third he burst into the room in a low run as behind him two more soldiers rushed in, aiming over his head and bringing all three rifles to bear at once.

An empty room, perfectly whitewashed walls, glass in a new window. A single bed and upon it the naked form of a young woman, her eyes closed, long blonde hair. Larry lurched upright, cautious as he searched the bed for any sign of a bomb or other improvised explosive device that had taken the lives of so many troops.

'Could be inside her.'

The gruesome suggestion of the trooper beside him was none the less tactically sound; the enemy could have inserted a motion–sensitive Improvised Explosive Device inside the woman's body. Nobody took chances out here, not with Islamic State moving around and seemingly devoid of the tiniest morsel of compassion.

'Check her out,' Larry ordered.

Within seconds, an explosives specialist in the team was inside the room and scanning the body. It took only a few moments to ascertain whether the woman represented a lethal threat to the company.

'She's clean.'

Larry eased forward, and he didn't need to pull out the image that his team had been provided with to tell that the woman on the bed was the target of their mission even through the blood on her face where she had been punched, blood oozing from her nose. He slipped off a glove to press two fingers to the woman's neck and felt a pulse throbbing vibrantly beneath his touch as the woman yelped in fright.

Larry flinched as she bolted upright on the bed, sucked in a deep breath of air and screamed as she saw the heavily armed men surrounding her. Larry jumped forward and wrapped his arms around her as she flailed in panic, and he spoke slowly and clearly.

'You're safe, ma'am. Lieutenant Larry Bryant, 18th Infantry, US Army. You're safe.'

It took three repeats of the sentence before the woman stopped thrashing in his arms, and Larry turned to look over his shoulder.

'Contact C&C, tell them we found Kiera Lomas.'

***

X

DIAC Building, Washington DC

'We've got another one.'

Ethan looked up as Jarvis hurried into the office, which was filled with paperwork as Lopez and Ethan ploughed through the onerous task of searching back through every deployment that General Thompson had ever been a part of in his long career with the U.S. Army.

'Where?' Ethan asked.

'Persian Gulf, less than an hour ago,' Jarvis replied as he tossed an image of an aircraft carrier deck engulfed in flames onto the table. 'A pilot in the Navy took his F–18 Hornet and bombed his own carrier before he flew it straight into the carnage he'd created.'

'Jesus,' Lopez uttered in horror, 'casualties?'

'Seventeen dead, thirty plus severely injured, reports are still coming in,' Jarvis informed her. 'This just got real serious, folks.'

Ethan looked down at the terrible images of what had happened. 'Any details on the pilot?'

'Commander, twelve years in the service,' Jarvis replied, clearly angered and moved by the horrific images. 'He was on his third combat cruise with the USS Carl Vinson. Patriot, all American boy, happily married with one young son back in Norfolk.'

'Any radio calls? Anything to connect him to our case at Fort Benning?' Ethan asked.

Jarvis sighed.

'His jet was vaporized by the impact and there was nothing left of the pilot to study as he did not eject. However, we do have his last radio call and it suggests a lack of complicity in what happened.'

'How so?' Lopez asked.

Jarvis appeared visibly shaken as he replied.

'He doesn't make a sound until the last instant, when he suddenly screams in horror. It lasts a second and a half before his plane went in and the radio was cut off.' Jarvis sucked in a deep breath. 'The pilot deliberately targeted and bombed his own people, then flew his plane up over a loop at low speed and dove straight for the deck. Then, suddenly, at the last moment he's afraid?'

Ethan bit his lip.

'That's not enough to convince us that this incident is related to what happened at Fort Benning,' he said, knowing how bad it sounded. 'It could be something else, no matter how bizarre.'

Jarvis shook his head.

'I had the NRO analyze the voice recording from the carrier's data, and they picked up an unusual transmission burst as the plane entered the carrier's circuit. The transmission continued sporadically throughout the landing cycle and ended abruptly with the pilot's death.'

'What kind of transmission?' Lopez asked.

'The data's too sketchy right now, but we're trying to pin it down. Either way, something was being sent to that aircraft, a signal that may have caused this entire event to unfold. Somebody on that carrier was in control of the pilot when he died.'

Jarvis had a file tucked under his arm that he opened and laid down on the table before them as Lopez, Ethan and Hellerman gathered around.

'Commander Sandy Vieron,' Jarvis announced. 'The Navy's keeping this under wraps for now as it occurred in the Persian Gulf and there were no media aboard the ship to cover the event. It's not going to take long though for the word to get out. I'm guessing that the Navy will put this down to a tragic accident or catastrophic mechanical failure once they're apprised of what truly happened.'

Ethan nodded.

'Veiron's record will remain clear of any wrong doing but this whole thing is already in motion. We're too late, there could be any number of military personnel both former and serving with these things in their heads and we won't be able to stop them being activated.'

'What's Veiron's medical history?' Lopez asked. 'Anything there that could connect him to General Thompson?'

'The Navy's looking into it right now,' Jarvis replied.

'What about the carrier?' Hellerman asked. 'Whoever was behind this must still be aboard.'

'Again, we've informed the ship's captain of what we know and he's already going through the process of organising a search of the ship in order to try to root out whoever was behind this. Trouble is the aircraft carrier has no less than five thousand personnel aboard, so it could take a long time to figure this out as they couldn't triangulate where the signals they detected were coming from with any accuracy, only that the transmitter was aboard ship when the event occurred.'

'And that transmitter is likely now sinking to the bottom of the Persian Gulf,' Ethan said. 'In the confusion after that crash it would have been easy for the perpetrator to dispose of any evidence connecting them to the event.'

Lopez leafed through Sandy Veiron's file and something leaped out at her from a page as she studied the pilot's medical history.

'This might be worth something,' she said as she laid the file down on the table. 'Veiron was admitted to a medical institution in Germany a year ago for a routine procedure to clear his sinuses.'

Jarvis leaned closer as he studied the same page of the file.

'Commander Veiron had suffered from headaches and blocked sinuses,' he read out loud. 'The condition was believed to have been further inflamed by a series of long–range, high altitude flights during a brief deployment to forward operating bases in west Germany. Naval aviation doctors diagnosed the blockages and scheduled him for the procedure.'

Lopez looked at Ethan.

'The US Army deploys to Germany from time to time, doesn't it?'

'Along with the Air Force,' Ethan confirmed. 'There's a good chance that Thompson would have been stationed at some point in Germany, and if we can tie him to the same hospital or the same surgeon…'

Jarvis pulled his cell phone from his pocket and speed dialed a number. Within a few minutes, data was spilling across a screen in Hellerman's office.

'Got it,' he said triumphantly. 'Major General Thompson was stationed for two weeks at the Dagger Complex, a military base in Darmstadt, Germany and part of US Army Intelligence and Security Command. According to this, the complex houses the National Security Agency's European Cryptologic Center, the agency's principal Signals Intelligence unit in Germany.'

'When was he there?' Ethan asked.

'Two years ago,' Hellerman said, 'and while he was stationed there he was treated for a minor sinus infection.'

'Just like Commander Veiron,' Lopez said. 'What's the time frame for their presence there?'

Hellerman looked at the data on his screen. 'Veiron was never stationed at Darmstadt, but he was treated at the Landstuhl Regional Medical Center, an overseas hospital in Germany operated by the US Army and the

Department of Defense. That makes sense as the hospital's near Ramstein Airbase, where Veiron would likely have landed.'

'Was Thompson treated at the same hospital?' Lopez asked.

Hellerman nodded. 'Yes, and the hospital is only fifty clicks south of Darmstadt.'

Ethan closed the file he was holding. 'Who treated them? Is there a name of a surgeon or anybody on the teams involved that links both men?'

Hellerman scanned through the pair of files on his system and then he looked up at Ethan.

'Doctor Heinrich Muller,' he said. 'The surgeon conducted both of the procedures under general anesthetic.'

'I want to know where Muller is, right now,' Ethan snapped.

Hellerman started work hunting the doctor down as Ethan glanced through the office windows and across the Watch Room's ranks of desks. The massive television monitors arrayed across the walls portrayed news events from around the globe, and right now half of them were carrying the same story.

'Kiera Lomas,' Lopez identified the image of the reporter, her bedraggled features captured by a sharp eyed photographer as she was helped off the back of a C–130 Hercules aircraft somewhere in the Middle East.

'The abductee,' Jarvis acknowleged as he too caught a glimpse of the reports, 'looks like they got her out.'

'Here we go,' Hellerman said as he pointed at his screen. 'Heinrich Muller is still in Germany, runs a private practice south of Ramstein.'

Ethan grabbed his jacket and looked at Jarvis.

'We need to have a chat with the good doctor and we need to be quiet about it.'

'We can't just snatch him,' Hellerman pointed out, 'he's one of ours and still enlisted as US Army Reserve. We don't have probable cause to pick him up.'

Ethan looked expectantly at Jarvis.

'We've had two major incidents in the space of a few hours already and we've no idea what Muller might have done to countless subjects during otherwise routine surgeries. We can apply for an international arrest warrant, wait for the required clearances, hope that Muller doesn't make a run for it and then talk to him for weeks with his lawyers present and hope that he 'fesses up while crossing our fingers that nobody in the military stationed at nuclear silos has also been hacked and launches a bunch of ICBMs at Russia while we're doing all of that…'

Lopez picked up the thread.

'Or we can go to Germany, grab him and find out who he implanted.'

Jarvis nodded as he dialed another number on his cell phone.

'Go, now. Get a flight down to McGuire Air Force Base in New Jersey. I'll liaise from here and arrange your transport to Germany.'

***

XI

FBI Field Office,

Virginia

'You're kidding me?'

'I'm not,' Hannah Ford insisted as she drove the pool car down the highway and tried to keep from getting too animated. 'That's what he wants us to do. Direct order from the top, from the horse's mouth in fact.'

Special Agent Mickey Vaughn was a junior agent not long out of Quantico and assigned to Hannah. Hannah was a ten year veteran of the Bureau and had already been disciplined twice for aggression in the field and an unlawful discharge of her weapon that had brought some disrepute to her field office and the wrath of Valery Jenkins, but now she held all the cards and was enjoying herself immensely.

'Director LeMay's got you on a covert operation and Jenkins has no control over what you do?'

'That's what he said,' Hannah replied. 'I report directly to LeMay until further notice.'

Vaughn let out a soft whistle. 'Jenkins is going to go ape when she finds out about this.'

'That's what I'm hoping for,' Hannah replied as she pulled into the field office lot and parked.

They walked together toward the office as Vaughn continued interrogating her.

'So what is it that we're after here? Did LeMay ask you anything about the research you've been doing?'

'He's interested in seeing Warner and Lopez brought to justice, was pretty much the run of it,' Hannah replied.

'Sounds like a revenge mission,' Vaughn pointed out. 'Is that even something you want to get involved with? What's LeMay's stake in this? Why does he want Warner's ass hung out to dry?'

'That much I don't know,' Hannah admitted, 'and I'm pretty sure the Director's not telling me everything, but then again I wouldn't expect him to.'

'It doesn't feel right,' Vaughn said. 'What about this Mitchell guy, the one whose blood you pulled from the homicide in Virginia?'

'Drew a blank,' Hannah said as they walked into the office. 'Sure, there's something there but LeMay's priority is Warner.'

Vaughn frowned but said nothing as they made their way through the office. They were barely half way to their desks when a voice hissed from an adjoining office.

'Ford!'

Hannah turned to see Valery Jenkins glaring at her from one side of the office. She turned and strolled casually across, fully aware of the half dozen or so agents who had looked up from their computer screens with interest to watch the exchange.

'Where the hell have you been?' Jenkins demanded, her tightly–bunned gray hair quivering with restrained fury as she stormed into her office.

Hannah followed her at a leisurely pace and leaned on the door jam.

'Had an appointment that I couldn't miss, case you forgot.'

Jenkins stood behind her desk. 'Tell me, now.'

'Can't do that.'

'What?!'

'National security, ma'am,' Hannah replied as she examined her fingertips. 'If there's anything else?'

Jenkins glared at Hannah over her thin–rimmed spectacles and for a brief moment Hannah thought that Jenkins might spontaneously combust.

'You're pushing me to the limit, Ford,' she growled. 'As your superior I am required to know what you're doing and where at *all* times. Your whereabouts are also a matter of national security.'

'Director FBI begs to differ,' Hannah smiled back calmly, her voice just loud enough for everybody else in the office to hear. 'Do take any issues you have to him as from this moment. I have work to do.'

Hannah spun on one heel and marched away from Jenkins without a glance back. She stifled a broad smile as she heard a faint curse and the slamming of a door somewhere behind her as she sat down at her desk.

'You're playing with fire,' Vaughn said as he observed the rest of the agents in the office quietly return to their work.

'Playing with fire is what gave mankind an edge over the animals,' Hannah pointed out as she switched on her computer.

'So, where do we start?'

The screen on Hannah's monitor glowed lethargically into life, and not for the first time she wondered about the agency's policy regarding technology. Her friends always figured that law enforcement agencies and especially intelligence outfits possessed the very latest in computer technology, but in truth they preferred technology that was a year or two old. The simple reason for that was reliability – new tech' was always plagued by bugs that took time to iron out as flaws were exposed by users. Only when computer programs were stable did the FBI and other agencies begin to adopt them.

'LeMay's essentially given me, and by extension you, *carte blanche* to dig into Warner and Lopez and find out what the hell they're doing. Our first job is to find out where they are.'

Hannah accessed a secure search engine and located the *Warner & Lopez* website.

'It's changed to Lopez & Warner,' Vaughn observed. 'Looks like I'm not the only guy being bossed about by a woman.'

Hannah picked up her phone and dialed a number.

'You're just going to call them?' Vaughn asked in amazement. 'Won't that alert them to the fact that we're watching them?'

'Yes, that's exactly what it will do,' Hannah said. 'I want Warner to know that I'm breathing down his neck. I want to become an irritation to him, get on his back and stay there until he gives some ground and starts talking.'

Vaughn cast a glance at Jenkin's office and smiled faintly.

'I have the sense you might succeed in annoying him.'

Hannah slapped the back of her hand across Vaughn's shoulder as she listened to the number she had dialed briefly ring and then switch across to another line as it was diverted.

'They're not in the office,' she said. 'I'm guessing it's switched to a cell.'

The cell rang briefly and then went to answerphone.

'It's Lopez,' Hannah said to Vaughn.

Hannah hung up the phone without leaving a message and then accessed another program on her computer. Connecting to the FBI's immense database, the program gave Hannah the ability to immediately trace the location of the receiving cell.

The *Hollywood* image of agents attempting to locate the bad guy by keeping them talking for long enough to get a trace had long ago become a thing of the past. A landline call could be originated immediately by the carrier, which in this case was Hannah's own desk phone at the field office. Likewise, using a digital trace to the receiving cell that had picked up the call could reveal the location of the user, if one had the FBI on their side and the complicity of the relevant phone company.

Hannah watched and waited as she saw a visual indication of the call trace being mapped out on a simple image of the United States before her. Moments later the image zoomed in on Washington DC, in particular an area just off the east shore of the Potomac River alongside Highway 295.

'Joint Base Anacostia–Bolling,' Vaughn read from the screen.

'Headquarters of the Defense Intelligence Agency,' Hannah murmured in reply as she leaned back in her seat.

'Looks like your boy Warner was telling the truth,' Vaughn said. 'They *do* work for the DIA. Which makes me wonder again why LeMay wants them in prison so badly?'

'Me too,' she replied as she stood up abruptly and grabbed her jacket. 'I guess there's only one way to find out.'

'What's that?'

'Get your coat,' Hannah said as she breezed past him. 'We're going to DC. I'm going to follow Warner and find out what he's really up to.'

***

XII

Anacostia, Washington DC

'I see them.'

Hannah Ford leaned on the window of the pool car and watched as Ethan Warner and Nicola Lopez travelled in a dark blue Lincoln with government plates through the traffic headed south on the Anacostia freeway toward DC's Capital Beltway. Vaughn followed a discreet distance behind the Lincoln, driving casual so as not to alert their targets to the tail.

The city was busy, but Warner's driver seemed to know the backstreets and the best ways to avoid the local choke points as he drove across the Potomac toward Ronald Reagan Washington National Airport. Their vehicle pulled up a short while later at a drop–off point before the airport's enormous concave entrance and both Warner and Lopez got out as Vaughn cruised by toward a massive lot and pulled into the first vacant space he could find.

'Where do you think they're going?' Hannah asked as they climbed out.

The sound of airlines soaring into the hard blue sky completed with the buzz of traffic as Vaughn shrugged.

'Who the hell knows with these two? Either way, we'd better corner them before they leave town.'

Hannah slammed her door shut and smiled behind her sunglasses. 'Leave that to me.'

Vaughn moved alongside her as she strode into the terminal entrance, Warner fairly easy to find and follow through the crowds, taller than most guys and with a slight swagger that was perhaps a remnant of his military days. Hannah stayed back a respectable distance and watched as both Warner and Lopez headed directly for the departures lounge, both with carry–on luggage of small back packs, no suitcases or other paraphernalia.

'Travelling light,' Vaughn observed.

'I get the feeling these two don't *do* luggage,' Hannah replied as she circled around the lounge as Warner and Lopez settled in to a couch after they had checked in.

'They won't talk.'

'They don't have to,' Hannah replied as she took a direct line, approaching Warner from behind where he could not see her. Vaughn drifted off to her right to watch from a nearby coffee shop as Hannah moved up behind Warner.

'Hello Hannah,' Ethan said without looking behind him.

Hannah felt her cheeks flush in irritation as she stared at the back of Warner's head.

'A bit of an amateur, isn't she?' Lopez murmured from alongside Warner as she leafed through a magazine.

Hannah looked up and saw in the glass windows of a convenience store opposite a shadowy reflection of the lounge behind her, her own form superimposed over it. Hannah mastered her dignity and leaned her arms on the back of the couch as she looked down at them.

'Going somewhere nice?'

'Far away from you,' Lopez smiled sweetly as she glanced up from her magazine. 'And your puppy dog over there,' she added with a tilt of her head.

Hannah managed not to glance at Vaughn, who was sitting at a coffee table and watching them. Instead she moved around the couch and took a seat opposite Warner.

'I'm not sure I can let you leave the country,' she said. 'You're both still suspects in an unsolved homicide.'

Ethan watched her for a long time, his gray eyes unnervingly still until he spoke.

'You just can't bear to be parted from me,' he murmured. 'I knew it.'

Hannah blurted out a laugh. 'You're a real fantasist, Warner.'

'She does keep hanging around though, doesn't she?' Lopez pointed out, new interest in her eyes.

'It's my job,' Hannah shot back at Lopez.

'To hound innocent civilians?'

'Let's not waste time playing games,' Hannah said. 'You're both on the DIA's official list now but that doesn't solve my crime scene.'

'I told you where to look,' Ethan said. 'I take it that you found something of interest and that you're here to ask questions about that something, because you and I know that Lopez and myself are innocent of any murder.'

Ethan Warner had a confidence about him that Hannah found oddly reassuring, despite the fact that he could just as easily be described as a confidence artist and con–man, the sort of person who could win the trust of just about anybody and then vanish overnight with their life savings.

'Innocent until proven guilty,' she reminded him.

'Mitchell,' Warner said abruptly. Hannah averted her eyes and saw Warner smile. 'So, you did find out something. Do tell.'

'I'm not here to talk about Mitchell,' Hannah snapped back. 'I want to know where you're going.'

Lopez smiled ingratiatingly at her. 'Bless. You just watched us check in and there are only two flights leaving in the next hour off that desk. One of them's going to Hawaii and we're not wearing beach shirts. Take as long as you like, *hon'*.'

Hannah's hand drifted of its own accord toward her side arm, and with a force of will she suppressed the urge to replace Lopez's smile with the magazine she was holding.

'You two should have a show of your own. You're like Bonny and Clyde, and we all know how they ended up.'

'Folk heroes and loveable rogues,' Warner grinned.

'Dead,' Hannah countered, her voice cracking like thin ice as her mirth vanished. 'You're both playing a dangerous game and this time I have the Bureau behind me.'

'LeMay?' Warner uttered. 'Got yourself a promotion did you?'

'I'm leading the investigation.'

'Into what?' Lopez asked.

'The both of you,' Hannah replied cheerfully. 'It seems that you've been involved in a number of major incidents over the years and the Bureau believes that you represent a serious threat to national security.'

'The only threat we represent to national security is exposing how useless it's becoming,' Lopez retorted. 'But we're off on our holidays now, so you can consider this green and pleasant land safe from our devious machinations.'

'What are you really here for?' Ethan asked Hannah. 'You know about Mitchell. What did you find out?'

Hannah shrugged dismissively. 'He served with the Marine Corps and the Navy SEALS in Vietnam, worked for the government after that. He died years ago.'

'He's about as dead as I am right now,' Ethan replied. 'Either that or he assumed the identity of someone already dead.'

'Funny how the guy is to be held responsible for your wrong doing and yet nobody, anywhere can find him and the only cover you both have for the things that you've done is from the Defense Intelligence Agency.'

'It's not by choice,' Lopez uttered, 'believe me.'

'Then why work for them?'

'Naive patriotism,' Warner replied. 'I keep hoping that the agencies that supposedly work for our country will actually keep doing that. What about Majestic Twelve? Did you uncover anything about them?'

'Y'know, I actually looked into that too,' Hannah said, 'and all that I found was a bunch of papers suggesting that some secret cabal was formed in 1947 by President Truman right after an alien spacecraft crash landed in Roswell, Nevada. It was real interesting, and as soon as I took the tin foil hat off my head I promised myself I'd never watch another episode of the *X–Files* again.' She smiled. 'The papers are considered by experts to be forgeries.'

'They would be,' Warner replied. 'Real conspiracies seem to have taken to hiding behind false ones. You ever heard the saying: *the best lies are mostly the truth*?'

'I'm not surprised that you'd know that,' Hannah said. 'Your record is full of half–truths, government redactions and other inconsistencies that just don't add up for me. You're a big bag of mysteries Warner, and one way or the other I'm going to get to the bottom of all of them.'

'Well, this has been fun,' Lopez said as she got up. 'But we have a plane to catch and you have a whole lot of time to be wasting instead of doing a proper job.'

'Why are you going to New Jersey?' Hannah asked.

'None of your business,' Lopez replied.

Ethan stood and lifted his backpack onto his shoulder. As he turned to leave, Hannah grabbed his arm.

'I just wanted to check in with you both, let you know that from now on I'm only ever going to be one step behind you.'

Ethan said nothing, but Lopez leaned around him and waved at Hannah.

'And that's probably as close as you'll ever get. Have a nice day!'

Hannah fumed and let go of Warner's arm, the former Marine's broad jaw touched with an infuriating half–smile as he turned away and followed Lopez through the departure lounge toward the gates.

Vaughn walked up alongside Hannah and watched their quarry leave.

'How'd it go?' he asked.

Hannah watched Warner disappear and then turned for the terminal exits. 'They're terrified of me and we've got them on the run.'

'Really?'

'C'mon,' Hannah said quickly. 'Let's head to the DIA and see if we can figure out what they're up to.'

***

XIII

Hajjam Island, Iraq

There were few things more beautiful than the desert at night.

The air was untainted by the human stain, the starts glittering with vibrant colors in the velvety black vault of the heavens above to cast a faint glow in the moonless sky that guided him on his journey.

There was no way that he could have crossed into Kuwait via the Safwan border crossing, which was too heavily guarded, as was Umm Qasr port far to the south east as he hiked across the silent hills, careful to stay below the ridgeline.

The journey down the Khawr–as–Zubayr Waterway from Basra had been a short but difficult one, made harder by the police checks routinely made on private vessels traversing south toward Umm Qasr and the Persian Gulf. There was much fear of Iranian sponsored terrorists seeking passage either into or out of Iraq, supporting the uprisings of Islamic State and its myriad splinter groups. It was hard for Abrahem to leave Iraq, but now he was alone and revelling in the solitude and safety the darkness provided, both from his enemies and from the burning hatred that seared his heart, consuming but not replenishing, focusing but blinding all at once.

He would miss his homeland, or at least what was left of it.

Hajjam Island was three kilometres long and provided access to the Persian Gulf for those with a will and a means to evade the Kuwaiti authorities. Patrol ships roamed the coast and inlets seeking out refugees, fugitives and smugglers alike, and were possessed of cameras that could see in the dark. Abrahem Nassir knew better than to travel across the open water at night, but for the time being he was safe.

At the southern tip of the island awaited a small craft that would take him around the floodplain cradling both Warbah Island and Bubiyan Island, the vessel staying within Iraqi waters although perilously close to the Iranian border. From there he would board a private vessel bound for Green Island, an exclusive resort in Kuwait City. Papers had been arranged under false names that would facilitate his exit via the international airport for the west.

All was in hand, so that the end could begin. The speed with which the American troops had closed in on captured journalist Kiera Lomas had surprised everyone, but Abrahem's people had succeeded in their mission and now her early rescue mattered little. In fact, it may have helped things along.

Abrahem felt a light touch to his step, a jubilance born of the vengeance that flamed in his heart and grew stronger with every passing day. His time had been long coming, and it sometimes felt that he had endured an age of repressed fury and injustice, of being ignored, forgotten, abandoned, the memory of so many lost names burned into his mind, tormenting him like ghosts in his sleep…

Abrahem forced the thoughts from his mind, for they cost him focus and drive. To be a slave to one's anger was to be imprisoned by one's life, a Bedouin elder had once told him. *Learn to let go of your hatred for it will only serve you well when you really need it, during the night of the long knives, the moment of retribution.* Abrahem let the cool night air soothe him as he descended toward the island's southern tip and saw a tiny light blink on and off in the infinite blackness ahead.

He descended onto the darkened sands, the sound of rollers whispering nearby as Abrahem saw the figure of a man waiting for him alongside a small motor launch that he had hauled up onto the beach.

'Salaam,' Abrahem greeted him.

'We must hurry,' came the response, tinged with panic. 'The patrols could return at any moment and if we're caught we will be…'

'Relax, Hakim, my friend,' Abrahem cut him off. 'The Kuwaiti patrols are timed and predictable, the crews as lazy as they are stupid. We shall reach the ship in time and then you shall be safely on your way.'

A nervous smile flickered like an errant wind across Hakim's features. 'There is much to fear, Abrahem. What you have done, it could.., it could be dangerous for us all.'

'What I have done will be a danger only for our enemies, Allah willing,' Abrahem replied. 'Have you brought good news from our associates?'

Hakim nodded, pulled a cigarette out from a packet that had been squashed into his shirt pocket. Abrahem reached out and forestalled Hakim's hand.

'The light from a cigarette carries far on a clear night,' he warned. 'Agreed?'

Hakim hesitated and then stuffed the crumpled cigarette back into its packet as he replied.

'There have been deaths, of the infidels,' Hakim informed him. 'A general shot his own troops and then turned the gun on himself, and then an American pilot bombed his own ship and crashed into it. We detected the transmissions, just as you said we would, and the Americans are concealing the events as you predicted.'

Hakim's voice was touched with true fear borne of a lack of understanding, the terror of the unknown laid bare for those with the knowledge to see what others could not. Abrahem smiled in the darkness as he gestured to the boat.

'That is the news that I had hoped to hear. Allah is with us, Hakim, and His wrath shall fall upon the infidels again and again until none of them remain. Come.'

Abrahem pushed the launch out into the rollers, Hakim leaping aboard and grabbing the helm as he pulled on a starter cord. The engine spluttered into life, a puff of oily smoke gusting onto the breeze as the launch turned and accelerated gently out of the bay, the waves helping to conceal the sound of the engine.

'I am not sure that Allah would approve of what has happened,' Hakim insisted as they travelled. 'It is not wise to interfere with His workings, especially the minds of men. And now one of them has escaped.'

Abrahem abruptly sat up in the launch. 'When? Where?'

'A woman, the reporter,' Hakim explained, 'the Americans found her in Basra and took her away.'

Abrahem sighed and sank back into the boat. 'She was allowed to escape, Hakim. She will soon be of use to us.'

Hakim's frown was visible even in the feeble light from the stars above.

'You allowed her to escape? But what if she remembers and is able to lead the Americans back to us? They will hunt us down, Abrahem, and they will not stop until…'

'She will not remember,' Abrahem snapped. 'There is no gain without risk, Hakim.'

Hakim fell silent as he guided the launch out around the edge of the islands, hugging the shorelines as they eased south. Abrahem found himself grateful for the return of the silence, weary already of Hakim's voice. *No gain without risk*. In some ways, Hakim was right. Abrahem had taken a calculated risk in allowing the Americans to liberate Kiera Lomas, given that their early arrival had cost poor Ismael his life at their hands, outnumbered and outgunned. It would attract great media attention and she was sure to undergo a medical examination to determine the state of her health, both physical and mental, before being released. That had been the reason for the appalling abuse by her captors on Abrahem's orders: to focus the attentions of the physicians elsewhere, to draw them away from the real threat.

None the less Abrahem realized that he could afford to take no further risks, to leave no other channels open to the Americans when they began their inevitable pursuit of him and those in his employ. They always did – the hard line followers of Allah liked to refer to the Americans as infidels and fools, but they were in fact a dangerous and cunning foe who always, as the American cop shows liked to put it, *got their man*. Abrahem was fervently hoping that this time they would also get their man, but only when it was far too late to matter. He wanted to be there to see their faces when their country collapsed around them, and for that to happen no further risks could be taken. Any plan was only as strong as its weakest link.

'There they are.'

Hakim's voice whispered to Abrahem in the darkness and he looked up across the surface of the ocean. The dawn was creeping across the horizon, clear and bright as they closed in on the yacht powering across the seas. Sleek, white, glossy, a chartered vessel hired by rich foreigners for scuba diving and island hopping off Kuwait's pristine shores, not for picking up illegal immigrants seeking to cross borders. The cost of the trip had been high for Abrahem, but it would be worth it.

Hakim slowed the boat down as the yacht likewise slowed, its powerful engines humming as it moved in gently alongside the launch so as to prevent the wash from its hull rocking the smaller vessel too harshly on the waves.

Abrahem looked up at the deck and saw at least three individuals silhouetted against the dawn sky. Another, no doubt, would be at the wheel.

'Salaam,' called one of the yacht's crew, touching two fingers to his forehead.

'One to come aboard,' Hakim called in hushed tones.

The crewman opened a gate in the railings running the length of the yacht's hull as Abrahem got to his feet and slung his backpack over his shoulders, tightened it in place as with one hand he slipped a wickedly curved blade from his pocket and held it concealed behind his wrist.

'It is time,' Hakim said. 'Good luck my friend, may Allah watch over you.'

Abrahem moved forward and threw his left arm tightly around Hakim's shoulders as he pulled the younger man close to him.

'And you Hakim, my friend.'

Abrahem turned the blade expertly over in his free hand and with a rapid, vicious swipe he plunged the silvery knife deep into Hakim's skull just below his ear. The razor sharp weapon crunched through thin bone and Abrahem felt Hakim stiffen as a sharp intake of breath was suddenly expelled and his body fell limp in Abrahem's grasp.

Abrahem released the body and let it fall over the side of the launch with a crash of water as he leaped up to the yacht's side and hauled himself aboard. The crewman before him barely had time to react, opened his mouth to shout a warning before Abrahem thrust the clenched knuckles of one hand deep into the man's thorax.

The crewman's throat collapsed, strangling off the warning as his eyes bulged and he staggered back from the railings. Abrahem slashed the blade across the man's belly and he gagged and bowed over at the waist, one hand instinctively trying to hold closed the deep incision that had split his stomach open and sprayed dark blood across the pristine white deck.

Abrahem grabbed the man's hair and hauled him backwards through the railing gate and hurled him over the side. The crewman hit the water even as Abrahem launched himself toward the bridge as a shout of alarm went up.

Two men charged him, shouting in Arabic as they rushed in across the deck, shadowy figures hunting him down like demons.

Abrahem slipped the pack from his back and hurled it into the face of the furthest man as he dropped down low and brought the blade up into the belly of the nearer. It was a clumsy blow, designed more to frighten and pitch him off balance than to kill him. The man yelped as he saw the blade coming and hurled himself to one side over a deck locker, and Abrahem turned to face the second man as the rucksack hit the deck alongside him.

Abrahem slashed out with the blade, caught the man's forearm with a faint spray of blood that provoked a cry of pain as his attacker jerked aside and swung a heavy–looking metal bar of some kind at Abrahem's skull. Abrahem ducked the blow easily and drove the point of the blade straight forward into the man's plexus. The weapon sank with a rasp deep into the man's body and he gasped, his eyes wide as Abrahem twisted the blade and yanked it out. The serrated edge tore at the man's flesh and the grooved surface of the blade allowed blood to spill in torrents as the man screamed in pain and fear and collapsed onto the deck.

Abrahem turned and saw the other crewman fleeing for the bridge. He dashed up the steps and slammed the door behind him, his panicked face looking out of the window as he locked the door.

Abrahem leaped across the deck and up the steps in pursuit. He could see the ship's captain screaming down the radio, his face contorted with fear, and the crewman cowering alongside his captain with his gaze fixed on Abrahem.

Abrahem smiled as he watched the captain staring at his radio in confusion, unable to understand why he could not raise the coastguard. *Fear of the unknown.* Abraham's rucksack contained a modulating frequency jammer sufficient to block all radio channels within a limited distance by decreasing the signal–to–noise ratio, a device stolen from the American soldiers when they abandoned Basra to anarchy and bloodshed.

Slowly, Abrahem turned and retrieved the rucksack from the deck, then carried it to the bridge. He unpacked the jammer and showed it to the captain through the window. Despair ripped across the man's face as he recognized the device.

'Give me the boat, and I shall give you your lives,' Abrahem called through the window.

The two crewmen looked at each other and then shook their heads in unison.

Abrahem shrugged and then pulled a 9mm pistol from the rucksack, aimed, and fired twice straight through the glass.

Both men barely had time to scream before they were hit. Abrahem turned and with a sharp blow from his right elbow he smashed the rest of the window and reached in and unlocked the door. He shouldered the door aside and strode onto the bridge to see both men lying on the deck, gripping their wounds and weeping as they begged for mercy. Both men had voided their bowels, a sickly stench permeating the air. Death, it was always so undignified, not like in the *Hollywood* movies where a single gunshot dropped the victim instantly. It was a gruesome, painful, drawn–out experience both for those dying and those witnessing. But it was also necessary, especially now.

'Go in peace, Inshallah,' he said.

Abrahem fired two more shots, both of them this time impacting the victim's skulls with a thud that silenced their pleas. Then he calmly put the pistol away and began the onerous task of disposing of the bodies over the side of the yacht, making sure that their bellies were slit open before he did so to ensure that the expanding gases of decomposition did not cause the corpses to float on the ocean surface to be found by the patrols or the coastguard.

As soon as his grim task was complete, Abrahem turned the yacht for the Kuwaiti coast and eased the throttles open. He had a long journey ahead of him, and he did not want to miss his flight.

***

XIV

Anacostia–Bolling Airbase, Washington DC

'It's important!'

'I understand that ma'am, but I don't have the authority to let you in regardless of your badge.'

Hannah Ford stood at the entrance to the Defense Intelligence Agency with Vaughn alongside her and fumed in silence as she confronted the security guard blocking her access to the Defense Intelligence Agency's DIAC building.

'We called in advance,' Hannah tried again. 'We were told to report to this desk and await further instructions.'

'And you have reported,' the security guard replied. 'Perhaps you should get on with the next bit?'

Hannah smiled a tight grin. 'I haven't got all day, genius. Y'know, criminals to catch, fugitives to hunt, things more important than standing guard?'

Vaughn took Hannah's arm as the guard's composed expression crumbled into a scowl.

'Come on,' he said as Hannah allowed herself to be led away. 'They're giving you the run around. You know how this works, we do it enough ourselves at the Bureau.'

Hannah sighed as she tried to contain her indignation. She did indeed know how the system worked when one agency simply did not want to talk to members of another agency. Meetings were booked then cancelled, or the subject would mysteriously not be available when agents arrived to question them. Documents would be promised but then never materialize or take months to do so, when they could be retrieved instantly using digital archives.

Hannah shook off Vaughn's grip as she rubbed her temples and slumped into a seat near the foyer entrance.

'This isn't going to help anything,' she protested, more to herself than to Vaughn. 'I'm going to get in there one way or another.'

'Maybe this is for the best,' Vaughn suggested. 'I've never felt that strolling right up to Warner was our best play. Why let him know we're coming?'

'He already knows who we are,' Hannah replied, 'and anyway, like I said it was to ruffle his feathers a bit.'

'Well, if he's watching now I'd say your plan backfired. We don't know where he's gone and the DIA isn't going to be telling us any time soon.'

Hannah closed her eyes and forced herself to breathe for a moment.

'You're right,' she said finally, hating herself and her temper. 'We need to think of a new way to get to him.'

'Good,' Vaughn said, 'because I have just the way to do it.'

'How?'

'Well, if you want to get to Warner you should think about talking to his family.'

'But they're not a part of his work and likely won't know a damned thing.'

'So?' Vaughn challenged. 'This isn't about them, is it? It's about bringing Warner out into the open.'

Hannah felt a surge of enthusiasm flood her system once more as she stood up.

'What are you waiting for then? Where do we start?'

'Natalie Warner,' Vaughn said, 'his sister. Natalie studied politics at the University of Chicago and gained an internment at the White House after her Honors Degree, and she once worked as an analyst for Congress at the Government Accountability Office in Washington DC. Who better to ask about suspicious activities at the DIA? Two birds, one stone.'

'Damn,' Hannah said. 'Let's go.'

The drive from the DIAC building to the Capitol where Natalie Warner worked was not a long one, and within an hour they were sitting in the plush office of a DC law firm as they awaited Natalie Warner. The former analyst emerged from a nearby office door ten minutes later and walked toward them, extending her hand and smiling brightly as Hannah stood.

'Hannah Ford? Natalie Warner.'

Natalie was a brunette a couple of inches taller than Hannah, her long hair flowing across her shoulders like a mahogany halo, but there was a familiar arrogance to the set of her shoulders and a recognizable gleam in her eyes as though they were reflecting the frigid waters of Lake Michigan, where she had been raised. Natalie Warner looked every inch the image of her brother.

'Thanks for meeting us at such short notice,' Hannah beamed in response, keen to maintain an affable air as she introduced Vaughn. 'We really appreciate it.'

Natalie beckoned them to follow her into her office, and she closed the door behind them.

'So what can I do for you folks?' she asked as she sat down at her desk opposite them and waited expectantly.

Hannah let her partner do the talking for a moment.

'We're here regarding your brother, Ethan Warner,' Vaughn said.

Natalie raised an eyebrow. 'What's he done now?'

'You don't sound surprised we're here,' Hannah said, somewhat startled by Natalie's lack of concern.

Natalie smiled, her eyes sparkling as she glanced briefly up at the ceiling as though for inspiration.

'Let's just say that Ethan has a remarkable knack for getting himself into trouble in the worst possible places. I know that he's not dead, so what's he into now?'

Hannah glanced at Vaughn, momentarily off guard.

'A homicide,' Vaughn said, 'Virginia, three months ago. A man named Stanley Meyer.'

Natalie nodded.

'It was on the news,' she said promptly. 'Both Ethan and his partner were being sought for the suspected homicide, but both were later cleared. Hard to miss that one, really, it was being paraded state to state before suddenly everything went quiet. It's a wonder Ethan doesn't have his own cable show by now.'

Hannah folded her arms, fascinated by Natalie's lack of concern.

'We're here with the FBI researching an unsolved homicide that may be connected to your brother and you're acting like *this* is the game show.'

Natalie leaned forward on her desk, folded her hands and kept an even smile on her face as she looked directly into Hannah's eyes.

'I've watched my brother serve his country for over two decades now in one role or another, and I've been directly involved in one of those investigations that almost cost the life of one of my colleagues and resulted in the murder of another. I've seen both Ethan and his partner, Nicola Lopez, hunted down by rogue elements of the CIA and entrusted with secrets of national security so classified you'd probably burst into flames if you laid eyes on them. Through all of that Ethan never once has lost his humanity, his patriotism or his willingness to lay his life on the line for causes greater than his own. If you think that he's involved in a homicide I have absolutely no doubt that you're right, just as I have absolutely no doubt that Ethan either did not commit the crime or did so in self–defense.'

Hannah sat in silence for a long moment in the wake of Hannah's riposte.

'Very eloquent,' Hannah replied. 'It doesn't change the fact that I'm looking for Ethan Warner in connection with a homicide and he seems to keep avoiding me.'

'Can't imagine why,' Natalie smiled sweetly.

'You said that you were involved in one of your brother's investigations,' Vaughn pointed out. 'That it resulted in the death of a colleague?'

'Ethan and Nicola were working a case for the Defense Intelligence Agency, which the CIA opposed as it would uncover programs they would have rather kept under wraps.'

'What kind of programs?' Hannah asked.

'Classified programs that involved the manipulation and abuse of American citizens,' Natalie explained. 'As a result, the CIA inserted an assassin inside a non–governmental–organization office in an attempt to ensure that none of the offending documents reached the light of day. I was working in that office and almost lost my life too.'

Hannah frowned, glancing at a series of notes she had made earlier.

'How did they get involved with you, exactly?'

'Ethan had asked me to help him out in a search for his fiancÃ©e, Joanna Defoe. Jo had gone missing five years earlier in Gaza, Palestine, presumed abducted by militants when she and Ethan were working there as journalists. No trace of her had ever been found and Ethan wondered whether I would be able to use my office privileges to see if there was anything in the records about Jo, which it turns out there was.'

Hannah blinked, scribbling as she went. 'And this Joanna, did he find her?'

'Yes.'

'And?'

'And *what*?'

'What happened?' Hannah snapped. 'Is she alive? Can we talk to her?'

'She's alive, but you won't find her,' Natalie replied. 'She went off the grid a couple of years back and hasn't resurfaced yet. Shame, I liked her. She has a way with people.'

'She does?'

'You wouldn't know,' Natalie smiled again.

Hannah felt color flush her cheeks with heat as she saw Vaughn fight off a smirk beside her.

'And where is Ethan right now?'

'Who knows?' Natalie replied. 'One minute he's in Chicago hunting down bail jumpers as usual, and then next he's called in by the DIA and I won't hear from him for a couple of months.'

'You said that you knew that Ethan's not dead,' Vaughn pointed out, 'that's why you're not concerned about our visit, right?'

'That's right,' Natalie agreed. 'He called this morning, said he and Nicola would be out of the country for a few days, a rush job of some kind for the usual suspects. That's a sort of code between us that means they're working for the DIA again.'

'You got any idea why they headed over to New Jersey?' Hannah asked.

'How long's a piece of string?'

Hannah felt prickly heat rise up over her head as she shot out of her chair and turned for the office door.

'Many thanks Miss Warner, you've been very helpful indeed.'

'Always a pleasure.'

Hannah was half way down the hall and storming toward the exit before Vaughn caught up with her.

'You've really got to reign in that attitude of yours, Hannah,' he said as they walked out into the sunshine.

'The hell I do,' Hannah shot back. 'That *cow* in there only just fell short of giving me the bird. Why do I think that if we visit Warner's parents we're going to get the same treatment?'

Vaughn sighed.

'Because Warner might actually be a stand up guy,' he replied. 'Maybe there's something more to this than we know about?'

'Yeah,' Hannah uttered, 'maybe. All we've got left now is his former commander in the Marine Corps, a Douglas Jarvis. His address is in the district but he's also DIA so he's going to be wrapped up tighter than a mosquito's ass.'

Vaughn shrugged.

'That doesn't mean he won't talk. Let's stick with it, maybe Jarvis will open up a little and we may even be able to figure out why Warner's in New Jersey.'

They walked together across the street and got half way to their pool car when two glossy black SUVs pulled into the sidewalk alongside them. Doors opened as armed agents stepped out and surrounded them.

'What the hell is this?' Hannah uttered as she reached for her badge.

An agent's hand shot out and forestalled her as the rest of the agents reached for their concealed weapons. Hannah froze, as did Vaughn.

'We're FBI,' Vaughn warned them.

'We know who you are. Step inside the vehicle, please,' said the lead agent, square headed, shaven hair, eyes hidden behind designer wrap around shades.

It wasn't a request.

***

XV

Ramstein Airbase,

Kaiserslautern, Germany

The enormous C–17 Globemaster III of the 305th Air Mobility Wing out of McGuire Air Force Base, New Jersey, landed at Ramstein with barely a rumble of wheels on asphalt as Ethan watched the base's massive illuminated control tower pass by to his right. The airbase was consumed by a pre–dawn darkness, bright lights demarking the runway and taxi ways around them.

The Globemaster had lifted off from McGuire and flown non–stop across the Atlantic on a routine supply mission to the USAF Europe headquarters based at Ramstein, allowing Ethan and Lopez to catch a ride on the DIA's ticket.

'You think anybody's tailing us this time?' Lopez asked as the massive aircraft taxied off the runway toward a service ramp.

Ethan knew what she meant. Since they had taken up again with the DIA they had encountered a new and potentially lethal enemy in the form of a cabal of powerful industrial and military leaders known as *Majestic Twelve.* Formed during an extraordinary meeting between military leaders and President Harry S. Truman via an Executive Order in 1947, the event had become the stuff of legend but the group had recently revealed themselves as all too real through the work of their chief field operative, a man named Aaron Mitchell.

'We'll have to assume so,' Ethan replied as the aircraft came to a stop and he unbuckled himself from his seat. 'MJ–12 has taken an interest in everything we've been working on since Argentina. They're always watching.'

Ethan led Lopez out of the huge aircraft as its enormous tail ramp lowered to facilitate the removal of the military vehicles with which he and Lopez had shared the aircraft's cavernous interior. Groups of USAF loadmasters hurried inside and began unchaining the vehicles as Ethan saw two agents awaiting them beside an unmarked vehicle.

'Warner, Lopez,' the taller of the two greeted them. 'We're your ride. Anywhere you need to go, just ask.'

No names. No unnecessary information. Just the way the DIA liked it after what had happened a few months before in Abu Dhabi, when an otherwise effective agent had resigned from the agency after witnessing a truly horrific murder. Whatever had to be done would be down to Ethan and Lopez, keeping official agents off the record.

'Do we have a location for Heinrich Muller?' Lopez asked, equally aware of the new rules.

'His residence is to the south,' came the brisk reply. 'We can take you there now and obtain him before he travels to his clinic.'

'Do it,' Ethan said as he opened the car's passenger door. 'I want this guy off the streets.'

Ethan climbed in alongside Lopez and within moments the vehicle pulled away from the aircraft servicing area, its passage smoothed by pre–warned security guards who allowed the vehicle through the various gates without delay.

'What are we going to do with this guy once we get him?' Lopez asked.

Ethan took a deep breath as he considered his reply. Nobody who had served in the military could fail to be aware of the issues surrounding information obtained by the measures implemented by the CIA under the Bush administration. Extreme rendition and "enhanced interrogation techniques", a sanitized name for agency sanctioned torture at prisons like Abu Ghraib, had provided intelligence often proven to be unreliable at best and outright false at worst, prisoners compelled to say *anything* in order to prevent their further suffering.

Ethan had never been a proponent of such methods, not wanting to cross the line in his mind that he believed separated him from the kind of people he was paid to hunt down. But now time was of the essence, and it was highly probable that Muller was their man and had something to do with the horrific deaths suffered by so many US military personnel.

'We do what we have to do,' he said finally, and then leaned forward and tapped one of the agents in the front of the vehicle on the shoulder.

'Do we have a secure safe house?'

'Yes sir,' came the reply. 'You can operate from there for as long as you require.'

Ethan nodded.

'Good. We'll need to pick up some things along the way. I'll write a list.'

*

Heinrich Muller awoke as he always did, with the dawn.

It was not as easy to get out of bed as it once had been and he could feel his advancing years aching in his bones. The room seemed colder than it used to despite the heat from the radiators, but he forced himself out from beneath the warm duvets and dressed slowly before making his way out of the bedroom toward the ornate circular staircase that descended through the mansion.

Nestled in the hills south of Kaiserslauten, Muller had lived in the house alone since his wife had passed away and his children moved out into new lives of their own. He had made his fortune both as a much–respected surgeon and for his willingness to offer his services to those who could afford them, whether those services were necessarily legal or not.

Muller reached the bottom of the staircase and rubbed his cold hands together, glancing instinctively at the digital thermostat on the wall and wondering whether there might have been a power outage during the night that had tripped the boiler's fuse. It was then that he saw the front door to his home, wide open.

Muller froze in mid–stride as he stared at the open door. The mansion was alarmed, and he knew that he had set it before bed the previous night because he was paranoid about such things and he never retired without double–checking the system.

Muller turned immediately for the nearest phone, set into the wall alongside a passage that doubled back beneath the staircase toward the kitchen. The phone was out of its cradle, missing. Muller barely broke his stride as he whirled and ran at a pace he had not achieved for years out of the front door, wondering just who it was who had breached his security and, more worryingly, what it was they wanted.

The blow caught him low in the belly as he passed through the doorway and he crumpled as he sank to his knees, stopped dead by the attack. He saw boots alongside him just before a black sack was thrust down over his head and fastened tightly about his neck, his arms yanked behind his back and his ankles bound all at once with startling efficiency.

'*Bitte, bitte,*' he gasped through the sack. 'Please, what do you want?'

Nobody replied as he was hauled to his feet and thrust into a waiting vehicle that he heard approach up the long, private drive, far from prying eyes. Muller was shoved into place on the rear seat, doors slammed all around him, and then they were on the move. A deep, angry voice growled at him through a distorter, the digitized oratory both impersonal and frightening.

'You knew this day would come,' it growled. *'Shut up, stay still, do as we say and you might just survive it.'*

Muller whimpered with fear but managed to hold his tongue for the drive. It felt as though he were cramped on the seat for hours when in reality it was barely twenty minutes before the car slowed and parked and he was dragged from its interior and guided unsteadily on his feet into a building.

The odours of stale air and bare wood drifted through his sensorium, the footfalls around him sounding hollow as though they were walking through the bare shell of a house, no furniture, no carpets.

'Ich verstehe nicht,' Muller mumbled finally. 'I don't understand.'

No response. Moments later, Muller was turned about and thrust downward onto a seat of some kind. His legs were swung up and around and then he was laid down, the back of his head cracking against solid wood. He felt straps securing his arms, chest and ankles and he began to weep inside the sack.

'Bitte, bitte!'

The sack was torn from his head and he blinked in the light as he saw four masked men surrounding him. They watched him in silence, and he furtively hoped that this was some kind of horrific mistake.

'Please,' he gasped, 'I work for the United States.'

'We know,' came the response. *'Tell us, everything.'*

Muller's mind raced. 'Everything about what?!'

The tallest of the men strolled to one side of the wooden board upon which Muller lay, and the old man saw a tray atop an old table nearby. On the tray were an assortment of power tools and a pair of garden shears.

'Mein Gott, nein,' he gasped as the masked man turned to look at him.

'Everything,' the man repeated.

Muller nodded frantically. 'I'll tell you everything about what you want to know! I don't have anything to hide!'

The man nodded to one of his accomplices and the other man pulled a sheet of paper out from his pocket, unfolded it, and pinned it to the wall of the otherwise bare room. Muller focused on the image and recognized the face upon it immediately.

'Mein Gott,' he uttered again in horror. 'It wasn't?'

The picture of Major General Frederick Thompson looked down upon him as the masked men closed in all around. Their boots crackled against something on the ground beneath the table, and Muller looked down to see a large sheet of plastic spread beneath him.

He wept again as the tall man looked down at him, an electric drill now held in one hand. The drill suddenly spun with a shrill whine that filled the room, a six–inch long steel bit gleaming in the morning light streaming through a grubby window nearby as he growled down at Muller.

'Talk.'

'I don't know what happened to Thompson!' Muller pleaded.

The masked man nodded to his accomplice, who stepped forward and with one mighty tear ripped off Muller's shirt and exposed the blotched, bare skin of his flabby belly. The man lifted the drill and lowered it toward Muller's skin, the bit spinning in a frenzied blur a finger's width above his defenceless flesh.

'Talk.'

'I don't know what happened!' Muller screamed in terror. 'I don't know!'

The masked man looked at his accomplice once more and the second man gripped Muller's head and forced it back against the board. Moments later the drill lowered and Muller screamed as raw pain tore across his stomach and the drill whined and churned as it sank into his flesh. A splatter of blood sprayed against the masked man's clothes as he worked and Muller screamed.

The drill was yanked free, dripping with blood as the masked man looked down at him once again.

'Last chance! Talk, now!'

'I'll lose everything!' Muller screamed in raw terror and pain. *'Everything!'*

The masked man turned away and lifted the drill once more and Muller's last feeble resistance withered away and he shouted out.

'I inserted the implant!' he cried, staring at the ceiling through blurred tears and praying that there would be no more of the terrible pain.

The drill whined down into silence once more as the masked man looked down at him and shouted in his face. *'Everything!'*

'They paid me!' Muller sobbed. 'Paid me to insert devices into the nasal cavities of my patients at Ramstein and Basra! I had to. They knew my family, my children. They said I would be well paid to do as I was told, that the patients would not be harmed!' Muller sucked in a ragged breath, his vocal chords twisted with agony. 'They didn't say that it was the patients who would be doing the harming!'

'Who paid you?!'

Muller closed his eyes, tears streaming down his quivering jowls.

'There were no names, only meeting places and private payments via off shore accounts. I was given names and dates, nothing else.'

There was a moment's silence as Muller's captors seemed to consider what he had said.

'How many?' the masked man demanded. *'How many implants did you complete?'*

Muller tried to think straight. The pain in his belly was subsiding, but he was shivering with fear as he realized that he would be unlikely to get out of the room alive.

'Twenty, thirty, I can't recall!'

'How much were you paid?' another, equally distorted voice asked.

'A quarter million dollars for each patient!'

'Over how long?'

'Five years.'

'When was the last one?'

Muller detected a ray of light as he realized that his captors were no longer shouting at him, that there seemed to be a hint of compassion or concern detectable even through the digitized distortion devices they were using. Muller realized that anything he said could not be used against him, that his torture would nullify any confession.

'Two months ago.'

'We want names,' a voice demanded, *'names of all the patients you implanted.'*

'I'll have to get them, they're at my office,' Muller said. 'Please, let me go and I'll help you!'

A long silence and then the masked man spoke again. *'Too late, Muller. We'll get the names ourselves.'*

The drill howled into life and Muller saw it jab downward as white pain seared his stomach and he screamed at the top of his lungs.

'Abrahem!' he screeched, and the drill fell silent as he sobbed in ragged breaths. 'Abrahem, that's all I know. Somebody in Iraq.'

Muller's body convulsed with a shudder and he passed out.

*

The masked men looked down at Muller for a moment and then the tall man ripped off his mask.

'You think that's all he's got?' asked another of his masked accomplices as they tore off their mask to reveal long dark hair and exotic eyes.

Lopez lifted an electrode from Muller's belly, along with the tube of fake blood she had sprayed across the drill and Ethan's clothes. The electrode was connected to a pair of car batteries concealed beneath the table, the current spread by the fake blood to prevent burns to Muller's skin.

Ethan tossed the drill aside. Psychology was everything, perceived pain and bloody gore almost more frightening than the act of torture itself. He had once read that the threat of torture was often a more effective means of obtaining confessions than the actual application of the pain itself. In Muller's case his awkward viewing angle and belief that his guts were being drilled out, accompanied by a mild pain that was vastly inflamed by his own imagination, had been enough to extract what they needed.

'He just passed out in fear,' Ethan said. 'There's not much else there, but we have a name and a location: Abrahem, Iraq.'

'That's not a lot to work on,' Lopez pointed out.

Ethan turned to the two DIA men beside them, who had now also removed their masks.

'Get in touch with the DIAC, give them what we know. Maybe they can figure something out from there.'

'What about him?' one of the agents asked, pointing at Muller's comatose form.

'Get him home, leave no trace, and then inform the local police of what he's suspected of doing. A search of his clinic should reveal the names we're after and provide evidence of his illegal activities. He'll be repatriated to the US for trial. Let's get this done and disappear.'

'Where are we going?' Lopez asked Ethan.

'Iraq,' he replied.

***

XVI

South West Waterfront Park, Washington DC

The unmarked SUV pulled up at an oval near the Titanic Memorial in south west DC, where the Potomoc's tidal basin met the Anacostia River at the Georgetown channel, the green waters sparkling in the sunshine.

Neither Hannah nor Vaughn had said a word during the short journey down from the Capitol, and their escorting agents had likewise remained stonily silent. As the SUV pulled up so one of them opened their door and stepped out, beckoning them to follow. As Hannah climbed out, the agent gestured toward a row of police patrol vehicles parked alongside the city's EMC Fireboat launch.

'You're safe here,' he said, apparently aware of their discomfort. 'Take a walk in the park, why don't you?'

Hannah rounded on the agent. 'What the hell is this? You have no jurisdiction to accost federal agents going about their lawful business in…'

The agent climbed aboard the SUV, closed his door and the vehicle pulled away long before Hannah could finish her sentence. Vaughn glanced at the nearby memorial park.

'We gonna take a walk then?'

'What else do you want to do for them?' Hannah demanded. 'Bend over?'

Vaughn grinned, immune as ever to Hannah's fiery retorts. 'I want to know what the hell this is about and I guess the answer is in there.'

Hannah glared at the nearby wooded glade as she yanked her sunglasses back down over her eyes and marched toward the park.

The park was half empty at this time on a weekday morning, a few casual strollers and dog walkers here and there minding their own business and paying little attention to Hannah as she walked along the riverfront. At the end of the walkway was a wide wall, atop which was a stone memorial plinth of a man with arms outstretched, looking out across the Potomac.

Nearby a series of park benches were unoccupied except for one, upon which sat an elderly man in a dark blue suit, his hands folded comfortably in his lap as he looked at her. Hannah instinctively made her way across to him with Vaughn following.

'Who the hell are you?' Hannah demanded.

'Nice to meet you too,' the old man replied. 'My name is Douglas Jarvis.'

'Warner's handler,' Vaughn recalled from their research. 'His name was mentioned back at that homicide scene in Virginia, remember?'

Hannah did indeed remember. Warner had spoken to a cop guarding the police line outside the hotel in which Stanley Meyer had been murdered, and later had been on the phone to somebody called *Jarvis*.

'Mister Jarvis,' Hannah greeted him with little warmth, 'is it customary to abduct federal agents?'

'No,' Jarvis replied, unconcerned. 'Agent Ford, I am here to offer you information for your own protection.'

'My own protection?' Hannah echoed, bemused. 'I'd have imagined that it was your people who need protecting, after everything I'm uncovering right now.'

Jarvis smiled. 'You ever heard of Pandora's Box?'

'I've read Hesiod,' Hannah snapped back. 'I'm not interested in mythology, Mister Jarvis, I'm interested in justice and I won't stop to get it.'

'Don't wish too hard,' Jarvis suggested.

'Why did you bring us here?' Vaughn asked, curious. 'You could have just called us in or allowed us into the DIA when we turned up earlier today.'

Jarvis slowly got up from the park bench and slipped his hands into his pockets as he stood before them.

'You've been given some kind of *carte blanche* by Director LeMay to go all out after Ethan Warner.'

Jarvis's forthright assertion of what had been a covert directive put Hannah off balance.

'The details of our operation are classified and cannot be shared with any outside party regardless of…'

'Take the stick out of your ass,' Jarvis muttered as he waved Hannah aside with an idle wave of one hand. 'You've stood in front of the DFBI and now you think that you're on a mission for the good of the world, best buddies with LeMay, untouchable.' Jarvis smiled faintly. 'Didn't stop me from grabbing you off the street, did it?'

Hannah frowned. 'You trying to make a point?'

'You're being sold up the river,' Jarvis replied. 'LeMay wants somebody expendable to pursue Warner to the ends of the earth, to do whatever it takes to prevent the DIA from exposing what LeMay's got his dirty little paws into. You think that you can't cross any lines, that you can walk roughshod over your superiors in your mission, and that when you've achieved it you'd be lauded to the world as a superhero and showered with plaudits for your valiant achievements.'

Jarvis looked at Hannah for a moment and then at her partner, Vaughn.

'Let me guess about her,' he suggested to Vaughn. 'Headstrong, impulsive, tenacious and likely to get herself into trouble before she even knows what she's doing?'

Vaughn raised an eyebrow. 'Hit it on the head.'

Hannah shot him a hurt look, then glared back at Jarvis. 'What's your point?'

'You'll be used by LeMay and then disposed of,' Jarvis replied. 'He'll use you as a means to get what he wants, and then you'll find yourself out of the Bureau before you even know what the hell happened. Non–disclosure agreements signed, healthy pension, everything they can offer to get you out of the building and off their minds, and if you fight back…'

'What?' Vaughn asked, although Hannah remained silent.

'Then they'll play dirty.'

Hannah scoffed. 'You're watching too much television, Jarvis. The Bureau looks after its own, as does the entire intelligence community.'

'Valerie Plame,' Jarvis replied, 'a CIA agent whose identity was exposed by the Bush administration after her husband, a former US Ambassador, criticized the intelligence used by that administration to go to war in Iraq. Valerie and her husband ended up taking members of the administration to court. They even made a *Hollywood* movie about it.'

Hannah gritted her teeth. 'The administrations have learned from the mistakes of the past.'

'You keep telling yourself that.'

'LeMay isn't going to suddenly turn on me.'

'It's exactly what he'll do because you're just like Ethan Warner.'

'I'm *nothing* like him.'

'You're exactly like Warner, because I originally hired him for the same reason that LeMay's chosen you: expendability. You're used to perform a task and then dropped like a hot rock. The only reason Ethan's still anywhere near the DIA is because he's so good at what he does and we have history going back to the Corps, something I'm not willing to betray. If he hadn't had that, I wouldn't have fought so long and hard to maintain him as an asset. You, Hannah, don't have a damned thing to protect you and Special Agent Valery Jenkins is champing at the bit for any reason to come down on you.' Jarvis smiled. 'You're about to become the perfect patsy.'

Hannah shook her head, chuckled.

'You're just covering yourself with scare stories,' she replied. 'I'd have thought somebody at your level could come up with something more original. You're worried about what I'll uncover.'

'That's right,' Jarvis replied. 'Agent Ford, I can't do this meet again. I brought you here in an attempt to ensure that we would not be observed by LeMay or any of his assets who I'm certain will already be looking for you. If you keep digging you're going to come up against people who are everything you see on television and worse. I wish I could reveal more but I cannot.'

Hannah glanced without concern across the Potomac's choppy waters. 'I'll remember to play nicely.'

Jarvis took a pace closer to her.

'I know about the blood that you found at the hotel in Virginia, Hannah,' he said. 'I know that you're looking into the man that it belongs to.'

Now Hannah's gaze snapped back to Jarvis. 'Mitchell.'

'Ethan has encountered Aaron Mitchell on two occasions, and on both of them he barely escaped with his life. You don't know what you're getting into here Hannah, either of you. These people will crush you like worms without the proper support, and while Ethan does have that protection I can assure you that you don't.'

'I have the Director of the FBI behind me,' Hannah protested. 'How does protection get more powerful than that?!'

'Because LeMay is part of the threat,' Jarvis replied. 'He's using you to fold up our investigation because we believe that he's a part of something called Majestic Twelve.'

Vaughn stepped up now, concern etched into his features.

'Warner mentioned something about an MJ–12,' he said, 'some kind of cabal, industrialists and politicians? We took it as fantasy.'

'It's real,' Jarvis assured him, 'very real. Forget television programs. MJ–12 has existed now for some seventy years and is on the record, despite attempts by the CIA to destroy those records during investigations in 1973 and again in 2004. Enough remained that the Government Accountability Office was able to mount a case against the agency, which resulted in its Director resigning.'

'Natalie Warner,' Hannah murmured, almost to herself. 'She worked there, at the GAO.'

'And was almost killed by Aaron Mitchell's predecessor,' Jarvis acknowledged, 'a man named Mister Wilson. At the time I had believed that I was working for the government, when in fact both I and my superiors had been working for Majestic Twelve – that's how highly placed these people are. Now, we're working against them and have both the DIA and elements of the administration supporting us.'

'The same kind of administration that you just berated for having betrayed Valerie Plame?' Hannah challenged.

'Like you suggested,' Jarvis countered, 'each administration can learn from the mistakes of its predecessors, and this one is not so beholden to the hawks in Congress and the Senate. LeMay is part of the old guard, a stooge of Majestic Twelve or perhaps one of its members. He wants you to stamp us out, to bring us to justice for real or imagined crimes, and thus remove the threat of exposure.'

'Or bring you to justice because you're the one working for Majestic Twelve,' she suggested in reply.

Jarvis grinned.

'That's the intelligence game for you,' he said. 'I can't prove one way or the other who the enemy is, Hannah – that's something that you'll have to decide for yourself. But believe me, LeMay will cheerfully see you betrayed and abandoned if it suits his purpose and there will be nothing that you can do about it.'

Hannah watched Jarvis for a moment in the bright sunlight.

'I could just arrest you right now, have you brought back for questioning.'

'Yes you could, and I would not resist. But then I would be freed, just as Ethan and Nicola were, and you would be back to square one.'

'That's the kind of power that this MJ–12 could wield,' Vaughn said. 'You're spinning us a tale but there's nothing to substantiate any of this.'

'Except Aaron Mitchell,' Jarvis countered. 'You have a choice. You can choose to obey LeMay and pursue Ethan Warner, who even now is on his way to Iraq in pursuit of another threat against our country's security, on the pretence of his having some awareness of the events behind Stanley Meyer's murder. Or, you can pursue a man whom you actually *know* was present at the unsolved homicide, who is supposed to be dead but isn't and keeps vanishing whenever local law enforcement appears on the scene.' Jarvis raised a questioning eyebrow. 'I know where I'd put my money.'

'You and I are not the same people,' Hannah said.

'I know,' Jarvis grinned, 'which is why I'm giving you this advice instead of letting you walk into the end of your careers and perhaps worse. It's your call what you do. Don't take my word for anything I've said, just be mindful that for now you can trust only yourselves.'

Jarvis walked past them and away down the path. Vaughn called after him.

'And what the hell are we supposed to do if everything you've said turns out to be true?'

'Call me,' Jarvis replied without looking back. 'By that time, I'll be the only friend you have.'

Hannah watched Jarvis leave, saw through the trees the SUV return smoothly to pick him up with their FBI pool car alongside.

'I'm not buying it,' she said finally. 'He's got every reason to try to derail us or convince us not to pursue Warner.'

'He's got no reason to tell us as much as I think he just did,' Vaughn countered. 'C'mon, Hannah, we both know the intelligence game isn't a black and white thing with good guys fighting bad guys. Jarvis said it himself, he's ended up working for the wrong people without even knowing it.'

'And you think that somebody in the position of Director FBI could be in the grip of some mysterious cabal? My ass, it's the last thing I'd bother with if I were in the Bureau's hot seat.'

'But maybe not if you were on the way to the top and needed a push,' Vaughn said. 'Crazier things have happened. We should do what Jarvis says and take a closer look at this Mitchell guy, see if we can pin him down. He's the link between all of them, this whole charade. If he is guilty of killing Stanley Meyer it proves everything that Warner and Jarvis are saying.'

Hannah thought for a moment and then her cell phone buzzed in her pocket. She retrieved it and saw the name on her screen.

'It's LeMay,' she said.

'You gonna answer it?' Vaughn asked.

'What the hell else can I do?!' Hannah snapped as she answered the phone.

'Ford.'

'Special Agent Ford, I need you to travel to Ronald Reagan Washington National Airport and catch Flight 275 for Hong Kong immediately. Seats have been reserved. There's been a breakthrough in the case.'

'Yes sir.'

'Report back to me when you reach Hong Kong. An agent named Bradley Hinkley will liaise with you at the field office inside the US Consulate Building.'

'Yes sir.'

The line went dead and Hannah looked at Vaughn. 'Looks like we're off to Hong Kong.'

'Just like that?' Vaughn asked. 'Why send us and not assign agents from the local field office?'

'I don't know,' Hannah admitted. 'He says we'll be briefed when we get there.'

'I don't much like this,' Vaughn said as they started walking. 'Maybe Jarvis really is onto something.'

'Yeah,' Hannah said without conviction, 'but what really interests me is why Ethan Warner is in Iraq – Jarvis let that much slip. What the hell is he doing out there and if it's connected with some great conspiracy involving this Majestic Twelve then what does it have to do with LeMay sending us to Hong Kong?'

Vaughn did not have an answer for her as they walked back through the glade toward their pool car.

***

XVII

Dalecarlia Reservoir, Washington DC

He felt bleak, despite the bright blue sky and warm sunshine filtering down through the canopy of trees overhead.

A narrow path wound through the woodland of Little Falls Park alongside the Potomac, a popular local destination where families gathered to picnic and unwind after a busy week. But he walked alone, favoring the solitude and the silence that the middle of the week brought to this area.

Aaron J Mitchell walked with a slight limp, still carrying the injury to his ribs he had sustained two months before when he had violently encountered Ethan Warner. Both of them were former Marines, although Mitchell had gone on to serve with the Navy SEALS and should have bested Warner despite his opponent's youth. Yet he had not, and it had only been chance that had allowed him to escape the encounter.

The wound to his pride ached with a far sharper pain than the wound to his body. Time was not on Aaron's side and for the first time it had cost him a victory in a game where the stakes were so high, failure really could be fatal.

It had occurred to him, on the few occasions when he allowed his mind to dwell on abstract reverie that his father would have glowed with pride at the sheer scale of that which Aaron had achieved. His father had served with distinction in the United States Army during the final year of the Second World War, a decorated soldier who had inspired in his fellow men the realization that anything was possible, even for a *negro*. As had happened many times before in an ancient and tragic irony, it had been the conflict of men that had thus conceived the respect of those fellow men hitherto considered inferior by the society of the time. Aaron, when his own time had come more than twenty years later, had followed in his fathers' footsteps, joining the United States Marine Corps just in time to find himself cast into the steaming jungles of South East Asia and a conflict of unimaginable, incomparable brutality that had ingrained into Aaron's mind the singular and special evil of mankind. Aaron had served two tours in Vietnam, had been himself decorated twice. During that period, a number of events that were to shape Aaron's life occurred.

The first was his father's death of chronic heart disease. The ailment, the result of years of smoking after the war, had afflicted his body during Aaron's last years with him, but the sudden loss of his father was a terrible blow to the young soldier, who once again returned to the battlefield because there was nothing left for him anywhere else on earth. There Aaron witnessed the sheer terror of battle, the fear of ambush, the brutal nature of the jungle and all of its attendant dangers.

Aaron had returned after his second tour to the United States, taking up a role as an instructor. For two years he had trained young men to take to the field against the enemy and watched them return in boxes, if at all. For two years he had wrestled with psychological demons, the nightmares and the self–enforced solitude, the images of those terrible jungles that infected his scarred and broken mind. Throughout that time he had believed that he may never recover the self that was Aaron James Mitchell, so brutalised was he by the terrors he had witnessed. Diagnosed with what was then termed "shell–shock", Aaron had been honorably discharged from the Corps in the midst of the public backlash against the Vietnam campaign. Unable to find work or even a home, like so many formerly decent soldiers he had become a vagrant, abandoned by the country he had fought for.

A year later, while scratching a meagre existence on Washington DC's hard streets, he had been approached by a man from the Pentagon who had taken him into a hostel down Rock Creek way, cleaned him up and provided him with food and shelter. Aaron, too weary to care why anybody would provide for him without asking anything in return, accepted the assistance. There were others in the hostel, all former soldiers with nowhere to go. After a few days of leisure, about half of them were gathered into a room and informed of why they were there.

Aaron had listened with interest to the hour–long lecture, during which a suit from the Pentagon informed them that they were being recruited into a covert unit. They were free to leave if they did not wish to serve, and that their service would be neither strictly military or government but somewhere between the two. There would be no medals, no public recognition, nothing other than a cause and a career.

Half of the men in the room left afterward to once again take their chances on the streets, too embittered by their abandonment by both government and the people to even consider serving once again. Aaron had looked out at those streets and realized that there was nothing and nobody out there for him. At least here he had a cause, something to work for. And work he had for thirty years, until he had reached a sufficient level of trust and superiority to discover that the Pentagon knew nothing of what he did and nor did the administration. Aaron James Mitchell worked for Majestic Twelve.

'You're late.'

The voice broke Aaron from his reverie and he looked to his right to see an old man join him from another path. The man was shorter than Aaron, aged now by the passing of so many years, but still recognizable as the suit who had first lectured Aaron and his fellow vagrants thirty years before.

'Past caring,' Aaron replied as they strolled.

Victor Wilms looked up at Aaron through rheumy eyes. 'Finally reached the limit,' he said calmly. 'It happens to everybody, Aaron. I'm surprised you've lasted this long.'

'You doubted me?' Aaron asked.

'Not at all,' Victor replied. 'I figured that at some point you would lose patience and execute every one of *us*! You know that you're the last man standing, don't you, from that class?'

'No, I did not.'

'They're all long gone, Aaron. Some quit, some got injured and were relieved of duty, some were killed and the rest vanished in various God–forsaken corners of the globe, never to be seen again.'

'I'll count myself lucky.'

'I'd count yourself good at what you do,' Victor snapped. 'You got your ass kicked for the first time in thirty years. It's not like you quit.'

'I thought that I would be replaced.'

Victor smiled and shook his head. 'MJ–12 prefers trusted operatives to fresher faces. You're too valuable and still an effective agent. Trust me, they're more than happy with your work over the years.'

'And who is it that I work for?'

'You know better than to ask me that, Aaron.'

Aaron stopped on the path alongside the reservoir, the smooth water perfectly reflecting the blue sky and drifting clouds.

'I've dedicated thirty years of my life to MJ–12, never once questioned my role or the things I've been asked to do. I've taken many lives on the orders of men I've never met, and now it may cost me my life to continue to do so. I want to know whether it's worth it.'

Victor stood before him, his hands in the pockets of his jacket as he directed a stony gaze at his former protÃ©gÃ©.

'You want to know whether it's worth it?' he echoed. 'What's brought all of this on, Aaron? I know damned well that it's not the fear of death, you've faced far worse, and a couple of broken ribs isn't it either.'

Aaron glanced out over the nearby water. 'Stanley Meyer.'

'Meyer?' Victor echoed as though shocked. 'You're getting cold feet about the man that could have destroyed this country's entire economy? Jeez, Aaron, and there was me thinking that this was serious.'

Aaron's own gaze was no less chilling and Victor's off–handed humor shrivelled.

'It's serious to me.'

Victor averted his gaze and gathered himself. 'The man was a fool Aaron, to think that he could somehow put the entire globe before himself, render our entire fossil fuel industry irrelevant overnight. Your disposal of Meyer cleared the way for a stable economy and re–levelled the balance of power back to where it should be.'

'Did it?' Aaron challenged. 'What Meyer had there, what he could have done would have ended the wars in the Middle East and removed Russia's choke–hold on the gas supply to Europe. It would have ended climate change and brought in a new era of power generation that would have broken up the big fossil fuel companies and levelled *that* playing field and yet we killed him, stole the technology and buried it.'

Victor took a pace toward Aaron.

'Yes, we did,' he snapped. 'Because there are too many people making too much money from those Middle East wars, too much money from fossil fuels, too much leverage from Russia's control of gas. Majestic Twelve is the industrial–military complex, Aaron, you know that and you're employed to protect them. That's what you do, it's what you signed up for and you're in far too deep now to just suddenly get a conscience and walk away.'

Aaron glowered down at his former mentor.

'When I become too old for this job, what happens then?'

Victor smiled. 'You become like me, Aaron. You continue to serve in a less physical role but you remain a part of MJ–12. It's like a family, Aaron, we look after our own.'

'So does the Mob.'

Victor's smile turned cold. 'If you walk away, Aaron, they'll hunt you down like a dog.'

'Some family.'

'I pulled you off the streets,' Victor snapped. 'Gave you a life again, gave you something to believe in!'

'You lied,' Aaron reminded him. 'You told us that we'd be working for the Pentagon, remember?'

'You do work for the Pentagon, for the administration, for the people and the country in their name. But they don't own America any more than the administration does. Industry owns America. The Presidents of the United States live in the White House because people like MJ–12 finance their political campaigns. We live in the glory of a free–market capitalist economy, and that's made MJ–12 not just bigger than government: they own it. The United States of America is a business, Aaron, just like any other. MJ–12 decides who does what, when, how and why, and what you, me or anybody else thinks isn't worth crap.' Victor took a breath and smiled at his own ingenuity. 'You work for the people in a way that can never be publicly admitted but you're performing a public service Aaron, one that is essential to the continued dominance of America's interests.'

'Business interests.'

Victor sighed. 'Are you saying that you want out, Aaron?'

Aaron shook his head slowly. 'No, not at all.'

'Then what's this all about?'

'I just needed to know where I stand.'

'Well, now you do.'

'Where can I find Ethan Warner?'

Victor smiled. 'Ah, so you wish to exact revenge for your hurt pride?'

'I wish to finish the job,' Aaron growled. 'Where is he?'

'He caught a flight to Iraq two hours ago,' Victor replied. 'He's back on the DIA payroll and he's after something that I want you to find and bring back to America for me.'

Victor produced a file, which Aaron took and briefly leafed through. He saw a series of images of metallic, splinter–like objects an inch long, marked as "cerebral implants", and the names of four National Security Agency operatives who had vanished in Kowloon some twenty years before. Beside their images were two words: *Mind control.* He looked up at Victor in surprise.

'The killings at Fort Benning?'

'Indeed,' Victor said. 'Our Islamic terrorist friends suddenly got all sophisticated. I don't need to remind you of how important it is that they should not be able to deploy this technology on US soil again. Recover it and bring it home.'

Aaron closed the file and slid it beneath his jacket. 'Warner has a head start in Iraq.'

'You're not going to Iraq,' the man said. 'You're going to Hong Kong to look for a man named Jin Chen. You'll be briefed on the way.'

'I want Warner,' Aaron growled.

'You'll get him in good time, my friend,' Victor said with a smile that held no warmth, 'Let Warner and the DIA track down the terrorists while you track down the technology, and this time you really are working for the security and benefit of the United States.'

***

XVIII

Basra International Airport,

Iraq

'Been a while since I've been here,' Ethan said.

The Arab Emirates connecting flight from Dubai had landed a few minutes earlier but the airport terminal was virtually silent as he walked with Lopez toward the exits, few international flights moving into and out of the country in the face of near–constant uprisings by Islamic State terrorists and other insurgent tribal groups vying for power and influence.

'I don't think much of our chances of hunting any of these people down,' Lopez replied as they stepped out into the blistering heat outside the terminal, her hair hidden by a native *hijab* to avoid offending the more religiously sensitive Muslims. 'The country's in chaos as much now as it was a decade ago. They could be anywhere, maybe even dead.'

Ethan nodded in agreement.

'Maybe,' he said, 'but they worked for our military and it's my guess they'll stay close to what they know.'

Before they had left on the flight to Iraq, Jarvis had provided them with documents taken from Heinrich Muller's office detailing a number of junior doctors and surgeons who had worked alongside the doctor during his tenure in Iraq.

'If the implant in General Thompson is the work of Islamic State or a similar organization, most of the people connected to it will likely have been executed,' Lopez said.

Ethan heard his cell phone ring and answered it, switching to speaker phone as they waited beneath the searing sun for a cab.

'Ethan, it's Doug,' Jarvis spoke to them both, *'there's been a new development while you were travelling and we may know the origin of the device we found in General Thompson's brain.'*

'Go ahead,' Ethan said. 'We could do with some leads.'

'The urgency of the mission has opened up some new channels through the Pentagon, and we've had reports that these devices were something being worked upon by the National Security Agency some twenty years ago, operating out of a safe house in Hong Kong.'

'You mean these things are ours?' Lopez asked in horror.

'The technology may have been developed by NSA experts,' Jarvis confirmed. *'But four of them went missing in Kowloon shortly before Hong Kong was handed back to the Chinese by the British, who had occupied and governed the city for some two hundred years. The technology was too sensitive for the NSA to dispatch military forces to recover it, and the four men were never seen again.'*

'The Chinese,' Ethan murmured, 'but how would they have come to be in Iraq?'

'I don't know,' Jarvis admitted, *'but if they grabbed the NSA's technology in 1997 and started work on it, who knows what they could have developed in the time since?'*

'We'll keep it in mind,' Ethan replied. 'We're on our way to Basra's hospital. I'll check in as soon as we know anything more.'

A battered taxi cab awaited them outside the terminal, coated in dust and with faded paintwork blasted by the desert sun. Ethan tossed his bag alongside Lopez's inside the trunk and got in as the driver smiled and greeted them enthusiastically.

Known as the *Venice of the East*, Basra was situated on the Shatt–Al–Arab waterway which flowed into the nearby Persian Gulf. Canals and streams intersected the city and were used for irrigation purposes, giving the city its comparison to Venice, but pollution and falling water levels had stripped most vessels of the ability to navigate the canals, further hindering the city's progress in the wake of the American occupation. The cab pulled away toward the city as Ethan went on.

'What we really need is a direct lead on this Abrahem that Muller mentioned,' he said.

'It might not be his real name,' Lopez pointed out. 'He might even be a she, or maybe they got into all of this more recently and haven't yet committed a crime.'

Ethan used the door handle to wind down the window and let the breeze into the hot interior of the car.

'It's not going to be easy and this place is lethal. Basra's under threat from Islamic State and what law enforcement exists won't have much left in the way of records after so many years of war.'

Lopez could not add much as the taxi drove them through Basra's city center, the site of so much conflict and suffering over endless decades of Saddam Hussein's iron rule and then repeated wars and bombings by both the American military and now militant groups vying for control. Despite the harsh conditions endured by Basra a rebuilding program was underway, largely initiated by the British and American forces stationed at Basra during the conflict, and Ethan could see that in places Basra looked something like it once had before the wars.

Al–Faihaa General Hospital was located in the north west of the city just a few kilometres from the airport. A low, wide white building with a horizontal blue stripe running the length of its first–storey windows, the parking lot outside was virtually empty as Ethan climbed out of the cab with Lopez and they walked inside.

The interior of the hospital was quiet with only a few staff walking around and many of the wards empty of patients. Ethan walked toward the reception desk, grateful that so many of the hospital's signs were written in both English and Arabic, and spoke to a woman sitting behind the main desk. Within a few minutes, a handsome man in a gray suit and blue shirt walked out to greet them.

'Mister Warner, I'm Doctor Alin Darwish.' Darwish's English was heavily weighted with a British accent. 'Oxford,' he explained as he noted Ethan's reaction.

'Thanks for meeting with us,' Ethan said. 'Is there somewhere we can talk in private?'

Darwish led them into a sparse office and closed the door behind them.

'We're looking for anybody at the hospital who might have worked with this man,' Ethan said as he handed Darwish a photograph.

'Doctor Muller?' he asked, recognizing the face immediately. 'He worked here for many years and for the military contingent at the airport. He is an excellent doctor.'

'You worked with him?' Lopez asked.

'I was an intern then,' Darwish explained. 'The war gave us opportunity to learn fast, sadly. Most of the doctors have long since left Iraq because of the violence and oppression suffered here since the British forces went home.'

'Why do you stay?'

'Because this is my home,' Darwish replied to her. 'Would you leave America if war came to your door?'

'No,' Lopez admitted.

'People here need my care and that of my colleagues. However, I thought that Muller also returned to America some years ago?'

'Germany,' Ethan corrected the doctor. 'It was there that we've learned he was working for militant groups.'

'Muller?' Darwish asked in horror. 'But he was one of the most generous doctors we ever had. He saved lives when we no longer had sufficient resources to do it ourselves, became something of a hero to the younger nurses and doctors working here, including myself. I don't believe that he willingly colluded with militants – he hated them.'

'He may not have worked directly with the fighters,' Lopez said, 'but he sure as hell worked with the organizations. He gave us a name: Abrahem.'

Darwish raised his hands in supplication.

'Such a name means the *Father of all Races*,' he said. 'It is a common name in Iraq.'

'Muller was likely paid from the top of the organizations, possibly even by benefactors in Iran and other nations sympathetic to seeing the American mission in Iraq fail. He took the money, Dr Darwish, in return for conducting medical procedures without the knowledge of his patients.'

'Not here he didn't,' Darwish snapped. 'This is ridiculous!'

Ethan slid another picture across the table to Darwish.

'This was Major General Frederick Thompson,' he explained, 'and he recently killed dozens of his own countrymen in a gun attack in Georgia.' Ethan slid another image across the table, this time of the implant found in Thompson's skull. 'This is what the autopsy uncovered. It was lodged in his frontal lobes.'

Darwish looked down at the image and frowned. 'What is it?'

'A device that penetrates the brain and allows indirect control of the person's actions,' Lopez replied. 'It was inserted by Muller at military hospitals in Berlin and Basra. We traced the origins of the devices back here. Somebody at this hospital must have been involved. Now, who worked with Muller who may have had sympathy or an allegiance to militant groups active during his tenure here?'

Darwish rubbed his temples as he stared at the image of the device.

'I didn't even know such things were possible,' he said. 'There is nobody here with even the remotest ability to create or surgically implant these kinds of devices.'

'We figured that,' Ethan replied. 'But who might have had cause to support such an action? Did anybody at all assist Muller in any way?'

Darwish looked up.

'One of our interns, Abu Hazim, was a major benefactor to the hospital during the darkest hours of the war. He worked here and also gave money to purchase supplies and often brought in casualties from the battles.'

Lopez frowned as she looked at the list of names Jarvis had supplied them with. 'He brought casualties here himself?'

Darwish nodded. 'We knew that they were probably militant fighters, injured during skirmishes with the British soldiers based here, but we needed the money that Hazim had access to. It was an unspoken agreement – medicines in return for treating injured militants.'

'Where is this Hazim now?' Ethan asked.

'He still works here,' Darwish replied. 'He's on the wards right now.'

Ethan stood without another word and looked at Darwish expectantly. The doctor took the hint and opened his office door and they walked out together. They were halfway down the hall when Darwish gestured toward one of the wards ahead and a young doctor standing over a patient's bed.

'There he is,' he said, and called out; 'Abu?'

Ethan saw a short, stocky doctor look at them through square lensed glasses, his eyes fly wide as he looked at Ethan and Lopez and then he whirled and dashed away down the hall.

Ethan broke into a sprint in pursuit of Abu, Lopez alongside him in an instant. They thundered down the corridor as Abu crashed through swinging doors ahead of them and turned left.

'He's heading for the exits,' Lopez called as she shouldered through the door just ahead of Ethan.

Ethan turned the corner in the corridor, saw the sign on the wall directing them toward the exits and Abu fleeing ahead of them. Nurses leaped out of Abu's way as he flew past them and then they saw Ethan and Lopez in pursuit. Two trolleys and a cloud of medical swab packs flew into their path as the hospital staff, fearing for their colleague's safety, hurled obstructions out in front of Lopez.

Ethan saw her vault lithely over the trolleys, barely breaking her step as he plunged into them and smashed them aside. The metal trolleys clattered noisily down the corridor as Abu smashed through the exit doors and outside into the bright sunlight.

Lopez shot through the doors just ahead of Ethan, who crashed through them into the brilliant sunlight of a courtyard just as a deafening crescendo of machine gun fire shattered the air around him. Ethan hurled himself to the left as fear pulsed through his heart, bullets impacting the walls behind him as he saw Lopez throw herself down behind a crumbling wall.

Ethan hit the ground and rolled sideways as bullets showered him with dust and mortar chips and he curled up in a narrow recess. He peeked around the edge and saw Abu Hazim vanish down an alley opposite the courtyard, his footfalls echoing away into the distance.

Ethan peered up and saw a gunman on the roof of a building across from the hospital, his silhouette clear against the bright sky as he fired a last burst and then vanished from sight.

'Clear!'

Ethan leaped out and sprinted toward the alley alongside Lopez.

***

XIX

Ethan sprinted out onto the street and turned left as he saw Hazim dash across to where a dusty looking sedan was parked alongside the sidewalk. The doctor scrambled into the vehicle and started the engine, which coughed a cloud of dirty black smoke before it took off to the east.

Ethan dashed across the street and saw a battered looking motorcycle leaning against a wall. He couldn't tell if the bike was parked or abandoned, but he rushed up to it and grabbed the handlebars as he climbed onto the saddle and saw an aged old key lodged in the ignition.

'Not motorbikes again?' Lopez uttered as she leaped onto the pillion seat.

Ethan reached down and opened the fuel valve, then flipped out the kick–starter and stamped down on it. To his delight and surprise the engine spluttered into life and the motorbike rattled and clattered as he stomped it into gear and accelerated out into the street. A crowd of Iraqi's shouted curses at him as they sprinted in pursuit of the stolen motorcycle, but their protests were drowned out by the hot wind and the clattering engine.

Hazim's vehicle had vanished around a corner and left a plume of desert dust behind it, and Ethan turned the bike gingerly in pursuit, unsure of whether the ancient old machine's tires could take the strain. The engine growled and complained until Ethan straightened up again and accelerated once more.

Rows of palm trees flashed by either side of them, market stalls and donkeys lining the road as Ethan weaved past a battered old van chugging down the street.

'Where's he running to?' Lopez shouted above the hot wind.

'The southern quarter!' Ethan yelled back. 'It's where the insurgency is the strongest. They're likely protecting him. If we don't get to him before then, we'll both disappear!'

'Great!'

Hazim turned right onto a main through fare known as Trading Street, a double lane highway heading south east through the city and packed with dense traffic. Ethan followed and began gaining quickly on the dusty sedan as it was held up by the flow of trucks and other trade vehicles.

Ethan twisted the throttle and the motorbike coughed and accelerated between two heavy goods trucks rumbling along the broad road, their engines deafeningly loud as he soared between them and got a better look at Hazim's sedan. It had once been white but was now a dirty rust–color, missing its rear fender and its windows smudged with grime.

Ethan allowed the motorbike to drift to the left as he pulled alongside the vehicle and looked into Abu Hazim's eyes. In an instant he saw two things there: genuine fear and the muzzle of a pistol aimed at him. Ethan squeezed hard on the ancient drum brakes and the motorbike jerked as though he had dropped an anchor into the asphalt beneath them.

The gunshot shattered Hazim's window and Ethan felt the shockwave as it rocketed by inches in front of his head. Lopez slammed into him from behind, caught out by the sudden braking manoeuvre as Ethan struggled to maintain control. The motorbike weaved to the right and he heard a horn blare from directly behind him. Ethan looked over his shoulder and saw one of the huge trucks looming close on their tail.

'He's bigger than us!' Lopez snapped.

Ethan accelerated clear of the truck as a huge, open plan junction with no warning lights or traffic control loomed ahead, ranks of vehicles warring for priority as they swarmed in a chaotic jumble across the junction.

'Perfect!' Lopez shouted. 'Now what?'

Ethan looked ahead and saw Hazim at the wheel of his vehicle, looking left and right as he approached the junction. But he was looking more right than left, toward the busy southern districts.

'He'll go right,' Ethan shouted. 'He wants to head south! Hang on!'

The junction was packed with vehicles honking their horns and vying for a passage as Ethan braked and allowed the two heavy goods vehicles to thunder past and conceal his path. He hauled the motorbike hard to the right and mounted a ramp onto the sidewalk as he took the right turn and then braked to a halt.

'Stay on us!' Ethan said as he jumped out of the saddle.

Lopez slid into the seat he had vacated as Ethan dashed out amid the traffic, ducking low as he sought out Hazim's battered sedan among the many similar vehicles jostling for position on the busy road. Drivers hollered at him in Arabic as he dashed between the vehicles, and then he saw Hazim's car appear as it swung in a hard right turn toward him on the opposite side of the road, held up behind rows of other vehicles all heading south.

Ethan stayed low as he reached the edge of the left hand lane, and then as Hazim's car approached he leaped out and sprinted toward it. Hazim saw him in an instant and swerved aside as Ethan hurled himself up onto the hood and tumbled onto the roof. Ethan grabbed hold of the edges in a grim bid to hang on as the vehicle's acceleration swung him around, and he looked down through an open sunroof to see Hazim's terrified eyes stare up at him even as he aimed the pistol up at Ethan.

Ethan had only a moment to react, the scene imprinted in his mind as time seemed to stand still. The pistol was a 9mm Beretta M1951, licence built by the Iraqis as the *Tariq*. Ethan glimpsed the Arabic writing stamped down the side of the barrel as he twisted to one side, reached down through the sunroof and grabbed the barrel of the pistol with one hand before Hazim could pull the trigger.

The barrel mechanism was hot but Ethan gripped it tightly and prevented it from moving, effectively neutralizing the weapon. Hazim's eyes widened as he tried to pull the pistol down from Ethan's grip, but Ethan slipped his finger behind Hazim's trigger and then pulled hard as he twisted his grip and pushed up from the sedan's roof with all of his might. Hazim's weaker arm was yanked upward and out of the sunroof as Ethan pulled him away from the steering wheel. Ethan hauled Hazim's arm sideways across the roof and slammed it down, bent it at the elbow and pinned it in place as he reached out with his other hand and twisted the weapon from Hazim's grip even as he heard shouts of pain from within the vehicle.

The sedan swerved toward the sidewalk and Ethan hung on grimly to Hazim's arm to prevent himself from sliding off the roof as the car slammed into the sidewalk and shuddered as it slid to a halt.

The sound of a motorbike engine screamed alongside the vehicle as Lopez skidded to a halt in front of the sedan and leaped from the motorbike. She dashed to the driver's door and saw Hazim's face twisted in pain, his arm half in and half out of the sunroof and twisted at an awkward angle.

Ethan released Hazim and rolled off the vehicle onto the sidewalk as he aimed the pistol at the Iraqi doctor.

'We need a word,' he uttered grimly.

Even as he held the gun pointing at Hazim a pair of Iraqi military trucks rolled up alongside them in support, and Hazim's shoulders sank in despair.

*

'Start talking.'

The interrogation room of Basra's police station in As–Saymar was one of crumbling, unpainted walls and a broken–tiled floor. Although in better repair than the old Jamiat station, which had been blown to pieces, it still reminded Ethan of some backwater KGB black prison where criminals and the innocent alike were sent to end their days in pain and seclusion, buried from sight of the world beyond.

That Abu Hazim knew of the reputation of Iraqi prisons was without doubt. He could barely keep his gaze from the two Iraqi prison guards standing beside the door, their rifles cradled in their grip.

'Never mind them,' Ethan snapped as he clicked his fingers in Hazim's face. 'Talk, now!'

Lopez leaned against the wall nearby, her arms folded as she watched Hazim with dark eyes devoid of compassion.

'Why did you run?' Ethan demanded.

'Because I was afraid!' Hazim shouted back finally. 'Because I did not know who you were, because I didn't know what you wanted with me!'

'Who were the gunmen who opened fire on us?!'

'I don't know!' Hazim insisted. 'I have been followed often to and from work by men who watch me.'

'They must be watching you for a reason,' Lopez pointed out. 'I'd say it's because they know something about you, Abu, just like we do.'

Ethan leaned closer to Hazim. 'You've heard of Guantanamo Bay, right? And Jamiat, the prison cells. You know what happens there, what they went through. We've already caught you Hazim. It's over. Start talking and you might just avoid jail here. Waste my time and I'll have you sent down for more years than you'll survive in a jail that nobody's heard of, where nobody will hear you scream and nobody will care what happens to you.'

'I don't know what you're talking about!' Hazim almost screeched, his wrists manacled to the table top.

Ethan smiled without warmth as he sat down on a wooden stool opposite Hazim.

'Yes, you do. If you want to have a life when you walk out of this room, start talking to us.'

'About what?'

'Start with Abrahem,' Ethan said casually, taking a chance. 'When did you last see him?'

Hazim looked up at the mention of that name, his dark eyes filled with foreboding.

'Who?'

'Don't dick us around!' Ethan snapped as he slammed a clenched fist down on the table, mostly to distract Hazim from his own attempts to formulate a convincing next line. 'We know about the procedures performed here by Doctor Muller. We know about the implants and we know about Abrahem! He'll sell you down the river, Abu, may already have done so! That gunfire, are you sure it was meant for us and not for you?'

Hazim's eyes wobbled in their sockets and he swallowed, his skin sheened with sweat despite the cool air in the unheated stone room.

'The hell with him,' Lopez snapped as she pushed off from the wall and headed for the cell door. 'Feed him to the damned Islamists or send him to the US, let them crucify his useless butt.'

Lopez yanked open the cell door as Ethan got up and grinned cruelly down at Hazim.

'Have a nice life, what's left of it,' he said and turned for the door.

He was almost out of the cell when he heard Hazim's voice call out.

'They will kill me!'

Lopez spat a cold laugh over her shoulder at him. 'Yeah sure, you would say that. This guy's not worth anything.'

She kept walking down the corridor outside.

Ethan stopped at the door and looked over his shoulder. 'That's your problem, Hazim. We don't need your testimony because you're not a big enough player. We'll get what we want, with or without you.'

Ethan turned away again and began walking as the guards moved to shut the door with grim smiles of anticipation. This time, Hazim's voice shrieked in pursuit.

'Abrahem Nassir!'

Ethan stopped as he heard the door to the cell close behind him with a metallic clunk that echoed through the corridor. Lopez raised an eyebrow as Hazim cried out again, his voice muted by the heavy door.

'I'll tell you everything, please!' he yelled. 'I know Abrahem Nassir!'

Ethan leaned against the wall for several long seconds, making Hazim sweat as much as possible before he turned back and opened the door. He walked back in, Lopez following and slamming the door behind her.

'He's making it up,' she said without interest, 'anything to save the coward's ass.'

'It's true!' Hazim shouted, directing a hurt look at Lopez.

'Prove it,' Ethan said as he re–took his seat. 'Last chance, Hazim. You don't give me something worthwhile right here and now you'll disappear from history, understand?'

Hazim ran his hands through his thick black hair, his voice resigned as he spoke.

'Abrahem Nassir is from Basra,' Hazim explained. 'He did a deal with foreigners for some technology that they wanted Doctor Muller to implant into American soldiers who passed through the hospital. They had money, lots of money, and they assured him that there would be no direct consequences. Abrahem hired us all on that basis.'

'To do what?' Lopez demanded.

Hazim stared at the table as he spoke, at his own manacled hands.

'Doctor Muller inserted devices into their nasal passages, up into the brain,' he said, 'while they were under general anesthetic. That was all. We did not know what the devices were, only that we were to say nothing to anybody.'

Ethan leaned closer to Hazim. 'Where is Abrahem Nassir now?'

'I don't know,' Hazim replied. 'I promise that I don't know. He took off a few days ago and then the men in suits turned up looking for him. I don't know who they were or who they worked for, but I know where they came from.'

Ethan waited and Hazim breathed a last, terminal sigh.

'They were Chinese,' he said.

Ethan's fists clenched a little tighter.

'How many of the devices did you insert into American service personnel?' he asked.

Hazim shrugged.

'Hundreds,' he said, 'thousands.'

Ethan whirled to Lopez. 'Get in touch with Jarvis, let's get this out in the open as fast as we can.'

Ethan turned back to Hazim. 'Tell me about Abrahem Nassir. Everything you know; where he's been, who's funding him and what his plans are.'

Hazim sighed, his head hanging low.

'I don't know. All I can be sure of is that he is being funded by a wealthy benefactor, and that he is intending to travel to the United States. I overheard his people saying that they had allies, in Africa.'

'Where in Africa?' Ethan demanded.

'Somalia.'

***

XX

American Consulate Building, Garden Road,

Hong Kong

The American Embassy in Hong Kong was perched at an awkward angle on a steep hillside surrounded by massive skyscrapers that overlooked the island's north shore and Kowloon Bay beyond. It looked to Hannah as though it had been built as an afterthought, a subtle snub to the distant yet global power of the United States.

The FBI vehicle that had picked them up from Hong Kong International Airport on the island of Chek Lap Kok, a few kilometres east of Hong Kong, pulled into the Consulate Building and a set of steel gates opened to allow it through into the parking lot under the watchful eye of a security guard. Hannah got out, slightly dizzy with fatigue as she walked into the Consulate Building with Vaughn alongside her, and they were greeted immediately by an attache who guided them through the building.

'You really think that these guys will have anything of use after all of these years?' he asked Hannah as they walked.

'The Chinese are voracious record keepers,' Hannah replied, 'and the offices here have paper logs going back decades. If we can link even a single operative to the abductions, we'll have a lead. I guess it all boils down to the state of the remains.'

Director LeMay had provided them with a brief before they had boarded their flight from the United States. Although it had contained little in the way of details, Hannah now knew that a body had been found washed up on the shores of Kowloon a day before. That body belonged to a former National Security Agency officer who had been stationed in Hong Kong some two decades before and been missing ever since. Hannah did not know what the NSA's operative was doing in Hong Kong at the time, but given that the territory had been handed back to Communist China by the United Kingdom in 1997, it seemed possible that the NSA and other government agencies had been clearing house of any sensitive documents and programs before the Chinese could access them.

The Consulate Building did not have its own mortuary – instead the local hospital where the autopsy had taken place under the Bureau's control had shipped images of the remains to the Consulate for viewing purposes. Hannah and Vaughn were led to a small conference room on the second floor and sat down, the windows overlooking the road below and giving them a glimpse of the bay to the north between the high rise buildings glinting in the sunlight. The FBI had numerous offices worldwide situated in consulate buildings and US Embassies, termed *legal attaches* and used as staging posts for federal interests around the globe.

Within a few minutes, Special Agent Brad Hinkley strode into the room. A Texan attached to the Hong Kong office, he brandished his own swaggering style of greeting, all firm handshakes and hugs before he sat down opposite them.

'So, what brings you folks all the way out here? Director LeMay said it was urgent and to do with the body we recovered yesterday.'

'1997,' Hannah replied. 'Four computer experts from the National Security Agency were abducted from Kowloon Bay while on a boat trip to the islands, presumed held by the Chinese ever since. The event occurred just before Hong Kong was repatriated to the Chinese by the British, allowing Communist elements to move more freely through the city.'

Hinkley nodded. 'The office at the time put everything it had into finding them, but they vanished without a trace. Of course China denied any involvement and put their disappearance down to drownings. The Consulate had been careful not to say how or where the operatives actually vanished from, so the fact that the Chinese were able to pinpoint the disappearances as being on the waters of Kowloon Bay said everything. I read the files and it was figured that in 1997, on the verge of receiving back their ownership of the island, China wouldn't do anything rash with their new prize. Big mistake.'

'Do you know anything about what these guys were working on?' Vaughn asked.

'Beats me,' Hinkley said, 'it's all so classified that I can't get close to it and neither could anybody here at the Consulate in 1997, but we do know that when they vanished they had something on their possession.'

'How so?' Vaughn asked.

'Because half the damned US Special Operations Service descended on both this office and the NSA's Hawaii base where the NSA guys were originally stationed. It's a listening post that monitors China, Taiwan and some of Russia. They were looking for something after the abductions all right, but they never found it and left empty handed as far as I know.'

'And now this body shows up,' Hannah said. 'What's the story?'

Hinkley opened a file and spread it before them. Hannah looked down and saw images of a young man in his twenties, and the gruesomely decayed remnants of the corpse fished out of Kowloon Bay.

'Stephen Ricard, age twenty seven years,' Hinkley announced. 'He was an analyst for the National Security Agency stationed at Hawaii and posted to Hong Kong to maintain an NSA watch station out of an apartment on the south shore along with three other agents. All were on the record as being employed by a local British IT company, and all attended work there while also performing their analysis of China's growing computer and cell phone network. He vanished along with his three colleagues in 1997.'

'Are you sure these remains are his?' Vaughn asked.

'The body was badly decomposed,' Hinkley admitted, 'and the teeth had been removed to hinder identification of the remains, something else that the Chinese would have reason to do and that wouldn't occur in a straight forward drowning. However the autopsy confirmed that according to the Medical Examiner, despite appearances, Stephen had died or been placed in the water only a couple of months prior to his discovery due to the presence of marine growth inside his body tissue, specifically various kinds of algae and such like. Although his teeth had been yanked, four minor fractures in his tibia, fingers and ribs from a childhood accident remained visible under X–Ray and confirm the remains belong to Stephen. He also had a small tattoo of a *Goldeneye* logo, some sort of computer game based on the *Bond* movie, on his left shoulder which is also just visible in the images.'

Hannah nodded as she saw a dark smudge beneath the yellow and purple flesh, smeared with what appeared to be a mixture of foliage and raw sewage that had clung to the body from the bay's frigid waters. The chances of the tattoo and the fractures both belonging to some other unfortunate soul floating in the bay were highly remote.

'Cause of death?' Vaughn asked.

'Purportedly drowning,' Hinkley said, 'but several more things rule that out. Firstly, there was evidence of damage to the interior of the trachea, consistent with a tube being forced down Stephen's throat to flood his lungs with seawater. Along with the limited level of decay, that supports a staged drowning. Secondly, it was the damage to the victim's brain that the Medical Examiner believes killed him.'

'The brain?' Hannah asked.

'Stephen had major trauma to his frontal lobes,' Hinkley explained, 'consistent with a foreign object being repeatedly inserted into his brain via his nasal cavity, which also showed signs of long–term damage. Whatever he endured at the hands of the Chinese it went on for a decade and a half and eventually killed him. The Chinese must then have dumped his body in the water and hoped the problem would float away and become fish food.'

'Do we have any idea what they were putting into his brain?' Vaughn asked, somewhat appalled.

'No,' Hinkley admitted, 'but whatever it was left a basic impression on the interior of the nasal cavities, which the Medical Examiner was able to scan and reproduce using a 3D–printer.'

Hinkley produced from his pocket a small plastic evidence bag, and inside it was a slim plastic cylinder barely an inch long. Hannah frowned as she looked at it.

'Small, no identifying marks.'

'Nothing that we could see,' Hinkley confirmed, 'but the brain's tissue is not good at retaining impression from something so small. Still, whatever this is it seems to me to be central to what everybody's out here looking for.'

'Everybody?' Hannah asked, confused. 'I thought that we were the only people out here looking for this?'

'There was some guy here this morning,' Hinkley said, 'big guy, African American. He was working for the FBI too.'

'The FBI? But we're here under LeMay's direct orders. Who the hell else could there be working for the Barn out here?'

'Beats me,' Hinkley said, 'but he was legitimate, had all the right credentials.'

Hannah shot Vaughn a concerned glance. 'Do you have any CCTV of this person, a name? Anything?'

Hinkley shook his head.

'The guy was an agency heavyweight, had priority access to the building through the car pool gates and carried enough authority to have the security systems disengaged down near the sally port. I had to meet him down there personally and talk this over with him.'

Hannah hissed a sigh out as she glanced out of the windows at the traffic outside.

'What kind of vehicle was he driving?' she asked.

Hinkley shrugged. 'Limousine, private plates, tinted windows. Didn't look like something the Barn would finance, but then this is Hong Kong. You kind of learn to expect anything.'

'Mitchell,' Hannah said to Vaughn. 'He's onto this as well.'

'Could be a coincidence,' Vaughn said without conviction. 'But if he's out here he may have the jump on us. He must be impersonating a federal agent.'

'But then how would he get in here so easily?' Hannah challenged.

'If he's high enough up the chain, he can go anywhere he wants,' Hinkley said. 'Who is he?'

Hannah stood up and shook Hinkley's hand. 'We're working on that. If anything shows up in the paperwork regarding Stephen Ricard, please do forward it to us.'

'Will do,' Hinkley promised.

Hannah did not speak again until she reached the sidewalk outside the Consulate, the traffic noise helping to shield her conversation with Vaughn.

'Mitchell's chasing the same thing as us?' Vaughn asked. 'You think he's on–side this time?'

'I don't know,' Hannah replied. 'If what Jarvis was suggesting is true then Mitchell is working for this Majestic Twelve, so presumably whatever the NSA lost out here will be something that they're looking to acquire.'

'So you're buying Jarvis's line now?'

'Not exactly,' Hannah replied, 'but if Mitchell's the enemy then it's our job to get to this before he does.'

'Or maybe he's actually working for the FBI,' Vaughn said, 'which would mean that LeMay at the very least knows about him.'

Hannah stared at her partner. 'Jarvis said we'd be hung out to dry.'

'If Mitchell gets whatever it is LeMay wants first,' Vaughn confirmed. 'We don't know that's the case, but whatever the hell's going on here our best bet is to beat Mitchell to whatever it is people are looking for out here.'

'Mitchell must also have left the Consulate empty handed,' Hannah said, 'so what would be his next move?'

Vaughn glanced around them at the city and then toward Kowloon Bay.

'If Stephen Ricard was only dumped a couple of weeks ago it's possible we could find evidence of the boat that did it, although it's a long shot with all the maritime traffic moving through the bay.'

'We could check currents, work backwards from where the body was found to give us an idea of where the body was originally dumped.'

Vaughn winced. 'There are too many variables and we don't know exactly how the body was placed in the water. It could have been upstream somewhere on the mainland, not out in the bay.'

Hannah felt her shoulders slump as she realized that Vaughn was right. Without more details they couldn't accurately plot the movements of the body, and that meant they couldn't pinpoint where Stephen's remains had entered the water. They had only one option left, and that was to let Mitchell do the work for them.

'We'll get traffic camera footage of the street out here and get the plate of Mitchell's vehicle,' she said finally. 'Let's find him instead and figure out what he's got in mind.'

***

XXI

El Hur,

Somalia

'Salaam, my friend.'

The old man greeted Abrahem with a warm embrace and held his shoulders firmly in his hands as he looked the younger man up and down in the darkness, the sound of waves crashing far behind them. Tariq Adel was elderly now but the fire of insurgency burned as brightly in his eyes as it had decades before in the killing fields of the Iran – Iraq war that had taken so many lives.

'Every day, you make your father proud Abrahem,' Tariq said. 'He would have smiled upon you here as he smiles upon you now from Paradise.'

'And I shall continue to do so, Tariq,' Abrahem replied.

'Come,' the old man beckoned. 'There is much to say.'

Abrahem followed Tariq up to the small village, an isolated group of low buildings huddled against the east African coast in the Harardhere District. Barren beaches stretched for miles to the north and south and there were no roads across the boundless desert wastes to the west. The village's presence in the darkness was betrayed only by a handful of flickering fires, beacons in the absolute blackness around them.

Abrahem's journey had been long, cramped aboard a tiny boat that had chugged its way out of the Persian Gulf and turned south along the coasts of Oman and Yemen, travelling through the night and all of the next day and then the following night also. The smell of grease, metal and smoke stained Abrahem's clothes with the hated odour of western civilization, their love of oil and petroleum like an addiction surging through their veins. He was grateful for the fresh breezes billowing across the Somalian coast and rippling through his shirt as he followed Tariq to one of the larger buildings, built the old way from compacted earth that had been baked into bricks in the harsh sunlight. He wondered how many long centuries these homes had stood, lived in by people who had known nothing of the troubles that would face their ancestors.

Dark eyes watched him from the blackness, reflecting the firelight that glinted off the smooth metal of Kalashnikov AK–47 rifles slung over the shoulders of Islamist pirates. Their ancestors had likely also been men of the sea but fishermen, not the callous murderers who watched him now, devoid of any morsel of humanity. Abrahem could not say it out loud for he needed their assistance, but he despised their bigotry, their ignorance and their addiction to death and theft. To Abrahem they were no better than the infidel Americans.

The interior of the building was filled also with the smell of smoke, but this pungent cloud was wood smoke and seemed somehow clean compared to the chemical taint of the boat, which had sailed on south after delivering Abrahem at the pre–arranged location on Somalia's dangerous shores. Fresh clothes awaited Abrahem and he changed eagerly as Tariq prepared food and drink for him nearby.

'When will I be able to leave?' Abrahem asked, and then realized what he was saying, offending his host. 'I mean only that I have little time to complete my mission. The Americans will not be far behind me.'

Tariq smiled as he poured thick, sweet coffee and turned with a plate in his hand filled with meats, fruits and vegetables, the harvest of kings when compared to what little the unyielding soil of Somalia produced.

'I know well what you mean,' he replied as he handed the plate and the coffee to Abrahem. 'As I know well what a rush the world is in these days, its people always thinking of tomorrow and never of today.'

Abrahem took the food gratefully as he sat down beside the fire, and with Tariq gave thanks to Allah for his safe journey and for the food before he began to eat.

'The Americans never sleep,' he replied, 'they never cease activity, like machines. If I should falter or allow myself the comfort of sloth, they will be upon us.'

'Then we shall deal with them then,' Tariq replied without concern. 'Now, it is time for rest. You have been successful so far?'

Abrahem nodded. 'Everything is in place. The Americans will not know what has hit them. They will question everything that they are, all that they have become. They will never be the same again.'

'Some would say that day has come and passed,' Tariq replied, 'during their World Trade Center attacks.'

Abrahem snarled.

'Acts of cowardice! The killing of civilians, not soldiers. What men were they? They achieved nothing but to provoke America to rape and pillage across our lands in return! They claimed to have killed Americans in Allah's name, but their own countrymen were bombed in their millions and all for America's damned black oil!'

Tariq watched Abrahem for a long moment as he ate.

'We strike back as we can,' he replied finally. 'We do not have armies and jets and bombs like the Americans. Open battle is not a possibility for us.'

'It's not the fight that matters,' Abrahem smiled grimly, 'but the outcome. The trade center attacks destroyed Iraq and Afghanistan. They provoked our own leaders to hunt down Al–Qaeda, to kill Sheik Bin–Laden, to persecute our people while they profited from the fruits of our lands. *Our* lands. Do you know, Tariq, how many children's bodies I dug from the rubble of Basra and Baghdad after the American raids?'

Tariq closed his eyes and did not respond.

'Babies,' Abrahem murmured, his eyes glazed, 'their bodies burned to powder or torn to shreds. My own family…'

Abrahem broke off, blinked and lowered his chin so that Tariq might not see his grief as it wrenched at his heart and tugged painfully at the muscles of his face.

'I know of your pain, Abrahem,' Tariq replied finally. 'It is shared by all of us, for there is barely a Muslim across the world that has not lost a member of their family to this scourge of our people.'

Abrahem nodded, keeping his head down and chewing on a slice of meat as he recovered himself.

'I shall not stop,' he said, 'until I have changed the face of America. This will be my legacy.'

Tariq's eyes widened as he looked at the young man before him, his face cloaked in shadows and his eyes dark with a vengeance that burned brightly and yet consumed the life force within him. The brightest stars, Tariq recalled, always burned the fiercest before dying young.

'Your life is worth more than this,' Tariq said carefully. 'Be not wasteful with it.'

Abrahem's dark eyes locked onto Tariq's with a fearsome gaze.

'Do not worry yourself, Tariq. Every last ounce of my being will be used to its full potential and America will suffer the agony of its loss for a thousand years. They will pay for what they have…'

Abrahem fell silent as his eyes rose to the sky somewhere above them outside. The wind rumbled and he could just make out the whisper of the waves rolling onto the nearby beach, but something else caught his attention. Something unnatural, rhythmic, man made.

Abrahem dropped his food and grabbed Tariq.

'We must leave, now!'

'Why?' the old man asked, confused.

'The Americans. They are already here!'

*

USS *Harry S. Truman*, US Fifth Fleet,

Persian Gulf

'Lone Warrior, Ranger One, in–bound Bullseye, ETA two minutes.'

Ethan heard the pilot of the Sikorsky SH–60 *Seahawk* call his position in the darkness, the horizon outside invisible and the cockpit aglow with green digital instruments, and then the co–pilot looked over his shoulder and give a brief thumbs–up to the occupants in the rear.

Ethan sat alongside Lopez in a jump seat, and around them sat an eight man team of US Navy SEALS, part of the Navy's Special Warfare Insertion division. Both he and Lopez has been flown out of Basra as part of a Carrier On–board Delivery flight to the USS Harry S. Truman, which had replaced the damaged USS Carl Vinson.

The elite troops surrounding Ethan were heavily armed and already briefed to expect resistance, and despite their training and skill listened patiently to Ethan as he spoke to them through his microphone.

'The target is Abrahem Nassir and he must be captured alive. We have evidence that he left Iraq and travelled on a merchant vessel down the coast of Somalia, and the carrier group's radar data suggests he made landfall here within the last hour. His assistance is essential to us if we are to prevent the attack that we believe he has planned. The capture of Nassir or any of his lieutenants may prevent another Pearl Harbor or nine–eleven.'

Ethan nodded once to clarify that he was done and the team leader gave him a thumbs up and moved alongside the *Seahawk*'s port side door, ready to lead his team out on rappel lines already coiled in preparation on the deck. He felt the *Seahawk* dip as it began to descend toward Somalia's rugged coastline, plunging downward and pulling Ethan up into his straps with negative G–force as the helicopter plummeted from the sky.

Suddenly Ethan's head was pulled down and his butt slammed against the seat as the *Seahawk* pulled up at the last moment, its rotors hammering the sky outside as the side doors were hauled open and he saw the SEALS hurl out their rappel lines and without hesitation they jumped in a rapid but orderly queue out of the helicopter and into the faint light of dawn outside.

Ethan held his position, knowing better than to get in their way as the soldiers deployed. A rush of sea air hit him, cold and brisk and vibrant, and was followed by a waft of jet fuel and then the crackle of small arms fire as the SEALs hit the beach and encountered the enemy.

'Let's go!' he shouted.

Lopez moved instantly as she clipped herself to the port rappel line and launched herself out into the vigorous downwash of the helicopter's rotors. Ethan followed on the starboard line and they plunged downward together, Lopez crashing into the surf at the edge of a broad beach that was just visible in the faint light.

Ethan crashed down alongside her and they both dashed up the beach as staccato bursts of gunfire raked the sand around them, returning fire from the SEAL's M–16 rifles clattering up into a tightly bunched gathering of low buildings perched on the edge of the beach.

'There's too many of them!' Lopez yelled above the gunfire.

Ethan could see multiple flickering fires amid the buildings and among them at least twenty rifles firing back at the SEALs storming up the beach. To his right two of the SEALS switched their firing mechanisms to the M–16's underslung grenade launchers. Two grenades popped in graceful arcs over the rifle fire of their comrades and thumped down amid the enemy.

Ethan shielded his ears as the grenades detonated with bright flashes of light, clouds of lethal shrapnel scything through the armed militants defending the buildings as screams competed with the gunfire. The SEALs immediately began charging into the hail of uncoordinated fire, advancing by sections with each man covering his buddy and presenting a continuous and withering field of fire to their enemy.

The *Seahawk* had pulled back from its vulnerable hovering position, climbing rapidly as it turned away and moved to cut off any escape route to the north.

'Come on!' Ethan snapped.

He jumped up and began running south down the beach, keen to cut off anybody who might make a dash from the cover of the village. The damp sand slowed his sprint as though he were in a childhood dream and fleeing from some unthinkable monster from the depths of his imagination. He struggled up the bluff, Lopez alongside him as they crashed through dense fields of long grass clogging the bluff.

'Enemy.'

Lopez's harsh whisper slowed Ethan and he crouched down, his chest heaving for air as he heard the clatter of machine gun fire nearby. Above it, faint but audible, he could hear the sound of running feet beating a hasty retreat toward their position. Ethan looked at Lopez and saw that she already had her pistol gripped firmly in both hands.

Ethan checked his own weapon and then he leaped out into plain view and aimed into the dim light to see a crowd of women and children rushing toward him, panic in their eyes as they staggered to a halt and threw their arms in the air with a crescendo of cries and pleas for mercy. All were dressed in long, black *burqas*, only their eyes visible as they held their arms aloft and shielded their children with their bodies.

Ethan lowered his pistol as Lopez moved out of cover alongside him, lowering her own weapon as she surveyed the terrified villagers.

'Abrahem Nassir,' Ethan snapped, keen to entrap the villagers while they were still in fear for their lives and perhaps figure out where their target had gone. 'Abrahem Nassir?!'

One of the women turned and pointed over Ethan's left shoulder, toward the south, and Ethan instinctively glanced in that direction.

'Ethan!'

Lopez's startled voice alerted him, but it was too late. Ethan turned back in time to feel something club him across the side of his head and the gloomy beach reeled as he was hurled to the ground. He saw Lopez being overpowered, realized with the last of his consciousness that many of the women concealed in the *burqas* were in fact men, and then everything went black.

***

XXII

'Warner!'

Ethan heard the voice from the distant periphery of his awareness, pulling him in along with the unwelcome embrace of a throbbing ache that permeated his skull. Something jabbed him in the chest and he sucked in a lung full of air as he bolted upright and bright pain lanced behind his eyes.

'Take it easy.'

The voice soothed him and he felt the gloved hands of two Navy SEALS supporting him, one with a rifle guarding them and the other with a water canteen that was offered to Ethan. He drank from it gratefully and suddenly the pieces of his memory reconnected themselves and he looked at the SEALs in shock.

'Lopez?!'

'We haven't found her yet,' the soldier replied, 'but we have prisoners and we don't think Nassir can have got far. You're lucky his people didn't shoot you in the head where you lay.'

Ethan nodded. 'Gunfire would have exposed them, and they probably didn't have time to hang around.'

'Neither do we,' the SEAL replied. 'We've wasted enough time looking for you so get off your ass and get moving. We've got work to do.'

The canteen was snatched away and the SEALs marched off. Ethan hauled himself to his feet and followed them at a jog back toward the village where the *Seahawk* helicopter was now landed on the beach, its rotors spinning slowly as the pilots awaited the SEALs gathered on the beach before them.

Ethan could see that in the soldier's midst, on their knees and with their hands behind their heads, were a small knot of ragged looking Somalians surrounded by a captured cache of weapons. Nearby, four more prisoners were hauling bodies down onto the beach. It took only a few moments for Ethan to realize that the SEALs had suffered no losses during the assault, but that there were at least a dozen Somalian dead lying on the cold sand as the dawn glowed weakly across the sky.

'Any injured?' Ethan asked the team leader as he held the back of his head in one hand and winced at the pain.

The SEAL's commanding officer shook his head.

'No casualties in our team. Twelve hostiles eliminated but our main target remains at large.'

Ethan looked down at the captured militants, all of them staring at the sand with their hands behind their heads. He looked up along the bluff, beyond the village to the deserts that stretched away into the empty wilderness. Abrahem Nassir, if he had been present in the village, could have travelled no more than a few miles at best, assuming he had a vehicle.

'Can we track them?'

The commander shook his head.

'We can't be seen over this country in broad daylight,' he replied. 'Even ignoring the international implications, the threat from shoulder–launched rocket propelled grenades to our *helo* is too great.'

Ethan knew that such basic weapons could be lethal to low flying helicopters no matter how advanced they may be, and the Somalians likely possessed them in spades.

'I want Lopez back,' Ethan said. 'If Abrahem escapes I can pick his trail up later but I'm not leaving my partner here.'

'We're not here to babysit the two of you,' the commander snapped back. 'She knew the risks. It's her problem now.'

'Would you leave one of your men out here?!'

'My men know the risks also and would take care of themselves.'

'And if an American woman turns up on the Internet, held captive by Islamist militants who claim she was abandoned here by American soldiers? How do you think that will go down with the folks back home?'

The commander sneered at Ethan. 'I'll let Congress deal with that.'

'Give her a chance. If we can't locate her in the next ten minutes, I'll stay behind and find her myself.'

The SEAL offered Ethan a grim smile.

'Your funeral, pal,' he said and then glanced at the prisoners. 'I've got an idea.'

Ethan waited as the SEALs ordered the captives to their feet. The SEAL commander seemed to scan each and every one of the men before him, assessing them with a practised eye, before he picked three of them out.

'Cut the rest loose.'

'You're letting them go?' Ethan asked.

'Kind of,' the commander replied.

To Ethan's surprise, many of the toughest looking men were freed and left standing on the beach as the SEALs dragged the three prisoners chosen by their commander back toward the *Seahawk*. The helicopter's engines began running up again as one by one the SEALs filed back inside, the Somalians forced to lay on the helicopter's deck as it lifted off.

Moments later three of the SEALS opened fire on the Somalians still on the beach below them, dropping them instantly in a hail of bullets as the *Seahawk* climbed away.

Ethan strapped himself in and watched as the SEAL commander talked to the pilots and the helicopter swung out over the ocean and headed south, climbing swiftly. The side doors had been left open, offering a vertiginous view of banks of misty cloud that soared past and then the helicopter broke free of them, climbing ever higher. Ethan guessed they were at five thousand feet before the helicopter levelled off and the SEAL commander spoke to their captors.

'There will be no negotiations,' he snapped, shouting above the roar of the engines and not bothering with a local dialect. 'I know that you can all understand me. You will tell me what I need to know or you will not leave this helicopter alive, understood?'

The three captives stared sullenly into the middle distance, their heads pressed against the metal deck and rifles pinned against their skulls.

The commander pointed at one of them. 'Him first.'

The SEALs hauled one of the Somalians to his feet, the militant unsteady as the helicopter rocked on the wind currents. The SEAL commander glared into the militant's eyes.

'Abrahem Nassir. Where is he going and what does he intend to do?'

The Somalian smiled, his teeth yellow.

'*Alluhah Akbhar*,' he snapped. 'God is great!'

The SEAL commander smiled grimly back at his captive. 'Not great enough to get you out of this!'

The commander nodded and without warning another SEAL yanked the militant backwards by the collar of his ragged shirt toward the open port door alongside Ethan. The Somalian's smile withered into panic and he opened his mouth to scream something, but the cry was lost as the SEAL commander jabbed his knuckles into the Somalian's throat. The militant's eyes bulged and he staggered backwards, his hands flying to his throat as the SEAL by the open door, one hand gripping a safety rail, hurled the Somalian out the side of the helicopter. The Somalian flew backwards out of the *Seahawk* and into the air, his eyes and mouth wide open in an expression of terminal horror.

Ethan stared transfixed as the militant spiraled down toward the clouds below them and then vanished, his fate sealed. For some reason, perhaps to veil the fact that he was witnessing a cold–blooded murder, Ethan recalled his own parachute training and his knowledge of what would happen. The militant would reach terminal velocity in a few seconds, well over one hundred miles per hour. At that speed, hitting the water far below would break every bone in his body as effectively as if he had hit concrete.

Ethan looked back at the remaining two captives, who were both staring wide eyed on the deck where they lay at where their companion had recently vanished into oblivion.

'Him,' the commander pointed.

The SEALs hauled another of them to his feet, and this time the man started babbling immediately, tears flowing from his eyes.

'Qeycad!' he whimpered. 'They are going to Qeycad!'

'What's there?' the commander demanded.

'A bush plane,' the Somalian replied miserably. 'Abrahem is to be flown to another country and out of Africa, that's all I know!'

The SEAL leaned close to the terrified militant. 'What does he intend to do then?'

'I don't know,' the Somalian wailed. 'They didn't tell us everything! They paid us to protect them, that's all!'

'Where did he come from?' the commander demanded.

'Iraq,' the Somalian said. 'Basra, I know that much. They said he was from Basra.'

The commander looked at Ethan, who nodded. The information was likely legitimate if the Somalian knew that Abrahem was from Iraq. But it also meant that Abrahem would once again vanish.

'Do you know where Abrahem Nassir intended to go after Qeycad?' the commander asked, his tone more reasonable.

'They didn't say,' their prisoner replied, his voice trembling. 'They just wanted to pass through the area.'

'How did they arrive?'

'A boat, from the gulf. It left immediately.'

'You're doing very well,' the commander growled at his captive. 'At this rate you may even live. Who was he travelling with?'

'An old man named Tariq, who arrived here the day before.'

'He was from Iraq too?'

'Yes, a sheik, very powerful. We did everything he said. He had a lot of money but I don't know where it came from.'

'A benefactor,' Ethan said, speaking for the first time since they had taken off from the beach. 'Where there's money, there's a trail.'

Ethan realized that the helicopter was turning gently, the dim light streaming in through the windows changing angle as the *Seahawk* flew over the coast once more, this time heading inland.

'Did they have vehicles with them?' the commander demanded.

'Yes,' the Somalian replied, 'two trucks.'

The commander turned to Ethan. 'Qeycad is ten clicks from the coast.'

'How long was I out?' Ethan asked.

'I don't know, but it only took us a few minutes to find you. The helo's are equipped with infra–red sensors that spotted your body.'

Ethan nodded as he tightened his harness. 'They could have travelled three or four clicks by now, half way to the town. If they get there we won't be able to find them.'

'And if we're identified over Somalian airspace it'll be my neck on the line back home!' the commander snapped. 'And it'll be much worse if we get hit.'

'Just get me close enough,' Ethan insisted. 'I'll do the rest.'

The commander forced the Somalian to his knees in the helicopter and turned to his troops. There was no spoken command needed, they simply responded by reloading their M–16's magazines and preparing once more for combat. The commander checked his watch.

'Fine,' he said to Ethan. 'We'll drop you in on them.'

Ethan nodded as he felt the *Seahawk* suddenly plunge into a rapid descent. Ethan's stomach lurched into his chest as he saw the commander listen intently to something the pilot was saying.

'We've got two trucks,' he reported. 'One headed north, the other west, and we only have time…'

'To get one of them,' Ethan finished the sentence. He slammed a fist on his knee and cleared his mind. Abrahem would want to escape, so he would likely be heading west toward Qeycad. Sending Lopez north would provide the diversion and time he needed to make good his escape, so in theory Ethan should pursue the northern vehicle.

But if Abrahem was as cunning as Ethan suspected he may be, he might try to make off with both his escape and a prize: Lopez. All or nothing, the course of a man without compromise.

Ethan looked up at the commander and hoped against hope that he was right.

'We go west.'

***

XXIII

'We've got them on radar.'

Ethan leaned to one side and craned his neck to peer around the corner of the *Seahawk*'s cockpit door and saw that they were descending through the wispy clouds hovering above the endless deserts that were now tiger–striped with long shadows as the sun rose behind them, illuminating Somalia in a rich golden glow.

A small screen in the center of the console portrayed the desert before them in shades of green and black, and in the center was a white spot following a faint trail through the deserts.

'They're running hard,' Ethan said. 'We can't shoot them without risking hitting Lopez if she's in there, and Abrahem might shoot her anyway if he thinks he's cornered.'

'No time to debate,' the SEAL commander snapped. 'Qeycad's only a few miles away and I'm not risking us being identified or attacked.'

Ethan watched the truck for a moment longer and then he made his decision.

'Put us overhead.'

The SEAL commander stared at Ethan for a moment. 'What are you going to do?'

Ethan smiled faintly. 'I don't know. I'm sort of making this up as I go.'

The SEAL shrugged and relayed Ethan's request forward to the pilots. The *Seahawk* surged forward as they accelerated, and the SEAL commander opened the helicopter's side door once more and allowed Ethan a glimpse of the wildly careering truck a few hundred feet below them as they thundered overhead.

'Let's make use of this human baggage,' the SEAL commander suggested to his men as he gestured to the captives. 'Maybe we can use them to slow that jeep down a little.'

Ethan heard the two Somalians pinned to the helicopter's deck squeal in terror, fearing that they were about to be jettisoned over the side as the SEALs hauled them to their feet. He got out of his seat and grabbed the SEAL commander's arm.

'Let them be, just get me onto that truck.'

The commander narrowed his eyes and glanced at the prisoners. 'They'll only go back to looting and raping. Why spare them?'

'Because we're *not* them,' Ethan replied. 'Right?'

'They can *identify* us,' the SEAL snapped. 'This is as far as the helo' goes, and it's your last chance to slow that truck down! It's not negotiable, unless you're giving these pirates the same human rights as their victims?'

Ethan stared at the SEAL but he had no viable response as the soldier turned and had his men force the two captives to their feet, both men weeping openly and begging for mercy. Even before Ethan could protest further, he was shoved to one side and the two captives were propelled from the helicopter to plunge down into the path of the truck.

Ethan saw their bodies spiral down, limbs pounding the air in a terminal attempt to prevent their impact with the ground, and then they hit the earth in the truck's path in puffs of golden dust as the *Seahawk* sank lower and the truck slowed as it tried to manoeuvre past the gruesome obstacles.

'Isn't it time for you to leave?' the SEAL commander suggested.

The *Seahawk* lowered over the desert sands rushing by below them, the fuselage bucking and gyrating in the wind currents as vast plumes of dust and sand billowed outward under the turbulent down wash from the rotors. Ethan stepped out to the edge of the open doorway, saw the truck swerve desperately to one side in an attempt to avoid the helicopter. Ethan looked right and saw the track weave to the right between dense clumps of hardy thorn bushes cluttering the landscape, and he realized that the truck would have to pass beneath them.

The hot desert wind tugged at his hair and shirt as he leaned out, the truck less than ten feet below him as the helicopter pilot skilfully guided them down, and then Ethan took a breath and jumped.

His stomach lifted into his throat as he plunged down and slammed into the back of the truck with a resounding thump just as the vehicle lurched to the right. Ethan slammed into the side of the metal doors in the rear of the truck, his legs flailing as he threw his hands over his head to protect it.

The *Seahawk* helicopter surged upward and away, turning east as Ethan scrambled for purchase in the truck and dragged himself forward. A grubby window looked into the cab, where he could see both the driver and a passenger inside. The driver, and old man with yellowing teeth, was looking back at him, a gun held in one hand as he tried to aim backwards over his shoulder while driving the truck.

Ethan threw himself aside as a gunshot cracked out. The dirty window shattered in a cascade of broken glass that showered across Ethan as the shot went by him. He rolled to one side of the vehicle, directly behind the driver's seat where he could not be attacked, and crawled forward as he drew his own pistol and prepared to put it against the driver's head.

The truck suddenly threw him forward as the driver hit the brakes and Ethan tumbled into the back of the cab and slammed against the unyielding metal in a tangle of limbs as the truck lurched forward again, the engine growling as it accelerated.

Ethan rolled down the back of the truck and barely grabbed hold of the side before he was thrown out of the back and onto the dusty track behind them, his legs dragging on the rough earth as he hung on grimly to the tail gate. Fury seared Ethan's guts as he dragged himself back onto the truck and realized that he had no choice. Another wild gunshot through the shattered rear window clanged off the bodywork to his right in a cloud of sparks that were snatched away by the hot wind, and he slammed himself down into a prone position in the rear of the truck and took aim at the metal panel behind the driver. The rough surface of the track jostled him and spoiled his aim, but with a large target so close before him he could hardly miss.

Ethan fired three shots, each of the bullets easily piercing the thin metal of the truck's cab and slamming into the driver's body. Ethan saw the driver's head quiver as the bullets impaled him and the sound of the truck's engine began to decrease as the driver's body slackened in the wake of the gunshots.

Ethan scrambled forward to the window and reached in through the shattered window as the truck swerved to the right toward dense thickets of thorn scrub. He pushed the wheel to the left and the truck straightened up as he realized that Lopez was strapped into the passenger seat, her head lolling this way and that and her chin on her chest.

Panic ripped at Ethan's heart as the truck rumbled to a halt on the desolate trail and the engine coughed into silence as it stalled. Ethan vaulted over the side of the truck and opened the driver's door to see the old man slumped in his seat, his eyes open and his chest heaving, blood pouring from wounds in his belly and chest.

Ethan could hear the air rattling into and out of his ruined lungs, but the man did not move an inch. The bullets must have torn through his spinal cord, and now blood bubbled in pink spheres on his lips as Ethan reached in to jerk his chin up with one hand and glare into the old man's eyes.

'Where is Abrahem?!' he demanded.

The old man looked at Ethan for a moment, his eyes briefly focusing in on him and then he smiled, his yellowing teeth stained with blood.

'*Alluhah Akbhar,*' he whispered.

Ethan scowled and jumped down from the cab as he hurried around to Lopez's side and opened her door. He reached up to her neck and pressed his forefingers to her throat, then almost shouted in glee as he felt a pulse throbbing strongly beneath his touch.

A damp rattle issued from the old man's lungs, and Ethan looked across to see his head sag, his beard pressing upon his chest as his eyes closed.

'Son of a bitch,' Ethan uttered, his voice sounding loud in the otherwise silent desert dawn.

The truck's engine was clicking as the hot metal cooled and contracted, and Ethan could see no sign of any water bottles or other survival equipment inside. All he could hope now was that none of his shots had perforated the engine or radiator and that he could get back to the shore before the *Seahawk* was forced to abandon them in this war–torn and desolate nation.

Ethan reached across and unclipped the old man's seat belt, then let his body fall from the seat to land in the dust at his feet. Ethan climbed aboard and shut his door just as Lopez lifted her head and stared at him blankly.

'Where are we?'

Ethan switched on the engine and began turning the truck on the track.

'Somewhere we don't want to stay,' he replied. 'Are you okay?'

Lopez nodded slowly, staring ahead as Ethan turned toward the coast. 'They hit me over the damned head. Where's Abrahem?'

'We lost him. We've got to get back to the coast or we'll become permanent residents here.'

Lopez turned and looked through the shattered window of the truck.

'Then get back to the coast faster,' she said.

Ethan looked back and saw several vehicles hurtling toward them down the trail, clouds of dust billowing behind them. He cursed silently and slammed the accelerator down as far as it would go and squinted in the brilliant sunlight streaming across the horizon as the sun began to rise. The Somalians must have heard the *Seahawk* even from miles away, and headed east immediately.

A deafening crack split the air between them and the windscreen of the jeep blossomed with fractures and exploded inwards, showering them with sparkling shards of glass.

'They're good shots!' Lopez shouted above the howling wind and she turned, pulled Ethan's pistol from its holster and tried to take aim through the shattered rear window.

Ethan glanced in his side mirror at the nearest vehicle, a hundred yards behind them and closing fast. The second was right behind it and obscured in the dust trail of the first.

'We've got about three miles to go!' he shouted.

Lopez fired a shot and Ethan saw the first sickly flicker of panic in her expression. Somalia was a no–man's–land of warlords, militants and deprived villages. If they were captured here they would vanish and never be seen again, the brutality of their captors well known.

The leading truck was within fifty yards now, two men in the front and several in the rear bearing rifles that were being fired at random, the puffs of smoke from their barrels visible in Ethan's mirror. Ethan heard shots zip past a few feet from his window and he ducked reflexively.

'Jesus!'

Ethan jerked the wheel from side to side and looked back to see thick dust clouds billowing outwards behind them, and almost immediately he lost sight of the leading vehicle some thirty yards behind as the dust concealed them from the gunfire. Another desperate shot rang out, rocketing by with a supersonic crack somewhere above their heads.

'It's not working!' Lopez shouted. 'We're not going to make it!'

Ethan looked about the jeep desperately and then he saw the truck behind them loom forth from their dust trail, heard the sound of its engine above that of the truck he was driving, saw the faces of the militants crowding the rear, their eyes wide and shining with mindless hate, pink mouths agape, ugly rifles and machine guns pointing at them.

'Hang on!' he yelled.

Lopez rammed her boots up against the dashboard as Ethan slammed his foot down onto the brakes.

The truck's wheels locked up on the dusty trail and it shuddered as it skipped and bounced across the rough ground. The truck behind it rushed up as Ethan dropped his head slightly and relaxed his grip on the wheel to prevent his arms from being broken as he took his foot off the brake pedal at the last instant.

The pursuing truck's engine noise rose to a deafening crescendo and then it smashed into the back of their vehicle even as he heard the wheels lock up and screams of alarm compete with the roaring engine. Ethan was slammed backwards in his seat as the truck was catapulted forward, and he heard screams as three bodies were hurled over the cab of the pursuing vehicle and slammed into the rear of his own.

Ethan slammed the throttle back down and the truck accelerated away as he heard the second pursuing vehicle slam into the first behind them with a crash of rending metal and the screams of injured militants as they toppled from the back of Ethan's truck. He turned and saw the first vehicle's exhaust puff a thick cloud of black smoke as it pulled away from the wreckage, the driver screaming something unintelligible as he accelerated away again. Ethan saw the injured bodies of the militants hurled onto the track quiver as the truck's tires crunched over them.

'Balls.'

Ethan turned to concentrate on the view ahead as Lopez took aim and fired two shots, both of them impacting the truck behind but none of them injuring any of the militants still aboard.

Ethan pushed the accelerator to the floor, but the truck wallowed and creaked as it weaved lazily across the trail.

'Go faster!' Lopez yelled.

'I can't, the impact must have fractured the back end!'

Ethan looked in his mirror and saw the truck pursuing them once more, this time with suicidal rage as the militants chanted and jeered, the driver's face smeared with blood from the recent impact.

Ethan saw the bluff ahead and the low buildings of El Hur and he realized instantly that the race was over: they'd run out of road. He was about to consider swerving off–road or even stopping and trying to shoot all of the militants behind them before they could be overpowered when a terrific crescendo of rotor blades hammered the air before him and vortexes of dense dust swirled in golden tornadoes into the blue sky.

From behind the bluff the SH–60 *Seahawk* rose up, its wicked looking side–mounted cannon pointed straight at Ethan.

'Get down!' Ethan shouted.

A crackling blast ripped the sky before them as the helicopter's guns opened up, hails of tracer fire rocketing over the truck and slamming into the vehicle behind them. Ethan glimpsed in his rear view mirror the truck vanish in a shower of bright sparks and a cloud of black smoke as it veered sharply left, hit the bank alongside the trail and lifted off, rolling in mid–air to slam down into the desert as militants' bodies flew from the wreckage, their bodies riddled with 20mm shells. Ethan saw the vehicle crash onto its back amid a cloud of twisted metal and spinning tyres.

Ethan's truck slowed as it reached the bluff, blundered up through the thick sand and came to a halt. He clambered out, Lopez joining him as they dashed down toward the beach to where the *Seahawk* was landing. Its side door opened and the SEAL commander reached out with one gloved hand and helped them aboard.

'Thought you weren't coming back?' Ethan challenged.

'We weren't!' the commander yelled as the helicopter lifted off. 'We spotted your vehicle fleeing the Somalians as we took off. Abrahem got away into the bush, probably on foot! He must've been among the villagers who attacked you.'

Ethan cursed as he strapped himself into his seat and shouted above the noise of the beating rotors.

'Contact the fleet, tell them that he's heading for America!'

'We don't know that for sure?!'

'That a chance you want to take?' Ethan challenged.

The commander gritted his teeth and relayed the command to the pilots.

***

XXIV

USS Harry S. Truman,

Persian Gulf

The SH–60 *Seahawk* touched down on the deck of the enormous aircraft carrier, and despite the ear protection he was wearing Ethan could hear the tremendous noise soaring across the decks as they climbed down from the helicopter's interior. A buffeting gale whistled across the carrier's flat deck as it sailed at twenty knots into the prevailing wind, the ocean churning by far below her massive hull.

Crewmen in colored shirts corralled them against the *Seahawk*, which had folded its tail back upon itself and turned its rotors into a single stack that lay back across the length of its fuselage to minimize the amount of space it required upon the ship. Steam from the launch catapults billowed across the deck from the bows as Ethan saw a Grumman EA–6B *Prowler* aircraft thunder down the catapults and roar off the deck into the turbulent dawn sky.

A terrific shriek made him flinch and he whirled in time to see an F–18E Super Hornet land just thirty feet away from where he stood, its arrestor hook catching the number three wire as fifteen tons of fighter jet was dragged from a hundred fifty knots to a halt in less than two seconds.

A crewman appeared before him and he waved for Ethan and Lopez to follow as they circled around the front of the helicopter. The sound of countless engines whining seared the deck, the smell of aviation fuel tainting the air as Ethan saw the carrier's enormous control tower looming before him.

The crewman led them down a series of steps along the edge of the carrier's hull, the ocean sweeping past in turbulent white eddies sixty feet below, and then they walked inside the ship and the crewman removed their ear protection.

'You don't have much time so we gotta move quickly,' he informed them. 'Follow me and do everything I say.'

Ethan obeyed without question as they walked, but the urgency of the situation demanded questions and answers.

'Please inform your captain that we need to send a priority signal to Washington DC, the Defense Intelligence Agency.'

'Your signal will be sent in the air. Right now you need to get to Saudi Arabia.'

'Why are we going there?' Lopez asked.

'You'll find out on the way,' came the response as the crewman led them to a doorway emblazoned with the legend: *Strike Fighter Squadron 81*. The door was open as they walked in and two pilots awaited them, both holding flight suits in their hands.

'Oh, not again,' Lopez murmured.

Ethan grabbed a proffered flight suit and began pulling it on as the older of the two pilots briefed them.

'We'll get you to King Abdulaziz Air Base in no time,' he said. 'Just sit back and enjoy the ride, okay? We've been told you've done this before?'

'F–15s out of Eglin in Florida,' Ethan confirmed, 'couple of years ago.'

'Air Force? Okay,' the pilot replied, 'that means you haven't seen anything yet.'

Ethan was handed a gray helmet with a glossy black mirrored eye–shield, an oxygen mask and a pair of fire retardant gloves. As soon as they were ready, the pilots led them back through the endless corridors inside the carrier and then ordered them to don their helmets before climbing the steps back out onto the flight deck.

The sound of jet engines shredded the air as they ascended onto the aft deck, and Ethan saw rows of F–18E Super Hornets parked tightly together, their wings folded up as crewmen swarmed across them. Two of the sleek, angular fighter aircraft sat with their canopies open as the pilots led them toward them, both aircraft's tails emblazoned with the 81st's emblems.

Lopez stared at the fearsome looking aircraft with some trepidation.

'This is down to Jarvis,' she said finally. 'He knows I hate this stuff.'

Ethan ascended a ladder beside the nearest F–18's cockpit and climbed as directed by the ground crew into the rear seat, the pilot climbing into the front. A galaxy of television screens, dials, switches and lights confronted him as he was strapped into the ejection seat by a crewman. To his right, Lopez was likewise strapped into her seat, her head leaning on one gloved hand as she shook her head in dismay.

The canopy on Ethan's F–18 closed and the raucous of the flight deck was silenced as Ethan heard the jet's turbofan engines whine into life, crewman pulling power hoses from beneath the jet even as, right in front of them, a massive Grumman E–2C *Hawkeye* slammed down onto the deck. Ethan's pilot called a series of radio commands to the control tower and within minutes they were taxiing across the crowded deck toward the bow catapults, directed by yellow–shirted crewmen using nothing more than hand signals, radios useless on the aircraft carrier's violent and noisy deck.

'You like fairground rides, Mr Warner?' the pilot asked over the intercom.

'That a leading question?'

The pilot laughed. *'Brace yourself.'*

The two jets lined up on alongside each other on the catapults at the carrier's bow as crewmen again swarmed around them and Ethan saw the F–18's wings fold down, the flaps being extended as the Hornet's nose sank a little under the tension of the catapult.

A series of barked radio commands that Ethan could not decipher crackled over the RT, and he saw the pilot give a thumbs up and a salute to one of the deck crews as the Hornet's engines whined up to full power, the jet vibrating like a leashed beast straining to escape.

Suddenly the aircraft jolted and then Ethan was shoved back into his seat as though he had been literally fired from a cannon. The deck flashed by in a surge of blurring motion and Ethan felt his lungs compressed against his spine and his head slam against the headrest as the F–18E Super Hornet was hurled from zero to a hundred eighty knots in a little over two seconds.

The deck blasted by and then suddenly the vibration was gone as the fighter soared into the air and banked gently right over the sparkling ocean. A scattering of cumulus cloud shot by, light and shadow flickering through the cockpit as Ethan saw the altimeter climbing through two thousand feet.

He looked over his shoulder out across the F–18's wing, and saw Lopez's aircraft move into close formation as they climbed up through broken cloud layers to twenty thousand feet, the bulbous canopy of the aircraft providing a spectacular panorama of the ocean below.

The pilot's voice sounded in his ear.

'I'm opening a data–link channel, stand by.'

Ethan waited for a moment and then Doug Jarvis's voice crackled in his ear as one of the screens in the cockpit showed the old man's face as he spoke from what must have been the DIA's Watch Center in Washington DC. A second screen showed Lopez's face obscured by her oxygen mask, dark eyes glowing with discontent.

'Ethan, Nicola,' Jarvis greeted them. *'I trust that you're enjoying the ride.'*

'Up yours,' Lopez muttered in reply.

'Many people would give their right arms to be sitting where you are now,' Jarvis chided.

'They can have mine,' Lopez shot back. 'What's the story?'

'Have you apprehended Abrahem Nassir?'

'No,' Ethan replied. 'He escaped us and is likely heading for America even as we speak.'

'I'll alert the relevant authorities,' Jarvis replied. *'We're already on high alert but it's not possible to figure out where Nassir might strike, or whether he has allies already in the country we can neutralize. Do we have any further intel?'*

'Abrahem was in the company of an older man with plenty of money according to the prisoners questioned by the SEAL team, somebody called Tariq.'

'We'll look into it,' Jarvis promised.

'There's also further evidence of Chinese involvement,' Lopez added. 'It looks like whatever Abrahem got his hands on, it doesn't belong to him. If this entire thing is being funded by one man then this Tariq is at the head of the money chain – pin him down and it'll lead to anybody else working for these two who are already Stateside.'

'I was worried about the possibility of China's involvement,' Jarvis echoed. *'The President is hosting a ceremony on the South Lawn of the White House tomorrow evening for the President of the People's Republic of China, some sort of major new Asian Trans Pacific Trade agreement.'*

'Abrahem might have plans to attack that ceremony,' Lopez replied. 'From what we can gather he may have obtained technology from the Chinese, perhaps the implants that were used to control Major General Thompson.'

Jarvis nodded.

'There have been some further developments here. The FBI has people on the ground in Hong Kong and Kowloon trying to trace the connection between four NSA agents abducted there in 1997 *and Abrahem's involvement now. They've sent a pair of agents, a friend of yours I believe Ethan?'*

'Hannah Ford?'

'The same. Quite an interest she has in you, courtesy of Director LeMay.'

'The FBI are fishing for the same technology out there,' Ethan said. 'If Majestic Twelve are behind LeMay, then Mitchell might also be out there. You need to send her a warning.'

'Correct,' Jarvis replied. *'But my men haven't been able to locate her yet.'*

'She could be in danger and we can't let that technology fall into the hands of Majestic Twelve, either through LeMay or Mitchell.'

'Where do we start?' Lopez asked Jarvis. 'We need to pin this down before Abrahem can make his move.'

'You'll be flown to Saudi Arabia, where an aircraft is waiting to bring you back to the States. I've obtained one of the highest security rating's our unit has ever achieved, because there's something waiting for you here when you get back and you're going to have to see it to believe it. Get your heads down, because whatever Abrahem has coming is

going to keep you very busy when you get back. For now, you'd best be on your way. Jarvis out.'

The screens in the F–18's cockpit blinked out, and Ethan saw Lopez's aircraft drift away out of formation until it was a bright speck on the horizon.

'Time to hustle,' the pilot said, *'I feel the need.'*

'The need for what?'

Then reply came back from the other Super Hornet pilot. *'Speed!'*

Ethan felt the F–18 rocket forward as the throttles were pushed to the firewall. Full afterburner punched the Hornet through the sound barrier and the G–force acceleration crunched Ethan down into his seat as the fighter's nose was hauled up into a steep climb as it searched for the rarified cold air of the upper atmosphere. The F–18 soared through forty thousand feet and rolled through the inverted, Ethan hanging onto his lunch as he was finally returned to right–side up. The sky above was a deep indigo blue and the clouds below tattered blankets of white stretched across the azure ocean.

'We're supersonic and heading for Mach Two,' the pilot informed him calmly, *'courtesy of Uncle Sam's Navy.'*

***

XXV

Tai Tam Tuk,

Hong Kong

'Are you sure that's the one?'

Vaughn kept a careful watch on the vehicle that was driving down a road toward Tai Tam harbor. Hannah drove, careful to keep her distance from the glossy black limousine as it cruised alongside a gorgeous mountain lake on one side and the sheer face of the Tai Tam Dam on the other, the harbor visible ahead and to their left.

'It's him all right,' Hannah replied as she drove. 'The plates match the traffic cam footage, but we can't be sure that Mitchell's aboard.'

Hannah could tell that Vaughn was uncomfortable with what they were doing. The brief from Director LeMay had been simple enough: track down Ethan Warner and Nicola Lopez and ensure that they were arrested and imprisoned for their crimes, by way of looking into the NSA abductions from 1997. Now, they were driving into unknown territory on Hong Kong Island, following a man known to be an assassin and completely ignoring LeMay's orders.

'And we don't know where Warner and Lopez are right now,' Vaughn pointed out.

'We've got nothing,' Hannah agreed. 'Right now, Mitchell is our only lead and also a link to Warner. LeMay will understand.'

'LeMay might think that you're working for Jarvis and not the FBI.'

'And what's he going to do?' Hannah challenged. 'We're following leads pertaining to the Stanley Meyer murder, leads that connect to both Ethan Warner and Aaron Mitchell. These leads could close the case. If he doesn't like what we're doing here then he's going to have a hard time reprimanding us about it – he damned well sent us!'

Vaughn gestured ahead. 'The limousine's turning.'

Hannah frowned as she looked ahead and saw the black vehicle turn right off the road and into a secluded forest. A barrier protected the entrance but it was open to allow tourists into the public park that surrounded the dam's reservoir.

'You think he's going for a stroll in the countryside?' Vaughn quipped.

'How far does this go?'

Vaughn glanced at a map of the island in his lap.

'Half way back to the city,' he replied. 'It's a tourist trail and nature walk and the road runs right along it for about five clicks before you reach the edge of the city.'

Hannah frowned as she followed the limousine, allowing it to disappear infrequently around turns in the road which wound its way between soaring forests cloaking the mountains. There was not a lot of traffic on the road and only the occasional tourists on pushbikes.

'What the hell is he doing all the way out here?' she asked out loud.

Vaughn frowned. 'If we know Mitchell, it's nothing good. Maybe he wants to get out of the way of Hong Kong's surveillance for some reason?'

Hannah did not reply as she drove, and then she saw the limousine pull over through the trees. Hannah eased the car by as she watched the limousine cruise into a small parking area in the woods. Through the trees she could see a series of trails vanishing up into the hills, the area devoid of tourists.

Hannah pulled over to the roadside and opened her door.

'Mitchell will have noticed us behind him,' she said. 'We can't risk pulling into the same lot. You drive on and find another, then double back for me. I'll stay on Mitchell.'

Vaughn shook his head. 'He's dangerous, you can't do this on your own. You saw what happened to Meyer and…'

Hannah got out of the car and shut her door before jogging away from their vehicle. She reached the edge of the tree line as she heard Vaughn drive away, no doubt cursing her to high heaven. She walked for a few minutes back up the road until she reached the parking lot.

The lot was deserted but for the black vehicle parked now alongside a narrow trail winding its way into the woods. The wind whispered through the leaves, dappled sunlight shimmering on the forest floor and reflecting off the vehicle's glossy paintwork.

In for a penny…

Hannah stepped out from behind the trees and forced herself not to draw her weapon as she walked across the lot toward the car. She could tell even from a distance that the windows were mirror–black tinted, veiling the interior of the vehicle from prying eyes. Private plates, the vehicle otherwise unmodified and equally unremarkable. She could tell that the vehicle was unoccupied as she peered through the front window, so she moved on into the forest and followed the nearest of the trails.

She could hear no birdsong as she moved, a possible indicator that somebody had recently moved up the trail ahead of her, silencing the wildlife. She had read once that a forest requires around fifteen minutes to return to normal after a human being has passed through, and she reckoned that Mitchell could only be a couple of minutes ahead of her.

The sound of a branch or twig snapping from somewhere off the trail caught her attention and she froze, one hand resting on the butt of her pistol as she looked ahead through the trees. A muffled wheezing sound drifted to her on the faint breeze. Hannah looked over her shoulder to ensure that nobody was approaching from behind before she edged forward to where a dense thicket of vines and foliage concealed a small clearing amid the towering trees.

Another twig snapped, and Hannah eased forward to the edge of the thicket and then she froze once more as she surveyed the scene before her.

Bound to a tree trunk, his mouth gagged, was a Chinese man perhaps in his late fifties or early sixties. His brow was sheened with sweat and his face pinched with agony as he writhed against his bonds.

Another sharp crack, and now Hannah realized that the man's arms were tied back around the far side of the tree and that she could see a tall, broad figure partially concealed there. The Chinese man screamed behind his gag and Hannah saw the shadowy figure wielding what looked like some sort of metal tool. She drew her side arm and waited, watching as the bound man wept, his head hanging low as the shadowy figure emerged from behind the tree with a pair of bloodied plyers in his hand.

Aaron Mitchell was physically larger than she had anticipated, the images she had studied for so long not doing justice to his frame. She figured maybe six four, two hundred fifty pounds and no fat that she could make out under a thin white shirt that bulged with muscle.

Mitchell moved to stand before his victim and waved the plyers in front of his face.

'Don't make me start on the front,' he growled as he yanked the gag from the man's mouth. 'Kowloon, 1997. Start talking or you'll never see your family again.'

The Chinese man's features twisted in a volatile mixture of pain and rage as he spat his response.

'Go to hell!'

Mitchell watched his captive for a moment and then shrugged. 'So be it.'

The big man drew back his elbow and Hannah realized that he was about to plunge the plyers directly into the victim's groin. The captive screwed up his face and gritted his teeth in anticipation of the unthinkable pain he was about to endure when Hannah stepped into the clearing and aimed her pistol at Mitchell.

'That's enough.'

Mitchell looked over his shoulder at her, an expression of mild surprise on his features as he remained motionless, the plyers inches from his victim's body.

'Drop the tool,' Hannah uttered, her pistol aimed between Mitchell's eyes.

Mitchell turned slowly to face her but did not drop the plyers. 'You don't know what you're doing.'

Hannah raised an eyebrow. 'Stopping you from killing somebody else, I'd say. Hands up!'

Mitchell did not move.

'You've got about four minutes before we're all dead,' he said calmly. 'I suggest you use them wisely.'

Hannah frowned at the big man. 'You don't expect me to believe that? Get down on your knees right now!'

'Less than four minutes,' Mitchell replied. 'Either I extract the information that I know this man possesses, or neither of us will find out what really happened in Kowloon in 1997.'

Hannah kept her aim steady. 'We can find that out at the Consulate'

'You're very naive,' Mitchell growled.

'And you're a murderer!' Hannah shouted. 'I've already got you for one killing and it looks like you're set for another right here!'

'Needs must,' Mitchell replied. 'Three minutes.'

Hannah felt her pulse begin to race as she looked at the elderly man bound to the tree.

'What does he know?' she demanded.

'Everything,' Mitchell replied. 'He works for Chinese intelligence as a hacker and has done so for many decades.'

'I'm a financial consultant,' the injured man whimpered, 'for Hei Sing Bank in Kowloon. Call them, they'll confirm it! And call the police!'

'It's a cover,' Mitchell replied. 'The bank has been infiltrated by hackers who use it as a staging post to attack western digital interests and military installations. We've known about them for some time.'

'That's a lie!' the captive wailed. 'He's insane, he's going to kill me! I have a family!'

Mitchell kept his eyes on Hannah. 'Three minutes, Agent Ford.'

'How do you know my name?'

'I know more than you about a lot of things, and right now the only thing standing between me and preventing another attack on our country is *you.*'

Hannah's grip on her pistol felt slick and conflicting emotions raced through her mind as she glanced at the man tied to the tree.

'This isn't the way to do it,' she snapped.

'On the contrary, this is the way it's always been done,' Mitchell countered. 'Not much more than two minutes, Agent Ford, before this man's associates arrive. Believe me, if you want to end up floating in Kowloon harbor you're going the right way about it.'

Hannah shot the Chinaman a glare. 'Start talking!'

The captive's eyes flew wide as horror paled his complexion. 'But I don't know any…!'

Mitchell whirled and the plyers clamped down on the captive's groin and were twisted violently. The hellish scream of agony that soared from the captive's lips was silenced by Mitchell's other hand that clamped down on the victim's mouth, virtually covering the smaller man's face as the plyers bit deep. Hannah's guts convulsed in sympathy as she witnessed his torture.

Mitchell yanked the plyers free and removed his hand. The captive's hellish cries faded into choked sobs that coughed from his heaving chest as he wept openly.

'1997, talk fast,' Mitchell growled.

The captive did not respond and Mitchell moved the plyers in again.

'We took them,' the captive gasped finally.

'Took who?' Mitchell demanded.

'The operatives, from the NSA,' the man whimpered. 'They were on Kowloon Bay, on a pleasure boat during a break from a neurotechnology symposium. Agents were sent in and they abducted them, took them to the north shore and then into China.'

***

XXVI

Mitchell glanced over his shoulder at Hannah, who lowered her weapon as she stared at the Chinaman's tortured face.

'Everything, Jin Chen, if you want to survive this,' Mitchell snapped.

The agonized victim sucked in a trembling breath as he replied.

'We'd been watching them for months, waiting to see what they were doing. We knew about the listening posts in Hawaii of course, but it wasn't possible to spirit NSA operatives away from there to China without being intercepted. Kowloon was much closer, so we focused on the embassies and CIA fronts based there.'

Hannah stepped forward. 'What happened to them?'

Jin Chen struggled for breath, mastering his pain.

'They were interrogated for weeks, deep inside the mainland. The purpose was to break down their will before then showing them kindness and compassion, winning their "hearts and minds" as you Americans say. It took time and a great deal of suffering on their part, but we were helped by America's media suggesting that they had died in a boating accident: the agent's families were not looking for them anymore, and the American government was more interested in hiding the existence of its listening posts than protecting its own people.'

'How far did they help you?' Hannah pressed.

'They were invaluable,' he replied. 'Our technology leaped immensely just from those four individuals, and the devices they carried revolutionized our understanding of neurology.'

'What's the connection to the attacks in America?' Mitchell pressed.

Chen drew another breath. 'I don't know about any attacks in…'

Mitchell slammed the plyers against the man's groin but did not twist them.

'Please, no!' the captive shrieked.

'Give me a reason not to.'

Chen's features imploded with the helplessness of his situation.

'We reverse engineered the neural implant technology that the NSA operatives were found with,' he said finally. 'Then we developed it over the next decade. We used the NSA operatives as test subjects, controlling them, improving the work.'

'What work?' Hannah asked, but was silenced by a harsh glare from Mitchell.

'What's the connection?' Mitchell demanded once more. 'How did they end up in the heads of our personnel?'

Jin Chen sagged against his bonds, sweating profusely from the pain wracking his body.

'We used the Iraq war as a means to test the devices more thoroughly by implanting them into the brains of American servicemen fighting in the conflict. We could not enter Iraq directly, so instead we used our finest operatives disguised as American soldiers to abduct an Iraqi software engineer's family on the threat that his family would be executed if he did not comply. We used him to smuggle implants into Basra's hospitals, where they were implanted into American service personnel.'

Hannah stared at the Chinaman in disbelief.

'You were trying to remotely control human beings?' she gasped in horror.

'What happened to the engineer?' Mitchell demanded.

'When we were done with him, we executed the engineer and his family, our people disguised as American soldiers,' Chen replied. 'We could afford no links back to us so they had to die. But one of them escaped, a teenage boy.'

Hannah felt a pulse of alarm surge through her. 'What was his name?'

'Abrahem,' came the reply. 'Abrahem Nassir.'

Mitchell glanced at Hannah. 'This could all be about revenge.'

Hannah nodded as she looked at the captive. 'How did the Chinese implant our service personnel after the war ended?'

Jin Chen shook his head. 'We didn't. The boy, Abrahem, he grew up during the occupation of Iraq and become one of a small team of smugglers we used to supply a German doctor in Basra, who was paid to implant the devices on our behalf into your servicemen. We didn't know it was Abrahem of course, so many years having passed by. On our last run, Abrahem did not deliver the devices to the American hospital and instead disappeared. We've been looking for him ever since.'

'How far did you get?' Mitchell demanded.

Chen sighed.

'The last known position of Abrahem Nassir was on a boat from Basra to somewhere on the African coast, but we don't know where. Intelligence suggests that countries like Somalia represented the best place for someone like Nassir to hide, but we had no known location to search.'

'What was his assumed destination?' Hannah asked, fearful that she already knew the answer.

Chen smiled through his pain, as though his answer was a bitter victory for him.

'America,' he said. 'Nassir thinks you killed his family, just as you murdered so many thousands of innocent Iraqis in your war for oil. The President of the People's Republic of China is already in the United States in preparation for a ceremony to mark China's integration into the Trans Pacific Partnership deal, and Nassir's likely target will be either him or the American President, or both. It is already too late to stop him.'

Mitchell looked across at Hannah. 'Where is your partner?'

Hannah's heart leaped in her chest as she realized that Vaughn had not yet shown up.

'Who's pursuing you?' she countered as she glanced over her shoulder in the hopes that Vaughn would be somewhere behind her.

The plyers hit her across the face even as she turned back to Mitchell. The blow caught her off balance, pain ripping across her scalp, but even as she fell she tried to swing her pistol around and take aim at Mitchell.

A heavy boot slammed across her wrist and her pistol spun from her grip as she crashed down onto the forest floor. Hannah's breath bolted from her lungs as she tried to get up, her right arm numb from the wrist up, but she saw Mitchell loom above her and then suddenly his muscular arms wrapped around her neck and tightened like a metal vice.

Hannah's eyes bulged and her throat collapsed as Mitchell squeezed with unbearable strength. Hannah reached out for his face, her nails scraping across his skin and seeking his eyes, but the powerful man buried his face in her shoulder to protect it and her arms flailed uselessly for a moment and then sank to her sides as though of their own accord.

Moments later, Hannah's vision turned to black and she lost consciousness.

*

The gunshots were loud in the otherwise silent forest as the men hurried up the hillside, their weapons drawn, their eyes seeking motion amid the towering trees and dense foliage. Dark suits, designer sunglasses, black hair and stern expressions.

They moved without words, silent glances and nods all that was required for them to systematically advance until they reached a clearing deep in the forest. They slowed, edging their way closer, weapons trained on the clearing and the body they could see lying on the forest floor.

A woman, dressed in heeled boots, gray slacks and a white shirt, a gun in her open hand.

Opposite her, a Chinese man with his skull shot through, the fingers of one hand bloodied and bent out of shape, his groin thick with matted blood and a pair of plyers in one hand. Behind him, a length of rope cut through with the plyers lay around the trunk of a nearby tree.

The armed men surveyed the scene and the wound to the woman's head where she had been struck, and then they moved forward as their leader, a stocky, older man, leaned down and searched for a pulse in the Chinaman's neck. He waited for a moment and then shook his head.

'He's gone. They killed Jin Chen.'

The leader stood upright as he turned and watched as from behind him his colleagues carried the body of a man that they tossed into the clearing. Vaughn's face was badly beaten, his eyes swollen as he slumped onto the forest floor and lay in silence.

'This must be his partner,' one of them said as he pointed to the woman. 'The FBI, they always work in pairs. They must have been torturing Jin Chen.'

Another stepped forward and aimed down at Hannah Ford's body. 'Let's finish them, right now.'

The leader's arm swung out and belayed the pistol, pushing it up into the air as he looked down at Hannah Ford.

'No,' he said. 'I have a better idea.'

***

XXVII

Joint Base Andrews, Prince George's County,

Maryland

Ethan felt the wheels of the Boeing C–40B *Clipper* aircraft thump down on the runway at Andrews, the enormous airbase flashing by as the aircraft's brakes and reverse thrusters were applied.

A squadron used for transport by members of the administration, the 89th Airlift Wing included the President's famous USAF VC–25, a converted Boeing 747 known as *Air Force One* when the President was aboard. Ethan was sat in a plush leather chair which he had extended fully, allowing him some precious sleep after the flight from the USS Harry S. Truman to Saudi Arabia. There, they had boarded the US Navy's *Clipper* and flown to Ramstein in Germany for a refuel before then continuing on across the Atlantic to Washington DC.

Ethan unstrapped himself from the comfortable seat as Lopez yawned and stretched nearby, glancing briefly out the window.

'Are we there yet?'

Ethan got up as he grabbed his jacket and back pack. 'Let's just hope we're here in time.'

A Navy Lieutenant hurried back to join them as the aircraft taxied in, his fresh faced appearance belying his experience and authority.

'A transport is awaiting you and your contact at the Defense Intelligence Agency is also ready to brief you. You'll be taken directly to the headquarters of the National Security Agency.'

A glossy black limousine rolled out across the servicing pan and slid in alongside them as they descended the steps from the huge aircraft, the lieutenant opening the door for them to climb aboard. Inside, Jarvis awaited them.

'Welcome back,' he said. 'We don't have much time so I'll be brief. There's been a major breakthrough and now we're looking at an imminent terrorist attack.'

'The ceremony on the South Lawn tomorrow,' Ethan confirmed as the limousine moved off. 'It's the perfect target for Abrahem Nassir, and the Presidents of two countries he may have a grievance against will be there.'

'We won't have long to locate and apprehend Abrahem,' Jarvis agreed, 'so we've been given Stellar Security Clearance courtesy of the administration and the Joint Chiefs of Staff. We're heading to the NSA, so you'll need to sign these.'

Ethan looked down at a pair of non–disclosure agreements as Jarvis handed each of them a pen.

'What have they got in there?' Lopez asked.

'Like I said, you'll have to see that to believe it,' Jarvis replied. 'I could barely believe it myself, and you won't be seeing anything until you've signed those NDAs.'

Ethan and Lopez signed the agreements, and Jarvis remained silent during the short journey from Joint Base Andrews to the NSA Headquarters.

Ethan looked up at the NSA's glossy black building, a gigantic rectangle of mirrored glass that reflected a shadowy version of the world beyond, the blue skies and white clouds muted and warped. Ethan knew that behind that mirrored glass were layers of copper and more glass to make sure that signals stayed within the agency, protecting it against electronic eves–dropping.

'Keep your mouths shut and your eyes straight ahead,' Jarvis said to them as the vehicle in which they were travelling pulled into the NSA's massive parking lots and began processing through the security check points. 'You're cleared to be here, but only because of the seriousness of the situation and the president's personal say so.'

Ethan expected Lopez to utter some quip, but she too seemed subdued as the vehicle closed in on the massive building.

The National Security Agency had been established by President Truman in 1952, its purpose simple and direct; protect the United States of America against the intelligence gathering forces of other nations, and simultaneously gather intelligence on said nations. Within that remit and with ever increasing levels of sophistication, the NSA had used the rapidly evolving technology known as SIGINT – *Signals Intelligence* – to pursue its purpose, that of absolute knowledge and absolute control of intelligence across the globe. Although many people around the world had heard of other agencies such as the FBI and the CIA, and despite the fact that the CIA was indeed the senior agency, it remained that few people knew of the existence of the NSA nor of the fact that all other agencies in the United

States of America relied upon it for both Signals Intelligence and cryptographic analysis.

Working alongside the United Kingdom's GCHQ, along with similar such agencies in Canada, Australia and New Zealand, the pooling of resources between these agencies formed the backbone of *Echelon*, a much discussed and equally veiled communications analysis network that enveloped the world's telecommunications. The satellites, optical fibre taps, Internet monitoring and cryptographic analysis resources of these combined networks made it possible, though not easy, to monitor the communications of almost any person on the face of the planet.

'Do we know if Abrahem Nassir is in the country?' Lopez asked as the vehicle eased through the security checkpoints.

'No,' Jarvis replied. 'There's no sign of him entering the US through a customs airport or seaport, which means that if he is here he can only have accessed the country via a private aircraft. We've been monitoring all flights into the continental United States from Africa, but he could have routed through Europe too.'

'He would have had to jump before landing to avoid customs airports,' Ethan pointed out, 'if an aircraft had been used. That's a tall order if you haven't done it before.'

'He must have sympathizers on our soil,' Lopez added. 'That could explain how this was all arranged. We know that there are US citizens supporting terrorist activities all the time, albeit in very small numbers. He must have moved from ally to ally across the globe to end up here.'

'Transport will most likely have been provided,' Jarvis agreed, 'along with other support to get him toward whatever destination he has in mind. Your questioning of the militants in Somalia revealed only that he was likely to be travelling here. Considering what I hear the SEALS put them through, I think it's fair to say that if they had known anything more they would have said so.'

'They were just pawns in Abrahem's big game,' Ethan said. 'We've got to assume that his target is the Trans Pacific Trade ceremony at the White House, for which he could have dozens of implanted serving and former military personnel all available as potential assassins. Hell, much of the police force is made up of former soldiers. We could prevent one attack only for Abrahem to initiate another instead so he's our only viable target. We've got to track this guy down or whatever's coming will be like another Pearl Harbor, another nine–eleven.'

'I know,' Jarvis said, 'which is why you're here and with special clearance into the NSA Headquarters. The CIA and FBI are in the loop but they're far behind the curve on this one, so you two have point right now.

Whatever we find out here will guide what we do next on the ground. I only hope it's enough.'

Ethan looked at his surroundings through the vehicle's tinted windows.

'So this is where *Echelon* is based,' he said as the vehicle descended into a below ground–level parking lot.

'*Echelon* was the old version of our SIGINT capability,' Jarvis replied as the vehicle whispered to a stop in the underground lot and he opened his door. 'What we have now is known as PRISM.'

Ethan followed Jarvis with Lopez alongside him as they walked at a brisk pace through the building, the seriousness of the situation giving the old man's pace new vigour as they descended via an elevator into what Ethan realized was a subterranean section completely concealed from the outside world.

'You need to play catch up here on what's happened and what the NSA's involvement is,' Jarvis said as they descended in the elevator. 'Echelon, a clandestine global surveillance and intelligence gathering initiative between many countries allied to the United States, was replaced with PRISM in 2007. The NSA uses PRISM to collect Internet communications from major US Internet companies and is operated under the supervision of the U.S. Foreign Intelligence Surveillance Court.'

'Is this the program that was leaked a few years back?'

'By Edward Snowden,' Jarvis confirmed, 'who is, depending on your outlook, a courageous patriot or an insane traitor. Either way, PRISM's existence went public and revealed not just the extent of the surveillance gathering but also a financial arrangement between the NSA's Special Source Operations and PRISM partners worth millions of dollars.'

'So what's the connection between this PRISM and our search for Abrahem?' Ethan asked.

'It's not Abrahem that's the link,' Jarvis replied. 'It's China. PRISM is responsible for more than ninety percent of all the NSA's Internet traffic acquired using FISA section 702 authority. The Edward Snowden leaks also exposed the existence of MYSTIC, a voice interception program used here at the NSA to record every single phone call made in a targeted country for thirty days, and that intelligence analyzed for potential targets of interest that may threaten US security. With the spotlight on these programs and the media focusing on them, the real conspiracy has been missed entirely.'

'What conspiracy?' Lopez asked. 'Do you mean Majestic Twelve?'

'For once,' Jarvis replied, 'MJ–12 are as behind the curve as we are. It's this way.'

Jarvis led them down a corridor of pristine white panels illuminated from behind and in deep contrast to the impenetrable blackness of the building's exterior.

'We're being scanned for recording devices,' Jarvis said as they walked. 'The scanners are implanted behind the walls.'

As they reached the end of the corridor a door opened and two armed soldiers stood to attention before checking their security passes against a log and then waving them through.

Jarvis led them through a doorway and into a large Watch Room that looked not dissimilar to the ones Ethan had seen at the Defense Intelligence Agency. Large screens ringed the walls at the front of the Watch Room in the manner of a space agency's control room, and rows of desks with operatives seated behind them monitored events across the world.

But this time, there was something odd about the images on the screens, the pictures indistinct, slightly blurred.

'The news feeds are out of focus,' Lopez said.

Jarvis shook his head. 'Those are not news feeds.'

Jarvis walked to one corner of the room and then turned to face them, speaking softly so as not to disturb the thirty or so operatives at work behind their desks.

'Welcome to The Identity Mine,' he said simply.

'The what?'

Jarvis gestured to the Watch Room around them. 'This room is used specifically to monitor the activities of thirty or so of the most wanted people on the planet,' he explained. 'Their activities are observed in a way that no other country on Earth has ever been able to do before so that the NSA is able to predict when and where they're going to strike next. This program is in its infancy, just a couple of years old and so clandestine that even Edward Snowden wouldn't have been able to get near it.'

Ethan frowned and looked at the screens. Several of them showed slightly blurred images of people talking to the camera and responses coming back from somebody out of sight. Others showed the view through a car windscreen as it drove along a highway, yet another the interior of a busy shopping mall. Several of the screens were almost black but filled with bizarre little points of light swimming and zipping about on them.

'I don't get it,' he admitted finally. 'What are they actually *watching* here?'

Jarvis smiled, clearly enjoying himself once again, standing in the center of something so secret that barely a handful of people in the world knew about it.

'They're not watching the criminals,' Jarvis said. 'They're watching what the criminals are *seeing*.'

Lopez stared at the screens for a moment longer and then her jaw dropped. 'This is what the criminals are doing, right now?'

'Right this very instant,' Jarvis confirmed, gesturing once more to the screen. 'Welcome to the future of intelligence gathering, where the criminal leads law enforcement directly to the scene of their next crime. You're not seeing through the eyes of a camera, and not even precisely through the eyes of the person in question. You're seeing what their *brains* are seeing, literally as it happens.'

Ethan blinked and almost missed a breath as he tried to digest what Jarvis was saying.

'Their brains? How is that even possible?'

Jarvis smiled, clearly as amazed as Ethan at the technology before them.

'You're watching the brain waves created by what they're seeing converted into moving images here in the Watch Room. Effectively, you're seeing their thoughts.'

***

XXVIII

'We're seeing their thoughts?' Lopez gasped as she surveyed the Watch Room's myriad screens. 'That's insane.'

Ethan shook his head in disbelief, his arms folded as he realized that the blurry images of talking people and the responses from off–screen were in fact ordinary conversations being conducted between two people.

'I myself wouldn't have believed it possible until I was given the clearance necessary to get full disclosure about this program,' Jarvis said, 'but this technology is in use today and has far–reaching consequences for law enforcement and personal privacy. If it was to become public knowledge, it would make Snowden's PRISM leaks look like a joke in comparison.'

'How does it work?' Ethan asked.

Jarvis leaned against the wall as he spoke.

'Almost a decade ago, researchers at the ATR Computational Neuroscience Laboratories in Japan figured out a way to sample electrical signals moving from the retina to the brain's visual cortex. They realized that for any given image witnessed by an observer a unique signal was relayed to the brain, and thus those individual signals could be recorded, analyzed and stored. They wired volunteers up to a series of simple electrodes and showed them around four hundred images, recording each signal into a database. When they were done, they then reversed the process and placed random images in front of the subjects. A computer in a room nearby recognized the relevant visual signal and produced an image of what the subject was seeing.'

Lopez frowned. 'That's not quite what we're seeing here,' she said.

'The technology was considered by the scientists involved to be useful in developing a better understanding of cognitive thought, dream analysis, psychology and so on,' Jarvis replied. 'But the NSA was way ahead and had recognized the tech' as being tremendously promising in the field of intelligence gathering, and they had made copies of earlier data during a discreet hacking operation from an NSA listening station in Hawaii.'

'And then they militarized it,' Ethan guessed.

Jarvis shrugged in agreement.

'Of course they did,' he said. 'I can't think of a technology that hasn't been militarized or emerged as a result of military research. The NSA realized that the technological leap to go from seeing thoughts on a screen to seeing real–time imagery was not particularly great, requiring only a larger database of source imagery, better and smaller hardware and a way of installing that hardware into an unsuspecting host.'

'That sounds like a virus or something,' Lopez said with an expression of disgust.

'In a sense that's exactly what it is,' Jarvis agreed. 'Effectively, the NSA was developing a program to hack the human mind; to intercept signals on their way to the brain, code them into data and send them back here.'

Ethan shook his head in wonder.

'And they did it,' he murmured to himself. 'How many federal and international laws does this Identity Mine of theirs break?'

'It would probably be quicker to ask how many of them it *doesn't* break,' Jarvis admitted, 'and the evidence obtained here could never be used in a court of law, much like that gathered by *Operation Watchman*. But it can lead law enforcement to catch criminals of all kinds in the actual process of committing their crimes. It's the next best thing to predicting the future – watching the present play out in the perpetrator's mind.'

Lopez shook her head. 'How did they go from a handful of recorded images to this?'

'The NSA picked up the technology but it was already moving quickly in the civilian field. The same Japanese firm that developed the initial technology then started looking into whether they could see dreams instead of thoughts. They started monitoring again, this time as the subjects were falling asleep and witnessing something known as hipnagogic imagery, the half–dreams we experience when falling asleep. They recorded the signals in the same way as before into a database and then let the subjects sleep while watching the monitors. Sure enough when the subjects entered REM, or Rapid–Eye–Movement sleep, which is normally associated with dreams, they could *see* the dreams in motion.'

'Jesus,' Lopez uttered. 'That's creepy.'

Ethan looked at the screens that were black, the ones with the strange lights leaping about across them.

'They're sleeping,' he realized.

'The observers see their dreams here too sometimes,' Jarvis confirmed. 'The lens of the human eyeball sees the world inverted, so it requires the brain to flip the image into something we can understand. When the subjects are dreaming, their brain automatically presents the images to them right–side up – so we then have to flip the dream images manually here on the screens to override the programming and make sense of what we're seeing.'

Ethan moved closer to a railing and leaned against it as he overlooked the operatives and the big screens before him. He could see the people talking on the screens but there was little sound.

'So they can see but not hear?' he asked Jarvis.

'The information from the subjects is visual only,' Jarvis confirmed. 'The lip reading skills of operatives assigned to this program and a small sonic implant ensure that some audio makes it through, enough to get a reasonable picture of what's being discussed. Phone records from PRISM often complete the picture.'

'How do they know the difference between what the subject's thinking or dreaming and what they're actually seeing?' Lopez asked.

'Different brainwaves,' Jarvis explained, 'the signals travel to different parts of the brain depending on if they're purely visual or the product of our imagination. Experiments at the University of California, Berkeley, were able to produce images of scenes and events when the subjects were asked to recall those scenes and events, without ever having had a picture presented to them. So they'd be asked to think of something obvious, like the Eiffel Tower or the Golden Gate Bridge. Observers monitoring the subject's brain waves in another room were easily able to distinguish the images and identify them. The feeds here in The Identity Mine are filtered to remove any thought signals, but they could also be altered to produce *only* images of the subject's thoughts.'

Ethan stared at Jarvis. 'Thought crimes?'

'Wouldn't be admissible as evidence,' Jarvis reminded him. 'We're not in *Minority Report* territory yet.'

'You're not damned far from it,' Lopez retorted. 'How the hell did these subjects of yours end up being able to be watched like this? And what's the link with China?'

'The four NSA operatives who went missing from Kowloon, on route to a symposium on neurotechnology,' Jarvis replied. 'They were carrying copies of that early data taken from the Japanese labs who developed this technology, ten years before the first images of thoughts were successfully screened, which included their own detailed analysis and projected ideas for radically improving the technology. It's now believed that the Chinese grabbed them, obtained the technology and then used the abducted computer scientists to make their own improvements.'

Ethan thought for a moment.

'So you think that the implant we found inside Major General Thompson's brain was fitted with this kind of technology?'

'Pretty much,' Jarvis replied. 'That's why the people who had control of Thompson didn't have to be right on the scene when they initiated their attack. They could see what he could see, in real–time.'

'Wouldn't that have taken a lot of processing power?' Lopez asked.

'Yes,' Jarvis agreed, 'that's why they needed a vehicle like their van, to contain a computer to decode the data and a monitor to watch the scene unfolding. But the implanted device need only be small and requires only enough power to transmit the data to the processing point.'

'So the Chinese got hold of this technology,' Ethan surmised, 'and then they went one step further and added the ability to *control* the subject as well.'

'That's what we think happened,' Jarvis agreed. 'One of the NSA operatives' remains washed up outside of Hong Kong a day ago. These guys were elite hackers, real computer geniuses. China would not have wanted to kill them without first extracting every last ounce of use from them. Who knows what they could have achieved in the last decade?'

'Hacking human brains,' Lopez murmured. 'And these guys you're watching here, they have implants too?'

'Very small ones,' Jarvis replied. 'NSA agents maintained a permanent watch and when the subjects went for normal procedures at dentists or hospitals that required sedation at any time, they were able to use that time to insert small implants that wired into the frontal lobes to intercept and transmit data as it passed through the optical nerves and on to the visual cortex, building a complete visual picture of the subject's field of view.'

'They attached something to the optical nerve?' Lopez mumbled in horror.

'Apparently it's quite easy,' Jarvis replied. 'Surgeons can pop the eyeball out of its socket and insert a small transmitter, then reposition the eyeball with the subject being completely unaffected. As long as they're sedated, of course.'

'And this occurs without their knowledge,' Ethan figured.

'What they don't know *will* hurt them,' Jarvis smiled in response. 'Obviously we can't risk apprehending these individuals directly, but using this technology means that we never have to get too close to them and they never actually realize they're under surveillance.'

Lopez peered at one of the screens, which appeared to show a man brushing his teeth in front of a mirror. To her amazement, the man's fuzzy visage on the screen closely matched his image in a photograph beneath the same screen.

'So, how does this connect with Abrahem?' she asked.

Ethan figured he had the answer.

'Abrahem must have done some kind of deal with the Chinese,' he surmised. 'The Chinese would not have wanted to dirty their hands in Iraq for fear of causing an international incident, so they would have instead hired Iraqis or suitably corrupt Americans to implant devices into senior American personnel for the purpose of spying.'

'First the surgeon, Muller,' Jarvis confirmed. 'He's already confessed to being paid tremendous sums of money by the Chinese to insert mind–hacking devices into soldiers like General Thompson and others, although he swears he had no idea that this would be the outcome. He believed that the devices were some kind of high–tech trackers or bugs.'

'So, China would have needed somebody to carry these devices into Iraq for them,' Lopez realized. 'That way, they could gain field access to senior military figures working in the country.'

'They used the hospitals,' Jarvis replied, 'and targeted injured soldiers or personnel being treated for minor ailments and such like. As far as Muller can recall, he hid the insertion of the devices while performing sinus drains under local anesthetic. The small size and design of the devices caused minimal discomfort for the wearer, but he has told us that they also caused nosebleeds from time to time.'

'The list of possible carriers could run into the hundreds,' Ethan said, 'and many of them may be civilians now, scattered across the globe.'

'We can't focus on that many people,' Lopez agreed. 'If we can't find Abrahem we're not going to be able to stop him.'

'If he's targeting the Trans Pacific ceremony purposefully,' Ethan said, 'that means he must have planned this attack for some months. He would have had to be sure that the Presidents of both the United States and China were going to be in the same place at the same time. That narrows our list of potential targets down.'

'To a couple of thousand,' Jarvis replied. 'The President has been informed of the threat but is showing no signs of backing out of the ceremony, so you'll have to brief the administration yourselves.'

'What?' Lopez uttered.

'You'll be taken directly to Pennsylvania Avenue to deliver your own briefing to POTUS.'

Ethan blinked in surprise as Lopez frowned.

'What's *POTUS*?' she asked.

Jarvis glanced at her, somewhat bemused. 'President Of The United States, genius. You'd best do your hair.'

***

XXIX

'Will the Chiefs of Staff be present?' Ethan asked as he climbed back into the limousine.

'I doubt it.'

'And the directors of the intelligence and security services?'

'I certainly hope not.'

Ethan glanced at Lopez as the limousine climbed out of the underground lot and into the late afternoon sunshine. 'That means LeMay won't be there.'

Jarvis leaned in conspiratorially as he replied.

'The President wants to be updated personally on our progress. He knows that what's happened at Fort Benning will break out globally through the media within days, and he wants every last piece of information at his disposal when the storm hits. That means us debriefing him now before we do anything else. Believe it or not he asked for the both of you personally.'

Lopez raised a perfectly arched eyebrow. 'Both of us?'

'You're a team,' Jarvis replied. 'And as it's now *Lopez & Warner Inc*, it would have looked odd not to have you both there.'

Ethan glanced out of the tinted windows as the limousine passed through the last of the NSA checkpoints and began heading for the cluttered skyline of Washington DC. He had last met the current President several years before when he, along with Lopez, had prevented a crazed pastor by the name of Kelvin Patterson from infecting the then senator with an alien virus that the pastor had believed was in fact the blood of angels.

Despite the remarkable nature of their encounter they had won the eternal gratitude of the senator and now, it would seem, the President's ear.

'If we can let him know about Majestic Twelve, about what's been happening, about LeMay's involvement,' Ethan began, 'we could really start to root out the twelve men behind everything and…'

'That's not going to happen, Ethan,' Jarvis cut him off. 'You'll put the President in a position where he'll not be able to trust his most senior advisors. Short of replacing his entire administration there's no way for us to let him know of what's happening without fatally flawing his presidency, and you're forgetting one important thing.'

'What's that?' Lopez asked.

'The President himself might be a member of MJ–12.'

Ethan stared at Jarvis for a long moment. 'He wouldn't have gone down that road – he was one of the staunchest senators when it came to government transparency and the reduction of corporate influence at the Capitol. It's what got him into power.'

'That's the public face of politics,' Jarvis replied as the limousine whispered along the asphalt. 'What happens out of the eyes of the media, behind closed doors, is another matter entirely. Right now the only people we can trust besides DIA Director Nellis are the three of us and my assistant, Hellerman, as he's too damned *Uncle Sam* to even think about taking MJ–12's coin against our country.'

'And yet we were working for them and didn't even know it,' Lopez pointed out. 'They didn't need brain implants to have us around their little fingers. A group so closely woven into the fabric of political life in Washington can't be unraveled overnight even if the President is on our side, because we can never know exactly who to take this to.'

Jarvis offered them a tight smile.

'That may not be true,' he said.

'What do you mean?' Ethan asked, suddenly cautious.

Jarvis leaned back in his seat and watched the suburbs of the city passing by outside beyond the tinted windows as the limousine crossed the Anacostia River on the 11th Street Bridge.

'I had an idea.'

'I don't like it when that happens,' Lopez replied.

'It sounds like government speak for "I've had a *dangerous* idea",' Ethan agreed. 'We're only in this to stop Abrahem Nassir, not run errands for the DIA and the Pentagon.'

'I haven't told them about this,' Jarvis replied. 'Not even Director Nellis.'

Ethan stared at Jarvis in amazement. The one person who had done more than any other to resurrect the covert unit that Ethan, Lopez and Jarvis represented was now being kept out of the loop for reasons that Ethan could not fathom.

'What's going on, Doug?'

Jarvis took a deep breath.

'You said it yourselves, we can't do anything because we can't trust a soul on Capitol Hill or down in the Pentagon. So, the only way we can get that trust is to ensure without any shadow of a doubt that we recruit people who are utterly loyal to us.'

Lopez shrugged.

'Back to square one then as we can't do that. We don't know how far MJ–12's reach extends.'

Jarvis nodded. 'Unless the people we recruit have no choice but to help us,' he said.

'That's blackmail,' Ethan said. 'That would make us no better than the people we're trying to bring down.'

'I wouldn't use blackmail,' Jarvis replied.

Ethan's mind went blank as he struggled to understand what Jarvis was suggesting, but beside him Lopez gasped.

'You want to implant people,' she said. 'You want to control our own people and find out what's going on using the same tech' that Abrahem's been using!'

Jarvis raised his hands.

'It's only an idea at this stage,' he said. 'But it represents a technological leap in our intelligence gathering capabilities and it cannot be cast aside simply because human rights lawyers are…'

'It's *illegal*,' Lopez snapped.

'The subjects would be carefully selected and would not be controlled, only monitored in the same way that the criminals under The Identity Mine program are observed.'

'Until somebody blows it wide open,' Ethan said. 'Another Snowden for instance, then what would we do? Can you imagine the fallout from something like that? It would make PRISM and MYSTIC look tame in comparison.'

'But the reach we will have in pinning down MJ–12 could be unparalleled!' Jarvis insisted. 'The ends justify the means in this case, as the individuals we implant will know nothing of the device in their brains, just like the criminals we're already tracking. The intelligence we've uncovered using The Identity Mine has solved countless law enforcement cases. With this technology we could extend that reach into counter–terrorism and in the case of MJ–12, counter corruption at the highest levels.'

Ethan shook his head.

'And those highest levels of corruption would have no problem with murdering anybody they suspected of informing against them,' he pointed out. 'You'd be putting innocent lives in harm's way and they would know nothing about it. It's like putting a child in a blindfold and letting them walk into a lion's cage.'

Jarvis waved Ethan's argument aside with a waft of his hand.

'They wouldn't be informing, they'd be listening on our behalf without ever knowing it and what we learn would be available to us in real–time. If we thought that somebody was in danger we could prevent an attack long before MJ–12 could put it into action. And besides, the goal behind my plan was not to implant any civilians or military personnel at all.'

'Who then?' Lopez demanded, and then she got it.

'LeMay,' Ethan murmured, almost afraid to say it. 'You want to implant the Director of the Federal Bureau of Investigation with an illegal monitoring device that hacks into his brain.'

Jarvis nodded, clearly aware of the magnitude of what he was proposing.

'If you want to kill the Hydra…'

'You can't keep cutting off its heads because they're replaced. You have to pierce its heart,' Lopez replied. 'Jeez, how would we even go about something like this? LeMay knows about what's happening, right?'

'Wrong,' Jarvis replied. 'The task force behind this is being held back by the President, remember? Nobody knows right now, because everybody wants it covered up. That means that MJ–12 may not yet have the full story, and we know that LeMay has dispatched Agents Ford and Vaughn to Hong Kong in an attempt to discover what's going on, presumably because they're aware of a connection to what we're investigating. I figure that means he knows squat, at least for now, because both Vaughn and Ford are missing.'

'They're missing?' Ethan asked.

'We intercepted communications between two FBI field offices,' Jarvis explained. 'The two agents disappeared somewhere on the south of Hong Kong island.'

Ethan looked at Lopez, who despite her dislike of Hannah Ford could not conceal her concern.

'Mitchell,' she said.

'We should have made more of an effort to warn them,' Ethan snapped at Jarvis.

'I did everything that I could,' Jarvis insisted. 'Ford wouldn't listen to me.'

'If both Ford and Vaughn are missing,' Ethan added, 'then LeMay's main source of information on the ground in Hong Kong is limited, unless Mitchell is working for him. LeMay might by now know about the implant technology.'

'Either way, you're ahead of them,' Jarvis pointed out. 'If we do this, we do it soon and get an implant into LeMay during the security operation around Abrahem Nassir at the White House.'

'But the security will be tighter than ever,' Ethan said. 'How do we get to him and pull this off?'

'I don't know,' Jarvis said, 'but remember; LeMay is in bed with MJ–12 and as such has already betrayed his country in favor of his own pursuit of power and financial interests. He has become the enemy. What we do now, however illegal it might be, could be the difference between justice being done and our country falling into the hands of businesses obsessed with their own profits over Americans' civil rights. This isn't about turning our technology on our own people, it's about using MJ–12's own techniques against them. Now, are you in or not? If Ford and Vaughn did uncover what's happening, joined the dots and decided to inform LeMay, then they're likely dead. Do you want their sacrifice to be for nothing?'

Ethan and Lopez exchanged a glance and then made up their minds.

***

XXX

Hong Kong

Consciousness came slowly, drifting toward her and then receding like dark waves on a beach at night. Hannah Ford was lying on her back on something hard and she could feel her skin as cold as ice, her bones aching.

The pain reached out to her, called her in, and she opened her eyes and stared into absolute blackness. For a moment she panicked, believed that her sight had failed her, and then she heard the faint sound of a breeze among the leaves above her, saw the subtle motion of branches against tiny stars in the night sky.

Hannah groaned as she forced herself up onto her elbows, her muscles stiff and her head throbbing. She rubbed her forehead with one hand and felt her skin caked with something dry that flaked off in her fingers. She reached down for her weapon but it was gone, along with her cell phone and her identification papers.

Hannah dragged herself to her feet and realized that she was in the same clearing in the forest as when she had been attacked by Mitchell. She turned as she heard a groan of misery from her right and saw another body lying in the foliage nearby.

She scrambled across and recognized Vaughn's stocky form and black hair as he rolled over. To her horror his face was bruised and swollen, his eyes dark slits that she could barely make out in the starlight.

'Vaughn?'

Vaughn groaned something as she helped him sit upright and he squinted at her as his eyes widened a little.

'What happened to you?' he asked, his voice distorted by his swollen lips.

Hannah realized that she too must have been beaten to some degree as she could taste blood on her lips, could feel it oozing from her nose.

'Mitchell got the jump on me,' she said. 'What about you?'

Vaughn shook his head to clear it, struggled to his feet.

'I parked the car, started up here, and then somebody came up and slugged me from behind. Before I knew it I was being hammered by a lot of guys and I passed out.'

'Did you get a look at any of them?'

Vaughn shook his head. 'I didn't see any faces, didn't hear anybody speak. Mitchell must have had back up. We should have known.'

'Forget it,' Hannah said as they clambered to their feet and started walking through the darkened forest, seeking the way back to the road. 'All we can hope is that they didn't know which car we were using. Do you have the keys?'

Vaughn reached into his pocket and nodded. 'Yeah, but my cell's gone.'

'Mine too,' Hannah said. 'Let's just get back to the Consulate and get in touch with Director LeMay. He needs to know about what's happened.'

Vaughn limped alongside her, and like two geriatric government agents they made their way down the hillside to the darkened road. The route was devoid of traffic at this time of night, although Hannah could not be sure of the precise time as her wrist watch had also disappeared.

'They've made it out to be a robbery,' she surmised as they hobbled through the darkness. 'Two FBI agents overpowered by common thugs, maximum embarrassment.'

'Mitchell's a clever guy,' Vaughn uttered. 'He's going to have been avoiding agents like us for years if he's doing his job completely under the radar.'

'I don't give a damn,' Hannah uttered. 'What matters to me is that he was interrogating a man up there that he'd tied to a tree, and I got his name. Jin Chen.'

'Who's he?'

'I don't know, but we'll figure that out when we get back. He confessed to Mitchell to being involved in the abduction of the NSA agents in 1997.'

Hannah looked up as Vaughn led her to a small wooded parking lot, and there saw their silver sedan still parked where he had left it. Hannah limped across as Vaughn deactivated the locking system and climbed in, Vaughn handing her the keys as he climbed stiffly into the passenger seat.

The drive back into Hong Kong was far quicker than the route out, but the city was still a dense galaxy of lights and moving traffic as they made their way back to the Consulate Building on Garden Avenue. Without papers, they had to wait at the main gates until their identities were verified to the guards, and even then when Special Agent Brad Hinkley walked out to them he was accompanied by two armed agents.

Hannah clambered wearily out of her vehicle and Hinkley hesitated as he saw her.

'Jesus Hannah, what the hell happened?' Hinkley turned to one of the guards before she could answer. 'Get a medical team down here, right now!'

Hannah saw the agent hurry off and she shook her head.

'There's no time,' she mumbled. 'I need you to pull anything you can on a Chinese man by the name of Jin Chen, who worked at a British bank in the city.'

'Jin Chen?' Hinkley asked. 'What's happened?'

'It's a long story, okay?' Hannah shot back. 'Just do what I'm asking and contact the FBI Headquarters. I need to speak to Director LeMay as soon as possible.'

Hinkley looked at his watch and shook his head. 'He won't be available for at least an hour or two.'

'Then wake him up!' Hannah yelled at the Texan. 'The Chinese are preparing for some kind of major cyber–attack, and if we don't let home base know about it what do you think will happen?!'

Hinkley raised his hands in supplication as he whirled and dashed back toward the offices, while in the other direction walked two medics.

'We need to debrief LeMay or at the very least get this written up,' Vaughn said.

'The hell with that,' Hannah muttered as she was gently led by the arm toward the offices. 'We need to get the hell out of Hong Kong and back to DC. Whatever's developing here is going to break on home turf and we need to be there to…'

Hannah was cut off as suddenly four armed police dashed out of the building, their weapons raised toward Hannah and Vaughn.

'On your knees, now!'

Hannah stared in shock as the police surrounded them, Hinkley hurrying out of the building in pursuit.

'What the hell's going on?' Hannah uttered in disbelief.

Hinkley approached them cautiously. 'You said that you lost your weapons, papers and cell phones?'

'We were attacked,' Hannah said as rough hands yanked her arms behind her back and cuffed her.

'That's not what the police are saying,' Hinkley said. 'Yours and Vaughn's weapons were recovered two hours ago at the scene of a homicide in down town, that of a respected businessman by the name of Jin Chen.'

Hannah stared at Hinkley as her heart felt as though it were plummeting into freefall inside her chest. 'Jin Chen was being tortured by Mitchell in the woods on the south of the island!'

Hinkley stared apologetically at her.

'Local police uncovered plyers with your fingerprints on them,' he explained. 'The bullets in Jin Chen's body have already been matched to your gun, Hannah. The police are requesting that you be detained in Kowloon until further notice.'

'You've got to be kidding me? I saw Mitchell torturing Jin Chen. He was involved in the abduction of the NSA agents in 1997! Mitchell got it out of him!'

The police yanked her aside as Hinkley replied.

'They're saying that you must have done this,' he replied. 'Nobody knows anything about anybody named Mitchell.'

'Aaron James Mitchell!' Hannah shouted. 'You need to locate him to corroborate what we're saying.'

Hinkley looked at Vaughn. 'Did you see this Mitchell?'

Vaughn stared at Hinkley for a long moment. 'No, I didn't. I was attacked before I made it to Agent Ford's location.'

'Can you identify the people that attacked you?' Hinkley asked him.

'No, but it's likely that they were the ones who also attacked Hannah. This is a set up, Hinkley. If the Chinese or Mitchell is behind it then they're trying to prevent us from getting back to the states.'

Hinkley nodded.

'I'll do what I can.' he promised. 'We'll get on top of this, okay?'

'You'll do what you can?!' Hannah screeched. 'Get us the hell out of the country!'

Hinkley managed not to shout back at her as he sucked in a deep breath and turned to the police.

'This is the sovereign territory of the United States of America, gentlemen, and I cannot allow my people to be treated in this manner.'

The police sergeant confronted Hinkley. 'These people are wanted for murder, Agent Hinkley! What do you think will happen to our countrys' international relations if they are allowed to leave?'

'They'll *survive*,' Hinkley snapped. 'Release them or I'll have you and your men detained here until this is all cleared up.'

A dozen FBI agents suddenly emerged from the building with their weapons drawn, all wearing uncompromising expressions as they confronted the four Hong Kong police officers.

'Cleared up?' the sergeant shot back. 'Don't you mean covered up?'

Hinkley did not reply as the police released Hannah and Vaughn and backed off as more agents from within the building arrived to support Hinkley. Outnumbered and outgunned, the Hong Kong police officers retreated under armed escort, their sergeant calling over his shoulder.

'This isn't over! We'll be back!'

Hannah watched as the police were led out of the Embassy and then turned to Hinkley.

'Good job,' she said.

'It needed to be,' Hinkley replied. 'You've been here less than twenty four hours and you're already wanted for murder. You need to be out of the country within the hour, understood? I'll arrange transport.'

'They'll intercept us,' Vaughn pointed out, 'and we can hardly maintain a low profile looking like this.'

'You'll travel on diplomatic plates, private charter. I'll sort it now. Get yourselves cleaned up and ready to leave. I'll check in at the Barn and find out what's been going on, okay?'

Hannah smiled at Hinkley as she turned to leave with Vaughn.

'I appreciate it, Brad,' she said, relieved that somebody outside of LeMay's direct influence was finally supporting them.

*

Special Agent in Charge Brad Hinkley waited until Hannah and Vaughn were out of sight before he pulled a pack of *Luckies* from his pocket and lit one, savoring the nicotine hit as slipped a cell phone from his pocket and dialed a number he had memorized some years before. It took only moments for the line to connect.

'Yes?'

'It's done,' Hinkley said. 'They're wanted for murder in Hong Kong and are now on their way. They'll be in DC by the morning, but they're officially fugitives from justice now.'

'Excellent,' replied the voice through dense digital distortion. *'We'll take it from here. Your career prospects will improve greatly within just a few days.'*

Hinkley smiled as the line went dead and he lowered the phone from his ear. He took one last drag of his cigarette before he dropped the glowing butt down a storm drain in one corner of the lot. The cell phone followed it moments later.

***

XXXI

1600 Pennsylvania Ave NW,

Washington, DC

The limousine pulled into the White House grounds after a thorough search of the vehicle by dogs and explosives experts. Ethan sat quietly and watched as the vehicle drove slowly up to the iconic building, one that he had seen perhaps a million times and yet never set foot in before.

Tourists were admitted to the White House every day but they saw only limited areas of the building, others highly classified and off–limits to the public. The limousine drove to an entrance on the west side of the building and pulled up alongside a heavy looking door guarded by Secret Service agents. The agents responded with robotic efficiency, opening the limousine's doors and ushering Ethan, Lopez and Jarvis out of the vehicle and inside the White House with the minimum of exposure.

The interior of the White House was pretty much exactly as Ethan had believed it would be; immaculate red carpets, chandeliers and elaborately framed paintings on the walls. The building was enveloped by a hushed atmosphere, perhaps because of the dense layers of electromagnetic protection built into the walls.

'This way, please.'

The Secret Service agents led them through the building, which seemed to Ethan to be surprisingly busy with members of the President's staff hurrying to and fro, weaving around Ethan and Lopez and casting curious glances at the two unfamiliar faces dressed in casual clothes. Ethan figured that at least Jarvis was wearing a suit, whereas he and Lopez looked as though they'd been dragged in from the street outside.

They were led down the hall to the Diplomatic Reception Room, used as the primary point of entry for the President and his family into the White House. Federal style furnishings were arranged in front of a spectacular panoramic landscape wall covering.

'This way.'

'Where are we going?' Lopez asked.

'The Deep Underground Command Center,' Jarvis guessed as they were led to a stairwell that Ethan figured was adjacent to the West Wing.

Ethan knew that the White House had a labyrinth of tunnels beneath it, some leading to the Capitol, others to DC's subway network with an entire station beneath the White House itself. But the DUCC was a more mysterious construction, built during recent years to allow the President and his team to relocate to a safe location in the event of a major crisis.

'He's already bunkered down?' Ethan asked Jarvis.

'The threat is both credible and direct,' Jarvis confirmed. 'If Abrahem Nassir is on his way here we can't be sure of when and where he will strike until we have further information. The President will stay here until the arrival of the President of the People's Republic of China tomorrow.'

The Secret Service agents led them down a corridor at the bottom of the stairwell, the plush carpets and elaborate paintings of the White House a memory now. Bomb proof walls, harsh lighting and polished tile floors led to an armoured door, outside which stood two armed soldiers. Both men stood to one side as the Secret Service agents accessed the door and it hissed open.

They stood aside and gestured for Ethan, Lopez and Jarvis to enter.

Ethan walked into the bunker and was surprised to see a warmly lit room dominated by a long table, around the far end of which sat the President and several of his advisors. The President smiled and stood the moment he saw Ethan, walking around the long table and extending his hand.

'Ethan Warner,' he greeted him with a firm handshake. 'We only ever seem to meet when I'm in jeopardy.'

'Just can't stay out of trouble, can you Mister President?'

Despite having met the President years before when he had still been a senator, Ethan found himself somewhat star–struck all the same. The man he had known seemed to have grown in stature, become more a statesman and leader than he had been all those years ago. The President turned to Lopez and shook her hand also before he gestured to the table.

'Shall we?'

Jarvis stepped forward. 'May we have the room, Mister President? You'll understand, once we tell you what we've discovered.'

The President glanced at his advisors. 'My team are here to both take records and advise, Mister Jarvis.'

'They can listen to a recording, Mister President, although once you hear what we have to say I don't think that you'll be passing the message on.'

The advisors all looked at one another for a long moment and then the President nodded and asked them all to leave. Only a pair of Secret Service agents remained, standing either side of the bunker door as it was closed behind them. The rest of the Secret Service would assemble in the

"Horsepower" command post, as it was known, in the basement of the West Wing. Ethan knew that the President's Oval Office contained a trap door that led straight down to the bunker in which they stood and the command post, a vital rapid escape route in time of emergency.

The President sat down at the table, as did Ethan and Lopez.

'So what it is that's so important that you don't want the directors of our country's chief intelligence agencies present, Mister Jarvis?'

Jarvis sat down and folded his hands before him on the table as he replied.

'Mister President, we believe that there is a coordinated effort on the part of radicalized terrorist outfits to take control of United States military personnel and use them as human avatars to infiltrate and destroy our country from within. The death of Major General Thompson and the soldiers under his command was the first test of a technology that will allow our enemies to perform such actions, to physically and mentally control a human being from afar and use them to cause harm to others.'

The President stared at Jarvis for a long moment and then glanced at Ethan.

'This is almost harder to believe than what happened with Kelvin Patterson all those years ago.'

'But no less real, Mister President,' Ethan replied. 'We already know that Major Thompson was implanted with a device that took control of the frontal lobes of his brain and allowed others to remotely control his actions, an act that led to the deaths of many of the general's recruits at Fort Benning. The same thing likely happened to Commander Sandy Veiron aboard USS Carl Vinson. We now believe these attacks have been tests before a major strike on our country.'

The President thought for a moment.

'I have a major ceremony to attend on the South Lawn tomorrow to welcome China into the Trans Pacific Partnership, and I can't simply cancel that or go out there and tell the people of this country that the person standing next to them may be some kind of flesh–and–blood robot intent on killing anybody they can get their hands on. It will send the entire country into panic. It would be like revealing that half of my military staff are all *Terminators* or something.'

Ethan realized that to some degree the President was right. It was no longer the stuff of *Hollywood* myth that perfectly camouflaged enemies of the state could attack at will the citizens of any country using utterly emotionless machines. The difference was that the machines were not cyborgs but ordinary people acting without control of their bodies or minds.

'There's more,' Jarvis said.

'Go on.'

'We have connected the perpetrators of this act of sabotage to two main groups: one is a terrorist outfit operating out of Basra, Iraq, and the other is a state–sanctioned unit of computer hackers and scientists based in China.'

The President nodded, almost smiled at the irony.

'China,' he echoed. 'Why doesn't that surprise me?'

China's recent military expansion and growing cyber–warfare capability were known to anybody with the ability to read the news. A recent breach of federal government computers at the Office of Personnel Management had compromised the records of four million employees, even as China was establishing military installations that threatened countries with US treaties in place such as the Philippines.

'They've already hacked our Department of Homeland Security and the Department of Commerce,' Jarvis pointed out, 'and have an active and skilled force of cyber–warfare specialists constantly probing US cyber–security in an attempt to find vulnerabilities. This is simply their latest and most technologically advanced step in the game.'

'How the hell did they acquire technology like this?' the President asked. 'Even *we* don't have the capacity to hack into human minds.'

'That's not quite true,' Lopez said, speaking for the first time.

'What do you mean?' the President asked.

'The Identity Mine,' Jarvis replied, 'is a highly classified Black Budget program tasked with monitoring criminals through their own eyes, by seeing what they see and hearing what they hear. It was developed using technology that was stolen from us by Chinese operatives, who abducted four National Security Agency staff operating out of Hong Kong in 1997. We developed The Identity Mine from that same technology, but the Chinese went a lot further than we dared, going beyond merely monitoring criminals.'

The President appeared to struggle to keep up with the revelations.

'So they stole something that we developed and then weaponized it?'

'That's pretty much what happened,' Ethan said. 'They forced the NSA abductees to perfect the technology and then tested it on them. The body of one of the abductees washed up on a Kowloon shore two days ago, his frontal lobes a mess. We're assuming the other three operatives are now dead.'

'What about the terrorists out of Basra? How do they connect to all of this?'

'They were hired by the Chinese to smuggle the technology into hospitals used by United States military personnel working in Iraq. During routine medical procedures, the Chinese had paid off senior medical staff to insert the implants into victims under general anesthetic, either within Iraq or at other military installations around the globe. We believe that this was how General Thompson and Commander Veiron were implanted.'

The President didn't take long to figure out the rest.

'Something with the deal goes bad, the terrorists take off with the technology and the know how to implant people and they head here.'

Jarvis gestured to one of the screens in the bunker, where an image of a rugged looking Middle Eastern man had appeared.

'Abrahem Nassir,' he identified the grainy image of a swarthy man photographed in a bustling market street in Iraq. 'His father, an engineer, is believed to have been forced by the Chinese to smuggle implants into Iraq to be inserted into American service personnel during the 2003 invasion. Abrahem's family were murdered shortly afterward in a place called Aljazaer Park, an act which we think he believes was conducted by American soldiers but we think may have occurred at the hands of Chinese spies disguising themselves as Americans, intending to clear up any loose ends.'

'So the Chinese ensure that Abrahem targets the United States,' the President surmised.

'That may have been their intention,' Jarvis confirmed, 'but we have information that Abrahem's wife and two children were killed in 2008 during an American bombing raid over the south of Basra. If he harbored any doubt over who was behind his father's death, he won't care about that any more. He's the one we're looking for because he has both motive and means.'

The President stood and looked up at the image of Abrahem; the dark and hooded eyes, the dense stubble on his chin, the thick neck and arrogant glare.

'Is he in the country yet?' he asked.

'We don't know,' Jarvis admitted. 'Despite tracking him down to a militant hideaway in Somalia, a Special Forces team that accompanied Ethan and Nicola here was unable to apprehend Abrahem. We're sure he's coming here from the interrogation of his accomplices, so we must assume that he is even now planning his attack and attempting to enter the country.'

The President turned back to Jarvis.

'Is this brain control even possible?' he asked. 'I cannot believe that we would have created technology like this, that we would have attempted something so inhumane?'

Jarvis sighed.

'Sadly Mister President, it's not the first time that something like this has happened and this time there may be elements of our own intelligence service hoping that Abrahem's attack goes through.'

The President froze in motion as he stared at Jarvis.

'That's a weighty claim to make, Mister Jarvis,' he rumbled. 'I hope for all our sakes that you have something to back it up.'

Ethan spoke for Jarvis as he looked up at the President.

'Our agencies did something like this once before,' he replied, 'and the country compensated the families of the victims as a result.'

The President sat down.

'Tell me, everything, right now,' he said.

***

XXXII

The President sat expectantly at the head of the table as Jarvis stood up and paced back and forth across the bunker as he spoke.

'The whole thing was started by the CIA back in the 1950s. They initiated a series of experiments that by any measure would be considered the stuff of science fiction even today, let alone back then. The whole initiative was operated under the umbrella of something called *MKULTRA*.'

'What was *MKULTRA*?' the President asked.

'That project's details are veiled under Executive Order three–zero–one–zero–five,' Jarvis replied.

An Executive Order was a directive signed by the President of the United States and a policy that transcended administrations.

'Which one of my predecessors signed,' the President reminded him. 'The Executive Order shields the project from the public, not from this office. Go on.'

'MKULTRA was the name of a covert project run by the CIA under various different guises throughout the second half of the twentieth century,' Jarvis explained. 'Its origins occurred during *Operation Paperclip*, a mission to apprehend German scientists after World War Two who had been responsible for torture under the Nazi regime. *Project Bluebird* developed from this operation and was tasked with the study of mind control, enhanced interrogation techniques and behaviour modification. It was renamed *Project Artichoke* in 1951 and run by the CIA Office of Scientific Intelligence, before then becoming Project MKULTRA in 1953. The program was run by the CIA's Technical Service Staff, via the designator *MK*, and it received the highest security classification rating, *ULTRA*.'

'And what did this project do?'

Jarvis continued to pace as he spoke.

'It started with a comprehensive study of the phenomena of hypnosis, before moving into exploratory projects using forced morphine addiction and withdrawal, the use of chemicals and deprivation of sensory stimuli to produce amnesia and vulnerability in subjects,' Jarvis explained. 'In a memo dated 1952, an officer involved stated that the project's main goal was being to ask: *"Can we get control of an individual to the point that he will do our bidding against his will and even against fundamental laws of nature, such as self–preservation?"*'

The President looked at Ethan. 'That's just the kind of mind control that you're saying the Chinese, and by extension Abrahem Nassir, are wielding.'

'The work of MKULTRA was semi–passive,' Jarvis said. 'It worked using drugs rather than direct manipulation of the brain, weakening the victim's resolve and resistance to suggestion. The project continued right through the 1960's with experiments on unwitting American subjects both military and civilian. Agents injected drugs like LSD into drinks and water supplies, hallucinogens were administered without the subject's knowledge or consent and so on. It eventually progressed to deep–hypnosis programs designed to create unwitting assassins who were then stationed in politically volatile countries and could, upon a given command, carry out attacks on enemies of the state. It was intended that their actions could be explained away as psychosis or similar, divesting any blame on the USA.'

'Sleeper assassins,' the President acknowledged. 'Similar programs were uncovered in Russia after the Cold War.'

Jarvis nodded.

'MKULTRA developed an overseas arm, MKDELTA, which was responsible for the spraying of aerosolized LSD onto the village of *Pont–Saint–Esprit* in France in 1951. The event resulted in an outbreak of mass psychosis, with seven French citizens dead and more than thirty committed to mental institutions.'

'Not our finest hour,' the President said, well aware of the now–public nature of the CIA's more extreme programs of the previous century. 'How does this all tie in with the United States government admitting culpability in all of that?'

'A man named Frank Olson,' Jarvis said, 'one of the CIA operatives involved in MKULKTRA who witnessed a terminal interrogation in Germany under *Project Artichoke*, resigned his position and was later found dead after a suspicious fall from a Manhattan building. He was buried without autopsy and his death ruled a suicide, but the family fought for and won an exhumation and an independent autopsy which resulted in a coroner stating that Olson died *before* the fall. In 1975 our government admitted that Olson had been dosed with LSD and that the CIA and the state of New York had been covering up the details of his death for a quarter of a century. The government settled with Olson's family out of court.'

The President fell silent for a few moments as he digested what Jarvis had told him.

'What's the connection between MKULTRA and this new threat?' he asked finally.

Jarvis gestured to the screens.

'The direct threat to our country's security comes at the moment from this man,' he said, 'Abrahem Nassir. However, we believe that he is only one component of a much larger threat that's been operating behind the scenes for many decades. Our agency has labelled this threat by the name it has used in the few documents that attest to its existence: *Majestic Twelve.*'

The President's eyes narrowed. 'Go on.'

'Majestic Twelve is a cabal of powerful industry and military figures,' Ethan explained after Jarvis gestured for him to speak. 'They were supposedly formed in 1947 via an executive order issued by President Harry Truman to control the recovery and investigation of alien spacecraft after the alleged crash in Roswell, New Mexico in 1947.'

'So we're back to aliens again?' the President asked.

'Roswell, if it actually happened, was merely the catalyst the formed the group, which was attached to the United States Air Force Office of Special Investigations,' Lopez said. 'The FBI actually took the existence of MJ–12 seriously enough to look into its existence some years ago, but they came up with nothing and reported that the cabal was likely a hoax of some kind. Chances are, the OSI simply ensured that the Feds could gain no access to any data supporting the existence of the group, the funding of which is reckoned to be either private finance or our government's own Black Budget.'

'That sounds too easy,' the President said. 'We can't sit here and pretend that the FBI couldn't get anywhere, that anything amounting to evidence of a conspiracy must remain hidden because it's in the Black Budget. That's how conspiracy theories start.'

Jarvis smiled. 'However, now we believe we know why they found nothing,' he said. 'We have evidence Mister President, that the FBI is at least in part tied–in to operations conducted by Majestic Twelve.'

The President leaned back in his seat, his eyes fixed upon Jarvis. 'You're accusing federal agents of being part of a conspiracy against this country, perhaps even against me?'

'I know how it sounds,' Jarvis admitted, 'but the evidence is mounting against the agency for harboring at least one individual who is working for, or perhaps a central figure within, MJ–12. It makes sense that a cabal dedicated to subverting United States policy for profit would ensure at least some of its members or affiliates occupied high office within the government or the administration. Such high–level intelligence would be invaluable to their success.'

'And how would such a cabal coordinate their actions?' the President asked. 'If they're so secret, how could they exist in a world where even our most trusted agents, such as Edward Snowden, can steal sensitive data and transmit it to the media of the world?'

'I've come to believe that the Bilderberg Group and its annual meeting is to some degree the vessel through which Majestic Twelve coordinate their activities,' Jarvis said.

'Bilderberg?' the President echoed. 'I've attended that meeting every year since I took the presidency. It's no conspiracy meeting!'

'No,' Jarvis agreed, 'but an annual gathering of the world's most powerful men, and one into which the world's media is not just uninvited but actively prevented from reporting on, does make the perfect location for men of power to conspire does it not?'

The Bilderberg Group, formed by Joseph H. Retinger and Prince Bernhard of the Netherlands, was charged with the post–war take–over of the democratic process. The measures implemented by the group provided general control of the world economy through indirect political means. The meeting itself allowed each of the hundred or more participants to speak their mind freely because no media representative was permitted inside; nor would there be any news bulletin about the meeting or the topics discussed. If any leaks occurred, the journalists responsible were "discouraged" from reporting it. Bilderberg took its name from the Bilderberg Hotel in Oosterbeek, Holland, where the first meeting took place in 1954.

'Bilderberg represents the perfect meeting point for the members of MJ–12,' Lopez said. 'And we think that we've identified one of them.'

'Who?' the President demanded, directing a stony gaze at Jarvis once more.

'Director LeMay of the Federal Bureau of Investigation,' Jarvis replied.

A long silence filled the bunker as the President stared into the middle distance as though frozen in time. For what felt to Ethan like hours he merely sat in silence as though reflecting on some memory, and then he spoke with a soft, almost resigned tone.

'And what is your evidence?'

Ethan took the lead, aware of how Jarvis had put himself in the spotlight by revealing LeMay's suspected involvement with MJ–12.

'For some time now, Nicola and I have been pursued in our work by a man named Aaron Mitchell, who seems both well connected and financed. We knew that he was working on behalf of MJ–12 but we had no idea who was handling him, so to speak, who was giving him his orders.'

Lopez picked up the story.

'A few months ago, a man named Stanley Meyer was murdered and for a time Ethan and I were suspects in the case, which was pursued with extraordinary determination by the Bureau despite being an otherwise unremarkable homicide. During our investigation we were able to determine that Mitchell had been at the scene of the crime.'

'How so?'

'Because as it turns out,' Ethan replied, 'Mitchell has supposedly been dead for a couple of decades. He's a former Marine and Navy SEAL, and having met him twice now I can personally vouch that for a dead man he's in surprisingly good mettle.'

Jarvis joined in.

'The FBI investigated Stanley Meyer's crime scene and analyzed the blood found there. That analysis reported that no DNA match was found in any government database.'

'So?' the President challenged. 'Doesn't that prove that he wasn't at the scene?'

'No,' Jarvis replied, 'because the FBI Agent in charge of the investigation for some reason decided to take a second sample that she did not send to the Bureau and instead had tested by a private lab. And guess what they found?'

The President folded his hands on the table before him. 'Mitchell's DNA?'

'Alive and kicking,' Lopez replied.

'How does that tie this Mitchell to Director LeMay?'

'Ethan and Lopez were dispatched to Abu Dhabi on another mission that again concerned things of interest to MJ–12,' Jarvis explained. 'They were being pursued by Mitchell while I was in a Joint Chiefs of Staff meeting with LeMay. The Director wanted to know where Ethan and Lopez were, so I gave him their location – except I made a deliberate mistake and sent him in the wrong direction. As expected, Mitchell turned up with agents at his side exactly where I'd informed LeMay that Ethan and Nicola would be.' Jarvis sighed. 'He's involved Mister President, and Mitchell is the agent he uses to get his dirty work done for him. Two men were killed at the site in Abu Dhabi, one of them crushed to death beneath a twenty ton shipping container. Neither Mitchell nor LeMay care whose lives they take and now we have a situation where Majestic Twelve may have reason to allow Abrahem Nassir the chance to slip through our net and attack you directly.'

'Why would they do that?' the President asked.

'Because your administration's policies on the restriction of free trade and support for red–tape preventing the excesses of major banks and corporations interferes with MJ–12's main business of profit making,' Ethan explained. 'The profits of major corporations are reduced if they have to care for their workers better or can't use overseas sweatshops, or their weapons are banned by international treaties that your administration supports. These men of MJ–12 make most of their money off the back of the suffering of others less powerful, Mister President, and everything that you're doing is threatening that. I don't believe for one moment that they would directly conspire to assassinate you, but if they have the means to know that Abrahem Nassir is in the country and intent on attacking you, and the FBI has the lead in protecting us from that attack…'

The President nodded silently, already knowing how such a conspiracy could play out.

'Some of the country's biggest corporations finance presidential campaigns in order to ensure that any administration is allied to their business interests,' he said finally. 'I managed to win the election without such support, but it wasn't easy.'

'Then now is the time to strike,' Jarvis said. 'They have no hold over you, no way to control you, but once your time in the White House is over how long do you think it will be before a new President with less moral fibre is sitting in that chair?'

The President folded his hands over and rested his chin on them for a moment before he spoke.

'Organize the Joint Chiefs of Staff and send word to the CIA,' he said finally. 'We can't just arrest LeMay, but perhaps we can let him implicate himself should Nassir make it into the city. Ensure that the FBI is prevented from accessing any of the information that we have learned and let's distribute Abrahem Nassir's image to every law enforcement agency in the country.'

Jarvis stepped forward.

'I suggest you hold off on tomorrow's Trans Pacific ceremony too,' he said as the President stood to leave the bunker. 'You're going to be a target.'

The President smiled. 'I'm always a target, Mister Jarvis.' He looked at Ethan and Nicola. 'You have my authority to stop Nassir any way you can, and I assure you that for the time being at least the FBI will not be able to stop you. Track him down and stop him; *whatever it takes.*'

***

XXXIII

Broad Kill River,

Delaware

The waters of Cape May's Harbor of Refuge were silent and black as the small boat chugged its way north west toward a long stretch of Delaware coastline known as Slaughter Beach. Abrahem Nassir could not help but feel a grim amusement at the choice of names for the location of his entry into the United States.

The state of New Jersey was visible across the bay to his right, betrayed in the darkness by twinkling lights that were reflected across the rippling surface of the water. To his left beyond the sparsely populated coastline, just a hundred miles to the west, was Washington DC.

The enemy was close, he reflected, but he was closer. The narrow escape from the American soldiers in Somalia had cemented in both his mind and that of Tariq that there was no longer any time to waste. The Americans would locate the vessel Abrahem had used to travel from Kuwait to Somalia, interrogate its crew and learn of his movements. Abrahem doubted that the Somalian pirates would have held any loyalty to his cause once overpowered by the Americans, and it had only been Tariq's quick thinking that had allowed them to escape among the women and children, overpowering two Americans on the way out and scattering into the sparse bush with the coming of the dawn. With too many targets to follow, the Americans had been misled and both Abrahem and Tariq had escaped south.

His journey across the Atlantic had been facilitated on a private jet owned by Tariq out of Jomo Kenyatta International Airport in Nairobi, Kenya, the customs officials at the airport easily bribed. The flight had landed in Dakar, Senegal, to refuel before making the long flight across the Atlantic Ocean to land in the Dominican Republic. From there he had boarded a maritime ship bound for Maine before once again leaving the vessel *en route* off the coast of Delaware and being picked up by a smaller boat out of the town of Bowers, on the shores of the equally grotesquely named Murderkill River.

A deck hand approached him with a small cup of hot, sweet coffee. Abrahem took the cup with a nod and a smile of gratitude, his bones still aching from the bitter chill of the North Atlantic. Despite the provision of a life raft and food, Abrahem had been forced to wait over an hour for the small boat to locate him as he floated alone on the dark waters, praying to Allah that the United States Coast Guard would not stumble across him first. Good fortune had been on his side and he had remained undetected. Now, he sat wrapped in blankets as he waited for his muscles to warm up once more as the boat approached the shore.

America.

He had never seen the country before, despite hearing so much about it and having hated it with all the considerable passion in his heart for almost half of his life. The tranquil shores and twinkling lights against the starry sky reminded him somewhat of Basra, and for a moment he once again allowed himself the thought that perhaps the people of the two countries were not so different. It was the politicians who were to blame, the warmongering *"hawks"* of the American Senate and their thirst for oil, money and power. Everybody in their right mind in the entire world knew that the invasion of Iraq had been a business venture, a hostile take–over undertaken beneath the thin veil of the liberation of a country from the rule of a tyrant. What they didn't shout so loudly was that one tyrant had merely been replaced by another, the flag waving democracy of the United States that had raped Iraq of its finances, its soul, and then abandoned it to crumble beneath the blind corruption of Islamic militants and warlords. Furthermore, it was now widely accepted around the world that America's administration of the time had lied in order to justify the war; there had never been any evidence of weapons of mass destruction in Iraq, and anybody who had raised such a point had been ridiculed and even betrayed by that same administration.

Abrahem's resolve hardened. The American people had voted for their leaders, who touted their democracy to the rest of the world as an example of leadership by the people, for the people, despite the fact that they then so brazenly acted without any consideration for those people in whose name they claimed their positions of power.

Abrahem recalled his youth, of the day when the Americans had first rolled into Basra to cheers and cries of gratitude. Abrahem had cheered with them, ecstatic at the presence of troops from a country where the voice of the people actually mattered, overjoyed at where their protection might take Iraq. And then the troops had fired all of the police and the army, and then the American companies had come into the city and begun rebuilding things that did not need rebuilding, repairing things that the Americans themselves had destroyed during their fighter–bomber attacks of "*shock and awe*", had refused to employ the impoverished builders and artisans of Iraq in favor of paying their own people via the American government.

Throughout this, the Iraqi people had suffered more hardship than they had under Saddam Hussein, and when the uprisings began in Mosul and Basra and across the country the American companies abandoned their unnecessary projects unfinished, claiming a "lack of security". Having created dissolution, poverty and dismay among ordinary Iraqis sufficient to cause a revolt, they then blamed that revolt for their failure to complete the rebuilding programs they had been paid such vast sums to undertake. They left, their pockets lined with all of the money in Iraq and abandoned hundreds of thousands of Iraqis dead or dying, Abrahem's beloved parents, siblings, wife and children among them.

The cup in his hand shattered and crashed to the deck. Abrahem blinked as he looked down and realized that he had crushed it, the jagged debris cutting into the palm of his hand. Blood glistened in the faint light as a deck hand approached, concern on his features.

'Are you okay?'

The young man's voice was tinged with the lilt of Arabic but also stained with the twang of an American. An immigrant, who had perhaps fled Iraq as Abrahem had been forced to do.

'I am fine,' he replied, his voice gravelly with pain and grief as he clenched his bloody fist. 'How long until we make landfall?'

'Ten minutes,' the boy replied. 'Our berth is just up river from here.'

Abrahem nodded but remained otherwise silent as he watched blood ooze from between his fingers and drip onto the deck at his feet. The deck hand watched him for a moment longer and then shrank away as so many people did, sensing somehow the unrivalled hatred that emanated from Abrahem like something alive. The time for his vengeance was now close and he vowed that this would be the last time the blood of his family would be spilled in the fight against American colonialism.

A sudden bright light flared to the north, swept across the water and shone directly at the boat as Abrahem looked up and heard an American voice echoing across the water.

'United States Coast Guard! Unidentified vessel in the channel, heave to and prepare to be boarded!'

Abrahem felt surprise and fear pulse like a bolt of poison through his veins as the captain called aft to him in a harsh whisper.

'They must already be looking for you!'

Abrahem should have known that the damned Americans would be waiting for him already. He had of course guessed that the Americans would assume his target to be in the United States but he enjoyed the thought of them panicking to reach him before he carried out his attack. The fear of his enemy was a pleasure for Abrahem, to be savored at every opportunity.

'Get out of sight below decks!'

Abrahem whirled toward the boat's stern and the hatch there that led into the depths of the boat. He opened the hatch and then let it close again with a dull thump before creeping further aft toward the boat's stern rail. The inky black water surged with foam as the engines churned the river behind the boat, and Abrahem could already feel the chill embrace of the icy water as he pulled off his clothes. He only had one dry kit with him, having planned to get wet only once, and he knew that he would not survive long if he reached the shore in damp clothes. He placed his dry clothes carefully in the deepest, darkest corner of the deck that he could find.

As the boat came chugging to a halt on the river and the engines coughed to a halt, Abrahem slipped over the stern of the boat and vanished like a dangerous thought into the black water.

*

'Prepare to be boarded!'

The crewman's loud hailer echoed across the otherwise silent water, bounced back by the tree line a half mile away. The eighty seven foot coastal patrol boat on which the captain stood slowly eased in toward the small vessel that had chugged its way up the channel from the open ocean. Ordinarily such an act would not have concerned the Coast Guard, but with Delaware's wide open coastline a haven for drugs coming up from the south, any boat in the channel at four o'clock in the morning was suspicious. More than once the Coast Guard had hauled hundreds of thousands of dollars' worth of high–grade street drugs off small vessels just like this one.

The tug was grubby, patches of rust lining its cabin, and he could see only two men at the helm. Both were dark skinned, foreign looking, their hands in the air and their eyes squinting against the powerful lights flooding the tug's deck. The captain had seen the reports issued by the Coast Guard alerting crews to a potential terrorist threat from illegal immigrants attempting to infiltrate the United States in Washington DC and the surrounding areas, and right now he felt tension aching in his joints as he called out again.

'Keep your hands in the air where we can see them!'

The Coast Guard boat slid in alongside the tug and the captain, a pistol held in both hands close to his body, jumped across onto the tug's deck. As the only part of the Department of Homeland Security that was also a part of the military, the Coast Guard patrol boat and its three crewmembers were all armed.

'Take it easy,' the captain said to the two sailors as he advanced upon the tug's small wheel house. 'Keep your arms up and turn around slowly.'

The two crewmen did as he commanded, turning around and facing the wheel as the captain moved behind them. He checked to ensure that he was covered by his comrades before he holstered his pistol and then cuffed them both.

'What brings you out onto the water this late at night?' he asked them as he turned them around.

'Fishing,' the older of the two said. 'The bigger fish come out in the early hours.'

'That's true,' the captain agreed. 'But you need nets to fish them, so where's your gear?'

'We use floating nets,' the younger man replied. 'We put them out off shore and will return to them with the dawn.'

The captain eyed both of the men, his instincts tingling with the sense that something was amiss. He pulled his flashlight out and scanned the interior of the tug. As he swept the beam across the stern, he saw a small pile of clothes close to the stern rail.

Concern flashed through him like a bolt of lightning and he turned to shout a warning to the patrol boat as one hand reached for his pistol again.

'You'd better call in, we've got a swimmer in the…'

The captain saw the bodies of his two colleagues lying on the deck of their patrol boat only for an instant before his view was blocked by a fast moving shadow that filled his vision.

The figure loomed at him, ghoulishly illuminated by the harsh white lights of the patrol boat. The captain glimpsed the naked man's muscular body, water sparkling as it snaked down his flanks, his hair wet and lank and his eyes dark and fearsome as something flashed between them.

The captain felt a thin strip of white pain sear his throat as the naked man gripped his wrist and stayed his pistol. Warm blood flooded thickly down the captain's chest as he was slammed against the wheelhouse, the naked man pinning him there as he struck with the blade once more. The wicked knife plunged deep into the captain's throat, and though he writhed with terminal desperation the weapon sliced his arteries within seconds and the life drained out of his body as the darkness and the cold seeped in.

*

Abrahem watched the Coast Guard sailor's body slump to the deck at his feet, which was now slick with blood still pumping from the deep wounds in the mariner's neck. Beside him, he heard the younger of the tug's two crewmen turn aside and vomit over the rail into the water.

'There is not much time,' Abrahem said as he turned to the older man. 'The Coast Guard will be here within minutes once they realize they cannot contact their comrades. We must make shore and disappear.'

The tug's captain glanced at the patrol boat and the bodies of the other two crewmen slumped against the controls. Abrahem had killed them silently, like some horrific beast of the night, and then moved back aboard the tug to finish off their captain. Now he stood in the harsh light, naked and smeared with thick blood, the blade dripping in his grasp.

'Move, now!' Abrahem snapped.

The captain and his crewman stumbled over themselves as they hurried to carry out his order, and Abrahem strolled to the stern and dried himself.

America will know now for certain that I have arrived, he realized.

And he smiled in the darkness.

***

XXXIV

Ronald Reagan Washington DC Airport

Hannah Ford walked off the Boeing 747–400 in a daze, her thoughts fuzzy as she followed the crowds by unthinking reflex through the terminal. Vaughn walked alongside her as they fought their way past the lengthy queues already forming heavy barriers between themselves and the terminal exits. A US Marshall led the way, having been on the same flight and informed of the importance of their mission.

The United red–eye out of Hong Kong had taken eighteen hours, stopping off briefly at New York, during which time Hannah had made a call to the Bureau and informed Director LeMay of what she knew. Since then there had been no contact and her cell phone was silent as she checked it for messages or missed calls.

'Nothing,' she informed Vaughn as they reached the security areas and passport control. It took only a couple of minutes for their identity badges to see them through the security check points, the Marshall turning back into the terminal.

'He's already here,' Vaughn said as they walked out of the airport and into the morning sunshine. 'Must be, and they've got their hands full searching for him.'

Hannah tried to push her lethargy away. Despite the length of the flight she had been unable to sleep, driven to distraction by the helplessness of being trapped aboard an aircraft and unable to act on her instincts and pursue the men that she knew were coming here to do harm to her country. Her eyes itched and occasional spells of dizziness swayed her as she tried to remember where they had left the pool car.

'It's over here,' Vaughn said as he spotted their vehicle.

Hannah followed him across the lot and saw the blue Lincoln parked where they had left it. She yanked up the trunk and tossed in their small travel bags before she made her way to the passenger's side.

'You not driving?' Vaughn asked in surprise.

'I've got a call to make,' she replied as she climbed in.

The interior of the car was warm as Vaughn drove and the sunshine beaming through the windshield lulled her into a warm lullaby of sleep.

Hannah closed her eyes and sat in silence, letting the motion of the vehicle turning through the parking lot and the whisper of the engine draw her ever deeper into sleep.

The shrill warble of her cell phone snapped her back into life and she stared vacantly down at it. A number she did not recognize awaited her, the screen glowing bright blue as she answered.

'Ford.'

'LeMay.'

'Sir, we need to talk.'

'You've been cut out,' LeMay replied. *'We all have.'*

'Cut out of what?' Hannah asked as she set the cell to speaker phone.

'The investigation,' LeMay snapped back, anger clear in his tones. *'The President has handed the entire investigation over to the Defense Intelligence Agency. We're out of the loop.'*

Hannah's addled brain struggled to focus.

'How can the FBI be out of the loop on something like this?!'

'I can only assume that Warner and Lopez are spreading disinformation about what's happening. Warner has personal history with the president, who appears to be taking his advice at face value. I don't know what he's said as I wasn't invited to a meeting they had at the White House yesterday afternoon.'

Hannah reeled mentally as she tried to think of something useful to say.

'We're sure that Abrahem Nassir is either in the country already or arriving shortly,' she said.

'He's in the country all right,' LeMay replied. *'Homeland just reported the murder of three Coast Guard officers out near Cape May, Delaware. Their patrol boat went incognito in the early hours and their bodies were later found aboard. They'd had their throats cut.'*

'Does Homeland have a trail?'

'They've identified the boat they think must have picked up Abrahem Nassir to bring him into the country, and another larger vessel that sailed up from South America yesterday for Maine. It looks like Nassir jumped ship a couple of times. His accomplices stole the boat that brought him in, but they're in the wind and so is Nassir. Homeland's working on it as we speak.'

'Damn it,' Hannah snapped as she slammed a hand down on her thigh in futility. 'He's got to be heading for a major target. He's come this far, he's not going to settle for bombing a convenience store. He'll hit the Capitol or the White House or something.'

'The White House is on full alert, but the President also has an open–air address this evening on the South Lawn as part of a Trans Pacific Trade agreement ceremony celebrating a new deal with China.'

Hannah's mind stopped working for a moment as she reflected on this new piece of information. She could feel her brain ticking over but it was almost as though she could not quite control the train of her thoughts.

'Who will be there?' she asked impulsively.

'Most of the administration, at least three former Presidents and First Ladies and Senators from fifteen states, along with the President of the People's Republic of China.'

'That's a lot of big wheels in one place,' Vaughn observed as he drove. 'He might try to hit them all at once.'

Hannah shook her head to clear it as she replied.

'He can't have travelled with any kind of incendiary device, so he'll have to make contact with somebody here. He has a network, finance, people supporting him and helping him on his way. If we can pin them down it might lead us to Abrahem before he can strike.'

'I already have teams on it,' LeMay said. *'We'll be arresting known Islamist sympathizers and already have half a dozen in custody. We're hoping that we can break Nassir's chain of support sufficiently that he cannot carry out his attack, but it's a long shot.'*

'Too long,' Hannah agreed. 'We can't take the chance that he'll not have something already prepared, something or somebody here ready to go. This whole thing is about revenge on the United States, and given the way that he's travelled he must have planned this for months, perhaps even years.'

'Everything must have been laid out in advance,' Vaughn said, 'he must have flown from Africa to South America to get here so fast. That means huge financial power behind him. The money trail's our best bet.'

'Agreed,' LeMay replied. *'Right now we're looking into the financials of several companies, including the one that hired a private jet out of Kenya for The Dominican Republic yesterday and is likely the route that Nassir took. I'll pass on the address of the company to you both.'*

Hannah nodded. 'What about Mitchell?'

'What about him?'

'He turned up in Hong Kong, had a Chinese operative by the name of Jin Chen tied to a tree and was torturing him for information. It was he who left me for dead at the hands of the Chinese, and his presence at the scene of Jin Chen's murder is the only thing that will prevent us from being arrested for the homicide. Mitchell means business and he's clearly as involved with this operation as he was with the death of Stanley Meyer. What's his connection, sir?'

'I don't know, but he's not the priority right now Agent Ford. Your priority is locating Abrahem Nassir and apprehending him before he can initiate a national tragedy. I don't want another nine–eleven on our hands because we dropped the ball here.'

'We haven't dropped the ball,' Hannah shot back, 'it's been taken from us and we're being hunted because of that.'

'That's not the way the media will see it if the White House lawns look like a scene from a horror movie tonight,' LeMay replied. *'I can't get any closer to this operation than I already am without attracting the attention of the DIA. As far as they're aware, you two are still pinned down in Hong Kong and are wanted fugitives – law enforcement will be looking for you if I pass on the information I received from our Hong Kong office and I can only hang onto it for so long. You're the only ones who can get close to this now and if you want to clear your names there's only one way to do it. Find Nassir and report back to me.'*

'Yes sir,' Hannah replied, and the line went dead.

She looked across at Vaughn, who raised an eyebrow.

'I don't believe this is happening,' he said finally. 'He wants us to go rogue and finish this on our own?'

Hannah nodded, fatigue weighing heavily on her shoulders as she looked in the rear view mirror and saw her reflection. She looked like crap, her nose still swollen and her eyes bloodshot and bleary.

'We're not exactly in the best of shape right now,' Vaughn added, as if noticing the direction of her gaze.

Vaughn's face was also puffy from the blows he'd received at the hands of the Chinese, and he looked as though he were some kind of street thug recovering from a particularly rough night out.

'At least for once we don't look like federal agents,' she pointed out. 'Maybe we can get closer to Nassir and his people this way.'

Vaughn thought for a moment.

'Do we have an address for the company that financed the private jet flight out of Africa?'

Hannah looked down vaguely at her cell phone and realized that LeMay had already sent a series of files to her. She opened one and scanned the contents.

'It's registered to an address on 8th Street South East,' she replied, 'Vantage Aviation Hire.'

Vaughn switched lanes as they crossed the Rochambreau Memorial Bridge over the Potomac.

'Let's get down there and figure this out.'

*

Dulles International Airport, Virginia

The Bombadier Global 6000 private jet touched down on Dulles' runway, Aaron Mitchell watching the terminals and taxiways race past as the aircraft engaged its reverse thrust system and the pilots applied the brakes. The large, sleek jet slowed dramatically before it turned off the runway and began taxiing to the executive terminal.

Mitchell pushed away the fatigue aching through his bones as saw a pair of glossy black limousines awaiting him near the aircraft parking area. He knew that Majestic Twelve were keen to obtain the technology that the Chinese had developed, although he still had no idea himself precisely what they intended to do with it. The constant lack of information was both troubling and frustrating for him: frustrating because he could not effectively apply what he didn't know to the search he was conducting, and troubling because he could not be sure of the group's motives on this occasion.

The jet came to a stop near the terminals and Mitchell stood and stalked to the jet's door. A stewardess opened it and Mitchell stepped out into the fresh morning air and descended the jet's steps. He strode across to the waiting vehicles, and was directed by a suited agent toward the limousine on the right.

The door opened and Mitchell climbed in and slammed it shut behind him.

'What news?'

Victor Wilms sat inside the vehicle, his gray eyes settling on Mitchell's. Opposite him sat FBI Director LeMay.

'The Chinese were behind the abduction of four NSA agents in Kowloon in 1997,' Mitchell replied, 'as we presumed. They have further developed technology stolen from the NSA agents that allows them to control human minds, and have managed to implant members of the United States military during the Iraq conflict. They used Iraqi citizens to implant the technology during normal surgical procedures, one of whom, an Abrahem Nassir, is now on the warpath here in the United States.'

Victor nodded slowly.

'This is what we feared. The use by the Chinese of unreliable runners to transport such sensitive technology through a war zone was always fraught with the danger of betrayal. Now the technology could be used against us at any moment.'

Director LeMay rubbed his chin thoughtfully.

'The DIA has taken the lead in the investigation and the FBI are out of the loop,' he said.

'Does the administration suspect something?' Victor asked with interest. 'Do you still have their trust?'

'I'm working on that,' LeMay replied, 'but it's worth considering the possibility that the president has been made aware of Majestic Twelve and its work. The DIA's Director Nellis has made something of a mission in hunting us down, and now they're taking things to the next level.'

Mitchell frowned.

'MJ–12 is secure, but the President is not. It could take weeks to find a thorough way to test all of his staff for implants and then implement that test. Nassir is likely to strike within the next forty eight hours and I don't think that escape is part of his plan. He'll finish what he's started or die trying.'

LeMay looked at Victor, who was staring thoughtfully out of the limousine's window.

'Do you have instructions?' LeMay asked the old man. 'On how best to protect the president?'

Victor thought for a moment before he replied.

'Yes,' he said finally. 'We don't protect the president. We prioritize recovering the technology for future use.'

Mitchell stared at Victor for a moment, his brain struggling to digest what he had heard. 'Say that again?'

'We don't need to protect the president,' Victor repeated. 'The FBI are out of the loop and Majestic Twelve has been looking forward to the president's second term coming to an end. If that should occur sooner, then so be it.'

LeMay's face paled slightly. 'You're talking about treason and murder.'

'Oh come now!' Victor chuckled. 'It's a bit late to be getting a conscience, Gordon.'

Mitchell said nothing as he watched Victor formulate his plan.

'You have agents on the ground, as promised?' Victor demanded of LeMay.

'Two of them,' LeMay confirmed. 'They're working directly for me and don't know anything about Majestic Twelve.'

'Good,' Victor said. 'Use them as your patsies, while Aaron here simply follows the DIA until they are able to obtain the technology that either Nassir or the Chinese have brought to the country. He will take that technology from them, but we must leave Nassir's players in place.'

LeMay's eyes narrowed. 'Why take such a risk?'

Victor turned to Mitchell, ignoring the Director's question.

'You will ensure that Abrahem Nassir achieves his goal,' Victor said. 'I will obtain you direct access to the target, once we know for sure who it is. The assassination of our President will both clear the path for a presidency more in line with the objectives of Majestic Twelve, and will generate suitable public outrage to justify both a new president with an active war–footing policy and further military intervention in rogue states and other overseas interests. Agreed?'

Mitchell said nothing, staring at LeMay as the limousine pulled out of the airport toward Washington DC.

***

XXXV

Murderkill River, Delaware

'This is it,' Lopez said.

Ethan slowed their car and pulled into the sidewalk alongside the river as they saw a police cordon raised around the jetties, a Coast Guard vessel moored nearby around which swarmed Homeland Security officers.

They got out and hurried down to the jetty, Ethan feeling somewhat more important than usual as he held up his DIA identification badge along with Lopez and they were allowed to cross the line into the crime scene.

A Homeland agent by the name of Briggs, stern faced and with short–cropped blond hair, intercepted them.

'You been sent down from DIA?' he asked.

'Jarvis sent us,' Lopez confirmed and then added: 'We're running point for the White House.'

'Ain't you the thing?' Briggs replied with a raised eyebrow. 'Homeland's been ordered to bring you up to speed. Three Coast Guard officers pronounced dead at the scene, which was out there in the bay. Got another vessel moored up nearby, a tug that we figure was used by Abrahem Nassir to get ashore.'

Ethan looked to where the rusty tug sat at its jetty, two more officers guarding it.

'How long ago did this happen?'

'Four this morning, which makes it two hours ago,' Briggs replied. 'They've got a good head–start on us. Local law enforcement blocked all routes out of the town within a half hour of the call coming in, but that was more than enough time for Nassir to high tail it out of here along with any accomplices he may have had with him.'

Ethan eyed the tug again. 'Too small for long distance sailing and too slow to have brought Nassir here from South America. Was there another ship involved?'

'Coast Guard's looking into it and has record of a trade vessel out of the Dominican Republic passing the shore headed north in the small hours. If Nassir jumped ship, he could have been picked up here and brought ashore. Coast Guard was already on the lookout for him so they likely pulled this tug over and that was it.'

'He's taking big risks,' Lopez said as she observed the sight of the three bodies being loaded into body bags and pushed away on gurneys toward waiting ambulances. 'Not hesitating to kill in cold blood.'

'He's enjoying it,' Ethan guessed. 'Nassir's no Islamist, but he's taking as many lives as he can between here and wherever he's headed.'

'We figure DC,' Briggs said. 'He'll hit the highest profile target he can with maximum punch, take out as many bodies as possible before he gets ventilated. He's sure got nothing to lose now with pretty much every law enforcement body in the country out looking for him.'

Ethan turned to Lopez as they walked toward the battered old tug further down the shoreline.

'He's going to a hell of a lot of trouble to kill as many people as he can,' Lopez said as she walked alongside Ethan.

'Yeah,' Ethan replied. 'That's what bothers me. He's virtually screaming at us that he's here, massively increasing the chances that he'll get captured. It only takes one lucky break for us to pin him down and I can't believe that he's come this far only to take such a huge gamble with his plan.'

Lopez frowned.

'You think that he's got something else up his sleeve?' she asked. 'We know he doesn't have to go in directly if he's managed to implant somebody close to the President but he has to be in the general vicinity of his target, right? Just like the guys who hit General Thompson. The District's only a hundred miles from here.'

Ethan nodded.

'Yeah, he's landed in just the kind of place that you'd expect him to. But if he'd simply gone quietly ashore we'd be none the wiser. I don't get why he'd hit a bunch of Coast Guard officers just to provoke us when he could likely have slipped away quietly instead. They were near the shore by all accounts. He could have made it.'

'Maybe he's not much of a swimmer,' Lopez countered. 'Maybe the Coast Guard went in a bit heavy and spooked him?'

Ethan climbed aboard the dirty tug, little more really than a wheelhouse atop a rusting hull with some cluttered ropes and jerry cans in the stern, some lashed into place, others loose.

'Not experienced seamen,' Ethan said as he observed the mess. 'Coast Guard said that the boat's unregistered and probably was abandoned here. They must have stolen it and then used it to pick Nassir up.'

Lopez crouched down alongside the wheelhouse and looked closely at a large, blackened blood stain on the deck.

'Throat cut,' she murmured.

Ethan watched as her eyes tracked a series of bloody foot prints that tracked to the stern and she speculated on what had happened.

'Barefoot, so he'd probably removed his clothes and slipped off the tug, then attacked the two guys on the patrol vessel….'

'Before coming back aboard and finishing off the last guy,' Ethan agreed, 'which means he's a pro, able to kill silently. But that's my point – if he was already in the water he might have got away.'

Lopez looked at the junk in the boat.

'Unless he wants us to follow his trail,' she suggested.

Ethan thought about that for a moment.

'Nassir wants revenge and he probably likes the idea of us panicking over his arrival in America. The bigger the trail of carnage he manages to achieve, the worse we'll look when word finally gets out.'

Lopez nodded as she stood.

'And it all leads up to the attack in Washington DC. The media will examine the chain of events and deem the intelligence agencies to have again failed to protect America.'

'Maximum embarrassment for the administration,' Ethan said, 'even if the President survives any direct attack.'

Lopez was about to reply when Ethan's cell rang. He answered it and set it immediately to speaker phone

'Ethan, it's Doug. We've got a trace on the company that hired the jet that flew Nassir to South America. They're based in DC, Vantage Aviation Hire.'

'You got any names?' Ethan asked.

'Nothing yet, and they're likely an intermediary acting as agents for whoever needed the flight. If we send Homeland in they'll bust the joint and the FBI are out of the game until we can corner LeMay. You need to get over there and see what you can find out.'

'We're on it,' Ethan promised. 'Nassir's here, we're certain of that.'

'I know,' Jarvis replied. *'There's one more thing. We just got information from Homeland that several Chinese agents were detected entering the country through JFK last night. There are at least eight of them all on different flights in from Hong Kong, Singapore and Beijing. Homeland couldn't arrest them due to lack of evidence, and they had no reason to detain anybody. They placed a watch team on four of the men but lost track of them when they reached DC on connecting flights.'*

Ethan glanced at Lopez. 'You think they're in on the act too somehow?'

'Nassir is believed to have reneged on a deal with the Chinese in order to obtain this technology for his own ends. That can't have pleased the Chinese too much, so maybe they're searching for him too?'

'If so, they might get in the way,' Lopez pointed out. 'Having a bunch of Communists running about DC looking for him isn't going to help us any. They're not going to be friendly.'

'And they might have an agenda of their own,' Ethan replied, 'something more than just hunting Nassir down. They have the same technology that he does and might try something themselves while they're here – they've hacked just about every other US computer system going, there's only the minds of the people left.'

'Get to DC,' Jarvis advised. *'There's nothing else for it. We've got to assume that Nassir is heading there and that he's planning to hit the President. I suggest that you split up, one of you staying by the President's side and the other in the field, and liaise as best you can.'*

'Roger that,' Ethan said. 'We're on our way. Stay in touch.'

The cell phone went silent and Ethan stared at it for a long moment.

'What?' Lopez asked.

For a moment Ethan could not reply as something nagged at him, a thought just out of reach. Lopez tugged at his arm.

'C'mon,' she urged. 'We've gotta move.'

***

XXXVI

Bethesda, Washington DC

Abrahem Nassir hurried out of the back of an unmarked white van that had parked close to the sidewalk alongside a series of lock–ups near a shopping mall, the bright sunshine much like that of his desert home but tinted with the muddy stain of pollution and smog. He wasted no time in crossing the sidewalk and entering the sanctuary offered by lock up number four.

The location, like everything else, had been chosen long in advance. All of the buildings were privately rented and occupied by vehicle repair companies and dry cleaning firms, most of which were yet to open.

'Salaam, my brother.'

Abrahem's eyes adjusted to the gloom inside as he saw Tariq emerge from the shadows, the old man's moustache gray against his dark skin.

'Salaam,' Abrahem smiled as they embraced. 'Your journey was good?'

'A touch more luxurious than yours, no doubt,' Tariq replied as he looked the younger man up and down. 'But then I am not yet a wanted man.'

'Give it time, my friend. Soon they will be looking for you too.'

'Which is why we must hurry,' Tariq agreed. 'Your work cannot be completed unless you remain in the shadows until the very last moment.'

Abrahem looked past Tariq to where a series of laptop computers were arrayed across a table, all of them switched on and their screens glowing in the otherwise dark room.

'Is it done?' he asked.

Behind the laptops sat two men, both of them typing quietly, their brows furrowed and their faces illuminated by the unnatural glow of the screens.

'They are completing the task as we speak,' Tariq replied. 'They have done well, my friend. Soon we will have complete control.'

Abrahem moved closer and watched as the men worked feverishly, lines of code spilling like digital rain down the screens.

Abrahem had been fortunate enough to have been educated in Saudi Arabia at a private school funded by his late father. There he had learned much about the rest of the world and the technological wonders it held. Although he himself was by no means computer literate, in the sense that he could not program computers or write code, he knew enough to understand than in the digital age a mastery of computers was the key to true power. Vast amounts of data crossed the United States every single second of every day, held its infrastructure together, allowed people to communicate across immense distances without delay. The networks now installed allowed video conferencing and satellite links to the other side of the globe, and all of it was controlled by computers.

'This is the future,' Tariq said as he moved alongside his young companion. 'No more bullets and bombs, no more thugs flying airplanes into buildings. With this technology we can strike at the very heart of our enemy with surgical precision, just as the Americans boast that they can do in our homelands.'

Abrahem nodded. He recalled his rage, boiling even now just out of sight beneath the lid he kept upon it, as he watched the images of American jets sending missiles with impossible accuracy into homes in Iraq, killing militants but also women and children. The Americans liked to play down how many civilian casualties had died in the Iraq wars, liked to pretend that their invasions had been clinically precise, but Abrahem knew that the figure was in the hundreds of thousands. Entire villages had been wiped out, generations of Iraqis lost to the hammer of America's *"shock and awe"* campaign, often bitterly referred to as *"shocking gore"* by a media largely opposed to the invasions.

In return, the Islamist militias that had risen up in the crumbling ruins left behind when the Americans had withdrawn from Iraq had then begun an equally barbaric campaign of their own to grab power in the provinces. With Sharia Law their banner, they had murdered and tortured and maimed and oppressed with all of the fury their firebrand mullahs could wield, ending the lives of countless more of Iraq's sons and daughters, until now all that remained was the battered, sun scorched remains of what had once been a strong and united country.

And all of it could be blamed upon one individual.

Now, Abrahem could strike back against that individual in a way that nobody had ever seen before. He smiled to himself, his fury momentarily satisfied as he thought of the carnage that he would cause so very soon. But in this horrendous act of international terrorism, unlike that of America's, there would be no significant civilian casualties but for those who stood directly in his way. Their suffering would come in a different form, the psychological terror that their country was not just unsafe but that their very minds and bodies were no longer their own, that *anybody* could be controlled.

America had laid waste to Iraq. Now one Iraqi would lay waste to the *American Dream* forever.

'How long before the networks are complete?' he asked, eager to begin.

'They will be at work for another hour,' Tariq informed him, 'and then it will be done. We will have control and nobody will know it.'

The screens to Abrahem's right showed not data streams but maps of Washington DC, and on those maps were points of light that denoted areas known as "dead zones", one of which they were occupying at that very moment. The dead zones were littered across the city and indeed every city in the western world, and Abrahem had selected two of them in Washington DC: Bethesda, and an area just to the north of Whitehaven Parkway on DC's west side, close to the Potomac.

'The direct links can be established after leaving the zones?' Abrahem asked.

'All is in hand,' Tariq assured him. 'Right now, all we have to do is ensure that the Americans are headed in precisely the wrong direction just when we want them to be. Before they know what they have done it will already be over, and every American in the country will experience a *shock and awe* all of their own as they watch their televisions and cower. The whole world will know what you have done my friend, for every single one of them will be watching it for years to come.'

Abrahem clenched his fists as a grim smile spread across his face and his dark eyes reflected the glow of the screens.

*

'Where is she?'

'Just wait a moment!'

The interior of the van was getting hotter by the minute, the sunshine outside flaring through the windscreen as the two technicians sat in front of their screens in the rear of the van and tapped commands furiously into their computers.

Jiang Sin stood behind the technicians with his arms folded as they worked, the van rocking as it drove along a road to the north of America's Capitol. Jiang was a tall man, a former soldier now employed by the People's Republic of China's Ministry of State Security. A patriot, he found himself on enemy soil on a mission that he would never have believed he would undertake, America's population toiling at their desks and offices and under the burning sunshine, unaware of the catastrophe mere hours away.

'There, we have her!'

Jiang Sin reached out to steady himself on the back of the technicians' chairs as he leaned forward and peered at an unsteady image on one of the screens.

It looked as though somebody were filming themselves driving with a hand–held camera, the image jerking this way and that, but Jiang Sin could see that she was sitting in the passenger seat of a vehicle and talking to somebody, presumably the driver.

'Is that definitely her?'

'Yes,' said the technician. 'We have software monitoring her vocal patterns. It's her.'

Jiang Sin gripped the back of the seats as he listened to the woman's voice.

'… we're not going to track these people down quickly enough if we go through the normal chain of command. We need to go in real hard and figure out where he is, fast, then make our move.'

A male voice replied from somewhere alongside her.

'We're not supposed to even be on the case, remember? If we make a big show of ourselves down here we'll be the ones in custody.'

'I don't care,' came the woman's reply. *'I want Nassir.'*

Jiang Chen finally allowed a smile to creep onto his features as he patted the shoulders of the two men before him.

'Maintain a close watch on her and keep us within a quarter mile of wherever they go, understood?'

'Yes sir!'

Jiang Chen pulled a cell phone from his pocket and speed dialed a number. As soon as the line connected, he spoke quickly.

'We have them. Stay close to us and be ready to move as soon as I say so.'

***

XXXVII

Vantage Aviation Hire, Washington DC

Ethan sat in the passenger seat of an unmarked Metropolitan Police Department cruiser as he waited for the word to go.

The building across the street was small, nestled among many others on a tree lined boulevard where a parade of former three–story homes had been converted into small shops and businesses. Most belonged to financiers, law firms and other professional outfits, polished brass plaques on the walls.

'You got a visual yet?' Ethan asked.

His voice was carried via microphone transmitter to one of several officers arrayed around the area, all waiting for the right time to launch the raid.

'Negative,' came the reply, *'no movement inside.'*

Ethan shifted in his seat and tried to get comfortable. The sunshine streaming through the windshield was uncomfortably hot, but they could not sit with the air conditioning running for fear of overheating the engine, and Ethan might possibly be recognized if he stepped out of the vehicle too soon.

He figured that whoever owned the offices would be showing up soon enough, and as soon as they did he would move in with the police and take all of the company's records for the staff at the DIA to sift through in an attempt to track down Abrahem Nassir's benefactors. He had a court's subpoena in his pocket, clearing them to confiscate anything that might lead to a much needed breakthrough in the case.

Ethan rubbed his eyes and sucked in a deep breath of air.

'You okay, man?' the officer next to him asked.

'Long night,' Ethan replied. 'When this is over I'm gonna sleep for a week.'

'Wish I could,' the officer replied. 'Two kids, both under three.'

'I'd rather take on these terrorists,' Ethan murmured in reply, still convinced that young children would be the end of him.

'Most days so would I,' the officer replied. 'Coming to work is a nice break, and…'

'We've got movement.'

Adrenaline shot through Ethan's veins and he sat up in his seat as he scanned the street behind him using the vehicle's mirrors for any sign of the company's owners. Almost immediately he saw a sleek, silver Mercedes pull into the sidewalk outside the building and a young man climbed out. He was dressed in a smart suit, his hair black and cut short, his shirt crisp and white, every inch the DC entrepreneur.

'Wait for him to get the door open,' Ethan whispered into his microphone.

The radio remained silent as the man strode up the steps to the front of the building and reached out with a key to unlock the door. Ethan reached out for his door handle, and as the suited man opened the door Ethan climbed out of the vehicle.

'Go, now!'

From all corners of the street police officers appeared with weapons drawn as they sprinted toward the building. Ethan ran hard, feeling slightly restricted beneath the bullet proof vest that he wore, and dashed up the steps even as the suited man whirled with eyes wide at the shouts coming from the officers.

'Stand still, hands on your head!' Ethan yelled.

The suited man panicked and tried to slam the door shut. Ethan leaned his shoulder in as he ran and smashed into the door just before the latch caught. The door flew open and the suited man was hurled backwards onto the tiled floor of the corridor inside as Ethan skittered to a halt over him with his pistol aimed between the man's eyes.

'Hands on your head!'

The man cowered with his hands over his head as the police barged into the building, Ethan moving to one side to let them pour in and apprehend the suited man. Ethan lowered his pistol as he watched officers flood through the interior of the building and clear the other rooms, thundering up the staircases and barging through doors.

'All clear!'

The police stood back from the suited man, who was now on his knees with his hands cuffed behind his back as Ethan holstered his pistol and grabbed hold of his collar. Ethan hauled the man to his feet and slammed him against the wall.

'Didn't your mother ever tell you it's rude to slam a door in somebody's face?'

A sliver of defiance broke through the suited man's fear. 'It's rude to kick somebody's door in too.'

'Why'd you try to shut me out?'

'I was afraid, I didn't know who you were.'

'Didn't the uniforms give you a clue?' Ethan asked as he jabbed a thumb over his shoulder at the watching police.

'I didn't see them first. I saw you and you're not wearing a uniform.'

'Name?'

'Rasheed,' the man replied. 'Rasheed Adel.'

'This your business, Rasheed?'

'Yes. I mean, no. I run it for my uncle but he's never here.'

'Who's your uncle, Rasheed?'

'Tariq,' Rasheed replied. 'What's this all about?'

Ethan looked over his shoulder to see the main office behind him, sunlight streaming through bay windows that looked out over the tree lined boulevard. He turned and dragged Rasheed into the room and sat him down at his desk, the police following with weapons still drawn.

Ethan pulled the subpoena from his pocket and slammed it down in front of Rasheed.

'This is signed by a court judge from the District, which means you have to do everything it says or you wind up in jail. It gives us the right to confiscate every single thing in this office, which is exactly what we're going to do. But you're going to help us do our job much faster than that, right Rasheed?'

Rasheed nodded frantically as Ethan jabbed a finger at the computer before Rasheed, the start button lighting up as the hard drive began to boot.

'You're going to bring up all of the records for flights into and out of Africa hired by this company. I want to know who flew where, and you're going to start by telling me all about your uncle and a man named Abrahem Nassir.'

Rasheed frowned. 'I don't know anybody by that name.'

'You will,' Ethan promised as he handed Rasheed another piece of paper with a tail registration written upon it. 'This aircraft, who hired it?'

Rasheed frowned.

'Nobody,' he said.

'You and I both know that's a lie,' Ethan growled.

'No, it's not! That aircraft belongs to my uncle. It's not been hired by anybody for some time.'

Ethan glanced at the screen as it lit up with Rasheed's access details.

'Your Uncle is called Tariq, you said?'

'Yes, Tariq Adel. He is from Iraq, but mostly lives in Dubai after the wars.'

'He owns a private jet?' Ethan asked.

'He owns twelve of them,' Rasheed replied. 'Tariq made his money in oil before the first Gulf War in 1991. Tariq did not agree with Saddam Hussein's antagonizing of the West and feared that his plans to invade Kuwait would place the country's economy in danger, so he sold his oil company and went into aviation hire. He moved to Dubai in 1989.'

Ethan turned to the police officers.

'Take the place apart and have technical get in here and go through the computers.'

As the police officers whirled to undertake their duties, Ethan turned back to Rasheed.

'Tariq, where is he now?'

Rasheed shrugged helplessly. 'I don't know. I haven't spoken to him in weeks and…'

Ethan grabbed Rasheed's collar and shoved him forward. The man's nose impacted the desk with a dull crunch and a squeal of pain. Rasheed's blood spilled across his crisp white shirt and was smeared on the desk as Ethan yanked him back up and glared into his eyes.

'You're right, I'm not a police officer and the law doesn't apply to me, so either you start talking real fast or by the end of this you'll wind up in Cook County Jail for a few years while I ensure that your case goes through *real slowly*. I'm guessing that sharing a cell with a couple of killers who like pretty young guys isn't something you want to check out?'

'You broke my nose!' Rasheed coughed in futile rage.

'Prison will break your will,' Ethan hissed. 'You got that broken nose resisting arrest, Rasheed. You shut the door in my face and dashed in here, and I pursued and detained you at your desk as you were trying to delete all of the files on your hard drive.'

'That's not true!'

'Nobody else cares, Rasheed. Your uncle Tariq is involved in something that could result in him being shot dead on sight, so if you want to stay out of jail and perhaps save your uncle's life then *start damn well talking!'*

Ethan shouted his last into Rasheed's ear and the younger man suddenly collapsed into sobs as he slumped in his seat.

'Okay, okay! Tariq flew from Morocco to Italy yesterday, and then to the United Kingdom. From there, he flew here and arrived in the early hours of this morning.'

'What's he doing here?'

'I don't know, honestly I don't know! He's not visited America in years! I only know that he's here because he called and asked me to arrange the necessary paperwork for his flight with customs!'

Ethan shoved Rasheed to one side and pulled his cell phone out as he turned away and dialed a number. Jarvis answered within seconds.

'Talk to me.'

'Tariq Adel, Iraqi national now living in Dubai. He's not on our radar but he's got money from Iraqi oil and a high–class aviation business. He's in the country, arrived last night. My guess is that he's the benefactor behind Abrahem's travel plans and funding. We find Tariq, we might find Abrahem.'

'We're on it,' Jarvis promised, and the line went silent.

Ethan shut the cell off and turned to two of the armed police waiting nearby and gestured them over. The two men strode into the office and aimed their rifles at Rasheed. Ethan looked down at the terrified young man.

'You really want to earn yourself some brownie points? Tell me where your uncle would stay while in the country. I want the location of every car hire, building rental and vacation resort he's ever stayed at in the United States, with emphasis on recent locations in the DC area, understood?'

Rasheed bobbed his head up and down, his eyes wide with panic, and Ethan allowed himself the thought that perhaps the young man was innocent of any involvement in what his uncle had been doing. He pulled a tissue from his pocket and handed it to Rasheed, softening his tone slightly.

'Get it done and you'll be free to go soon.'

Rasheed took the tissue and used it to stem the flow of blood from his nose as he turned to the computer and began typing.

Ethan turned to the window and was surprised to see a Lincoln parked across the street and an auburn–haired woman sitting watching the building from behind sunglasses. Despite himself, a smile curled from the corner of his lips as he recognized Special Agent Hannah Ford watching him. To his surprise he realized that he was glad that she was okay and had obviously returned unharmed from Hong Kong.

'He's got something,' an officer said from behind him.

Ethan turned back to Rasheed and saw on the computer screen a digital receipt.

'A lock up, near the east side,' Rasheed said, his voice now somewhat distorted by the blood clogging his broken nose. 'It was rented a few weeks ago, but nothing's stored there and it's the most recent purchase made in DC by my uncle's company.'

Ethan scanned the address and nodded.

'Good, take him to get some medical attention,' Ethan said as he pulled his cell out again. Jarvis answered even more quickly this time.

'Bethesda, District Container Storage, Lot Four,' Ethan said as he read off the screen. 'I'm heading there now.'

'I'll send back up,' Jarvis replied.

***

XXXVIII

Washington DC

'They're on the move.'

Hannah watched as Vaughn slipped the Lincoln into drive and moved smoothly into the flow of traffic headed north. Ahead, three SUVs and two unmarked police pursuit vehicles had just departed the site of Vantage Aviation Hire, which had been ringed with police cordon tape and a couple of patrol cars parked outside to prevent prying eyes.

Even then, two TV cameras had been showing up just as they had left the scene.

'Traffic's going to be hell within an hour or so,' Vaughn pointed out as they drove, keeping a reasonable distance behind the police convoy. 'Once the dignitaries start showing up on Pennsylvania Avenue the whole city will go into gridlock.'

It was a good point, and one that had been occupying Hannah as they had waited for Ethan Warner and his team to make their next move. With the Capitol on lockdown due to the imminent Trans Pacific Partnership event at the White House, rush hour to begin at the same time as the President's arrival at the ceremony and with so many tourists, patriots and sightseers all keen for a glimpse of the President and his entourage on the South Lawn, getting anywhere fast was going to present a major headache.

'Warner knows about the event,' she said as they drove. 'He's going to want this whole thing resolved before it begins.'

'Then he hasn't got long,' Vaughn replied, 'and we don't have the first clue as to where Abrahem Nassir is. More to the point, we don't know where Mitchell is either.'

Hannah felt her jaw ache as she clenched it instinctively at the mention of Mitchell's name. The need for revenge against the assassin, which was what she had come to believe him to be, was almost overwhelming. In her mind the best kind of revenge would be to put a bullet from her pistol straight between his eyes, but she knew in reality that she would much prefer to bring the man to justice, her evidence of his blood at the scene of Stanley Meyer's murder her undisputable evidence of his crime and of their innocence of the homicide in Hong Kong. That, and the fact that Mitchell had supposedly died two decades before.

'He's here,' she said with clairvoyant certainty. 'Mitchell's as tied up in this whole thing now as the rest of us and he was working to uncover the identity of the abductors of those four NSA agents in China too. Whoever he's working for, DIA, NSA, CIA, I don't care. He's going down for what he's done and I'll stop at nothing to find him.'

Even as she said it Hannah felt a sharp pain behind her eyes and she winced as a throbbing pulsed through her skull. It felt as though her head was in a vice and somebody was alternately compressing and releasing her skull.

'You okay?' Vaughn asked.

Hannah blinked as she saw stars sparkling in front of her eyes and then the pain eased and she rubbed her face.

'I'll be fine,' she replied.

'You haven't slept properly in thirty six hours,' Vaughn insisted. 'You need to get some rest.'

'I'll sleep when this is done,' Hannah insisted. 'Right now we have a terrorist to catch and I want to get to him before Warner does. You got any idea where we're headed?'

'Can't be sure of anything other than they're heading out of the district, toward Bethesda I guess.'

Hannah glanced at the road signs, and as she did so the sunlight caught her eye as it flickered through trees lining the road. A weighty lethargy weighed her down and her eyes closed slightly as warmth enveloped her. She sank back into her seat, and then something flashed into her mind and she sat bolt upright as she sucked in a deep breath.

'What is it?' Vaughn asked.

Hannah spoke without conscious thought. 'District Container Storage, Lot Four. He's in Bethesda.'

Vaughn stared at Hannah for a moment. 'Say what now?'

Hannah blinked, trying to understand what had just happened. 'I saw it,' she said, already becoming aware of how ridiculous she sounded. 'Lot Four, District Storage. Take a left onto Wisconsin and hit the gas, we'll beat Warner and his team to it.'

Vaughn did not reply as he peeled off from following the SUVs and then slammed the accelerator down and lit their pursuit lights up. The Lincoln surged forward as Hannah shook her head in an effort to clear it. Vaughn shot her a sideways glance.

'So, you're using the *Force* now?'

Hannah stared out of the windshield into the middle distance as the Lincoln turned right and accelerated as its tires squealed, Vaughn pushing the vehicle hard, swerving in and out of the traffic.

'I don't know what happened but I saw the building and I know where he is. If I turn out to be wrong you can shoot me yourself.'

Vaughn did not reply as they raced over the District and Maryland border. Hannah glanced right in the hope of seeing Warner's convoy across to the north east, but she could see nothing as they raced toward the storage facility.

'We're almost there,' Vaughn warned her. 'What the hell do we do when we arrive? If by some miracle Abrahem's there, which will for sure freak me out by the way, we can't call for back up. We're not even supposed to be here.'

Hannah reached for her pistol and checked it before she glanced at her cell phone. She knew that if Abrahem was in the building she would have to call for support of some kind – the terrorist presented too great a threat to let inter–agency squabbling get in the way of his arrest.

'Be ready to call in,' she said to Vaughn finally. 'If this goes south, we'll have to use Warner for support.'

'Warner?!' Vaughn gasped. 'You're going to call the person we're supposed to be apprehending?!'

'Let's see if we can't grab Nassir first, okay?'

Vaughn said nothing as he shut off the Lincoln's lights and slowed down as they approached the lock–ups, located on a large lot surrounded by a twelve foot chain link fence. Hannah saw two potential exits, both open, and a number of vehicles parked in the lot.

'Stay clear of the lot,' Hannah said. 'Let's park around the block and move in on foot.'

'If they see us coming, we won't have an effective escape method,' Vaughn cautioned.

'Warner and his team will be here in minutes. We either get Abrahem pinned down or we'll lose the collar and access to the case. Let's move.'

Vaughn drove around the corner of the block and pulled in, several other cars lining the sidewalk ahead and a small number of business workers standing outside in the sunshine, perhaps on their lunch breaks, some smoking as they chatted.

Hannah got out of the Lincoln and began walking back toward the lock–ups. A high pitched wolf whistle from behind her made her turn to see a small group of male workers on the opposite side of the street watching her with leering smiles. Hannah pulled the side of her jacket back to reveal her FBI shield and pistol and immediately the men turned away and shrank back inside their workplace.

'I'll go in,' Hannah said. 'You cover me from outside in case they make a run for it.'

'You'll be outnumbered,' Vaughn insisted.

Hannah pulled her pistol from its holster and held it low by her thigh as they reached the lot's main entrance.

'It's worth it Vaughn,' she said. 'Just cover me, okay?'

Hannah's lethargy had fallen away from her like ice melting beneath the warmth of the summer sun, and she could feel adrenaline coursing through her body as she turned into the lot and saw immediately a large *4* on a storage building further inside the lot and to her left. Outside the building was parked a white van and a jeep with private plates and glossy black paint.

Hannah kept her breathing under control as she walked toward lot number *2* instead, hoping to delay any suspicion until the very last moment. Even as she strode through the lot she saw two men of Middle Eastern origin head toward the black jeep. Her legs felt as though they were guiding themselves, carrying her along without conscious effort, and then without any thought she turned directly toward *Lot 4*.

'Hannah?' Vaughn whispered in despair from nearby.

Hannah heard nothing, saw nothing except her targets as they looked up and noticed her approaching. Both of their eyes locked onto the pistol in her hand and they responded instantly, both reaching beneath their jackets.

Hannah raised the pistol and without hesitation she fired twice. The gunshots cracked the air like thunder and the closer of the two men took the first round straight through his chest and was hurled back against the jeep even as Hannah fired her second shot.

The second man ducked behind the vehicle and yelled something in Arabic as Hannah kept moving, firing round after round into the side of the jeep. She heard Vaughn screaming from somewhere behind her, but her focus was entirely on the rounds smashing into the side of the jeep's doors. She knew instinctively that vehicles were no real defense against bullets at such close range, and she was rewarded with the sight of the second man tumbling to the ground, blood pouring in torrents from the back of his head.

'Hannah, stand down!' Vaughn yelled.

Hannah reached the jeep and circled around it even as the door to the storage lot opened and a man rushed out screaming, an assault rifle in his grasp. Hannah saw the barrel come up but she continued walking and fired from almost point–blank range.

The shot hit the gunman in the shoulder and he spun aside and slammed into the wall of the building, then whirled and aimed again. Hannah pulled her trigger and the pistol clicked as she realized that she had emptied the magazine.

The gunman aimed his rifle at her, and an ear–shattering gunshot thundered in her ears as her world spun wildly and she collapsed onto the hot asphalt.

*

'Shots fired at District Storage, Bethesda!'

The call came across as Ethan saw the lot and the low rows of storage buildings ahead and he almost screamed at the driver.

'Go, now! All units, go!'

The vehicles screeched into the parking lot, the police driver aiming straight for lot number *4*. Ethan could already see bodies strewn across the asphalt and a man crouched over one of them with his pistol in one hand and a cell phone in the other.

Ethan leaped out of the SUV even before it had stopped moving and dashed toward the crouching man. Already he could see that the body lying before him was a woman, her long auburn hair snaking across the ground. Special Agent Vaughn looked up at Ethan as he sprinted toward them and pointed frantically.

'Four men, running out back!' he yelled. 'Go!'

Ethan dashed past the black jeep, Vaughn and Hannah Ford as he saw the bodies of three foreign looking, armed men lying in pools of blood around the entrance to the storage building.

He kept moving, sprinting hard and pumping his arms to keep his chest open and air flooding into his lungs as he built up speed and rounded the far corner of the storage buildings.

He immediately saw three men clambering up and over the fences toward a small copse of trees that led into the parking lot of what looked like a nearby shopping mall. One of them was already over the fence, something on his back in a rucksack, and for a brief moment the man looked up and saw Ethan running toward him. Dark eyes, a broad jaw thickly forested with black growth, closely cropped hair and the glitter of radicalism flaring like a distant supernova in his gaze.

Abrahem Nassir.

Ethan ran harder but the two men on the fence jumped back down and pulled weapons from their jackets. Ethan changed direction for the parked vehicles to his right and threw himself down into cover as a hail of gunfire showered the cars. Ricochets zipped up over his head and pinged off hot bodywork as he rolled out of sight and pulled his pistol out.

The two men were twenty yards away and at that range they could hardly hope to hit Ethan, the bodywork of the vehicles strong enough to slow and catch the rounds being fired before they got to him.

Moments later a thunderous broadside of assault rifle fire erupted from Ethan's left as his support team rushed to his aid. Ethan broke cover, coming up over the hood of one of the parked vehicles and aiming at the two men in time to see them cut down by the savage gunfire.

'Hold your fire!' he yelled.

The rifles fell silent as Ethan saw Abrahem Nassir and an older man hurry out of sight across the mall's parking lot and vanish into the crowds. Ethan spoke quickly into his microphone as he emerged from behind the vehicles, the DIA team advancing on the fallen gunmen.

'Suspects on foot, headed north through the mall lot, Abrahem Nassir and Tariq Adel confirmed. All available units pursue immediately.'

Ethan cursed as he heard sirens wailing across the city and jogged back toward where Vaughn was still crouched over Hannah.

'What the hell was that?!' he demanded.

Vaughn stood up, his hands open toward Ethan. 'I don't know. She just went for it, almost got herself killed and now she's out cold. She wasn't even shooting straight, just aiming at anything that moved, and then she kind of woke up and just stood there as someone was aiming a rifle at her. I barely got the last guy before he took her down. She wanted to arrest Abrahem Nassir before you guys got here.'

Ethan looked down at Hannah for a moment and saw blood trickling from her nose.

The sound of an engine starting caught his attention, and he turned to see a white van pull away from the sidewalk nearby and begin accelerating down the street.

Ethan broke into a run without conscious thought as he sprinted out of the lot exit and onto the street.

***

XXXIX

Ethan ran hard as the white van accelerated away, turning in the middle of the street as it sought to escape back toward the south and the district. Ethan heard the squeal of its tires on the asphalt as it spun round and saw the face of the driver as he hauled on the wheel.

Oriental, maybe thirty years of age.

The van's rear quarter presented itself to Ethan as he ran, and he stretched out and jumped up onto the rear step as the vehicle rushed away from the storage buildings. His hands slipped on the surface of the van and Ethan's heart missed a beat as he flailed and thought that he was going to slip and fall. He let his gun fall from his grasp as he reached out and his fingers gripped the edges of the closed door, barely hanging on as the van lurched from left to right in an effort to shake him off.

The rear door of the van burst open alongside Ethan and a Chinese man poked his head out, a pistol in his grip as he turned and looked at Ethan in surprise.

Ethan grabbed the man's collar and hauled himself up again as the gunman grabbed the door rail in terror and he tried to stop himself from being pulled out of the vehicle. Ethan pulled hard on him as though to throw him out onto the asphalt racing past inches beneath them, and then purposefully shoved him back into the vehicle.

The unexpected change of motion caught the gunman off guard and he tumbled back into the van as Ethan grabbed the open door and launched himself inside. The gunman crashed onto his back in a tangle of limbs alongside two men sitting at computer consoles who were staring in wide eyed terror as Ethan flew past them and crashed down on top of the gunman.

Ethan's left hand clamped around the gunman's wrist and smashed it down against the metal floor of the van as he let his right knee plough deep into the gunman's plexus. The Chinese man's eyes bulged and he folded up at the waist as his head raised toward Ethan in sympathy with the blow, and Ethan ducked his head down and thrust it forward in time to smack into the man's nose with a sickening crunch.

The gunman's eyes rolled up into their sockets and he slumped back again, the back of his head hitting the floor of the van with a resounding thump as Ethan grasped for the pistol.

'Don't move!'

Ethan froze, one hand on the weapon as he swiveled his gaze to his right and saw both of the computer technicians standing, reared up against their consoles as the open door of the van swung against its hinges. One of them was holding a pistol close to Ethan's head, the man's aim trembling as he spoke in heavily accented English.

'Hands behind your head!'

Ethan hesitated, then glanced at the cab where the driver and another passenger were looking over their shoulders and waiting to see what would happen. Ethan looked back to where the technician was aiming the pistol, barely inches from Ethan's temple. *Too close, within easy reach.*

Ethan nodded slowly, released the gun he was pinning to the floor of the vehicle and began slowly to raise his hands, his right hand only inches from his assailant's pistol. As he did so, the gunman took an instinctive step back to give himself space, lifting one foot off the floor of the van to do so.

'No!'

The driver's warning was too late as Ethan's right hand whipped sideways and knocked the pistol away from his head. Ethan drove upward with one foot and turned as he swung his left fist and it impacted the technician's jaw with a loud crack.

The technician's body whirled and flew sideways as it hit the open door at the back of the van and flew out into mid–air. Ethan saw the man's body smack down onto the hot asphalt behind them and roll to a halt in an unconscious tangle of limbs as vehicles swerved in chaos to avoid it.

The second technician's right hand swept toward Ethan's throat in a scything motion designed to collapse his thorax and choke him to death. Ethan jerked his left forearm up vertically and blocked the blow as he turned on one heel and slammed his right knee up into the Chinaman's groin.

The technician's eyes bulged like fishbowls as Ethan's knee crunched into his testicles and he folded up with an agonized gasp. Ethan pivoted to his left and lifted his left boot up as he drove his right elbow down into the back of the technician's skull, just behind his right ear. The blow sent the smaller man sprawling across the floor of the van as Ethan ducked down, grabbed the discarded pistol from the floor and aimed it into the cab.

Ethan offered the two occupants a breathless grin. 'Fancy a chat?'

The two Chinamen looked at each other, and Ethan could see that they both knew that they had no plays left. The van began to slow as the driver sought a place to pull over.

The impact came from behind Ethan, his only warning the sound of a screaming engine. He turned in time to see through the open rear door the shape of a dark blue Chevrolet just as it smashed into the rear quarter of the van with the force of a fallen angel. Ethan was hurled across the rear of the van and smashed into the sidewall even as he heard cries of fear and pain from the cab.

The van mounted the sidewalk and as Ethan was smashed into the computer terminals he heard the engine roar and felt the vehicle lift off. He glimpsed through the windshield leaves and branches looming before them before the van suddenly smashed into a large tree.

Ethan crashed into the rear of the cab as though he had been hit by a train. His vision starred and dimmed and he sensed rather than felt himself collapse onto the floor in the rear of the vehicle as the computers smashed into the rear of the cab and toppled down onto him, the body of the gunman and technician landing alongside the equipment and pinning Ethan in place.

Ethan lay stunned and silent for a few moments, became aware of an acrid burning smell wafting through the vehicle. He tried to get up but his limbs felt numb and the weight of the computer equipment and two bodies was too great for him to budge. A bolt of nausea poisoned his guts as his vision swirled. He closed his eyes for a moment as he waited for the nausea to pass so that he could reach out and once more make a grab for either of the pistols on the floor of the van.

The rear of the vehicle moved, sank down, and Ethan opened one eye to see a figure vault lithely inside and move toward him, the bright sunlight from outside flaring and forcing Ethan to squint. Ethan shifted his hand to where he thought a pistol might be and instantly the shadowy figure lunged forward. A heavy shoe pressed down on Ethan's wrist and pinned it in place.

The man leaned down and picked up the pistol, and then he looked at Ethan and aimed the weapon at him.

Ethan lay on his back, disorientated and pinned down by the computer equipment as he looked up into the eyes of Aaron Mitchell. The assassin looked back down at Ethan as in the distance the sound of wailing sirens grew louder.

'What are you waiting for?' Ethan croaked.

Mitchell looked down at Ethan for a moment longer, and then with his free hand he reached out and grabbed hold of a computer hard drive that was hanging by a set of leads from the twisted wreckage of the desks. Mitchell yanked the drive free and then looked back down at Ethan.

'The right time,' he replied in his deep, gravelly voice.

Mitchell lowered the pistol as he turned and jumped down from the rear of the van, and then vanished from sight. Ethan fought to right himself and sat up, pushing the wreckage off his chest bit by bit until he was able to struggle to his feet. Beside him lay the Chinese man he had struck first, groaning now as blood oozed in thick lumps from his shattered nose, his labored breath rattling in his throat. The technician was still unconscious, as were the two men in the front of the vehicle, their faces lost in impact bags that had burst from the dashboard before them. Ethan dragged the first gunman onto his side, fearful that he would suffocate, and then stepped down out of the vehicle and looked around.

Mitchell was nowhere to be seen, and Ethan slumped wearily onto the rear step of the van and sat there until SUVs screeched to a halt nearby and DIA agents sprinted toward him.

One of them vaulted up into the vehicle and crouched down alongside Ethan, handing him back the pistol he had dropped when he had pursued the van.

'You okay, man?'

Ethan nodded as he slipped the gun back into his shoulder holster.

'Two more in the cab,' he gasped. 'Get these assholes out of here and back to the DIAC building. They've got some talking to do.'

'Roger that,' came the reply.

'Did you see the other guy? Six four, two hundred fifty pounds, African American?'

The agent looked at Ethan strangely. 'I didn't see anybody else in the vicinity.'

Ethan sighed as the agent held out a hand and hauled Ethan to his feet. Mitchell was here, and that meant that the MJ–12 now had the Chinese technology that Ethan had been trying to hunt down.

Ethan clambered to his feet as armed police rushed toward the vehicle and yanked the cab doors open. The two men were yanked from the vehicle and pinned down to the ground, a young man who remained stoically silent and an older man with a defiant set to his expression. The older man shouted a warning in heavily accented English.

'You'll kill them all!'

'Stay on the ground!' the police yelled in unison as Ethan covered them with his pistol as they manacled the two prisoners.

'We'll kill who?!' Ethan demanded.

The older man glared up at Ethan, rage radiating from his expression.

'We were trying to help! Now you've ruined everything!'

Ethan glanced at the police.

'Get them back to the station as fast as you can, and get the techs' to put these computers and screens back together. I need to know what they were doing.'

*

'I want a name.'

The Chinese technician sat in the police interrogation room, his hands manacled to the Formica table top and his ankles likewise gripped in steel cuffs. He had been strip–searched, his clothes burned and was now dressed in a loose fitting gray jump suit, his nose swollen and the side of his face puffy and bruised.

Ethan sat opposite him, two law enforcement officers and two DIA agents accompanying them in the tiny room.

'I don't know any names,' the technician replied miserably.

Ethan smiled bitterly.

'I don't think that you understand quite what's happening here,' he said, trying to restrain his anger. 'All that's standing between you and a major international incident is us, and you're not helping. Who is your commanding officer? Who were you watching? Who sent you to Washington DC and why?'

The technician, who had revealed his name to be Sung, stared at the table top, his black hair glistening in the harsh white light from the ceiling, dried blood encrusting his lips.

Ethan smashed his fist down on the table before Sung and the Chinaman jerked in his seat and stared at Ethan.

'I don't know any names,' he repeated in a monotone voice.

Ethan leaned back in his seat and folded his arms.

'It's your superior officers you're afraid of, right?' he suggested. 'If you go home now, having told us everything, you think that you'll be sent into some prison somewhere for betraying state secrets.'

Sung's oriental features were hard to read, somehow less expressive than those of other races, but Ethan saw the technician's eyes wobble in their sockets as he thought of whatever hellish prison awaited him back home for his perceived failure.

'It's not going to be much better here,' Ethan said as he leaned forward on the desk. 'You're in the country carrying out illegal surveillance on US assets on behalf of China. You'll be tried, sentenced and imprisoned in a high–security facility where you'll be on permanent lockdown twenty three hours per day. On the hour that you do get out there will be killers, drug dealers, Hell's Angels and every other maniac you can think of who'll just love to get to know you *real* well, and being a foreigner who tried to kill members of our military, just how much sympathy do you think you'll get from the guards?' Ethan let a smile crawl across his features. 'There'll be nothing left of you come this time next year.'

Sung swallowed but remained silent.

'Or, we can cut a deal,' Ethan suggested. 'You go free.'

Sung looked up in surprise at that. So did the police officers and DIA agents.

'I don't know that we can offer him that after…' began one of them.

'Hear me out,' Ethan said as he raised a hand to forestall the objection and then turned back to Sung. 'You're a computer operator, right? Are you the superior officer?'

Sung thought for a moment and then shook his head.

'So you were just doing your duty,' Ethan said.

Sung nodded and Ethan went on.

'If this attack you've planned goes ahead, our countries could find themselves at war, Sung. China could find itself under attack, which will then draw other nations such as Russia into the conflict. Before we know it we could all be fighting each other in World War Three. Is that something you want to be responsible for Sung? Because that's what's going to happen. Your failure will be not helping us and seeing millions of innocent people die both here and in your own country because you didn't have the guts to stand up and help us stop this attack before…'

'We're not attacking your country!' Sung shouted.

Ethan looked at him for a moment.

'You're here,' he replied, 'you've implanted people, you were watching them on your screens Sung, I saw the video feeds before the crash.'

Sung glared at Ethan, hatred radiating from his dark eyes.

'You Americans, always so sure of yourself and yet so simple in your thinking. We're not attacking your country, we're trying to *stop* an attack.'

Ethan frowned and leaned back in his seat.

'Sure you are, Sung. You came all this way to protect our interests.'

'Abrahem Nassir,' Sung growled.

The mention of that name got Ethan's attention and he leaned forward again. 'What do you know about Nassir?'

'He stole our country's technology and we're trying to get it back before he does anything else to provoke conflict between our nations.'

Ethan stared at Sung for a long moment. 'You mean the technology that *your* country stole from ours, way back in 1997? The technology that you took from four National Security Agency employees and then killed them for it over many years?'

Sung averted his gaze, his anger deflated. 'I was not involved in that operation. We are trying to make amends.'

'How were you planning to do that, Sung? Who are you controlling?'

Sung smiled, his eyes still cold and black.

'Your agents,' he said, 'maybe people in this room. Maybe people you know.'

Even as Ethan was about to ask who the technician was referring to, the door to the room opened and an officer urgently beckoned Ethan to join him.

'You need to see this.'

Ethan got up and followed the officer to a second room down the corridor, where the computers and screens from the captured van had been set up again.

'I don't know what the hell we've got here,' a police IT expert said as he sat before the screens, 'but it's like nothing I've ever seen before.'

'I thought that the hard drive had been stolen,' Ethan said. 'I saw it taken.'

'It has,' the IT man said, 'but the other drives were recording much of the data the Chinese must have collected since they arrived here. You're looking at footage a few hours old.'

Ethan looked at the screens before him. Both showed images of the view through a windshield of a car driving through what looked like Washington DC, and Ethan peered at the images for a moment as he tried to figure out whose eyes he was observing the scene through.

He turned to a man sitting manacled to a chair in the same room, the older Chinese agent they had captured in the van.

'Get him over here.'

The police hauled the man to his feet and dragged him across as Ethan pointed at the screens.

'Who are these people?'

The man remained silent, his lips thin and straight and his gaze directed somewhere over Ethan's shoulder. Ethan stepped forward, reached down and grabbed the man's testicles in one hand as he twisted them and yanked them brutally upward.

The man jerked as though electric currents were seething through his body as he went up on his toes and Ethan growled into his face.

'Ten seconds and I'll twist them clean off! Your name and the names of those people on the screens!'

'Jiang Sin!' the man squealed. 'I can't tell you their names!'

Ethan twisted harder for a moment and then he released Jiang Sin. The Chinese man sagged, coughing and tears streaming from his eyes as he spoke.

'We're trying to stop Abrahem Nassir,' he said weakly.

Ethan peered at Jiang. 'Prove it!'

'Nassir is trying to assassinate the Presidents of both our countries!'

'Both of them?'

'Yes!' Jiang insisted. 'His plan is to start a war between China and America, and that's something that we do not want!'

Ethan stared at the screens for a moment longer. 'But you were watching through the eyes of *two* people.'

'Yes,' Jiang said, 'the second signal was not ours! That person is being controlled by Abrahem Nassir! We intercepted it and were trying to track them down using the person we implanted!'

Ethan stared at the two screens, and then he saw the person in the car look across a quiet street at a row of buildings, one of which Ethan recognized instantly. *Vantage Aviation Hire.* He heard Jarvis's words echo through his mind.

During the attack, several witnesses reported noticing that the general was suffering a nosebleed. The small size and design of the devices caused minimal discomfort for the wearer, but he has told us that they also caused nosebleeds from time to time.

Ethan whirled to the police officers.

'I've got to move, now! Keep these men in custody, no matter what!'

***

XL

Ethan dashed out of the police station, his cell phone in his hand as he hurried toward his vehicle.

'Jarvis'

'Hannah Ford was implanted,' Ethan said as he reached the pool car. 'The Chinese must have got to her when she was in Hong Kong.'

'But she was checked, scanned!' Jarvis protested. 'She was clean when they passed through the airport!'

'Well, somehow the Chinese got something into her and they're not telling us what!'

'Where is she now?'

'She's in custody,' Ethan replied. 'She got into a gunfight with Nassir and he got away, started shooting the place up before we got there.'

'I just got a call from her partner, Vaughn,' Jarvis revealed. *'They're starting to understand what's happening here and that they're being set up somehow. I think they might come over to our side.'*

'I can't be sure if the Chinese wanted to help Nassir escape or were trying to gun him down, but Hannah wasn't in her own mind. It's possible that they might have been using Hannah to catch or kill Abrahem.'

Jarvis's voice brooked no argument.

'Get to the White House,' he ordered. *'Nassir will head there while he still has enough time to take the President down. He'll have to be close by, near enough that he can see his plan come to fruition before his eyes. He's not going to want to watch this go down on a television somewhere.'*

'Agreed. What about Hannah?'

'I'll worry about her! You get to Nassir before he gets to the President!'

Ethan stood alongside his car and looked at the traffic building up on the nearby freeway, lines of stationary vehicles, horns honking and bodywork glinting in brilliant flares of white light in the heat.

'There's no way I'm going to get to the Capitol by car,' he replied. 'You're right though. Nassir's a hands on killer, he's not going to stand by and watch this from afar. My guess is that he'll be on foot, maybe in the crowds somewhere.'

'I'll get the MPD onto it with their helicopters,' Jarvis replied, *'they'll be able…. see more than… and pick him up more quickly… we could on… own.'*

'You're breaking up Doug,' Ethan replied as he looked about. 'I must be in a dead–zone or something. I'll have to call you back and…'

Ethan's train of thought slammed to a halt and he stared at his cell phone again.

'You there, Ethan?'

'Yeah, I'm here,' he replied, still staring at his cell's screen.

The screen was showing a signal of two bars, but Ethan recalled reading somewhere that nobody actually knew what the bars on cell screens really meant. It was possible to hold a cell phone call with one bar, or be cut off with five. The signal icon on his cell at least suggested that the reception was weak, perhaps affected by the heat and the high buildings surrounding the police station.

'What is it?'

'Damn me,' Ethan said finally. 'I think I know how they're getting signals to the victims, how they control them.'

'How?'

'Grab cell phone data from the date of the attack at Fort Benning! Run it against any of the signals detected coming *out* of Fort Benning, anything at all!'

Ethan waited as he heard Jarvis and Hellerman running the data onto one of their computer screens. A few moments passed and then Jarvis came back on the line.

'According to this the cell towers between Parkwood, where General Thompson set off, and Fort Benning both recorded an identical cell phone signal that remained active from just before the general left his home until the moment he took his own life. The frequency of the transmission matches precisely that detected at Fort Benning – eight hundred eighty hertz.'

'Genius,' Hellerman whispered in the background, audible now as Jarvis switched his own cell to speaker, *'absolute genius.'*

'They used cell phones to relay the signals, didn't they,' Ethan said.

'Cell phones, everybody's got one,' Hellerman said. *'They're one of our most ubiquitous devices and we carry them on our person. They hacked the general's cell phone and used it to relay signals to the implant in his skull. I'll be damned, it's like they dialed into his brain.'*

'Can we trace that cell?' Ethan asked.

'They'll have tossed it,' Jarvis said.

'It's their Achilles Heel,' Ethan said. 'Hannah attacked Nassir's storage depot, but according to her partner half way through the attack she suddenly faltered and looked as though she were waking up from a dream. If Abrahem Nassir is using cell phone networks to control his victims, then it makes sense that he would set up shop in an area where cell phone reception is weak. The area of Bethesda he was in is a dead–zone, hardly any reception at all, and it may have caused the Chinese to lose their control of Hannah.'

'Which would prevent anybody from using his own technology against him,' Jarvis surmised, *'and make it harder for them to track him down. But surely the White House must be protected against cellular signals?'*

'Maybe the White House but not necessarily the lawns. If Majestic Twelve are hoping for Abrahem Nassir to succeed, they'll have somebody on those lawns boosting the signals. We need to figure out who and fast,' Ethan said. 'The District isn't known for being the best when it comes to cell phone reception and I can't believe that Abrahem wouldn't have known that when he came here.'

'I'll inform Lopez and the Secret Service,' Jarvis said. *'Get to the White House as soon as you can. I'll get Lopez to identify the source of the signals both inside and outside of the White House.'*

'Don't risk letting Abrahem finish his mission,' Ethan insisted. 'If we have to shut the ceremony down, then do it!'

'Leave that to me. Jarvis out.'

Jarvis cut off the line and Ethan stared at his cell phone for a moment longer. General Thompson had been in possession of his cell phone when he had died, the device in the pocket of his uniform. Commander Sandy Veiron had also had his cell phone on him in the cockpit of his F–18E Hornet when he had ploughed into the deck of his aircraft carrier, pilots often using the devices to take photographs of other aircraft while flying operationally.

A cell phone was carried by almost every human being in the western world and the perfect vessel through which to pass signals to the devices implanted into the heads of victims of the Chinese or Abrahem Nassir. Ethan knew that there were devices capable of blocking all cell phone signals, disrupting communications and preventing Nassir and his people from taking control of human minds, but there was no way that the entire network could be protected all at once. If Nassir had a person on the inside, then Ethan knew that if he was close enough he would be able to boost his signals and get anybody in the vicinity who had been implanted to attack the President from close range.

Ethan glanced at the nearby traffic once again and made his decision. He turned away from his vehicle and hurried across the lot until he saw what he wanted. Ethan hurried across the lot and crouched down alongside a massive Harley Davidson Sportster 883, hurriedly pulling wires from behind the clocks and after he had examined them for a few moments he cut two of them and then stood up. He used a pocket knife to jack open the seat compartment and expose the battery, then touched one end of the bare wire to the twelve volt positive terminal. He connected the other end to the feed wire on the coil, then took his second wire and connected the solenoid and the starter. The big V–Twin engine coughed into life as Ethan secured the wires in place and slammed the seat back down over the battery.

'You done there, boy?'

Ethan turned and saw four bikers standing watching him, their muscular arms folded across broad chests and bulging bellies, eyes hard and cold. The sound of the motorbike's rumbling engine had masked their approach. One of them slipped a blade from beneath his jacket, the steel glinting in the sunlight.

'I need your bike,' Ethan replied. 'If I don't use it, we may be facing World War Three.'

The bikers stared at him for a moment and then they chuckled grimly. Their leader, a man with a thick and drooping moustache that framed his thin lips, smiled back at Ethan.

'Well why didn't you say so? I'll call *Iron Man* for you.'

Ethan didn't want to shoot them, but the man with the blade moved toward Ethan so he reached beneath his jacket and whipped his pistol out.

'Bad idea,' he snapped at the knifeman.

The knifeman smiled as his companions immediately pulled knives of their own and sneered at Ethan.

'*Real* bad idea!'

Ethan didn't have time to argue with the bikers and he sure as hell couldn't fight all four of them but he could see that despite their bulging biceps and chests they were old, fat and out of shape. He jumped backwards onto the Harley's seat and swung one leg over the saddle as with one hand he closed the clutch. Then he stamped down on the gear lever with his boot even as the bikers' lunged toward him and swung their blades. The Harley's engine changed note and Ethan opened the clutch a fraction as he reached back and twisted the throttle.

The Harley thundered into motion, the big–bore engine jerking Ethan away from the bikers' grasp as two of the blades flashed down and scraped across the bike's tail. Ethan let the bike roll across the lot, looking over his shoulder as he turned for the exit between the ranks of cars. The bikers lumbered in pursuit, screaming obscenities at him, but their faces were already sheened with sweat and he could see that they would never catch him. Their leader threw his knife, which whistled past Ethan's shoulder and clattered against a parked Ford as Ethan left them behind.

Ethan reached the exits, stopped the bike and then turned around on the seat before kicking the Harley back into gear. Within minutes he was riding the up ramp onto the freeway and began scything through the traffic heading north toward the Capitol.

The only way to pin down Abrahem now was to find the vehicle that would be used to control whomever his people had implanted, which Ethan knew would have to be capable of emitting signals with a high enough intensity to break through the lousy reception range in the vicinity of the White House. He rode one–handed as he pulled his cell phone out and dialed a number, gambling that his elevated position on the freeway might get a signal through.

***

XLI

The White House, South Lawn

'Lopez.'

Nicola Lopez answered her cell on the second ring as she lingered on the south lawn and watched hundreds of dignitaries waited patiently for the President, the First Lady and the President of the People's Republic of China to emerge from the White House.

'It's me,' Ethan said, sounding as though he was in the middle of a hurricane.

'What's happening?'

'It's the cell phones!' Ethan yelled. *'They're using the cell phones to relay their signals! They must have a booster somewhere, somebody acting to get the signal through the electromagnetic shielding around the White House!'*

Lopez covered one ear as she struggled to hear Ethan above a sudden rapturous applause as the guests on the White House lawn stood, the President of the United States emerging from the White House with his wife and the Chinese President beside him.

'Do we have a suspect or a target?'

Ethan shouted from the other end of the line.

'The Chinese are involved, possibly intending to target the President himself but I can't be sure! There's got to be somebody in the crowd who's helping them! Mitchell was here… took the hard drive… could be there….'

'Ethan you're breaking up!' Lopez gasped. 'Do we have a target?!'

'… likely to be… who's helping them… apprehend them now…'

The line went dead in Lopez's ear and she cursed as she shoved the cell back into her pocket and scanned the crowd. With them all standing and clapping, she figured that nobody would be able to fiddle with their cell phones. Maybe they wouldn't have to do anything at all, just keep them switched on and let the Chinese hack their way into an unwitting assassin's mind and unleash hell across the South Lawn.

The only people carrying weapons were the Secret Service and Lopez, and with a sudden start she realized that she could have been implanted. Her weariness clouded her thinking, made her question herself and for a moment she was lost in a delirium of silence, her eyes focusing on nothing and her legs feeling numb as she swayed on the spot. The applause before her died down and a blissful silence enveloped her as she literally began to sleep on her feet.

'Lopez.'

She jerked awake and looked to her right as a Secret Service Agent peered at her. 'You done napping?'

Lopez nodded, both ashamed and angry at herself as she focused on the gathering before her. She watched as the two Presidents, accompanied by their wives, walked down onto the lawns and a plethora of dignitaries moved forward to greet them.

Lopez scanned the crowds but she could see nothing that suggested an assassin was preparing an attack. Ethan had mentioned Mitchell and that he had grabbed a hard drive of some kind. Presumably the Chinese had been involved and perhaps that hard drive had contained the data necessary to control the assassin, whoever they may be.

Lopez's microphone hissed and she heard Jarvis's voice on the line.

'Lopez, we've got a plan. We've got a feed here from the Chinese computers we captured, and we're trying to hack into it now and figure out who has been implanted at the ceremony. It turns out they were watching through the eyes of whoever Abrahem Nassir managed to implant in Iraq, but they couldn't figure out who it was. You need to get to the Horsepower bunker and relay the feed through from us here at the DIA.'

'You can see what they see?'

'If we can hack the signal,' Jarvis replied. *'The Chinese were using a modulating frequency to hide their activities and they don't have a way of deactivating it after the computers were damaged in the crash – it's all part of their state's efforts to prevent their exposure here in the United States. If the computers were shut down their signals were scrambled and erased. Hellerman's working on a code to reactivate the signals based on the original modulation but it's taking time. You need to be ready.'*

Lopez looked at the Secret Service Agent alongside her, who nodded once as he heard the same transmission.

'I'll take you down there but we only have a few minutes. The ceremony's begun and if they're going to make a move, it's going to be real damned soon!'

'Get on it, Nicola,' Jarvis urged. *'This is the only way to stop the attack without causing a major international incident!'*

*

National Security Agency, Maryland

'Hurry it up!'

Doug Jarvis followed Hellerman like a ghostly shadow as he hurried into the National Security Agency's Identity Mine Watch Room and rushed toward a vacant seat among the operating consoles. He sat down and immediately began accessing files, then slowed as he saw the screens arrayed before him showing the world through the eyes of criminals.

'Wow,' he uttered as he stared in amazement at the technical fecundity. 'I wouldn't have believed this possible in my wildest dreams.'

'Your wildest dreams are about to become your wildest nightmares if you don't get to work,' Jarvis snapped. 'The only reason you got security clearance to be in here at all is because I asked for it. How long?'

Hellerman did not look up as he worked feverishly at his console. 'The code is complex, unsurprisingly, but I can have it cracked in an hour or two.'

'We have a *minute* or two,' Jarvis pointed out.

'Which is why I'm creating a work–around,' Hellerman said as his fingers flew across the keyboard. 'It won't give us a permanent signal but it will be enough to give Lopez a decent look through the eyes of our unwitting assassin. I only hope it's enough for her to identify them.'

'She won't need long,' Jarvis figured. 'An eye–point position can be triangulated, and the Secret Service can move in and quietly remove whoever it is before they can be made to act.'

Hellerman nodded as new data flooded down his screen.

'I've got signals traffic at eight hundred eighty hertz in the vicinity of the White House,' he said, his voice touched now with excitement. 'Can't pinpoint the location but it's definitely there. Somebody's acting as a booster in the crowd.'

'So we're looking for two people,' Jarvis muttered. 'Can you locate the booster?'

'No,' Hellerman said, 'but I can do the next best thing. I can give you their number.'

Jarvis watched as on a second screen a cell phone number popped up. He didn't need to look at it for long to know whose number it was.

'LeMay,' he said finally. 'Damn it, MJ–12 *do* want this attack to go ahead.'

'The Director FBI is in the crowd,' Hellerman confirmed.

Jarvis felt his cell phone vibrate in his pocket and he answered it immediately. 'Jarvis?'

'It's Vaughn,' came the reply. *'We just did a scan of Hannah's frontal lobes and we found the device.'*

'Good,' Jarvis replied, 'where are you both now?'

'We're on our way to the White House just like you ordered, but isn't that the last thing we should be doing?'

'How the hell did Hannah's implant get through the X–Ray scanner without being detected?!' Jarvis asked, ignoring Vaughn's last.

'Because it's not metal,' Vaughn replied. *'It's made from a biodegradable polymer, a synthetic mesh that mimics human tissue. It looks like the Chinese got further down the road with these implants than we thought. They don't even use conductive probes any more, but instead the implant has a mesh rolled up inside it that is injected through a needle just one micrometer thick. The mesh unravels once the implant is in place. Believe it or not, the mesh actually melds with the victim's brain tissue once injected and remains there for a limited time before breaking down and disappearing, and is designed to allow the interception of communications between the brain's neurons. It's based on some kind of advanced technology being developed by Harvard to treat neurodegenerative disorders – the Chinese must have copied the tech' and incorporated it into their devices. Even the internal chips are biodegradable, and the whole thing unravels and embeds itself in the brain in less than half an hour. We've only tested this on mice in the US, but the Chinese have gone much further.'*

Jarvis stared into space for a moment before replying.

'No evidence left behind,' he said finally. 'Is the implant still in place?'

'Yeah, the doctors don't want it out of her until they're sure they can remove it without causing permanent damage.'

Jarvis took a deep breath before he replied.

'Good,' he said. 'Leave it there and get Hannah into the White House right now. We have control of her chip, so she won't do anything that she shouldn't.'

There was a long pause on the line. *'What are you going to do?'*

'That's a matter of national security, literally,' Jarvis replied. 'Get her there and I'll take care of the rest, okay?'

Jarvis shut off the line and saw Hellerman looking up at him from the corner of one eye as he worked.

'What are you looking at?' Jarvis snapped. 'I know what I'm doing.'

'I know,' Hellerman replied, 'but I don't know if what you're doing is the right thing.'

*

Ethan weaved the Harley Davidson through the dense lines of traffic, the big bike's loud engine helping to clear the way as drivers heard him coming and pulled aside to give him more room. The Sportster was slim enough to slip through the gaps he was offered, the rumbling engine echoing through the ranks of traffic.

Ahead, a large Ford Ranger occupied by a beefy looking man in a white vest pulled across and blocked Ethan's path. Ethan saw the shaved head and cruel grin of the driver reflected in his rear view mirror as he looked back and chuckled at the sight of Ethan's Harley pinned among the traffic behind him.

Ethan slipped the bike into neutral, took his hands off the bars and reached beneath his jacket. He pulled out the 9mm pistol and aimed it at the Ford's rear view mirror. The big driver's smirk dissolved into panic as his eyes widened and then Ethan fired.

The bullet smashed into the mirror and shattered it into thousands of sparkling pieces that showered down onto the road as drivers to his left and right cried out in horror. The Ford Ranger's engine growled and it pulled over. Ethan slipped the pistol back into its shoulder holster, kicked the Harley into gear and pulled past the truck, not dignifying the driver with even a glance as he continued on his way off DuPont Circle and south toward Pennsylvania Avenue.

***

XLII

'It'll work, trust me. We've just gotta work fast!'

Nicola Lopez sat in the Secret Service "Horsepower" bunker and watched the screens before her. The agents not assigned directly to the President's side had set her up in the bunker with seven screens; two of them overlooked the White House south lawn, four more the streets surrounding the building via traffic cameras, and a final screen that was at that very moment blank.

Secret Service Agent Daniel Hopkins loomed over Lopez's shoulder. He was in his forties but in supreme physical condition, his gray suit barely containing his muscular frame, his jaw broad and an air of confidence surrounding him that marked him out as likely a former Special Forces soldier.

'I don't like this at all,' he muttered as he looked at the screens. 'We can't do a damned thing from in here if this doesn't work.'

Lopez sat and waited patiently for the seventh screen to show an image.

'We have top people working on this,' she said without betraying the slightest shred of doubt. 'We know how they work and our best people are right now about to figure out how to show us who is targeting the President.'

'That so?' Hopkins murmured. 'And how would they be doing that?'

'It's long and complicated,' Lopez said. 'But as long as we can intercept the signals and get a trace on their origin, we can bring this entire attack to a close without a single shot being fired.'

'And if you can't get a trace or intercept these signals you're talking about?'

Lopez smiled tightly as she stared at the screen and hoped against hope that Hellerman was on top form, because she still did not know who was going to make an attempt on the President's life.

Her lack of a reply did nothing to instill confidence in her Secret Service escort.

*

National Security Agency, Maryland

Hellerman began accessing a new signal feed and inputting data into the signal streams, long lines of code that to Jarvis seemed to be little more than numbers and characters he did not recognize.

Jarvis looked up at the screens and saw one displaying a rhythmically shuddering close up of the grimacing face of a naked young woman lying on her back on a large bed as some criminal or other had his way with her. Wads of cash were visible in one corner of the screen on a bedside table, along with the smoldering remains of two cigarettes.

Jarvis glanced down and saw Hellerman transfixed by the same screen.

'Stop perving and get working,' Jarvis snapped.

Hellerman's fingers rattled across the keyboards again but his gaze did not break from the display screen before them.

'The signals at eight hundred eighty hertz are those emitted by all cellular phones in the United States,' he said as he worked, apparently thinking nothing of performing three complex tasks at once. 'We can piggy back on those that are being used around the White House and target any in the direct vicinity of the South Lawn.'

'Won't the electromagnetic protection around the White House prevent any signals from getting in or out?' Jarvis asked.

Hellerman nodded.

'Yes, but we're looking for signals that come from within that electromagnetic boundary,' he replied, 'and then matching their communications with anything outside the boundary but within a short distance. If our terrorists are outside the White House and trying to control somebody inside, then we know that they'll be using some pretty powerful transmitters to break through the electromagnetic shielding. Even the most powerful equipment won't breach the interior of the White House, the shielding is just too strong, so if they're going to hit the President it's going to happen on the lawn before the state dinner.'

Jarvis watched as the screen full of data before Hellerman suddenly stopped flowing as his fingers ceased motion and the cursor came to a rest at the bottom of the screen. Hellerman finally took his eyes off the prostitute's ecstatic features as he turned to Jarvis.

'You ready?' Hellerman asked.

'Stop pulling my chain and start the program already.'

Hellerman hit the keyboard's "*Enter*" key and instantly the data streams vanished and a small spinning logo appeared as the computer began working.

Jarvis looked up expectantly at the blank screen before them in the Watch Room, and a silence descended on the other operators as they watched and waited for the program that Hellerman had created to latch onto any signals crossing the White House's electromagnetic boundary.

'What if we can't break through?' Jarvis asked.

Hellerman briefly shook his head.

'We'll get through all right, our signals are on a frequency left open by the White House,' he replied. 'What matters is whether we can ensure that we catch both the killer and the people in control of them.'

Jarvis looked up at a news feed screen running on a smaller monitor nearby and saw the President of the United States, the First Lady, and the President of the People's Republic of China walking onto the White House lawn.

'We're out of time,' he said.

*

'We're too late,' Agent Hopkins insisted.

Lopez stared at the blank screen and felt the burden of failure begin to weigh down heavily on her shoulders as the Secret Service agents began to prepare to move out of the Horsepower bunker and up to the White House lawns.

'Just give them a couple more minutes,' she pleaded.

'We don't *have* a couple of minutes,' Hopkins snapped. 'We're of no use to the President down here, and your friends at the DIA have failed to give us a head–start on who the assassin really is. Once the President starts mingling any advantage we might have had will be gone anyway – we need to be right by his side, right now.'

Lopez cursed as the Secret Service agents hustled out of the bunker and began rushing away to ascend into the White House and disperse onto the lawns in a flanking maneuver that would surround the President with a second layer of armed protection.

'Come on, Hellerman,' Lopez urged the blank screen, 'don't let me down.'

The monitor remained stubbornly blank as Lopez sat in frustrated silence, fighting the same urge that had taken the Secret Service; to do something tangible to defend the President instead of sitting in the bunker staring uselessly at a monitor. She was about to leap to her feet and sprint in pursuit of Hopkins and his team when the monitor flickered.

Lopez leaned forward, a pulse of excitement fluttering through her heart.

'Come on,' she urged the signal.

The image on the monitor brightened, and then suddenly it sharpened into focus and Lopez saw both of the Presidents and their wives standing just beyond the edge of dense ranks of dignitaries all waiting to shake the hands of two of the most powerful men on Earth.

The viewpoint of the implanted assassin was lower than the people around them, sufficiently so that Lopez was able make one positive statement.

'You're either a woman,' she whispered, 'or a real short guy.'

Lopez tried to figure out who the person was, but with the crowd around them and no sound it was impossible to figure out who they might be with enough accuracy to warn the Secret Service team. Lopez was about to make a sprint for the lawns when she saw the figure look down at her side and saw a white handbag. Slim hands reached in and produced a small vanity mirror.

'Oh God, please yes,' Lopez whispered.

The woman lifted the mirror to her face, eager to appear perfect for her meeting with the President, and Lopez got a shadowy glimpse of her.

Lopez's direct line in the bunker rang, the sound startling her as she reached out and picked up the receiver.

'Give me some good news!'

Hellerman's voice reached down the line to her from Maryland.

'The signal's being piggy backed from the corner of 17th Street, less than two hundred fifty yards to the west of the White House!'

Lopez was on her feet and running without even replying as she keyed her microphone and yelled at the Secret Service agents arrayed around the south lawn.

'The target is in the crowd, Kiera Lomas, female! Use the signal blockers on her cell, cut her off! I'll head for the signal's source!'

Then she had an idea. Cell phones were weak when calling but SMS messages, being smaller packets of data, often got through when calls could not.

Lopez began typing furiously as she ran.

***

XLIII

Kiera Lomas stood among the crowds of politicians and dignitaries from both America and China as she prepared to shake the hand of the man who had ordered the raid that had saved her life in Basra, Iraq.

She knew that the small number of journalists and television crews that had been admitted to the South Lawn would be watching her, that she had become the poster child for her country's withdrawal from Iraq, the last–ditch effort to save her life giving the President a huge boost in popularity as he neared the end of his second term.

Despite her gratitude, however, she intended to continue on her crusade with every fibre of her being. The President's failure to crack down effectively on gun control in the United States and his apparent inability to quash the well funded lobbying of the National Rifle Association, marked for her a tragic and regrettable collapse of common sense political activism, a golden opportunity missed by an administration that could have changed the face of American history by reducing the enormous number of deaths suffered by its citizens, both innocent and guilty, every year. That and the shocking aftermath of the previous administration's ventures in Iraq and Afghanistan had convinced Kiera like nothing else that her crusade was just, the influence of big business in Washington its target.

The President and his entourage mounted the dais erected before the watching crowds, and after more rapturous applause had died down the President's voice carried clearly over the crowds as Kiera watched, one hand on her bag beside her as she prepared to take the stand.

'We're here to celebrate a trade agreement that spans the largest ocean on Earth and one that I believe, personally, to be long overdue. The Trans Pacific Trade agreement now welcomes China aboard as a partner, in a deal that could finally overcome the historic rivalry between our nation and the rising tiger of the East. We all know how China has grown as a nation both economically and technologically over the past two decades, and only a fool would believe that such growth will come to an end soon. To join our friends across the Pacific in a trade deal that will secure and enhance both of our nation's futures for many decades to come, to embrace prosperity over enmity, is an achievement that we should all be proud of, and I personally applaud every single person involved in the deal for securing a partnership that I hope will last long into our futures.'

A ripple of applause fluttered through the crowd.

'Closer to home, it's been a hard road to freedom for our country and for that of the people of Iraq, for the end to a conflict which we did not start but which was left to us to complete, but today we can confidently say that our time in Iraq has come to an end and it came to that end in spectacular style. Members of our military were able to liberate a voice with whom so many of us have become so familiar over the years, a voice that was silenced by Islamic State jihadists intent on stifling the truth. They attempted to cast a veil over the opinions and broadcasts of one woman, and as any of us men know that's a task that's not easy to achieve under any circumstances.'

A ripple of chuckles fluttered across the audience as the President gestured to Kiera.

'Ladies and gentlemen, I'd like you to welcome among us journalist Kiera Lomas.'

A rapturous applause filled the lawns as Kiera stood, smiling broadly for the cameras and for the President as he stood back from the dais and applauded along with the guests as two Secret Service agents moved either side of her and escorted her to the dais. Kiera climbed the steps, the agents remaining nearby, as she approached the President and took his proffered hand.

'Welcome home,' the President said with a warmth that Kiera realized was entirely genuine.

The President embraced her briefly and then stood back to give her the dais and the attention of the crowds gathered before them.

Kiera moved to the microphones and saw the immense crowds gathered outside the White House grounds, flocked in their thousands and able to listen intently as the sound of the applause died down and there was suddenly a deep silence all around her. To Kiera's amazement, in the center of Washington DC she could have heard a pin drop as all activity ceased and it seemed the entire capital city of the United States of America hung on her next word. Former presidents watched from their homes across the country via satellite link, senators and other powerful figures all waiting to hear what she would say.

Kiera's mind fell silent as she stared across the hundreds of faces watching her expectantly, and she thought she heard a voice whisper in her head.

Kill him.

Kiera frowned, blinked, and began to speak.

'It's hard to put into words how much my life has changed since I was liberated from captivity in Iraq by the brave men and women of our armed services…'

Kill him!

'... who risked their lives in order to save mine, so that I might return here and continue my work in pushing for greater transparency of government, reduced corporate interference in politics and exposing corruption and injustice in our legal system. I guess you could say that when the President gave the order for me to be rescued, he kind of shot himself and most of Washington DC in the foot.'

Laughter rippled across the crowd as Kiera felt her arm twitch slightly of its own accord, as though urging her to move.

'And that,' Kiera went on, 'is perhaps the greatest tragedy of all and an ironic statement on my part. I have seen at first–hand what happens to a country when its law enforcement, judiciary and military collapse and its citizens are left at the hands of marauding bandits hell bent on destruction and mayhem. It doesn't matter what religion they follow, all that matters is that they can bear arms against others without fear of retribution, safe in the knowledge that there is no law preventing them from carrying the weapons of war as easily as the rest of us carry a cell phone.'

Kill him, now!

'Our country's constitution enshrines our right to bear arms, but that constitution was written in a time when law enforcement wasn't a phone call away, when marauding bandits plagued our lands just as they do Iraq's now. But our country has changed immensely since those days and now the United States is officially recognized as the world's number one gun crime murder capital. We have as many firearms in this country as we do people. It's hardly surprising that our children are shot in their schools by people of unsound mind who are still presented with no barriers to purchasing high powered assault rifles, pistols, shotguns and other weapons that have no place on today's streets.'

Kill him, right now!

*

The traffic became even more dense as Ethan carved a path toward the White House, the roads solidly blocked, and Ethan cursed as he pulled off the road and up onto the sidewalk. Pedestrians cried out in alarm as Ethan thundered down the sidewalk between trees and parked bicycles and scooters, sunlight and shadows racing past him in rapid succession, then slammed back down onto the intersection and began weaving through the vehicles again, the sun hot on his bare arms and clouds of heat from the engine billowing around his legs.

His cell phone buzzed in his pocket, and Ethan fumbled for it as he rode and read the message on the screen from Lopez.

Blue van, corner of G & 17!

Ethan yanked the Harley hard left onto K Street and wound the throttle open as he accelerated toward the target.

***

XLIV

'Blue van, corner of seventeenth and G!'

Lopez shouted the command in her microphone as she burst out of the White House security exit and onto the north lawn, her own cell phone screen holding an image sent to her by Hellerman of traffic camera footage of the vehicle parked there.

She heard a Secret Service Agent's reply come back to her moments later.

'The traffic's too dense for pursuit vehicles, officers are joining you on foot!'

Lopez sprinted down the White House drive around the North Lawn, the security post ahead of her already unlocking the gates that opened out onto Pennsylvania Avenue NW. She sprinted through the gates and turned hard left, tourists with cameras staring wide eyed as she ran by.

'Get out of the way!'

Lopez shouted at the densely packed citizens all watching screens erected on the north lawn showing the ongoing ceremony on the south lawn, the crowds parting for her as they saw the shield clipped to her belt and the gun in its holster beneath her shoulder.

The corner of 17th and G was only two hundred yards from the north lawn, Lopez sprinting alongside the Eisenhower Executive Office building and then out across the street.

Lopez could hear the sound of Kiera Lomas's voice as it was broadcast on radio and on television screens erected around the perimeter of the White House.

"... our government has ceased to be a voice of the will of the people, has ceased to become a democratically elected union of servants of this great country. It is possible, as we have seen in the past, for an administration to come to power despite losing the popular vote. It is possible, as we have seen in the past, for them to come to power and then act with complete disregard for the will of the people they purport to serve. It is possible for our country to be governed by those who have not been democratically elected and who do not act upon the will of the people. How can that be? It is possible because our country is not run by its government, but instead is bought out by the deep pockets of global mega–corporations who pay for our presidents to come to power on agendas favorable to corporations over people?"

Lopez saw the van almost immediately and then saw two police officers sprinting up from the south, their weapons drawn and their shouts echoing above the noise of the traffic.

'Stand down!'

Lopez's scream was drowned out by the sound of gunfire and the squeal of tires as the blue van suddenly lurched into motion. The gunfire cracked the air and Lopez saw one of the police officers tumble to the ground amid the ranks of cars as the van made to get away.

'This is what happened in Iraq, a country destroyed by our government in a war that was both illegal and not wanted by us, the people. That country was raped of its wealth by powerful arms and industrial corporations, and the remains left for the people who live there. Our country has become the vassal through which global corporations become more wealthy, where trade trumps human rights, where profit conquers altruism, where war vanquishes peace in the name of our right to oil or the right to bear arms!'

The blue van mounted the sidewalk alongside the rows of traffic and accelerated to the sound of screams from pedestrians. Lopez dashed onto the sidewalk in front of the vehicle, her weapon drawn as she took aim at the windshield.

The vehicle's engine screamed higher as it accelerated toward her and Lopez held her breath for an instant before she fired.

Three shots burst from her pistol and shattered the blue van's windscreen into a spider's web of fractured glass that sent the vehicle swerving from side to side as it crashed past a fire hydrant and sent a tower of glistening water high into the air.

Lopez hurled herself sideways as the van careered past her and thumped back onto the road, its fender smashing off the side of a truck's chassis and then rolling to a halt in the center of the lane. Lopez sprinted to the driver's side of the van and aimed into the cab to see a Middle–Eastern man slumped against the wheel, his skull shattered into a bloody mess by one of Lopez's rounds.

She turned and hurried to the rear of the vehicle and grabbed hold of the rear door.

To her shock the door flew open and she was thrown backwards as two men burst from the interior. As Lopez staggered she swung her pistol to bear upon a burly, bearded man who leaped out of the van with a rifle in his hands, and an older man with gray hair and a wispy beard, the cold eyes of a killer glaring at her.

Lopez hit the asphalt hard on her back as she fired, her shot hitting the upper lip of the rear of the van and ricocheting to one side as she heard two more shots fired.

Lopez felt her body shudder as though the ground had shifted beneath her, a double thud that blurred her vision as she felt her arms go strangely numb. Her lungs constricted inside her chest and for a moment she wondered who had fired the shots and why the two men in the van had not fallen, and then she realized that Tariq Adel was aiming his pistol at her, a cruel smile on his face.

Lopez stared at the scene before her, and then she realized that her legs were tingling and her shoulders sinking and the world spun around in a blur of color. The horizon tilted over and she plummeted onto her back on the lawns but strangely felt nothing as she landed, the bright blue sky filling her vision as clouds drifted quietly through the heavens.

'This very city in which we stand has the highest homicide rate of any in the developed world. Nine thousand Americans died last year as a result of gun crime, more than died in automobile accidents. The National Rifle Association will tell you that it is our right as Americans to bear arms. They won't tell you that saying so keeps the revenue rolling in for them, even though in this day and age we have armed law enforcement to protect us from those who would harm us in every city. This is not Iraq, but some days Washington DC is starting to feel worse than Basra!'

Tariq and the bearded man dashed toward the front of the vehicle. Lopez tried to get up, but her body would not respond and a savage pain ripped across her chest. She slumped onto her back as the engine to the vehicle started, the dead driver's body thumping down onto the road as the battered van pulled away in a cloud of exhaust fumes.

Lopez stared up at the blue sky and realized that she was struggling to breathe as citizens broke from cover and ran to surround her, their eyes wide with horror and concern as the sound of a large, thumping engine thundered between the buildings and vehicles.

Hannah Ford's face appeared as if from nowhere before Lopez, the agent crouching down alongside her and pressing against Lopez's chest as Agent Vaughn, his face bruised and battered, covered them both with his pistol and shouted at the surrounding civilians to get back.

'Stay with me, Nicola!' Hannah urged.

Lopez blinked, still unsure of what had happened until she felt the growing numbness in her chest, saw the blood oozing from between Hannah Ford's fingers, and she realized that she had been hit and that she could taste blood in her mouth. Suddenly she could not breathe, despite gasping and trying to inflate her chest for all she was worth, and she knew without a shadow of a doubt that at least one of her lungs had been punctured.

Hannah looked back down at Lopez, her face pained.

'Where's Ethan?!' she demanded.

Lopez realized that Ethan had not shown up at the scene and that he had his cell phone on him. She swallowed the blood in her mouth and managed to speak a final sentence.

'Ethan might be implanted,' she gasped. 'He didn't show.'

Lopez's head sank back wearily onto the grass. Amid the chaos and the shouting, Lopez lay in a vacuum of tranquility and stared up at the serene sky above her as she heard Kiera Lomas's final words.

'If America is truly to become great again we must become a nation of the people, for the people. Are you all going to live your lives knowing that corporations control our country's government, its capital city, even its presidents? Will you continue to let your children die from gunshot wounds in your schools just because a Constitutional right written two hundred years ago is held up by the NRO as a reason to continue making profits? Or will you take back control of your own country and demand the right to be heard, the right to true governance by democratically elected leaders who are not in the thrall of big business? Who will have to die before the people will wake up to the fact that the right to bear arms, and the right of corporations to control government, is killing us all day by day?'

Lopez smiled as she realized that Kiera Lomas had not made an attempt on the lives of either of the two Presidents standing beside her on the south lawn. She felt herself relax, felt relief wash over her.

For a moment Lopez was reminded of the skies of her native Guanajuato, of the mountains and of how far she had come in the years since, and then the sky fell into darkness and all was lost to her.

***

XLV

Ethan hauled the Harley Davidson onto 17th Street as a crowd of people gathered around something in the street, and in the distance a blue van with a smashed windscreen accelerated toward him.

Ethan wound the Harley's throttle open even as the blue van flashed by on his left as he hit the brakes and counter–steered the big Harley into a slide, the fat rear tire squealing and blue smoke spiraling onto the hot air as he turned the bike around and accelerated back up the street in pursuit of the vehicle. It weaved left and right, fighting its way past slower moving vehicles as Ethan tried to pick a moment to use the motorbike's superior power and acceleration to slip past.

The rear–view mirror showed the face of the driver, watching Ethan intently as he swerved hard right and broadsided a blue Prius that careered to the left and smashed into the side of a tree on the sidewalk with a crash of rending metal and shattering glass. Ethan jerked the Harley to the left and just missed the rear of the Prius as it skittered to a halt, its front wheel warped and buckled and the tire flat as it rubbed along the sidewalk.

Ethan could see a major intersection ahead that joined K Street, a through fare running east – west through the city on the edge of downtown. If the van got out there it would have more room for manoeuver and Ethan did not have the time for a protracted pursuit.

A smaller intersection appeared and Ethan closed up on the rear of the van. As they rocketed across the intersection, Ethan kicked the Harley down a gear and twisted the throttle wide open as he swerved first right and then left to fool the driver. The van jerked about in an attempt to block Ethan and then the Harley roared past, the engine loud in Ethan's ear as it was amplified between the passing buildings and the side of the van. Ethan passed alongside the van and the saw an articulated truck looming dead ahead.

The truck's horn blared and Ethan's heart skipped a beat as he leaned the Harley over and flashed through the rapidly closing gap. The truck swerved right to avoid him as Ethan shot by and out in front of the van and immediately kicked his heel down on the rear brake.

The Harley's rear tire locked up in a cloud of blue smoke as Ethan twisted the handlebars against the bike's slide. The heavy motorbike shuddered as it slowed and then its tires regained their grip. The Harley flipped upright as Ethan deliberately released the handlebars and launched himself out of the saddle.

The Harley high–sided and slammed down on its right side on the asphalt in a billowing cloud of sparks as chrome bodywork and metal scraped along the road. Ethan hit the ground and rolled over, coming up onto his feet as he looked back and saw the van hit the brakes, its tires squealing.

The van hit the Harley and the big motorbike wedged itself under the van's front fender as a deafening crescendo of tortured metal screeched and echoed between the buildings lining either side of 17th Street. Ethan leaped out of the van's way as it thundered past in a cloud of bright sparks that flared from the Harley's engine block as it was forced on its side along the hot asphalt, the bike's sheer size and weight bringing the van to a halt.

Ethan turned and sprinted to the van's side even as the driver opened his door and hurled himself out of the vehicle. He turned in time for Ethan to swing a punch that impacted the driver's bearded jaw with a sharp crack and spun him backwards into the open door. Time seemed to slow down as Ethan looked into the eyes of a burly, bearded man of Middle Eastern origin, the assault rifle held in both of his hands swinging up to point at Ethan as from the other side of the van a second man turned to flee.

The fleeing man was older, his hair and narrow beard gray, his eyes cold and cunning like those of a hawk and a smile that looked more like a sneer painted across his face as he looked back at Ethan.

Ethan hurled himself out of the line of fire even as the assault rifle shook and a flare of flame burst from its barrel. Ethan rolled by the vehicle's front fender as he heard screams from pedestrians as the gunshots rattled out through the streets, bullets smashing through the open passenger door where he had been standing moments before.

Ethan pulled his pistol from its shoulder holster and rolled along the hot asphalt beside the ruined Harley Davidson as he took aim beneath the van. He could see the gunman's booted feet as he hurried around the rear of the vehicle to catch Ethan as he appeared on the other side.

Ethan did not wait for the gunman to appear as he took aim and fired beneath the van.

The 9mm round smashed into the gunman's ankle at a range of no more than ten feet and he heard a great roar of pain as the bullet shattered bone and the big man toppled down onto one knee at the rear of the van. The barrel of the emerged but moved no further as the crippled gunman growled in pain and began crawling the last few paces to bring the weapon to bear on where Ethan lay.

Ethan was already up and running, and as the assault rifle appeared around the rear fender so he swung one boot and smashed it up under the barrel to send the rifle spinning up into the air as it was wrenched from the gunman's grasp.

Ethan turned around the corner of the wrecked van's rear fender and saw the bearded gunman on his knees, his hands raised beside his head and a grim smile spreading on his face.

'Alluhah Akbhar!' he shouted.

The sound of screaming sirens echoed across the streets as Ethan circled around the kneeling gunman and with one hand managed to unclip a set of handcuffs from his belt and secure one of the big man's wrists.

'Get up!'

Ethan hauled the gunman to his feet, his pistol jabbed under the big man's ribs as he hustled him to the driver's door and then shoved him face first into the vehicle as he cuffed the man's wrist to the steering wheel.

Ethan turned and began running in pursuit of the old man, Tariq Adel. To his delight and amazement, drivers in cars trapped within the dense traffic shouted and pointed up the street where Tariq had fled. Ethan pumped his arms and sucked in deep breaths of air, running hard down the street as he saw pedestrians cowering in driveways and crouching behind walls, evidently having thrown themselves into cover as Tariq rushed past with his rifle.

Ethan burst out onto the main intersection and heard screams ahead even as he heard rifle fire and saw Tariq standing on the sidewalk alongside Farragut Square, the rifle cradled in his grasp as he fired at Ethan.

Ethan hurled himself down on the ground as a shower of bullets smacked the sidewalk around him. Tariq was screaming obscenities as he fired at Ethan, the rifle's recoil too strong for the old man to aim properly. Pedestrians screamed in their hundreds as they scattered away from the gunfire, and Ethan aimed his pistol and held his breath for a moment before he fired twice.

The first bullet hit Tariq low in the belly, the second high in the chest and the old man staggered backwards on the sidewalk and tried to bring the rifle to bear on Ethan while seeking an escape route. Ethan, lying prone on the hot asphalt, fired again. The round smacked into Tariq's shoulder and threw him onto his back as the rifle spun from his grasp and clattered down alongside him.

Ethan jumped to his feet and sprinted across the road, weaving between vehicles as he rushed up to Tariq's body, his pistol still aimed at the old man.

Tariq was lying on his back, blood spilling onto his hands as he clutched the wound in his belly, his shirt a bloodied mess where Ethan's bullet had entered his shoulder and then exited his neck. Bright blood pulsed from severed arteries and Ethan realized immediately that the third wound was fatal.

Tariq seemed to know that he was doomed as he squinted up at Ethan, a slim, curved blade held tightly in one bloodied hand that he pointed at Ethan to prevent him from coming any closer.

'It's over, Tariq,' Ethan insisted. 'The President won't be dying any time soon and it's not worth you dying now. Let me help you.'

Tariq smiled, his white teeth stained pink with blood.

'It's not over,' he rasped, his chest surging as he fought for every last breath. 'It's only just begun.'

'The Presidents of America and China are safe,' Ethan snapped. 'You failed, Tariq. It's over.'

'Is it?' the old man asked. 'Then where is Abrahem?'

Ethan felt a sudden premonition of doom sweep over him. 'You tell me, Tariq.'

Tariq's smile did not slip even as Ethan heard police sirens wailing ever closer, fighting their way through the dense traffic.

'To fight is to be courageous,' Tariq whispered, 'but to deceive is to be wise.'

'Where is Abrahem?!' Ethan snapped.

Tariq's grip on his blade faltered and the weapon clattered to the sidewalk as his chest stopped moving and he gasped one final sentence.

'Getting his revenge before he joins me in paradise.'

Tariq's smile remained in place even as the light of life faded from his eyes and his hands slumped from his wounds to slap down onto the sidewalk.

Ethan stared at the old man for a long moment and then he heard the President's voice on the screens erected in the park nearby, saw him addressing the crowds on the South Lawn of the White House. There, on the image, were satellite links to other dignitaries not present at the ceremony but watching from afar.

And finally, Ethan understood what Tariq had meant. *Deception.*

'Oh no.'

Ethan whirled and sprinted across the park as he sought a means of transport. He knew that he had only minutes to act.

***

XLVI

Travilah, Maryland

The sun was low in the sky, sheets of molten metal flaring behind the rows of trees lining the asphalt road that weaved between vast estates and ranches nestled within deep forests and rolling hills.

Travilah was one of the United States' most exclusive residences, a place where those with the means could retire to a life of leisure far from the turbulence of Washington DC but close enough to feel the distant pulse of the country's beating political heart. Broad green fields, lush forests and tranquil lakes dotted the countryside in the late afternoon sunshine as Abrahem Nassir walked up the long drive of a massive colonially styled mansion.

Abrahem did not know precisely what panic he had managed to cause in the capital city of America, although he did know that the city was gridlocked. The Presidential meeting on the South Lawn of the White House was captivating the world, and the traffic through the city was ensuring that nobody would be moving anywhere fast for a good few hours. The radio he had listened to on the drive out of the city had hinted at several police actions around the Capitol area, police chases and other events that suggested perhaps the capture of people who intended harm to the country. Abrahem smiled, for he knew that while the law enforcement agencies of the most powerful country on Earth were otherwise engaged, he would now play the ace in his sleeve that none of them had seen coming.

America would now have its own moment of *shock and awe.*

Abrahem could not help but compare his elegant surroundings with the killing fields of Iraq and the battered, sun scorched ruins of Basra where children ran in bare feet and ragged clothes, ever fearful of attack by Islamic militants and American air strikes alike; where water was a luxury, not a given; where life was short, cheap and often filled with suffering.

But here in America was the paradise that so many of the militants spoke of, not as part of some supposed afterlife but in the here and now. A warm sun, a blue sky, rolling fields, water everywhere, luxury everywhere, nothing to fear.

Nothing but Abrahem.

The security guards at the main entrance to the home had been easy to kill. Despite Abrahem's obvious Middle Eastern origins, they had suspected no foul play when he had pulled in alongside their post to ask for directions. Both had been happy to assist him, both had scrutinized his map at his request and both had collapsed as 9mm slugs punctured their internal organs. Moments later, two more rounds had pierced their skulls.

Abrahem had opened the main gates and then hauled the bodies into his vehicle's trunk before driving slowly toward the house, the drive of which wound back and forth between ranks of tall, elegant aspen that were aesthetically pleasing and yet tactically disastrous for the occupants of the house beyond. Abrahem knew that they lived safe in the knowledge that despite their heinous crimes they would never be brought to justice for them, would never face a trial for the wars they had started, for the lives they had taken.

Abrahem slowed his vehicle and watched the house for a moment, then he killed the engine and climbed out, closed his door quietly. He knew that most of the occupants of the house would be sitting in front of the television, watching intently and indeed be being watched by millions of Americans. Despite the confidence he had in his plan Abrahem was surprised to feel somewhat nervous as he approached the front door. Perhaps it was because he had waited so long, yearned so much for this moment? He pushed the emotion aside as he reached the front door of the house, and then reached into his pocket and pulled out a cell phone.

Abrahem tapped in a text message and pressed *send.* Then, he waited. In his vehicle was a transmitter, which was signalling an implant inside the home.

Within two minutes the door to the massive house opened and a smartly dressed man confronted Abrahem. He was broad shouldered, with a thick neck and the closely cropped hair of a former military soldier. 1st Infantry Brigade Combat Team, to be precise, which had deployed to Baghdad, Iraq in 2008. Corporal James Larson, rifleman, twenty nine years of age, now a security specialist assigned to the permanent protection detail of a former President of the United States. He had been implanted after a minor bullet wound had required surgery in a field hospital near Basra.

Abrahem moved quickly, quietly, the blade flashing across Larson's neck. The soldier did not flinch, seemed almost asleep as the razor sharp blade opened his throat with a crisp sound, blood spilling in copious floods down his white shirt.

Abrahem watched, fascinated, as the soldier's legs slowly gave way and the light of life faded from his eyes. Like a giant statue he toppled slowly forward and Abrahem side–stepped Larson's body as it plummeted down and smashed into the steps in front of the house.

Abrahem grabbed hold of the former soldier's ankles and hauled him inside, then closed the door once more.

*

Hannah Ford hurried inside the White House feeling as though she were dreaming, the colors around her more vivid than she recalled them ever being. Her fatigue suddenly vanished as she turned a corridor, two Secret Service agents escorting her as she laid eyes on FBI Director LeMay.

The White House state dining room was filled with guests, the air humming with conversation beneath the ornate chandelier hanging over dining tables laid with Lenox gold charger plates and cutlery.

'The threat has been successfully neutralized,' came Secret Service Agent Hopkin's voice over the radio. *'Olympus is safe.'*

Hannah fumbled to get her microphone into place quickly enough to reply, her access to the White House cleared only minutes before by Jarvis via the President himself.

'Negative,' she snapped, 'I say again, negative, the threat has *not* been neutralized. All stations, stay alert!'

Her eyes sought out Director LeMay once more. The Director was talking to a pair of Chinese delegates, a flute of sparkling champagne in one hand and a cell phone in the other. Hannah began heading toward the Director, possessed of a determination that she had never felt before in all of her years. To her left she could see the President of the United States talking to the President of the People's Republic of China, surrounded by a small army of delegates all keen to shake the hands of the most powerful man on earth.

The state dining room was the largest in the White House, but less than fifty by forty feet overall. A bomb, detonated in or close to the room, would be devastating.

Hannah started to move more quickly as her mind raced and everything went into slow–motion. She saw Director LeMay and nothing else in the room, as though the rest of the world were merely an irritating blur.

Get him out of the room.

'Director?'

LeMay turned to Hannah and a glimmer of surprise flickered across his features.

'Agent Ford, what brings you here? How did you gain access?'

'There has been a major development, sir,' Hannah replied. 'I need to speak with you urgently, right now.'

LeMay raised an eyebrow but he excused himself from the room and followed Hannah into the hall outside, where White House staff were shuttling back and forth with trays of champagne flutes and *hors d'oeuvres*. Hannah led him to a quiet corner, two Secret Service agents following, and turned to confront him.

'What's this all about, Agent Ford?' LeMay asked.

Destroy his cell phone.

Hannah lunged for Director LeMay's cell. She ploughed her shoulder into the Director's chest and smashed him into the wall, the cell phone tumbling from his grasp to land on the carpet at their feet.

Hannah turned, lifted one heel and smashed it down onto the cell phone. The heel crunched through the phone and bent it almost in half with the force of the blow, the screen flickering out to darkness as LeMay staggered away from her.

'Special Agent Ford, what the hell do you think you're..?'

Hard–duke the son of a bitch.

Hannah turned and swung her right fist with all of her might and rage and punched Director LeMay square on the nose. The Director's face collapsed in on itself in pain as he staggered backwards and crashed down onto his back, Hannah ignoring his plight as she picked up the cell phone that she had stamped out and turned to the Secret Service agents.

'This cell phone is evidence that will implicate Director LeMay in the attempted murder of the President of the United States, the President of the People's Republic of China and the shooting of a DIA officer,' she said. 'Please secure it and let nobody, and I mean *nobody*, tamper with it, understood?'

LeMay staggered to his feet, blood pouring from his nose.

'That is my private cell and I'll be taking it with me! This is absolute nonsense! Arrest her!'

The Secret Service agents were not accustomed to taking orders from anybody, but LeMay's tone silenced any protest they may have made as they grabbed Hannah and pinned her against the wall. One of them picked up the damaged cell phone and handed it back to the Director.

'What about your partner, Vaughn? Where is he?' LeMay demanded, holding a bloodied tissue to his nose.

'This isn't over!' Hannah shouted, loud enough to attract glances from dignitaries within the state dining room further down the hall. 'Ethan Warner is still out there and we haven't captured Abrahem Nassir!'

Secret Service Agent Daniel Hopkins dashed into the corridor along with four more agents as they confronted LeMay and Hannah.

'What the hell's going on here?' he demanded in a harsh whisper, conscious of the delegates in the room nearby, then turned to his men. 'Get both of them out of sight, now!'

Hannah looked at Hopkins. 'Lopez was shot! LeMay's behind it all!'

Director LeMay stared at Hannah as though she were insane. 'I don't know what's got into her, but she's about to be arrested for assault and battery and is wanted for murder in Hong Kong!'

'The President isn't safe!' Hannah insisted to Hopkins. 'This isn't over! You have to find Ethan Warner, Aaron Mitchell and Abrahem Nassir!'

'Who the hell is Aaron Mitchell?' Hopkins demanded. 'And both of the Presidents are safe, so what the hell are you talking about?'

Hannah was about to answer when her earpiece crackled, along with that of every single Secret Service Agent on the south lawn. The coded message was as concise and clear as any she had ever heard.

'Olympus is compromised!'

Hannah looked up and saw both of the Presidents safely enveloped within the human shield of their Secret Service bodyguards. Confusion mounted in her addled mind and then she turned slowly and looked up at a television screen on a wall further down the corridor that was still displaying the feed from numerous Presidential homes around the country.

There, on one of the screens, a former President of the United States of America sat staring back at them, a gun held to his head.

***

XLVII

Travilah, Maryland

The family was seated on a wide leather couch in front of an enormous television screen that spanned an entire half of one wall, the screen a concave that prevented any reflections from marring the ultra–high resolution image presented upon it.

The carpets beneath Abrahem Nassir's feet were thick, plush, a light cream color devoid of even the slightest stain. The magnolia walls were tastefully decorated with photographs and paintings, softly lit by the sunlight streaming in through broad windows that overlooked the immaculate lawns and the woods beyond.

'You don't know me.'

Abrahem Nassir stood to one side of the screen, knowing that his voice was being broadcast live to the delegates inside the White House. Abrahem knew, of course, that live did not exactly mean "live" any more. The television networks always ran on a thirty second delay, ensuring that they could cut the feed if anything untoward occurred during a broadcast. However here at the former President's home, the feed to the White House was both truly live and direct. It could be cut off, of course, but Abrahem knew that the security agencies would want the feed to remain live as they attempted to make contact with him and prevent a tragedy.

The former President of the United States had not held office for some years now and had aged considerably. Abrahem, a man in the prime of his life, had been surprised by how short the former President was. He had expected a giant of a man surrounded by an aura of potency and competence. Instead he was more than a little disappointed that the diminutive individual who confronted him was both softly spoken and probably weighed less than a hundred eighty pounds, his hair silvery gray and his back slightly hunched with age.

'No,' the President replied, the barrel of Abrahem's gun aimed directly at his head. 'I don't know who you are. Why are you in my home?'

Abrahem leaned back on an expensive, polished wooden cabinet that lined the wall behind him. It would not have surprised him to learn that the cabinet cost more than he would have earned in five years in Iraq. He would not rush this moment, for Abrahem knew that it would be his last. There would be no survivors in this confrontation, and if he faltered then for him at least America would win again when their soldiers and police stormed the house and gunned him down with their patriotic fury. Abrahem would ensure that they would never get the chance, for he would personally bring this to an end much sooner.

'Why did you enter my home?' Abrahem challenged.

'I don't understand.'

'No,' Abrahem agreed, 'I don't suppose that you do. Allow me to explain. You ordered your country to war against Iraq and invaded my country. Before doing so you embarked upon a campaign that you proudly named *shock and awe*. Do you remember that, Mister President?'

The President nodded.

'Why did you do it, Mister President?'

'I don't have to answer to you.'

Abrahem smiled, pushed off the cabinet and took three long paces to where a young girl, perhaps twelve years old, was perched nervously on the edge of a couch. Abrahem grabbed her by her hair and yanked her to her feet as he pushed the pistol against the side of her head.

'Leave her alone!' the President snapped as he struggled to his feet. 'You can do what you like to me, but leave my family alone!'

'Oh, Mister President,' Abrahem murmured, 'if only you had given a thought to how many Iraqi fathers, mothers, sons and daughters cried the same thing all those years ago. Now tell me, why did you invade my country?'

'I did what had to be done for the security of our nation.'

'You lied,' Abrahem hissed. 'Your people lied, your intelligence services lied, your politicians lied, and your lies cost a hundred thousand Iraqi men, women and children their lives. *Shock and awe*, quite a title, no? And what did you intend that shock and awe to achieve in Iraq, Mister President?'

The President swallowed thickly as he recognized where the conversation was heading.

'It was designed to negatively affect the will, perception and understanding of an adversary to fight or respond to American strategic policy, to render them unwilling to resist through overwhelming displays of power.'

Abrahem nodded quietly as he echoed the President's words, the girl's hair still wrapped tightly around his bunched fist.

'Overwhelming displays of power. It must have been easy Mister President, to have given those orders while sitting in the Oval Office, far from danger. I wonder if you ever thought about how it feels to be on the other end of a shock and awe campaign? Have you ever wondered how it would feel to see your children's bodies blasted into pieces by bombs?'

The President's stoic demeanor began to crumble.

'Leave my granddaughter alone,' he croaked.

Abrahem looked at the young girl, her long brown hair and pale, soft skin.

'They burned, most of them,' he said idly as he stroked her hair. 'The bombs usually cooked them alive, but of course they don't show that sort of thing on your televisions. It might *offend.*' Abrahem glared at the President as rage overcame him. 'They don't show what really happens when America invades another country, or when Israel bombs hospitals and civilians in Gaza, because they don't want your poor American viewers to get *upset!*'

Abrahem yanked the girl's head back and rammed the pistol against her jaw.

'Are you getting *upset, Mister President?!*'

The President nodded as tears began streaming from his eyes. 'Yes.'

*

Ethan killed the engine of a stolen Honda motorbike he had liberated from a parking lot in Sumner Row, jumped off the saddle and slipped through the security gates of the mansion. He ran up the lawns at a sprint as he spotted the blood stains splattering across the asphalt near the empty guard house.

The sunlight cast long shadows across the lawns, the horizon blazing with golden light and the mansion aglow with an orange haze as he hurried toward it, running in a low crouch and hoping that he could reach the walls without being spotted by either Abrahem or anybody else the terrorist might have brought with him.

The front door to the mansion was closed so Ethan instead skirted the walls, moving cautiously past each window and peeking in as he sought some sign of the occupants and prayed that Abrahem had not yet managed to gain access to the family. He made only another few steps before he came to a large bay window that looked into a massive lounge, one wall dominated by a huge widescreen television. Inside and sitting on the couch were several members of the former President's family, and standing with a young girl in his grasp was Abrahem Nassir.

Ethan's heart plunged as he realized that his earlier hunch had been correct. Nassir was not a man who wanted to kill people remotely, using drones or cerebral implants or anything else. Abrahem Nassir wanted to wreak his revenge with his bare hands. He wanted to feel the life draining from his victims, as he had witnessed it draining from members of his own family so long ago in the burning wastelands of Basra in the wake of America's campaign. The incumbent President of the United States had never been his main target: the man who had led the administration when Iraq had been humbled before America's military might had been the President that Nassir sought, the President he held responsible for so many hundreds of thousands of Iraqi lives lost in the conflict.

Ethan knew that by now the police and the intelligence agencies would be swarming toward the house and that Abrahem knew it too. The Iraqi's plan did not involve his escape from the house for he knew that it was impossible. Abrahem intended to die here, and Ethan guessed that he intended to take the former President and his family with him.

Ethan moved on past the window and scouted around the back of the house. It was sufficiently large that he felt certain he could break into the building from the far side without being heard. He could only hope that any security alarms would be of the silent type that would alert the authorities without revealing Ethan's presence to Abrahem.

Two birds, one stone.

The rear of the house featured beautifully manicured gardens, tall hedges and a fountain that sparkled like a pile of shivering golden diamonds in the sunlight as Ethan eased his way past the most obvious entrance point, a set of French doors that led into what looked like an office. Instead, he headed for a smaller window in a door that appeared to open into a kitchen judging by the food waste and recycling trash cans arranged neatly against the wall.

Ethan grabbed a rock from the ornate hedges nearby and then hurried across to the window. He pulled off his shirt and wrapped it around the rock, and then after a quick glance into the kitchen to ensure that it was deserted, he smashed the rock into the window's edge.

The first blow did nothing and neither did the second, but Ethan's third blow fractured the window with a crackle of splintered glass. Ethan used the rock to knock more and more of the glass out until he could reach in and grab at the handle and locks. Within moments he had unlocked the door and opened it from the inside, and he slipped inside the kitchen and closed the door behind him.

The interior of the house was silent, large enough that whatever was taking place in the lounge Ethan wasn't close enough to hear it. He pulled his shirt back on and pulled his pistol from its holster, checked the magazine before he began easing into the house.

The corridor outside the kitchen was equally silent, sunlight streaming in beams across paneled walls, dust motes drifting like lost stars as Ethan crept forward, the pistol held low in both hands as he advanced. Paintings hung on the walls, aged oils speaking of Colonial vessels striking out across turbulent oceans in search of new lands, the New World.

Ethan reached another corridor and turned left, heading toward the front of the house and the lounge he had seen on the way in. Now he could hear something, voices in the distance. At first they were mere whispers but then he caught the tension in the short, sharp words as an old man replied to a question demanded of him.

Ethan slowed, listening intently as he approached a large foyer where twin staircases ascended to the upper floors either side of a large painting of what looked like Pickett's Charge, Gettysburg, the Union's rifles repelling the Confederate's infantry assault.

Ethan saw on his left the entrance to the lounge, the doorway wide open. From his vantage point he could see some of the President's family sitting on the couch and he could finally hear Abrahem Nassir's voice clearly as it carried out into the hall.

'Are you getting *upset*, Mister President?!'

Ethan crossed the hall and hugged the wall beside the entrance, his eyes closed as he focused in on Abrahem's voice. He was still standing where Ethan had seen him from outside, tucked up close to the television, most likely with the girl still in his grasp. Ethan had not been able to see a weapon in Abrahem's hands but he had to assume a pistol, or at the very least a knife, was the assassin's weapon of choice.

Ethan knew that he would not be able to shoot accurately enough to hit Abrahem and kill him outright without risking the life of his captive. Such sharp–shooting was the stuff of television legend, not the real world, as was the chance of a single shot dropping a subject there and then. Criminals had been known to fight after taking shotgun shrapnel in the head, others had taken sixty rounds and lived to tell the tale and in one remarkable engagement a US soldier in Vietnam fought for six hours despite nearly forty serious bullet, shrapnel and bayonet wounds, as well as performing an eighty yard run with a rifle round in one knee.

Ethan kept his eyes closed as he heard Abrahem Nassir's voice.

'I shall not leave this life without putting you through the same pain, grief and suffering that I and so many others have endured at your hands.'

The response came immediately, grief stricken.

'Please, leave her be!'

Ethan shoved his pistol into the back of his jeans beneath his shirt, turned and stepped into plain view.

'Hello Abrahem.'

***

XLVIII

'Set up a perimeter and don't let anything get within a quarter mile of that house without my say so!'

Secret Service Agent Daniel Hopkin's voice boomed like a cannon down the radio as the SUV rocketed along the country road, Hannah Ford hanging on for dear life as the team deployed to Travilah. She could see behind her a long stream of government vehicles all armed to the teeth, and behind that a pair of helicopters swiftly gaining on the convoy.

Hopkins turned to her, his broad jaw tense and his gaze penetrating in its intensity.

'According to the President, you're on point for this operation. I don't like it, Director LeMay is spitting flames about it and right now you're wanted for a homicide in Hong Kong so whoever is backing you must have some serious influence.'

'The Defense Intelligance Agency knows what's been happening,' Hannah shot back. 'Once this is over, everything will be explained, just get us to that house.'

'Where is this guy Warner, right now?'

Hannah shook her head. 'He took off and we don't have a location for him. The only thing we can assume is that he identified Abrahem Nassir's real target and headed directly there.'

'What are the chances that he's under the control of a hostile via one of these supposed implants?'

'Minimal.'

Hopkins nodded and keyed his microphone again.

'All units, consider all non–household entities to be hostiles. Repeat, all non–household entities to be hostiles.'

'Hey!' Hannah protested. 'I just told you Ethan Warner's on our side!'

'No, you told me his chances of subversion were minimal. That's not good enough for me to prioritize his safety over that of the President and his family, and we have reports from the Metropolitan Police Department that a man matching Warner's description has stolen vehicles and opened fire on members of the public! You either get me proof that he's safe to consider a blue or he's going down!'

Hannah stared in disbelief at the agent. She knew damned well, as did Hopkins, that there was no way in hell they would have the time to figure out what side Ethan was on before the Secret Service would storm the property and take Abrahem Nassir down.

'Do we still have the video link?' she asked.

Hopkins nodded as they were driven to a spot within one mile of the mansion.

'It's being maintained, but the feed at the White House was cut off prior to the appearance of Abrahem Nassir, so right now nobody knows what's happening and I want it to stay that way.'

'The media can't get in here, can they?' Hannah asked. 'The President's home has an aerial exclusion zone around it, right? Nothing can get close enough to film?'

'Don't underestimate the resourcefulness of the media,' Hopkins snapped back. 'They have drones with telephoto lenses that can shoot rock steady footage through a window from a couple of miles away. I want this situation contained within the next ten minutes before this asshole Nassir gets his revenge or whatever it is he wants. If I have anything to do with it this whole situation will never have happened, understood?'

Hannah hesitated as she looked at the agent's uncompromising glare, and then she nodded in agreement.

'Okay, fine,' she replied. 'But at least let me lead and get to Warner first. If he's in there he may be the one person close enough to Nassir to stop him from taking any more lives.'

Hopkins grinned ruefully as he checked the magazine of his pistol and then shoved it back into its holster as the vehicle slowed.

'Judging by Nassir's recent history, I don't think that's going to happen.'

The SUV came to a halt below the crest of a hill less than a mile away from the former President's residence, and Hopkins jumped out and jogged to the crest of the hill. Hannah followed as the agent crouched down in the foliage lining the road and pulled out a pair of binoculars, scanning the house for any sign of movement.

'Anything?' Hannah asked.

Hopkins shook his head.

'Nothing, but we'll know more when the snipers get into position.'

'They're not going to be able to pull off a headshot from out here,' Hannah insisted, 'even I know that.'

Hopkins was about to reply when he pressed his earpiece tighter and frowned as he listened.

'What is it?' Hannah asked as the agent looked up at the building.

Hopkins pulled his cell phone out and accessed a new file that he had been sent. 'The former President had two new members of staff on his security team, permanent assets hired only recently to provide extra security in the home.'

'Do we have identification details?' she asked.

Hopkins showed her two images on the cell's screen, and immediately Hannah pointed to one of them.

'We've got a real problem,' she replied.

From the screen of the cell the face of Aaron Mitchell stared back at her.

*

Abrahem Nassir turned abruptly as Ethan appeared in the doorway, a pistol pressed to the jaw of the young girl.

Ethan only had a brief moment to survey the big room. The former President's family were arrayed on the large couch and two armchairs either side of it, all of them wearing stricken expressions. Behind them stood a tall, dark man with his hands in the air, his pistol on the carpeted floor nearby and out of reach.

Ethan almost gave a start of recognition as he recognized Aaron Mitchell's intimidating form looming there but managed to focus on Abrahem instead,

'Who the hell are you?' Abrahem Nassir snapped.

'You don't need to hurt these people, Abrahem,' Ethan replied. 'They don't know who you are and probably don't know what the hell you're talking about. Look at that girl you're holding – she wasn't even alive when Basra first got bombed.'

Abraham's dark eyes glowed with malevolence and he almost spat his response in Ethan's direction.

'She's related to that bastard,' he growled, gesturing with a nod of his head toward the former President. 'I don't care if she was born yesterday, she's about to become as much of a victim of his policies as my family were, as all Iraqis were!'

Ethan raised an eyebrow and shrugged as he leaned against the wall. 'Fine, have it your way.'

Abrahem's eyes narrowed. 'You're bluffing, trying to buy time until the Secret Service and the Navy SEALS and the police come blasting their way here. It won't do any good; we will all be dead long before they can stop me.'

'I know,' Ethan replied. 'I just came here to watch the fireworks, to see if it was all worth it.'

Abrahem's features twisted upon themselves in fury as he tried to figure out what Ethan was getting at. He backed further away from the President, the young girl tight in his grasp and the pistol pressed so hard against her jaw that it seemed to have punctured her skin.

'What are you talking about?' he sneered.

Ethan knew that Abrahem would not be able to resist, would *need* to know what Ethan was doing there and what he was hinting at. It was human nature, an uncontrollable desire to find out what was going to happen next, and Ethan was counting on it to give the Secret Service snipers enough time to get a bead on Abrahem and at least try to take him down.

'All that we did,' Ethan said as though Abrahem should know everything. 'All that we did to fix your country, was it worth it? Did it make you the man you've become, or are you just some radicalized asshole who likes killing young girls for pleasure.'

'I'm not radicalized!' Abrahem shouted, the girl in his grip flinching with fear and whimpering. 'This is revenge! This is justice, the kind of justice that men like him believe that they're immune to!'

Ethan glanced at the former President, who was clearly both as upset and as baffled as Abrahem as to what Ethan was doing. Ethan looked back at Abrahem and judged the distance to his foe as perhaps eight feet. The distance to the windows beyond that looked out over the lawns and would be used by the snipers to shoot Abrahem was another ten feet, so any bullet fired would have to come in extremely low and with a low–aspect to the window to avoid the glass from deflecting the bullets from a true path.

Mitchell was standing at least ten feet from Abrahem and behind the couch, far too distant to make a move of any kind.

'Justice,' Ethan murmured in reply to Abrahem, 'to commit the same evil that you consider this man to have committed? To become the very thing that you so claim to hate, to bring more suffering when there has been suffering already. You do know that an eye for an eye just makes the whole world blind, right?'

Abrahem nodded.

'I do,' he replied, 'and better for a whole world to be blind and have learned from its mistakes that to see and continue to oppress and murder and maim for profit!'

Abrahem pushed the pistol harder against the girl's jaw, lifting her almost off her feet as he snarled at Ethan.

'Get on your knees!'

Ethan stayed where he was. He knew that Abrahem would not bluff, that he had no fear of killing, but Ethan also knew that in his own twisted way he wanted justice and that his main target, the ultimate target, was the former President. If Ethan could divert his attention for long enough to give the cavalry time to act…

'I don't kneel for cowards,' he replied.

Abrahem almost pulled the pistol away from the young girl to aim it at Ethan, but he resisted the temptation at the last moment and sniggered to himself.

'Lose the gun then or I'll shoot her dead anyway. I have nothing to lose.'

'On the contrary, you have everything to lose,' Ethan replied.

The distant sound of a helicopter reverberated through the windows and Abrahem briefly glanced in the direction of the sound, but he was too far away for Ethan to make a move.

'My family is dead,' Abrahem replied, 'my friends are dead or the prisoners of America. I have nothing left but to slay this family and take them with me into oblivion!'

'That won't bring your own family back,' Ethan pointed out. 'In fact, if we humans really are judged on our lives and actions after we die, I'd imagine that such an act of evil as yours would condemn you to a terrible punishment. I'd imagine that never, ever seeing your family again would be just such a punishment and…'

'The afterlife is imaginary!' Abrahem snarled. 'An invention, a lie used to get people to enslave themselves to mosques and churches! I will never see my family again because they no longer exist, and if Allah did exist he would not have allowed such injustice to happen year after year in my country! My war is not with the Great Satan that is America, it is with the evil people who used that country to murder millions and steal the wealth of my Iraq!'

Ethan took a pace forward, his eyes fixed on Abrahem's. 'Then your war is with me.'

'What do you mean?!'

'I figured it wouldn't matter to you all that much,' Ethan replied, 'and I guess that the guys were right all along. We should have finished you off though, done a proper job instead of letting you escape.'

Abrahem snarled at Ethan.

'Your people could never have caught me in Washington DC! Nobody let me escape and I…'

'Aljazaer Park,' Ethan cut him off.

Abrahem froze as though in time and stared at Ethan, the rage gone, replaced by a wide eyed stare as though Ethan had driven a sabre through Abrahem's heart.

'What?' the Iraqi uttered.

'There were eight of us,' Ethan replied. 'United States Special Forces, deployed to root out terrorist units operating near the river in the park's south east corner. Your father was an engineer, building bombs for Shia militia groups, Improvised Explosive Devices that had killed dozens of American troops.'

Abrahem was still staring at Ethan, the pistol no longer shoved under the girl's jaw but now resting against her cheek as he tried to speak, the words barely getting out.

'How did you know…,'

'We knew what he was doing,' Ethan uttered. 'Hell, he was handing the Shias two weapons per day, all primed and ready to go. We wouldn't have known about him if a previously built bomb hadn't prematurely exploded as the terrorists carried it to their car, which was under surveillance. How we laughed as we watched them burn.'

Abrahem's throat worked, his mouth apparently dry, the pistol wavering as though it were too heavy for him to hold.

'He was helping you,' Abrahem croaked, 'helping the Americans, but the militia threatened to kill us all if he did not build more bombs.'

'I know,' Ethan replied. 'We insisted that he continue in order to protect you all and so that we could follow the bombs back to the terrorist camps and annihilate them. It was working well, too, but then they caught on to what we were doing and traced it back to your father.'

Abrahem's pistol fell further, pressed now against the girl's throat.

'You killed him,' he gasped. 'You killed my family.'

Ethan shrugged as though he cared little for Abrahem's loss. 'He could identify highly placed informants among the Shia militia, men crucial to our staying one step ahead of the enemy. We knew that he'd be broken quickly – your father wasn't a heroic man, more a pragmatist. So we took him down, and then to ensure that nobody else could pass on any information we shot the rest of your family too. That's war, Abrahem. It sucks.' Ethan smiled at him. 'But we shot them quickly to minimize their suffering. After all, we're not barbarians and they were only Iraqis.'

Abrahem Nassir stared at Ethan for a moment and then with a cry of fury he hurled the girl aside and charged at him with the pistol pointed out in front of him as he opened fire.

***

XLIX

Ethan ducked out of sight into the foyer as Abrahem screamed and charged for the doorway, the gunshots smashing the wooden doorframe and sending splinters flashing past Ethan's eyes as he then plunged back in and collided with Abrahem as the Iraqi burst from the room.

The force of the Iraqi's charge propelled Ethan backwards and out of the lounge and he landed on his back on the tiled floor of the foyer as Abrahem landed on top of him. The hard shape of his pistol dug into Ethan's back as he crashed down, and Abrahem's own weapon rushed down toward his skull.

Ethan threw his hands up and blocked the savage blow, catching Abrahem's wrists in his hands and holding him at bay as the Iraqi screamed and snarled with inhuman strength as he forced Ethan's hands back over his head and brought his head crashing down.

Abrahem's forehead smashed into Ethan's nose with a burst of white pain, hot blood spilling down his cheek as the Iraqi fought with the strength and fury of the insane. Ethan pulled his head away from the pain as Abrahem lifted his head and crashed it down again into Ethan's, impacting just above Ethan's left eye.

Ethan's vision starred as the Iraqi smashed his head up and down, spittle flying and his maniacal cries soaring through the foyer. Ethan saw the former President and his family rush past behind Abrahem, hustling up the huge staircase as Abrahem smashed Ethan's head against the tiled floor.

Ethan waited, fighting against Abrahem but not throwing him off until the President's family were out of sight before he released his grip on Abrahem's hands and grabbed the assassin's face with both hands, one cupped beneath Abrahem's jaw and the other around the back of his skull as he twisted with all of his might.

Abrahem's neck was yanked sideways and he toppled off Ethan onto his back as Ethan hooked one leg over Abrahem to pin him down as he grabbed for the Iraq's pistol again and managed to overpower the assassin. Ethan came up on top and smashed his free fist down into Abrahem's nose, crushing it in a splatter of blood as he felt a sharp pain pulse through his knuckles under the impact.

Abrahem jerked a knee up and it slammed into the center of Ethan's back, pain ripping up Ethan's spine as Abrahem drove his hands under

Ethan's jaw and shoved him backwards, one leg hooking over Ethan's head and locking beneath his neck as his back was arched painfully over.

Ethan gagged as his throat was crushed, fighting to hold onto the assassin's pistol and prevent him from shooting as Abrahem screamed something in Arabic and began pushing Ethan's spine to breaking point.

Ethan grasped Abrahem's leg with his free hand in a desperate attempt to dislodge him, but Abrahem was already up on his elbows on the ground and now driving forward with ever greater leverage, pushing Ethan's head back toward his own ankles in some kind of advanced martial arts move design to break the opponent's spine.

Ethan felt white pain spear his back, heard something pop as though tendons were breaking under the strain, and then suddenly the unbearable pressure vanished as Abrahem rolled away and released Ethan and took aim with the pistol as he wrenched it from Ethan's grasp.

Ethan flipped upright and almost collapsed alongside Abrahem as he heard a deafening clatter of gunfire erupt beside him as Abrahem fired over Ethan's body at somebody near the lounge door.

Ethan rolled over and smashed Abrahem's pistol upward, his shots going high as a single returned round slammed into Abrahem's shoulder and jerked the Iraqi backwards. Ethan whirled and saw the large, dark figure of Aaron Mitchell tucked in against the entrance to the foyer, his pistol barely visible as he aimed it at Abrahem.

'It's over, Abrahem!' Mitchell boomed. 'You're done here!'

Abrahem looked to where the President and his family had been, the couch now empty and the family missing.

'It's never over,' he hissed as he jabbed the pistol against Ethan's ribs, using Ethan as a human shield, Mitchell's bullet apparently barely affecting the Iraqi.

Mitchell laughed, a great booming laugh that seemed to fill the house as he replied.

'Go ahead, kill him! You'll be doing me a favor! But know that I'll kill you just the same. You'll never hit me enough to stop me from there, but trust me when I say that I won't miss.'

Abrahem snarled something in Arabic as he grabbed Ethan's collar and yanked him to his feet, keeping Ethan's body between himself and Mitchell.

'He doesn't need to be alive to be of use,' Abrahem pointed out as he began backing away from Mitchell and toward the staircase.

Ethan looked at Mitchell, fully expecting the operative to open fire, but to his surprise Mitchell did not.

'Shoot him!' Ethan shouted.

Mitchell hesitated, and suddenly a deafening crash reverberated through the house as the front door was blasted inward and was followed by a cacophony of shouts as soldiers burst inside the building.

'Time's up, Abrahem,' Ethan hissed with a grim smile.

A salvo of shots rattled out and Ethan saw Mitchell duck out of sight as he was showered with debris. Ethan hurled himself clear of Abrahem's grasp as bullets peppered the hall and the Iraqi was forced to retreat up then staircase. A bullet skimmed Ethan's thigh with an excruciating wave of pain and Ethan rolled across the floor of the hall as he saw Abrahem sprinting up the staircase in pursuit of the former President and his family, his pistol in his hand.

Ethan, his right leg almost numb with pain, grabbed hold of the staircase banister and began hauling himself up in pursuit of the assassin as he sought his quarry somewhere above. He limped up to the first floor and heard a scream coming from somewhere toward the rear of the house, heard more shouts below and behind him as the Secret Service and their support teams flooded into the house.

Ethan broke into an awkward run as he drew his pistol from beneath his shirt and hurried toward the sound of the screams. He heard a crash and the splintering of wood ahead, and turned into a hall to see Abrahem rush shoulder–first through one of the bedroom doors as a high pitched woman's voice screamed in desperation.

'No, please, don't!'

Ethan sprinted with an awkward gait to the bedroom door and heard a single, deafening gunshot. His heart almost stopped in his chest as he burst into the room.

An ornate four–poster bed dominated the bedroom, the former First Lady cowering on her knees behind the far side of the bed. In front of Ethan stood Abrahem Nassir, his pistol pointed at the former President. The President was lying on his back on the thickly carpeted bedroom floor, a hole in his shirt where a bullet had impacted his chest.

Abrahem turned the pistol to aim at the First Lady as he spotted Ethan, a grim smile of satisfaction spreading on his dark features.

'So much for shock and awe,' he sniggered. 'Drop the pistol!'

Ethan held his ground, knowing that his gun was all that was keeping the First Lady alive as he staggered into the room. 'It's over,' he said weakly, barely able to stand and his pistol weighing his arm down it seemed. 'You've killed him.'

'Time to finish the game,' Abrahem snarled back.

Abrahem whipped the pistol around to aim at him, too fast for Ethan to respond, and Ethan heard a deafening gunshot that almost shattered his eardrums as he scrambled with his hands to try to protect his body from the bullet that would kill him.

***

L

The shot hit Abrahem in the side of his head, a fine spray of blood and bone bursting from the side of his face as the bullet smashed through his skull and embedded itself in the bedroom wall fifteen feet from where Ethan crouched.

Abrahem appeared to remain on his feet for a timeless moment, the muscles in his body randomly clenching and holding him upright as the last flickering neurons in his brain faded into silence. The assassin's body crumpled at the legs, slammed down onto its knees and folded over as though Abrahem were prostrating himself toward Mecca, his gun still clasped at an awkward angles in his hand as his forehead hit the carpeted floor with a bloodied thump.

Ethan turned to see Hannah Ford standing four–square in the bedroom doorway, both hands gripping the pistol that she had fired. Ethan's ears rang incessantly from the gunshots as he turned and vaguely heard Abrahem's final breath spill from his lungs in a low rasp.

The First Lady leaped up from her hiding place and rushed around the bed, tears streaming from her eyes as she cried out.

'Help him!'

Ethan staggered forward as his injured leg gave way beneath him and he slumped to the floor. Ethan stared blankly at the President's body, knowing that the bullet must have passed directly through his heart, Abrahem far too good a shot to have missed the vital organ in his last victorious moment. The First Lady plunged down alongside her husband and ripped his shirt open to reveal the dense black padding of a bullet proof vest.

Ethan's eyes widened as the President rasped a weak sentence.

'He didn't take the head shot.'

Ethan stared down in disbelief at the President as his wife helped him up into a sitting position.

'You had a vest,' Ethan gasped.

The President nodded. 'Always have a backup plan,' he rasped, clearly in pain from the bullet's impact. The President must have donned the vest before purposefully confronting Abrahem in the bedroom, directing the assassin's revenge away from the family and giving Ethan enough time to catch up. 'I only hoped he wouldn't shoot for my head. But I guess the malicious bastard wanted me to suffer.'

Ethan rested his hand on the President's shoulder, relief pouring through him as he replied.

'He would have been trained to make sure of a kill, even at close range,' Ethan said. 'He'd aim for the torso and if the first shot didn't kill…'

'It would surely maim, letting him fire a second into the head,' the President nodded as he replied. 'I'm lucky he didn't use a double–tap.'

The double–tap was a Special Forces technique, where the shooter would pull the trigger twice in quick succession – once to hit the torso, and the second shot on the recoil of the first, which would push the barrel upward slightly and cause the second round to go through the face or skull.

Ethan looked round to see Hannah Ford watching over them as Secret Service agents swarmed into the room.

'Stay still, hands on your head!'

Ethan complied as he saw the agents surround him, despite the President's assurances that he was an ally. Ethan looked at Hannah, and she pointed to his nose.

'You've got a nosebleed,' she said.

'Abrahem,' Ethan replied as he was cuffed by the agents. 'I'm not implanted. Mitchell?'

Hannah beamed in delight at him as she holstered her pistol. 'Apprehended, he's downstairs.'

Hannah's delight melted away and Ethan saw the concern etched into her features. He was about to ask her what was wrong, when he had a sudden premonition of doom as he stood up on legs unwilling to bear his weight.

'Nicola?'

Hannah did not respond for a moment, but then she spoke softly.

'She's on her way to George Washington University Hospital,' she said. 'She was hit. I don't know how bad it is.'

Ethan felt his world sway around him and he slumped back down onto one knee, fatigue finally overwhelming him as Hannah moved to his side.

'You need a hospital too,' she pointed out. 'How about we get you there right now?'

*

George Washington University Hospital,

Washington DC

The intensive care unit was quieter that Ethan would have imagined. It had taken some time for the Secret Service and local law enforcement to assure themselves that he was not in fact some deranged biker intent on murdering anybody who crossed his path, and that he had not been implanted with one of the nefarious devices.

Lopez lay entombed amid a tangle of tubes, intravenous lines and other medical paraphernalia. Her eyes were bruised and closed, her breathing controlled by a ventilator and her chest swathed in white bandages that looked clinically clean but to Ethan were merely a veil across the terrible damage wrought by the bullet that had passed through her.

A doctor stood alongside him at the foot of the bed and spoke as though from another world.

'The bullet severed her right subclavian artery, passed through her right lung and exited her left chest in the middle of the ribcage. She lost a lot of blood before the paramedics got to her, and was barely breathing by the time she reached the ER.'

Ethan swallowed, didn't take his eyes from Lopez as he spoke.

'What's her condition and prognosis?'

The doctor sighed softly before he replied.

'There is a reasonable chance that she'll pull through this and survive the shooting,' he said finally. 'But we can't predict what condition she'll be in when she does. Her brain was starved of oxygen for a considerable period of time.'

Ethan was unable to look at anything else but Lopez's face, her body seeming so small and vulnerable now as it lay on the hospital bed, her life hanging by the thread of modern technology. He knew there and then that without the intervention of paramedics, who had forced their way through the dense traffic to reach her, Lopez would have died at the scene along with the shooter.

'Who pulled the trigger?' he asked finally.

'I don't have that information sir,' the doctor replied.

Ethan turned and stalked out of the room. Outside in the corridor waited Hannah Ford, her green eyes swimming with concern. Ethan registered a moment of brief surprise that she was even still here.

'How's she doing?' Hannah asked.

Ethan struggled for a moment to speak. It felt as though somebody had shoved a sock down his throat.

'Touch and go,' he uttered finally. 'They can't predict her condition if she does survive.'

'Christ, I'm so sorry,' Hannah said.

Ethan could not bring himself to look at her as he spoke. 'Who shot her?'

Hannah looked up at the ceiling briefly before she replied.

'Ethan, going on a rampage isn't going to help you any and it sure as hell won't help Lopez.'

'You don't know that.'

'It didn't do Abrahem any good, did it?' Hannah challenged.

Ethan stalked past her and continued down the corridor, Hannah following.

'Where are you going?' she demanded.

'Am I under arrest?'

'No, you're under stress. I don't want you wandering off and doing something you'll regret.'

'Since when do you care?'

Hannah gripped Ethan's arm with enough force to pull him up short.

'We're on the same side,' she said. 'Doesn't matter about what's happened up before. Director LeMay's working for Majestic Twelve, I know that now.'

Ethan sighed and glanced out of a window, the iconic skyline of Washington DC's Capitol visible in the distance.

'He's untouchable, you know that too. They all are.'

'Maybe,' Hannah replied, 'but everybody has weaknesses and nobody is untouchable forever. We have Mitchell, remember?'

Ethan clenched his fists. 'Mitchell might have saved the President's life as much as put it at risk.'

'He's the enemy,' Hannah insisted. 'He murdered Stanley Meyer and Jin Chen in Hong Kong, stole the hard drives from the Chinese that contained the data we were searching for to hand over to Majestic Twelve and he still represents the very people who have been trying to bring us down!'

'Us?' Ethan uttered as he shot a glance at Hannah.

'Like I said, we're all on the same team, right?'

Ethan regarded her for a moment longer, and then he turned and walked away down the corridor toward the hospital exit.

***

LI

Lake Michigan, Indiana

The wind whipping across Lake Michigan had swept away some of the cloying summer heat and churned the surface of the water into charging armies of white rollers, the green waves glittering in the sunlight breaking between turbulent clouds scudding above as Ethan walked.

The rendezvous had been agreed, strictly off the record despite his official status as a Defense Intelligence Agency operative and asset. Ethan had driven east across the border to Marquette Park, near the Aquatorium, then parked up in a deserted lot on the south shores of the lake and walked east along the golden sands of the beach.

He didn't have to walk far before he saw Jarvis waiting for him, sitting on a low bench against the bluffs and watching the rollers coming in off the lake. He strolled up to the bench and sat down, not looking at the old man.

'Any news?' Jarvis asked.

Ethan shook his head, and Jarvis thought for a moment before speaking.

'I'm sure she'll pull through,' he said. 'She's a tough girl and she won't go without a fight.'

Ethan's jaw cracked with the briefest ghost of a smile that was snatched away by the brisk wind.

'What's the score?'

Ethan asked the question out straight, not in the mood to beat about the bush. Jarvis took a breath before replying.

'Hannah Ford and Michael Vaughn were wanted by the Hong Kong police for homicide. We couldn't let Mitchell go because he's being questioned here and is too valuable an asset to release, and the Chinese needed something in order to play ball. We sent the Chinese operatives you captured in DC back home, in return for Hannah and Michael's charges to be dropped.'

'Neat and tidy, as always,' Ethan murmured without passion. 'Where was Nicola's back up when she took on Tariq and his bodyguard?'

'The traffic slowed down law enforcement as well as federal and DIA agents,' Jarvis said. 'Nicola wasn't supposed to go bashing their door down on her own, she was just the first on the scene after two police officers were gunned down by Tariq.'

'You know what she's like.'

'I know what you're *both* like,' Jarvis shot back. 'and I wouldn't have either of you any other way, but sooner or later something like this was going to happen Ethan. It's not a game.'

'Don't patronize me,' Ethan growled. 'What about LeMay?'

Jarvis took a deep breath before he replied.

'LeMay was injured by Hannah Ford in the White House, after Lopez was shot. It turns out she punched the Director and broke his nose. While the Director was having his nose re–set that evening under general anesthetic, we took the opportunity to implant him with one of the devices we retrieved from the Chinese.'

Ethan slowly turned his head to look at Jarvis.

'But Hannah was implanted,' he said. 'You could have stopped her from doing something so stupid if…'

Ethan broke off as he saw the way that Jarvis was looking at him, the sly grin on his face and the knowing gleam in his eye.

'I'll be damned,' Ethan said finally. 'You *made* her do it.'

'We needed a broken nose for the Director,' Jarvis said by way of an explanation, 'and to be honest it didn't take much conditioning or signaling to give Hannah Ford sufficient motivation to knock LeMay on his ass. She was the one who found Nicola.'

Ethan stared out across the lake for a moment.

'You risked both of their lives.'

Jarvis looked across at him. 'You're going to argue the toss about this now?'

'No. I've got used to the dirty little games you all play, and the lives that get lost while you're playing them.'

'That's hardly fair,' Jarvis pointed out. 'We're all on the same side.'

'That's what Hannah keeps saying, but it's becoming tough to know,' Ethan replied.

Ethan watched Jarvis for a long moment, and the old man relented.

'Hannah was on her way to the White House to deliver her final blow when we picked up the emergency calls from the scene of Lopez's shooting,' Jarvis said. 'I diverted Hannah straight there when I realized who had been hit. Lopez's survival was more important to me, to us, than implanting LeMay.'

Ethan looked back out over the ocean. 'And Mitchell?'

'Uncertain,' Jarvis replied. 'He is definitely working for Majestic Twelve, but we're not sure in what capacity now. I'm beginning to wonder whether MJ–12's support for a terrorist group's plan to murder the president was a step too far even for him.'

'I wouldn't have been able to stop Abrahem Nassir if Mitchell hadn't been there already,' Ethan said. 'LeMay must have assigned him to the former President's staff, which means…'

'That LeMay must have known Abrahem's true target before we did,' Jarvis finished the sentence for Ethan. 'MJ–12 must have known all about Abrahem Nassir's plan for revenge and been helping him from behind the scenes for some time.'

Ethan rubbed his temple wearily, the bruises where Abrahem had head–butted him still sore and swollen.

'Surely a powerful organization such as MJ–12 would not want to see a terrorist attack on American soil succeed? What good would that do them?'

'That depends,' Jarvis said. 'The group may have military or defense contractors among its number who would stand to make great profits were another major war to be launched overseas. Justification for those wars is required to convince Congress of the need for conflict, to convince the American people that another war is worth fighting for our country's security.'

'I think that there are enough terrorists and enemies out there for a war to always be a possibility.'

'But not a certainty,' Jarvis replied. 'Businesses can't be built on uncertainties. Look at Iraq – we invaded on lies about non–existent weapons of mass destruction and American companies made billions off the back of a war financed by the tax payer. Yet nobody wants to go to war with China, Russia or North Korea, countries with definite chemical, biological and nuclear weapons capabilities that could harm us, despite the fact that Russia just annexed Crimea and is now making noises about Eastern Europe and the Baltic states "belonging to Russia". War isn't about territory or defense any more, Ethan, it's about making money and the big defense contractors don't want that revenue to dry up any time soon.'

Ethan folded his arms.

'So that's who we're up against now?' he asked. 'Big business people?'

Jarvis nodded.

'It's through them that we'll hurt the members of Majestic Twelve, and now we literally have eyes on one of their members. Director LeMay was implanted while under general anesthetic to fix a broken nose he thoroughly deserved. Whatever he is told or tells them, we will have on the record. This was a big score, Ethan, a huge step on the road to dismantling Majestic Twelve.'

'At what price?' Ethan uttered. 'You take one cabal down, another will fill the power vacuum to take its place. If arms companies have such a hold over Washington then we'll never be able to operate without one intelligence figure or another trying to trip us up. It's going to be a never–ending mission and like you just said, sooner or later we're all going to wind up dead trying to complete it.'

Ethan got up off the bench.

'So that's it then?' Jarvis asked. 'You just quit?'

'I quit once before,' Ethan pointed out. 'Lopez was the one who convinced me to come back in and now her life's hanging by a thread in a hospital in DC while I'm back here contemplating apprehending a bunch of low–life bail jumpers.'

'Then come back to DC,' Jarvis said, standing as he did so. 'Come back and start doing a proper job. The DIA wants you, hell the President still wants you on this case. He's as keen as anybody to achieve something against Majestic Twelve before his second term is up. Are you really going to let Nicola's courage and sacrifice be for nothing?'

'Don't use her name like that,' Ethan snapped. 'Nicola was reluctant to work for the DIA because she got tired of being crapped on by the government.'

'Well, now is your opportunity to go over their heads.'

Ethan frowned. 'What's that supposed to mean?'

Jarvis turned and looked over his shoulder. Ethan glanced in the indicated direction, and saw Hannah Ford waiting beside a black limousine.

'Fact is, you've been exposed to so many high–level classified projects that the President has cleared you COSMIC, as well as Nicola when she recovers.'

'She might not,' Ethan pointed out. 'Security clearances don't matter much to people when they're dead.'

'She's not dead yet,' Jarvis countered, 'and neither are you. You're blaming yourself for what's happened to Nicola, but the people who put her in that hospital are still in power Ethan, are probably already embarking on their next crusade for money and influence, and every single person who quits in this battle against their corruption is a victory for them.'

Ethan saw Hannah standing with her arms folded, the brisk wind rippling through her long auburn hair as she squinted into the afternoon sun from across the parking lot.

'Hannah hasn't been arrested or charged?'

'Presidential veto,' Jarvis replied. 'Hannah doesn't work for the FBI anymore and nor does her partner, Vaughn. They're DIA now, special clearances all completed, non–disclosure agreements signed. We're assembling a team, Ethan. After what happened here, the President has recognized the need for a larger and more comprehensive unit to combat the new technologies that are landing in the hands of the enemies of the United States. Majestic Twelve is the enemy within, and he wants them rooted out one by one and brought to justice or…'

Ethan watched Jarvis for a long moment and realized the veiled threat against the members of MJ–12. Root them out, *or eliminate them.*

'He'd go that far?'

Jarvis shrugged. 'MJ–12 has repeatedly gone that far and further to get what it wants. Fight fire with fire, is the President's personal view on this. We have a Presidential Executive Order behind us, Ethan. We're going to war against Majestic Twelve. Are you with us, or not?'

Ethan looked again at Hannah Ford as she waited patiently beside the limousine, and then he made up his mind.

***

Also by Dean Crawford:

The Warner & Lopez Series
The Nemesis Origin
The Fusion Cage
The Idenitty Mine

The Ethan Warner Series
Covenant
Immortal
Apocalypse
The Chimera Secret
The Eternity Project

Atlantia Series
Survivor
Retaliator
Aggressor
Endeavour
Defiance

Independent novels
Eden
Holo Sapiens
Soul Seekers
Stone Cold

Want to receive notification of new releases? Just sign up to Dean Crawford's newsletter via: www.deancrawfordbooks.com

ABOUT THE AUTHOR

Dean Crawford is the author of the internationally published series of thrillers featuring *Ethan Warner*, a former United States Marine now employed by a government agency tasked with investigating unusual scientific phenomena. The novels have been *Sunday Times* paperback best-sellers and have gained the interest of major Hollywood production studios. He is also the enthusiastic author of many independently published Science Fiction novels.

www.deancrawfordbooks.com